# SANTA BÁRBARA, CALIFORNIA

Harper's
House

anta Bárbara Mission

El Presidio
de Santa Bárbara

EL CAMINO REAL

PACIFIC

OCEAN

# GHOST
# WOMAN

◆ ◆ ◆

# GHOST
# WOMAN

◆◆◆◆◆◆◆

*Lawrence*
*Thornton*

◆ ◆ ◆

*Ticknor & Fields*
*New York*

For information about permission to reproduce
selections from this book, write to Permissions,
Ticknor & Fields, 215 Park Avenue South,
New York, New York 10003.

*Library of Congress
Cataloging-in-Publication Data*
Thornton, Lawrence, date.
Ghost woman / by Lawrence Thornton.
p.     cm.
ISBN 0-395-61592-5
1. Indians of North America — California — Fiction.
I. Title.
PS3570.H6678G48   1992   91-45624
813'.54 — dc20   CIP

Printed in the United States of America

VB 10 9 8 7 6 5 4 3 2

*To Toni*

# GHOST
# WOMAN

◆ ◆ ◆

# PROLOGUE

Soon after she was born her father entered the hut. "Look how beautiful she is," her mother said. "Yes," he answered, "she is perfect." He ran his hands lightly over her arms and shoulders, and then he looked at her face a long time, searching for clues. After a while he went to the mesa and returned with a handful of herbs, knelt beside the child, and rubbed the ball of his thumb back and forth over the leaves, which left a fine green residue on his fingers. As he held out the fragrant leaves for the child to smell, he named her Sage. The word required a catch in the throat, a glottal stop at the beginning, so that her name burst forth suddenly on her father's tongue.

In the first winter after she reached the age of understanding, Sage and five other children were sent to the storyteller's hut to learn about the universe. They had seen the old woman many times in the village. She was thin as a tule reed and her face was a tapestry of wrinkles, but she looked different in her hut. Light fell through the entrance, making an oblong of yellow all the way across the floor, where she sat working her mouth, getting ready to talk. Seated cross-legged on the clean earth, arms hugging her knees as she watched them coming in, she seemed powerful as a shaman.

After they had gathered around her in a circle, she cleared her throat and warned them that they must listen very carefully, because the words of stories were more rich with meaning than those they used every day. There was a special way of telling that lay halfway between speech and song, and they had to pay attention to the rhythms; otherwise they would not learn what they had to know. Listen to what I say, she said. Take it with you and let it seep into the marrow of your bones.

Her eyes mirrored strange and wonderful things when she began to tell the stories. There were three worlds, she said, the one where they lived, the one above, and the one below. Upper World was the home of Sun, Coyote, and Eagle, whose black wings held Upper World in the air. He stretched his wings when he grew tired, and that caused the phases of the moon. If there was an eclipse, it was because his wings covered the silver disc completely.

Middle World, where human beings lived, was supported by two huge snakes whose writhing caused the earth to shake. It was flat and circular, and the island where they lived was at its center. Supernatural beings lived there as well as in the sky, and of them the swordfish were most dangerous. Eight of them hid in a cave beneath the sea, where they hunted whales and ate them raw. Evil as they were, they benefited people by driving whales ashore for them to eat and use their bones for houses.

The storyteller sang that Lower World was the home of the Nunasis, who came out after dark to work their power, and she warned them always to bathe early in the morning before the Nunasis returned from going around the world, for later the water would be steaming because they bathed there too.

One of the Nunasis took the form of a man who put trees and rocks into his mouth and swallowed them without chewing. Another had a broken leg and went hopping around the world, making trouble for human beings. He lived on the mainland, and they could see the smoke of his cooking fire if they looked very hard. His brother made sounds in the trees like a newborn baby. This Nunasis looked like a cat, and whenever he cried, someone was about to die.

She sang of death in a soft, lilting voice, telling them that the soul stayed at the grave three days and visited familiar places one last time before traveling to the Land of the Dead, where it waited to be reborn. On the way across the ocean these souls might be seen as shining balls of light arcing through the sky. The place where they were going could be reached only by crossing a bridge above a dangerous body of water, where they could look down and see the damned undergoing punishment for their sins in life.

Take this knowledge with you, she said, looking at the children before her. Let it seep into the marrow of your bones.

She waited a little while until she was certain that her words had taken hold, and then she began again, her voice pitched higher, as she explained that the universe was an orderly but uncertain place ruled by supernatural beings. It was they who made the seasons come and go, commanded rain to fall, and allowed plants to grow in all their greenness. The happiness and sorrow of human beings, their lives and deaths, depended on old man Sun, who lived above the sky and followed a trail around the world wearing nothing but a feathered headband, so proud was he of his naked power. Every night he returned to a crystal house filled with animals that walked and crawled and flew at his bidding. The crystal house was many times larger than the chief's lodge, and its walls and ceiling and floor were thicker than the trunk of the stoutest tree. Think of the brightness of the midday sun, the storyteller said, and then imagine the whole sky like that, and you still would not know the power of this light, which is so strong that you might look into the eyes of any of the creatures living there and see into their skulls.

Then she said that the crystal house was the badge of the power of the sun. It was there that Sun decided their fate in a gambling game, theirs and that of all their families and of their ancestors who had gone before. After Sun went home with the light of the world, he called the other supernaturals to him. Sun and Eagle sat across the crystal floor from Coyote and Morning Star, and Moon hovered outside, looking down as referee. From a shiny box Sun removed a pair of dice like those their fathers used in games, and then he removed the counters. When they thought that they heard thunder, it was the sound of dice on the crystal floor.

The supernaturals played throughout the nights of every year and finally, at the time of the winter solstice, Moon spoke through the ceiling and said that now they must decide who won. The counters were arrayed in stacks, and when the winner was declared, there was a great rejoicing. If Coyote won, there would be plenty of rain in Middle World, and the rain would bring more than enough to eat. But if Sun emerged the victor, the debt to him was paid in misery and human lives.

She looked at each of the children in turn before dismissing them with a gesture of her hand.

Take it with you, she said. Let it seep into the marrow of your bones.

*One*

# THE SACRED
# EXPEDITION

◆ ◆ ◆

# 1

◆ ◆ ◆

Living as they did at the center of the world, Sage's ancestors had no way to know that a pair of earthly dice had been tossed across a table in Mexico City three days before Christmas in 1769 when the *visitador-general* in New Spain dispatched a band of friars and soldiers on a sacred expedition into Alta California. But they heard the rumble of thunder over the next twenty years as the missions sprang to life and the friars lured their brothers on the mainland into the compounds with gifts of colored cloth and strings of beads, playing on their love of beauty. Once the villages surrounding the mission of Santa Bárbara were emptied, the friars set their hearts on the salvation of the islanders, and there was a great commotion in the sky. Soon a deputation accompanied by a Chumash translator sailed to San Nicolás, and shortly after returning with a small group of Indians, Captain Walter Stafford, owner of a schooner called the *Enterprise*, was commissioned to remove the remaining members of the tribe.

On the day of the ship's departure clouds hovered low on the horizon to the north. A storm was brewing, and the *Enterprise* made good progress on its winds, dropping anchor in a bay called Dutch Harbor an hour earlier than Captain Stafford had calculated. He did not like the look of the sky and quickly ordered the crew to lower the longboats and make for shore, where the Indians waited, unaware that in the crystal house Sun was already raking in his winnings.

While it was still dark that morning six men lit pitch torches from the cooking fires and everyone in the village set off for the ridge that ran the length of the island. Sage, her husband, and daughter walked in the middle of the procession, but the sputtering torches frightened the child, who did not stop crying until her father lifted her onto his shoulders. Once the girl was quiet, Sage deliberately fell behind as the flames moved up the hillside, wavering left and right with the bearers' steps. It seemed important to watch her people make their way to the cliff where they would wait for the first sight of the ship, but their shadowy figures quickly merged with the darkness until nothing remained except moving flames. She felt herself floating in the darkness, alone with the gods whose shapes were held in arrays of fading stars. She had not been afraid since the fighting ended, but she uttered a little cry because of the loneliness, quickened her pace, and hurried up the path until she once again saw familiar figures outlined by the flames and heard her husband's labored breathing.

After they reached the cliff, the six men sank the sharp ends of their torches into the ground, and the flames bronzed their faces as they gazed toward the still-dark channel. A stiff breeze bit at the otter skins everyone wore against the morning chill. It blew the torch flames into dancing shapes. When the eastern sky reddened, sea elephants in the cove below slithered from their caves to flat rocks above the sea, and soon the great males were roaring in disputes over territory. Gulls rose from their nesting places and wheeled in pink light before swooping down for remnants of fish abandoned by the sea elephants, whose barking echoed from the cove as the people waited for the ship coming from the thin blue line of the mainland. Children fretted, parents admonished, mothers nursed infants, and Sage waited for someone to speak. She wanted words for the same reason she had fallen behind in the procession — because she needed to understand this momentous day. Yet the silence did not surprise her. Over the last few years they had used up their tongues in talk of fighting, exhausted what remained of their words weeks before, when the ship had glided through the black rocks to the cove below their village and anchored close to shore. White men in longboats came to them, and among them was a man from a strange tribe who understood their language. He said that the white men's priests would give them a home in a place surrounded by fields where all manner of food grew in abundance, said that there would be more to eat than they could find on the island now that the traders had killed all the otters.

Sage remembered everything as she looked across the channel at the mountains running north and south as far as she could see. The land always seemed large, but this morning it was enormous, and she was afraid of going there. She stared hard, as if by effort alone she could see the great lodge where tonight her family would gather around a fire for their first meal in their new home, but all she saw was the endless stretch of land and the sharp ridges of the mountains.

She was so intent upon the land that she did not notice the white speck on the sea until her husband and two women pointed. At first she saw only whitecaps; then the square shapes of sails and the dark hull appeared. The ship did not seem to move for a long time, but suddenly it became larger and rode high on the sea. One of the young hunters who had worried that the white men meant to steal their possessions and leave them to die without weapons or provisions apologized for his fears. She had not been afraid in that way, but the sight of the ship made her feel small, as if she could hold herself in her hand.

When the ship came closer, its whole length became visible. As it sailed parallel to the island everyone remarked on its strength. Men wondered aloud how the white men had built such an enormous thing. While they speculated about the ship, Sage was studying the sky. A steady wind had been blowing since they reached the cliff. Clouds massed low and heavy on the horizon to the northwest, and the wind moaned in the trees. Heavy swells began buffeting the ship, and an elder sitting beside her husband said they should hurry to the cove and be ready for the longboats, for the sea would soon be dangerous.

The burned-out torches stood abandoned on the verge of the cliff. As the people descended the path, the edge of a dark cloud masked the sun so that Sage could look at it without pain in her eyes. She judged the speed of the storm against the veiled sun as gulls flew low overhead, rushing for cover. Beyond the black shapes of the dead torches the roars of the sea elephants were lost in the wind. She wanted to tell her husband that they should slip into the woods behind the village and hide until everyone was gone, but even as the idea formed, she felt like a silly girl who could not accept things as they were.

Four longboats waited at the edge of the beach. White men wearing shiny black capes and hats impatiently helped her people into the boats. They all wanted to be with their families, and there was much confusion because the wind was howling so loudly now that they were forced to shout at one another. Her husband and child disappeared in the crowd. She tried to follow them, but a bearded sailor took her by the arm and guided her to another group, where she found her parents.

It began to rain. Sheets of driving water blew parallel to the sea as the boats set out across the cove, bobbing up and down on the swells and almost disappearing behind a shadow of rain.

In a little while she saw people looking down at her from the ship's railing. The boat dipped suddenly, and she had to grip the sides to keep from being tossed overboard. Sailors threw down lines, which their companions used to pull the longboat close. One by one, the islanders climbed the rope ladder and were pulled over the side.

She was the last to come aboard. As soon as she felt the deck beneath her bare feet, her husband took hold of her. She welcomed his embrace, but instead of holding her he pushed her away at arm's length, asking for their child. She answered that she had seen the girl with him on the beach. "No," he said. "I thought she was with you."

There was no sign of her daughter. Breaking her husband's grip, she pushed through the crowd toward the bow, where sailors worked the rigging. When she reached them she saw her daughter running up and down on the beach. She screamed her child's name, grabbed the nearest sailor. As she pointed to the beach, the ship began to turn in a slow, shuddering arc. She found the man who knew the white men's words and begged him to tell the captain to stop the ship. The captain listened, shook his head, spoke quickly, and walked away. The man told her that the sea was too dangerous to put a boat ashore. The captain would return for her child the next day when the weather was better.

The ship leaned to the right, jerked level, rose on a huge swell. Across the deck her husband and parents were pointing at the beach. Shouting her daughter's name, she ran to the railing, mounted, and jumped feet first into the sea. The frigid water struck her calloused soles, forced itself into her nostrils. She went down and down, spread her arms, felt her dress rise over her head and then subside as she lost momentum and rose with flailing arms and kicking feet. When her head broke the surface she drew in a draft of air and struck out blindly, paddling like a dog chasing sticks thrown into the sea. She coughed, gagged, arched her head. A wave loomed, blotting out the island. She felt herself rising, felt the rough vines of the kelp dragging against her arms as she was carried to the crest of the wave; from there she saw her child running up and down. She raised her left hand, shouted the girl's name, but the water stopped her words as she careened down the face of the wave and a length of kelp twined round her neck as she plunged to darkness.

Something ran across her face.

Torches sailed like arrows through the air, fell on her, burned her flesh.

She heard the rumble of thunder, the screech of gulls.

When she opened her eyes only one let in light. The sun burned straight overhead. She closed her eye against the glare, heard the surf again, the gulls, and also something she did not recognize, a soft and sliding sound.

Later she moved her arms. When she tried to straighten her legs, a sharp pain came from deep inside her bones. She heard the sliding sound again, voices that were not voices, a roar that was not the surf.

She opened her eye. A huge sea elephant stood twenty paces away. Beyond him others crowded together on the rocks. The male's mouth was open, his head tilted to one side as he watched her. She tried pushing herself away, but when she moved, pain made her cry out and the animal roared and rushed. His large, pointed teeth looked made for killing.

Her arms trembled with fatigue. She was afraid to move, but she knew that she could not sustain her weight much longer. She slowly brought her left arm up to her side, then her right. The animal watched as she rested her weight on her elbows. Then it rushed again, closing the distance between them by three or four paces. When it roared again she wet herself. She felt the warmth against her thighs. She could not move. She willed her body to become a bruised and bloody stone, tried to control her breathing, to move nothing but her one good eye.

In the cave behind him females stared placidly as cubs sucked their teats. She remembered sliding down the wave, the silence, the kelp around her neck, her daughter looking out to sea. She called her daughter's name, and the dry, croaking syllables were answered by the sea elephant's roar.

The cove lay many paces from the beach where her daughter was. She imagined the child huddled beneath a tree on the embankment, talked to her, told her to find a place in the sun, told her that she was coming.

She heard the creature breathing. Its black eyes gleamed above scars that ran down its neck and sides, some narrow, some wide and smooth. She remembered how the great males fought, remembered horrible wounds and gushing blood. She imagined the teeth sinking into her neck. Then she had a more terrible thought. Perhaps her daughter had wandered up to the cliff above the cove. If the animal killed her, her child would see it happen. She studied the rim of the cliff. Nothing but a clean line against deep blue sky.

She could not think clearly any longer. Her side ached, her arms ached and went numb. She closed her eye, but she still saw the sea elephant and her child. She felt herself slipping to the sand, tried to stiffen her arms, heard the roar.

The animal was eating her child. She sat up screaming, but the cove was empty and so was the cave. All that remained of the animals was the heavy scent of their droppings. She cried with relief that it had only been a dream. She breathed deeply, and as she stood, the pain made the sea blur. Her otter skin dress was stiff from dried salt water, crusted inside and out with sand. She looked at the rocky point. The tide was coming in. She had to go now if she was to escape, because soon the water would cut off her route to the beach where her daughter waited.

Her first step made the pain blaze like a hot ember in her side, but she continued walking through the animals' tracks. The pain eased by the time she reached the rocks, and when she came down on the far side she saw the northern end of the cove. She had told the child that if she was ever lost, she should stay where she was; someone would find her. She was a good, obedient girl; she would be waiting near the beach. Sage called her name, searched with her good eye. Kelp and tree limbs were scattered everywhere. It had been a terrible storm, and this knowledge made her call again as she went to the place where the girl would be. It was empty. She turned to the channel, hoping to see the boat bearing her husband and family, but the sea was empty and smooth as the inside of an abalone shell. The land where her people had gone was a distant blue shape in the mist.

On the embankment she found a basket of utensils, picked it up, pushed through the undergrowth, ignoring the branches that scratched her arms and the brambles that caught her feet. She stumbled, rose, and plunged on to the village, where she found huts untouched by the storm; the place of worship with its great curved whalebones stood solid and enduring. A wild dog she had befriended appeared from the trees and ran forward, wagging its tail and whining. She burst into tears at the sight of the dog, called to it, knelt down, and scratched its head. As she did, she glanced at her family's hut. The hide used to cover the entrance was closed; she remembered tying it open the morning they packed their possessions. She rose and ignored the pain in her excitement as she shouted her child's name and rushed across the clearing, tore the hide away, and saw the girl curled like a dark half-moon.

That night she made a fire in the shallow pit on the floor of the hut and lay down, wrapping her arms and legs around the shivering child, who whimpered her mother's name once before falling asleep. She pressed herself against the child despite the pain, would have pushed her back inside her womb if she could. In the middle of the night she felt the child trembling, and as she pressed closer she told herself that the ship would return in the morning. She dreamed of the day she bore her child, dreamed of the ship on the sea.

When she woke at dawn the child was shivering more violently. Sage pulled her dress over her head, wrapped it around the child, and whispered that she would return very soon. It was cold under the trees leading down to the beach and she was ashamed that the white men would see her naked body, but all that was important was that the men put her child in some safe place on their ship.

The sun warmed her skin as she waited. When it was overhead and the ship had not come, she went back up the embankment. It would come tomorrow, or later in the day. On the way back she passed a fresh water spring. A stone bowl lay at the edge and she filled it. As she returned to her hut the wild dog came out of the woods and followed.

She raised her daughter's head and rested it on her lap. She spoke, but the child did not answer. Parting the girl's lips with the thumb of her left hand, she dipped the fingers of her right hand into the bowl and let drops of water fall into the child's mouth. The girl coughed, swallowed, twisted away.

That afternoon she coaxed the dog near with the bowl of water. When it began to drink, she struck the animal on the head with a stone and it fell to its side, shivering and making strange sounds. She struck again and again until it no longer moved.

The basket of utensils contained a bone knife, a bone needle, a sea elephant's tooth, a scraper. She made an incision the length of the dog's stomach, parted the skin, cut through the muscles, and removed the intestines. She skinned the dog and cut the meat into strips so thin that light shone through when she placed them on the drying rack. She scraped away every bit of flesh from the hide before securing it to the rack and making a small fire beneath it. Then she returned to the hut. From time to time she left the child to test the skin for dryness. That night she wrapped her naked body around the child and fell into a dreamless sleep.

The next day the skin was dry. She removed her dress from the child and put it on. Its warmth astonished her as she carefully wrapped the child in the dog's skin. She made a fire and cooked a strip of meat, then she chewed a small piece, biting through the tough fibers. After reducing the meat to pulp, she put it between her child's lips, but the girl did not wake to eat, not even when Sage shook her.

The shivering and sweating stopped. Sage told herself that this was good. She tried not to think of how the child's skin looked like the belly of a fish, or how her breath was labored and without rhythm. She remembered children who had been ill and how, days later, they had run through the clearing. She imagined her child outside. She saw the ship as it would look coming into the cove. She ate the meat.

The next day she cooked another strip, chewed it to softness, and put a small portion to the child's lips. When she did not respond, the woman wondered whether she should force the meat into the small mouth, but she was afraid of choking her. Once again she ate the food, telling herself that it was good the little one was resting. The girl's breath came more regularly now, though it was so shallow that Sage put her hand on the thin chest to relieve a fear that had come upon her when she woke.

She went to the beach, and the sea was blue and the sun sparkled on the water. As she gazed at the emptiness, she realized that her injured eye was letting in light through a narrow slit. She had feared that she was blinded, and now that she could see a sudden happiness came upon her. It was a good omen. Today the ship would come. She sat down, determined to stay until she caught sight of the sails. The mainland was very clear. She could see the veins in the distant mountains and tried to imagine what her people were doing.

The day grew warm, and the sea was motionless except for thin surf. There was no wind, and she told herself that was why she had not seen it. The ship lived on wind. In the afternoon it would come. The wind always sprang up then. Never in her memory had it not.

When she entered the hut she saw her daughter's open mouth. A fly crawled on the upper lip. She brushed the fly away and sat down, cradling the girl in her arms. All afternoon she never took her eyes off the child's face. For a long time the word tried to come, but not until it was dark could she say it. Then she screamed, and wild dogs barked in response.

She carried her child to the burial ground on the ridge above the village. She tried to think of the spirit world, repeated as many rituals as she could remember.

Afterward she set out along the ridge, realizing that this was the first time in her life she had been alone. The only thing that made her feel alive was grief. If it were not for her grief, she could have been a leaf blown on the wind. The sea and the island had always been her friends, but now they were only things. The power invested in them by the tribe's beliefs meant nothing. She felt betrayed, and cursed the land and the sea.

At the northern end of the island she descended the ridge to a narrow beach, and the wind blew her dress tight against her body. Surf hissed. Gulls cried. Everything was the way it had been at the moment of creation.

When the pain in her side disappeared, she wished for its return.

When her injured eye opened fully, she wished to be half blind again.

She wanted to sleep in the sea elephant's mouth, dream its teeth, wake to the sensation of a sand creature running across her face, because if she felt pain and could only half-see, her daughter would still be alive.

After she ate the last strip of dried meat, she killed another dog, but once the animal lay dead at her feet she knew that she could not eat it. The preparation would remind her of all she had done to save her child. That afternoon she carried the body into the woods and left it for the hawks.

She trapped birds in snares and roasted them in hot ashes.

She foraged for herbs and berries, nuts and roots.

She made baskets of reeds, walked in the woods, spoke to birds and dogs.

Sometimes her mind made pictures that frightened her, and when they came she shook her head quickly, as if bees had lighted in her hair. After some time it did no good, and she began to live with strange imaginings.

One day she found herself at the cove where the ship had come. She did not know how she got there. The beach looked as it always had, and she wondered whether there had ever been a storm, a ship, a husband, and a child. She was no longer certain that the man she called her husband had chosen her, or that they had gone to his family's hut, where he had pressed his sex inside hers. She thought she might have dreamed of entering the birthing hut, felt her body open, held the newborn. Yet she remembered the child's face, her mouth, the way she ran. Her mind filled with pictures, her ears with voices. She did not so much take hold of these things as observe them, like a swarm of butterflies. Deep within her mind she began to think that she had always been alone.

Once she thought she was on the mainland, going toward the great lodge, but it was only the cliff above the sea elephants' cove. She looked over the edge to where the animals basked in the sun, talked to herself, wept, laughed. It was cold. She did not know how many seasons had passed since the storm, but she knew that she wanted to die.

She ate poisonous plants and felt pain in her stomach and head beyond anything she had ever endured. Afterward her mind was washed clean and she was not unhappy. She had wild dogs for friends, tame birds, vague memories of a small child, a belief that sometime a ship would take her to a place where she was supposed to be.

It was during this time that she wandered to the far end of the island and let herself be blown by the wind like a dried leaf. She found herself on a narrow beach where the wind held her dress tight against her body. Surf hissed, gulls cried. It would have been easy to walk into the sea and let herself be carried out to the deep water. She had almost drowned once, but the memory of the pain was nothing like the pain she now felt. And it was then that she happened to look toward the northern end of the beach and saw a large canoe, the kind the men used for fishing, dragged far up on the sand. She looked at it a long time, searching for signs of damage. It was too much to believe that it was seaworthy, but when she walked around it, she saw that every plank was tight. When she dug the sand from the bottom with a shell, there were no holes and there was a paddle, its handle worn smooth from the long work of many hands. All she could think of then was getting it into the water, and she pulled with all her strength, but it would not move. She pushed and it would not move. Her freedom lay heavily in the sand, but she was not defeated. She remembered that when the makers finished with these canoes, they placed logs on the beach and pushed them over the logs to the sea.

For two days, from first light to dusk, she cut and trimmed limbs as large as she could carry and placed them from the bow all the way down to the sea. She dug the sand from beneath the bow and pushed a limb into the hole. She did the same at the midpoint of the canoe, but it did no good. She pushed and pulled until the strength went out of her. Only then did she admit that it was so heavy, it would take six strong men to move it from its place.

She gathered the stalks of dreamplants and then began a fast, breaking it only to take a little water. Three days later, when she judged her body purified, she stripped the stalks and squeezed their milky juice into a cup and drank. She scattered a handful of sand over the embers of the fire outside the hut so that a line of smoke rose into the darkness. Then, so suddenly she was not even surprised, her head snapped back and she could feel the veins pulsing in her eyes. She tried to cover herself with the otter skin, but her hands had lost their strength. Soon winged canoes were flying through the air and the sky was tumbling, rainbowed with vivid colors. Great birds pierced her flesh with arrow beaks. She was dragged to the woods by wild dogs, set upon by eyeless men, plunged into the sea where swordfish waited. Water filled her lungs and she felt herself becoming part of the sea. Then she was floating, and though her mind was still gripped by the dreamplant, she saw her power. It came upon her as a small thing in the corner of the eye; it widened, spreading out until she saw nothing other than her spirit ship.

The next day she was too weak to do anything but think of the spirit ship, the house of the sea. Long ago, when she was still a child and knew no better, she climbed the rocks above the place where the *'altomolich*, the makers of canoes, were hard at work some distance from the village. Only the master and his helpers were allowed there, and as she remembered what they did, she saw her spirit ship come into being, plank by plank. Old men whose faces she could not see planed its boards and fitted them so carefully that if it were not for the narrow bead of tar, squeezed out by the pressure of the bindings, no seam would have been visible. Then the old men vanished and the hull sprouted two tall masts, and upon these masts appeared sails the color of purple lupine, and from these masts and sails rigging intricate as a spider's web sprang forth.

In the morning she ate flat cakes of meal; she went into the woods and cut tender branches from young trees, which she carried back to the village and stripped of their bark. She boiled water in a stone bowl and in this water placed the branches so that they would soften. When they cooled, she fixed their ends together with a length of cord and bent the branches into the curved shape she had envisioned. To match the purple lupine of the sails, she mixed crushed berries until the color appeared in the mortar, and she painted pieces of bark cut into the shape of sails. She set snares in the woods, and after several days found two splendid birds whose feathers she sewed to the skeleton of the hull.

She fixed her spirit ship with cords in the crotch of a tree not far from the cove, and when she looked at it from a little distance it floated not only on the sea but also on the air, binding island and mainland one to the other in a stitchery almost too delicate to see. This was her power, and she gave herself to it, confident that it would not fail.

Every day, whether in sun or rain, she went there and sang snatches of old songs. Every night in her dreams, the *Enterprise* came into the cove. As the seasons passed, the bark of the spirit ship loosened, the masts tilted; at last only a skeleton remained in the tree.

# 2

◆ ◆ ◆

That morning at the dawn of the nineteenth century, Fray Xavier Santos as usual wakened to the sound of the mission bells calling friars and neophytes to prayer. Since it was his turn to say Mass, he dressed quickly and was waiting at the altar when the Indians entered through the main door, where some of the brothers separated the men and women, sending them to opposite sides of the church. He disapproved of this measure even though experience had proved it necessary, and he was equally unhappy that men had to be stationed in the aisle with whips and goads to enforce silence and keep the neophytes in a kneeling position. Just as he was about to begin, a young Indian was pushed through the door, rubbing his shoulders, where he had undoubtedly been whipped for lagging behind. He whimpered loudly throughout Mass.

Afterward there was a delay in serving the morning meal, so the Indians were nearly an hour late going to work in the fields. A newcomer, Fray Olivares, had been put in charge of the kitchen, and because Fray Santos was especially impatient that morning he spoke to the younger man more sharply than he meant to. When Henry Harper did not appear by noon, Fray Santos found Olivares and told him to keep an eye out for his visitor. He was going up to the canyon, he said, and asked the young friar to come for him as soon as Harper arrived. His emphasizing the importance of the meeting seemed to mollify Fray Olivares, and with the misunderstanding smoothed over, Fray Santos went out to the portico. Twenty long-haired Chumash musicians were arrayed in a semicircle around Fray Humberto's music stand, all following the precise beat of his thin baton. Many of Fray Santos's brothers believed the Indians were incapable of improvement, and although he was more optimistic, the purity of the orchestra's melodies stunned him. He had long ago concluded that the quality of the music could be attributed only to Divine Intercession.

Had this been a normal Saturday, he would have stayed to listen, because he loved the way music sounded in the portico. But he wanted time to think about the woman lost ten years earlier and his recent meeting with Henry Harper, so he descended the stairs and set off for the canyon; he reached it fifteen minutes later, sweating and out of breath from the climb.

Fray Santos walked into the hills whenever he could in order to be alone in a small grove of trees beside the dam. He had discovered the retreat by accident one day soon after arriving in Santa Bárbara. He had been raised in Seville, and while he never doubted the call to the priesthood, which came when he was fourteen years old, he had not been prepared for the sparsely populated settlement on the coast. He took to walking into the hills whenever he could in an effort to calm his nerves and focus his attention on the great task of conversion that lay before him. Much as he loved the mission, he needed a place to be alone, and it was his good fortune to have found this quiet clearing marked by a fledgling angels' trumpet tree, which he interpreted as a sign from God. After an Indian carpenter made a simple bench for him, the clearing became his special place to meditate or work out problems having to do with mission business.

As he settled down to catch his breath, light filtered through the branches of the tree patterned his round face, still unwrinkled although he was now forty-nine. The voluminous brown cassock descending to his sandals did little to disguise his girth, and the white rope that belted the robe sat high on his stomach, suggesting the waistline of dresses worn by wealthy women of the parish.

Whenever he needed to concentrate, he fingered the rope belt, and as he gazed down toward the mission and the town the thumb and forefinger of his right hand rhythmically inched the rope into his palm until he reached the knotted end and released his grip to begin again.

Now that he was alone, the urgency of trying to anticipate Harper's demands was not as compelling as it had seemed. He was always overprepared, and today was no exception. After Harper agreed to see him, he had worked out his position with the care of a mathematician, and he realized somewhat ruefully that it would be best to relax and calm himself as much as possible.

From the bench he could see the double front doors of the church, flanked by six pink columns rising to twin bell towers. Oak groves surrounded the mission, and there were fledgling palms whose seeds had been gathered in the desert foothills by priests of the San Bernardino mission and sent as gifts to the brothers in Santa Bárbara. The tile-and-stone aqueduct flowing from the dam to reservoirs branched right, into the grain fields and orchards. A smaller tributary snaked left, where it fed a fountain in front of the church as well as a rectangular *lavandería*. He watched women washing clothes and beating them clean on the smooth sloping stones that drained the wash water into hedges.

Fray Santos loved this view. He had lived in Santa Bárbara long enough to see the mission develop from its first rude structures to an elaborate complex whose beauty was not limited to façades, tiled roofs, and tended fields where the Indian laborers appeared scarcely larger than ants. The building enclosed more delights, for the walls, windows, ceilings, lintels, doorways, and niches were decorated with elaborate designs copied from pattern books brought from Mexico, along with an architectural treatise of Vitruvius which had supplied other models for the Indian artists. Charcoal, indigo, cinnabar, copper ore, and verdigris supplied the pigments for the floral and geometric designs covering the walls. The altar pieces were also carved and painted, and many rooms displayed wainscoting and paneling made to look like marble. Simple bands of color framed the doors, although the west entrance was decorated with rows of triangles with laurel branches flanking the jambs and a large six-petal flower that was painted above the arch and always pleased him with its symmetry.

During his time at the mission Fray Santos had become something of a legend because of his work with the Indians, but he always reminded himself that he was merely a humble servant harvesting the fields of God. Despite his successes, he was never satisfied; every convert made him think of those who had not yet been brought into the fold, and many of the hours spent beneath his beloved angels' trumpet tree were devoted to thoughts of the spiritual condition of the lost souls. He thought of them in light of the Scriptures as well as in the writings of the early fathers, but when Fray Bernardino prevailed on the superior to allow him a telescope, Fray Santos's thinking changed.

One night the old friar invited him into his room to gaze at the stars. It was the first time he had seen the heavens with other than his naked eye, and as soon as he adjusted the focus and saw Venus shining as brightly as the moon, he discovered his image for the unconverted. It seemed that the blackness of space was swirling around the distant stars, and nothing he had read or thought of so perfectly conveyed the condition he had meditated on so long. Even before he relinquished the telescope to Fray Bernardino, he named it the Wind in the Void, and imagined all the lost souls in the universe swirling about in the vast interstellar darkness.

Since that winter night several years ago he had incorporated the idea into his discussions with the neophytes, who were especially susceptible to images. The idea soon became his trademark. He explored it further in a few poems and at great length in his journal. But rich as it was in widening his understanding, it was not until two months ago, after he had spoken to an Irish sailor, that the idea took on its present urgency.

O'Reilly had called him aside after Mass and begged to speak to him. They went out to the portico, and as soon as they sat down on a bench he began what seemed like a pointless story concerning himself and several companions who had decided that after the passage of many years it might still be possible to find sea otters on the island of San Nicolás. The smell of whiskey on O'Reilly's breath was pronounced, and the thought that the man was simply engaged in drunken rambling angered Fray Santos. O'Reilly said that he had taken only a few drinks to steady his nerves. "Be patient, Father. I'm coming to it as best I can."

O'Reilly had persuaded an acquaintance with a sailboat to take them out to the island. On the second afternoon, as they started up a ridge to admire the view, one of his companions reminded him of the story of the woman who had drowned in the cove years ago. He admitted that they had all been drinking that day, and that may have been why he felt her presence as soon as he reached the ridge. "She was there, watching, and I didn't feel drunk then, Father, not on your life." As he descended he thought he saw a shadowy figure disappear behind some rocks, and when he reached the boat he was positive that a dark shape was visible in the trees at the edge of an embankment. His voice quavered as he added, "I know something was there. It must have been her ghost."

Fray Santos remained silent after O'Reilly finished. Perhaps a minute passed, perhaps more. It was not until O'Reilly said, "Father, what do you think?" that he gathered himself sufficiently to chastise the man, warning him that belief in ghosts offended God. He sent him on his way with the provision that he think no more about such things and say ten Hail Marys.

Since it was a sunny day, he thought it would be pleasant to go up to the dam, but he was so impatient that he did not get any farther than the Sacred Garden, where he sat down heavily on a bench in the shadow of the statue of Santa Bárbara. Only then did he allow himself to think about this extraordinary revelation.

Like everyone else in the town, Fray Santos knew the story of the woman of San Nicolás Island. It was commonly assumed that even if she had not drowned, there would have been no hope for her, since the *Enterprise* had been dispatched the very next day and went down in a storm off the coast of Carmel. The sadness of her fate bore down on him long after he learned of it. At first he thought of it as being in a class with other disasters that illustrated the precariousness of human life. He did not realize how narrow that view was until he woke one morning, before the first bells chimed, with a clear and glittering idea. She had been on the verge of salvation when she threw herself into the sea, dying without the knowledge of God's grace. If against all odds she and the child had miraculously survived, there was an extraordinary opportunity for salvation at hand. When he remembered other splendid conversions, it seemed that this prospect shone just as brightly. He contemplated the poignant details of her rescue and conversion, and the sun felt warmer than usual, the scent of flowers very sweet.

Late that afternoon he went to see Fray Velásquez, and after he had vigorously presented a case for the positive effects her rescue would have on the community, his superior agreed to fund an expedition, authorizing a substantial fee to any shipowner willing to undertake the voyage.

As soon as Fray Santos began thinking of the logistics of the venture, it was obvious that he had to discount the sailboat owned by O'Reilly's friend. He would need a ship capable of carrying a number of men and considerable provisions. There were only three prospects, and by early the following week he had eliminated his first two choices. Diego Madrigal's vessel was undergoing repairs, and Marcus Whitby had accepted a contract to haul lumber from Monterey to Los Angeles. That left Henry Harper. All Fray Santos knew about him was that he owned a coastal schooner and lived on a small ranch north of the mission. He attended church infrequently, but his wife, Elizabeth, was a deeply spiritual woman who attended Mass every Sunday. He had come to know her well soon after she and her husband arrived in Santa Bárbara; she sought him out after Mass one day and they talked for an hour about a spiritual matter he could no longer remember. Since then, they met regularly, and he had the impression that something was bothering her, though she never spoke about her personal life. She read a good deal, and he was surprised by the depth of her knowledge of literature and theology. None of the other parishioners was capable of carrying on such interesting discussions, though he was sometimes distracted because her blue eyes always seemed sorrowful.

He had not spoken more than a dozen words to Harper, all of them limited to pleasantries on the stairs in front of the mission. As far as he could determine, Harper was a self-sufficient man, absorbed in his business. He would have preferred dealing with Madrigal or Whitby, but Harper was his only choice, and he cast about for the best method to approach him. When he decided to present his case to husband and wife together, reasoning that Elizabeth's piety might be useful, the deviousness of the plan bothered him until he reminded himself that it was to facilitate a noble cause. After that he was able to see his action as free of any ethical taint, and he rewarded himself with an afternoon on the beach, his eyes never straying from the islands.

Luckily, the Harpers attended Mass together the following Sunday. Although Fray Santos would have liked a few more days to think about his plan, he knew it might be weeks before he found them together again. He was not a man to hang back where his interests were involved, and when Mass was over he hurried outside. It was a warm summer morning, and women had opened their parasols to shade themselves from the sun. When he saw the Harpers halfway down the drive talking to three other couples, he went straight to them, refusing to talk to anyone on the way. He said there was a matter of some urgency that could not wait and quickly guided them through the crowd and up the stairs to the portico, where he led them into a room and closed the door. There were two long oak tables with candelabra and reading stands as well as a bouquet of red and white carnations. The walls were covered with eight large paintings dully reflecting light from the windows that opened onto the portico. It was a somber, formal room, perfect for a serious discussion, and Fray Santos, without speaking, pulled out two of the tall, rush-bottomed chairs in the hope that his manner would convey the seriousness of the occasion. Elizabeth looked worried, but Harper was curious; as soon as he sat down he said, "What is it?"

Fray Santos was certain that they knew the story of the lost woman, but it seemed prudent to recount it briefly. As he talked, he was attentive to both of them, trying to gauge the effect of his revelations in their eyes and faces. Harper listened without giving any indication of his feelings, but Elizabeth was deeply moved, and he congratulated himself because he was certain that he had touched her conscience. To make sure, he emphasized the pathos of the story, infusing it with religious sentiment.

"Think of it," he concluded. "Ten years alone on the island, mother and child."

Harper had been watching him carefully, and now there was a sparkle in his eyes. "If she's there, why didn't she give herself up to this Irishman?"

"The question has bothered me, too," Fray Santos said, and he was ready with what he believed was a plausible answer. "We know that hunters decimated the otters and killed many of her people. No doubt O'Reilly and his friends reminded her of them. If his companions are at all like him, they may well have been among those who pillaged the island."

"Would she have been so scared that she'd have given up the chance of being rescued? If you want my opinion, I think this Irishman's pulling your leg."

"Fear does strange things. I admit it seems unlikely that she would not have made her presence known, but then neither of us has been threatened with death, as she no doubt was many times in the old days. It is more than conceivable that she would have preferred to stay."

"Have you ever been to any of the islands?"

"Henry, please. It may be true. Isn't that good enough?" Elizabeth asked.

Fray Santos was grateful that she had spoken up. He judged the time had come to mention that Fray Velásquez had agreed to pay for the use of Harper's schooner.

Harper looked out the window for a moment before putting his hand on Elizabeth's, who seemed to shrink at his touch. "No one could have survived that long, but give me a few days to mull it over."

He did not hear from either of them during the week. On Sunday he saw Elizabeth at Mass, but he was delayed afterward by an old woman whose husband had recently died, and by the time he sent her on her way there was no sign of Mrs. Harper.

By the following Wednesday he had all but given up on Harper and had begun to think he would have to wait until Madrigal's ship was repaired. But a note, delivered by one of Harper's ranch hands, said that Harper would come to the mission sometime the following Saturday. There was nothing in the note about what he had decided, but Fray Santos was confident that he would not come to decline the offer. The pleasure he took in the certainty that Harper would provide his ship was undercut by the man's refusal to mention a specific time. The more he thought about it, the more likely it seemed that Harper was trying to unsettle him so as to increase his advantage in whatever bargaining would take place. This was one of the reasons for his going up to the dam: Harper would think he too had other things to do.

As he gazed down on the fields he had no doubt that the woman was alive, and he began to think of the work of her conversion. He was aware of the opportunity she presented. She would be his special convert, and he intended to make an example of her. Not only would his brothers find her remarkably well versed, but perhaps others as far away as Los Angeles would, also. It was, to his mind, within the realm of possibility that the news might reach Rome.

His plans were forming up nicely when he saw Fray Olivares coming up the path. Eager as he was to see Harper, he wished that the man had been even more tardy. It was pleasant to think about the effect of the conversion while sitting beneath his splendid tree, and he did not move until Fray Olivares pushed aside the branches. As he rose, he worked the last few inches of his belt through his fingers and then, satisfied, let it fall.

The orchestra was still practicing when he hurried up to the portico, entered the room where Harper was waiting, and saw him standing in front of a painting of the Assumption and Coronation of the Virgin. As soon as he greeted Harper, he invited him to the far end of the room. Fortunately, the drums ceased, as did the horns, and he had to contend only with a mournful song played by the pipers. When he offered Harper a chair, the man said that he preferred to stand.

He was, as far as Fray Santos could judge, about thirty-five. His face was large, his jaw square beneath a short beard, and his eyes had the look of a man accustomed to getting his way. He seemed altogether different without Elizabeth, even more obdurate than he had been during their first meeting.

"I'm grateful that you've agreed."

"In principle. We need to settle on the bounty."

The word struck him as unpleasant. Even fee had sounded crass when Fray Velásquez used the term.

"I prefer to think of it as remuneration for a deed of mercy."

Harper's face softened and his voice became conciliatory. "No offense intended."

He paused before saying that he could not undertake the voyage for less than a sum that was considerably beyond what Fray Velásquez had suggested, but Fray Santos was in no mood to argue. Although he realized that he should at least present the appearance of bargaining, now that he was face to face with Harper he did not want to risk alienating him. Besides, giving in now might prove useful later. He was more worried about how he was going to extract the additional money from Fray Velásquez, though he did not for a moment question his ability to do it. "Agreed."

"Good. I also want an Indian who can talk to her, and this O'Reilly you told me about will have to show me where he saw her."

The friar assured Harper there would be no problem with a translator. Though he was fairly certain that illness had killed off the Nicoleños years before, he was confident that one of the workers at the mission, Jesús, knew at least a few of the islanders' words. Convincing O'Reilly would be more difficult.

"And you too. In case something goes wrong, I want someone I can rely on."

During the interminable wait for Harper's response Fray Santos had taken into account a range of contingencies. He had been prepared for Harper's demand for more money. He had made plans to free Jesús from much of his work so that he could translate for him once the woman was brought back, and he had already thought about ways in which Fray Velásquez might rearrange his duties so that he would be able to spend as much time as possible with her. But the one prospect that had not occurred to him had been broached by Harper, who was looking expectantly at him now, apparently surprised by his hesitation.

"Yes, of course I understand," he said. The truth was that he was completely unprepared for this demand. The journey from Spain to Mexico many years ago was the most frightening thing that had happened in his life. There had been two terrible storms, a man had been washed overboard, and he had been wretchedly sick almost from the beginning. The moment he reached Veracruz he thanked God for saving his life and swore that never again would he set foot on a ship. Months passed before the nightmares ceased, and several years afterward he still could not think about the ocean without shuddering. His dream of the ocean raised its head as suddenly as a ground squirrel sitting up when it senses danger. Just as quickly it vanished, replaced by excitement and a perception of an unforeseen opportunity. He imagined the scene vaguely, as if he were seeing it through fog or distorted glass, but it was still splendid, and in that instant he overcame his fear.

"I understand," he repeated, trying to remain calm. "It is only fitting that I accompany you."

As soon as Harper left, Fray Santos presented himself to his superior. He had given Harper no indication that it would be necessary to obtain permission to leave the mission. While Fray Velásquez hesitated when Fray Santos made this unusual request, the superior was also excited by the prospect of finding the woman, and in the end he acquiesced.

In the days that followed, Fray Santos fulfilled his part of the bargain. As he suspected, none of the islanders had survived the illnesses that had struck the neophytes' village during the last ten years. He insisted that Jesús question everyone regarding his knowledge of Nicoleño, and the young man produced two middle-aged brothers, Antonio and José, who claimed to know the dialect. He invited them to a sunny bench in the cloistered garden where a half-hour's discussion convinced him that at least some rudimentary conversation would be possible. After he promised them a reduction in their work load, as well as larger portions of food at dinner for the next two months, they reluctantly agreed to go along.

When he insisted that it was O'Reilly's Christian duty to help in the rescue of the woman, the Irishman protested that he wanted nothing more to do with her and cursed the moment he set foot on San Nicolás. But Fray Santos persisted, entering his fear of the mysterious like a doctor probing a wound. O'Reilly was unmoved, saying that if he had actually seen a ghost, she must have been intent on doing him irremediable harm. That was their way, if the priest understood his meaning. Fray Santos angrily pointed out that it was sinful to harbor such ideas, and reminded him of the church's position regarding such heretical beliefs. The fight went out of O'Reilly as soon as the priest started in on the future of his soul. Although his view of the invisible world was founded as much on Irish superstition as on Catholic doctrine, men of the cloth had intimidated him from childhood, and this one was no exception.

Harper had set a date for the middle of June, and in the intervening weeks Fray Santos went about his duties more assiduously than ever. In his spare time he retreated to the foundry, where he indulged his passion for ironwork by designing a grille for Fray Velásquez's west window as a way of expressing his gratitude and also easing the way for further requests for money in the event of unforeseen developments.

Two weeks before the departure he was summoned to Fray Velásquez's office, where he found his superior in a black mood. The mission was plagued by backsliding among the neophytes, who seemed to believe that they could embrace Christianity while continuing to worship their old gods. Fray Velásquez informed him that there was evidence of a new outbreak of superstition, and when he asked Fray Santos to look into it, the friar gratefully accepted the charge. He was flattered that the superior had such confidence in him, and was delighted to have something more to do.

He told Mariano, the *mayordomo*, what he wanted to know, and a few days later the man approached him in the foundry, where he was working on the crossbars of Fray Velásquez's grille, saying that a young woman named María had developed a reputation as a sorceress after having had a vision. There was evidence that she had been performing forbidden rites late at night in one of the huts. Fray Santos dispatched Mariano to find her, and the three of them went directly to the superior's room; there, Fray Santos interrogated her with the help of the *mayordomo*.

While she freely admitted to her practices, she was unrepentant, and she described how her people worship their gods by offering them seeds, and then fasting and dancing in their honor. Her vision had empowered her to prescribe certain herbs, roots, and feathers that could free people from illness as well as enemies. "From you and the soldiers," Mariano said.

Until then she had looked only at Mariano, but when Fray Santos demanded to know more about her vision, she stared defiantly at him as Mariano translated.

"Everything she dreams has come true," Mariano said. "Her last vision was from herbs given to her by a shaman she will not name. She took them, and in her dream she met Chupu, who told her that all Indians would die unless they renounced baptism by bathing in the tears of the sun."

Fray Santos was outraged but not surprised. He had encountered superstition from the beginning of his work at the mission, but he was disheartened to learn about the cult because it might take months, even years, before her influence could be banished.

"We need to make an example of her," Fray Santos answered. "The best way is the painful way." But when he suggested that she be whipped, he did so with a heavy heart; he disliked physical punishment even in such grievous cases.

The episode with María did not affect his thinking about the woman on the island. On the contrary, it encouraged him to believe that converting her would be relatively easy, since she would not have been plagued by shamans or sorceresses. He was certain that without the influence of spiritual leaders she could not have maintained much in the way of belief after all those years.

When he thought about this time later, Fray Santos attributed the discovery of his picture to the calm that preceded the voyage to San Nicolás. After María's punishment, everything had returned to normal. Once his work was done he sat in the cloistered garden, admiring the trees and flowers, or walked up and down the halls with his hands clasped behind his back as he looked at the paintings on the walls. When he first arrived, the allegorical representations led him to meditate on the great moments of his religion, but as the years wore on their power began to fade. Although he continued to believe in them as a means of improvement for parishioners and neophytes, they lost their ability to move him personally and came to seem little more than decorations; he would pass through the building, unconsciously directing his gaze to other things that were more interesting.

That was why his renewed interest came as a surprise. It began with small details. Despite the static poses and strange landscapes, the representations of Jesus, Mary, saints, and common people suddenly emerged from the picture planes and affected him both physically and emotionally. When he examined *The Adoration of the Magi* he found himself attending not only to the figures of the Infant and Mother, but to the people around them. He was aware that he was searching the painting like a student, trying to decipher the principles of composition and the means by which the artist had achieved his effects.

Then, two months after O'Reilly came to him, he began rearranging some of the scenes to conform with his own imaginings. He was so disturbed that he thought it might be advisable to consult one of his brothers, but he judged that to be excessive and decided that all he needed to do was refrain from looking at the pictures altogether. The next day, when the details of half a dozen of the paintings came to him as he was eating lunch, he suddenly understood what had happened. Portraits of the Virgin, even faces of women in crowd scenes, had assumed qualities that he associated with the woman the day he discovered that she might still be alive. As he ate his pozole, he found himself substituting an image of an Indian woman in native dress for certain holy figures in the paintings. This proved unsatisfactory not only because it seemed blasphemous, but because the images in the pictures did not conform with his idea about his relationship with her.

The picture evolved slowly, over several days. Then one evening, as he was listening to the Poor Souls' bell, it came to him all at once. She knelt demurely before him, holding her child close as he made the sign of the cross. There was a bit of the sea visible in the background, and the ridge of San Nicolás Island. As he looked on, golden light began to creep in until it surrounded them as if they were figures in an illuminated manuscript. Moreover, people in the background who solemnly acknowledged this holy moment bore striking resemblances to many of his brethren.

Now, whenever he conjured it up, he experienced a troubling mixture of excitement and guilt that led to penance for the sin of vanity. But even though the picture made him uneasy, he found consolation in the belief that her rescue and conversion would sit like a crown on all his good works, and despite the sting of conscience that always accompanied these thoughts, his eyes would narrow a little, crinkling at the edges as he indulged in his secret pleasure.

Mariano drove Fray Santos, Jesús, and the brothers to the dock, where Harper was already on board the *Elizabeth's Delight*. O'Reilly loitered beside a stack of boxes some sailors were loading onto the schooner. When Fray Santos greeted him, he smelled whiskey, but there was no point in admonishing the man now. After they reached the island he would warn O'Reilly that it would be hard on him if he did not stay sober.

The sun was up by the time the crew cast off the lines and the ship headed into the channel. The wind had blown the sky so clean that the islands' ridges and canyons were surprisingly distinct, belying the distance that separated them from the mainland. Fray Santos loved the mysterious nature of the islands. After an east wind their cliffs, arroyos, and even stands of trees were clearly visible. At other times mists veiled them so that they no longer seemed anchored in the sea at all, but appeared to float on the horizon, stretching themselves like large, sleek creatures, awakening.

San Nicolás was a low, violet shape on the horizon. In a matter of minutes, it became larger, as if he were seeing it through a telescope. Sand dunes sloped to the sea at the western end, and the eastern rose precipitously to a giant escarpment that towered hundreds of feet above the sea. Within the hour they were close enough for him to make out the details of its surface and to smell the rank scent of decaying seaweed scattered in green and purple coils upon the rocks. What had seemed interesting in the distance was now stark and melancholy. In his picture he had imagined the island's contours as softly pleasing, but everything was sharp and abrupt, as if San Nicolás had been carved into shape with quick thrusts of a dull knife. The mottled surface of the rock opened to a cove where sea elephants sunned themselves and watched the passing ship as indifferently as the ospreys, kestrels, and swallows that flew in lazy profusion, patterning the sky with spirals and circles all the way up to the lip of the escarpment. He heard faint roars from the sea elephants, cries from the multitudinous aviary that swirled above them, but he was aware too of a heavy and abiding silence that hovered behind the sounds and seemed to dominate the place, pressing down from the sky like the palm of a great invisible hand.

His reading had led him to an old map of San Nicolás that he had taken to his room only two nights earlier. He had studied it carefully as he reconstructed what was known of the woman's fate, looking for a long time at the half-moon indentation of Dutch Harbor, where she was said to have thrown herself into the water. Now the cove lay straight ahead, and the black rocks flanking its southern and eastern sides reminded him of the waves that had threatened the ship bringing him to New Spain. Harper was standing by the leeward rail, having given the helm to his mate, and he was looking at Fray Santos with the same expression he had worn that day at the mission, when he appeared to be taking his measure. "Don't worry. We won't fetch up against them."

The assurance relieved Fray Santos, though it was disturbing that the man seemed able to read his mind. He had not given Harper the credit he deserved, and decided to be more careful.

"Look over there. You can see how the tide runs at an angle to shore. Anyone in the water would have gone straight onto the rocks."

It was true. The pattern of the riptide moving against the grain of the surf was as clear as the warp and woof in a piece of cloth. He tried to imagine what it would be like to swim to shore as he watched the breakers rolling toward the beach; a wild dog came out from a stand of bushes and trotted down to the water's edge.

"And the child?"

"The dogs would have made short work of a child," Harper said, adding, "We can still go back."

Now that Fray Santos had seen the dog, and understood the dangers posed by rocks and tides to anyone trying to swim ashore, his confidence in their survival began unraveling. Not long ago he was walking on the beach when a drowned man was pulled from the surf, and he could not avoid thinking of the woman's pale, bloated body washed up on the beach, or the child hidden beneath a pack of ravening dogs. He imagined Fray Velásquez through the rents and tears of his lovely picture, his face red with anger as he chastised him for wasting so many pesos.

At that moment he was inclined to believe that Harper's view was at least as valid as his own, but then he remembered O'Reilly's fear. The man was a drunkard and a coward, but he had been utterly convinced by what he saw. As the dog ran off down the beach, the friar turned to Harper, shaking his head. "No, we go ashore."

They camped at the southern end of the cove where the escarpment slanted down to a grassy area above the dunes. The crew had pulled the three boats well up onto the beach before rigging a shelter of canvas tied to poles and oars for themselves and separate ones for Fray Santos and Harper. Antonio, José, and Jesús made a place for themselves between the boats.

Fray Santos was tired from lack of sleep, and after dinner he retired to his shelter, declining Harper's invitation to join the crew at a bonfire they had built against the evening chill. While they ate, the sun had guttered out, a candle flame consumed by blue wax, and now the eastern sky had taken on the violet color of the sea. A steady wind blew from the approaching darkness, and no one had to tell him this was a permanent condition on San Nicolás. It was imprinted on the descending night not as a ferocious, devouring wind such as those which came down the mountains, but rather as a nagging presence that reached to the nerves. Never to be free of the sound and the feel of it against his skin was inconceivable. He could endure it for a day or two, but if he had been here all those years, if he had had to live with it . . .

Sympathy warmed his heart. Again he was convinced that she was out there, living a life that seemed to him even more unthinkable, now that he was here and had begun to understand its terms. That fledgling knowledge was what lay behind the melancholy he felt when he was close enough to see this strange, unearthly place. He watched as bats roamed the sky above the camp, moving with astonishing speed on silent wings, their tiny shapes clear against what was left of the light as they ascended and disappeared into darkness. Perhaps she was watching too. Or she might be looking down at the bonfire from a hiding place somewhere on the jagged edge of the escarpment, where she would be able to see the tiny figures of the men. She would be frightened as she wondered who they were and whether they intended to do her harm. Until then she had remained an abstract figure whose features were composed of details from a dozen paintings and the faces of female neophytes that he knew. Now he felt close to her, intimate, as if by entering her mind he had made her truly alive.

Long after night came he continued to gaze toward the invisible edge of the escarpment, and when he finally lay down it was with a clear image of a woman dressed in rags, a face marked by years of wind, and eyes reflecting the sparks blowing off the fire and rising into the darkness like burning beads.

The cries of sea gulls woke him, and he sat up, unaware for a moment of where he was. He had been dreaming, but he could remember nothing besides the sound of a boy's tenor. As he pushed the doorflap aside, he saw that a large fish had washed up on the beach not far away and gulls were fighting one another for the privilege of its flesh. The Indians had a fire going. Jesús, seeing him, held up a tin plate. Fray Santos shook his head, closed the flap, and said his prayers.

When he opened it a half hour later Harper was standing beside the fire, rubbing his hands together while two sailors prepared food. O'Reilly sat nearby; even at a distance Fray Santos could see that his face was puffy and his eyes bloodshot from last night's drinking. Harper did not look much better.

"Good morning. How did you sleep?" Fray Santos asked.

"I missed my bed," O'Reilly replied.

"Well, if we have any luck you'll be back in it in a night or two."

"A year is what it will be like to me." O'Reilly looked sourly at the sailor who was stirring something in a blackened iron pot. "Where did you find such awful drink?" he said accusingly.

The sailor laughed and offered an obscene reply that Fray Santos pretended not to hear.

After they had eaten the porridge, which was tasteless even by mission standards, Harper called everyone together in front of his shelter and said that they should fan out the length of the beach and then move inland, keeping each other in sight. Anyone who saw the woman was to fire his pistol. Those who were not with the group that flushed her were to go in the direction of the shots.

"Enjoy yourselves," O'Reilly said. "I'm sleeping off this poison."

"I want you along," Harper said.

"What for?"

"Not the pleasure of your company. I want to know where you saw her."

O'Reilly groaned. "I told him everything," he whined.

"Tell me. I don't intend to stay here any longer than I have to," countered Harper.

O'Reilly looked pleadingly at Fray Santos. The man was suffering, but the friar felt only anger. "You have only yourself to blame. Perhaps tonight you will show some restraint."

When they reached the crest of the dunes they were struck with a gust of wind that flattened the sparse sea grass and pressed the friar's cassock tight against his body. O'Reilly cursed the wind and looked away when Fray Santos glowered at him. As they headed up the southern slope of the escarpment, Fray Santos studied the ridge line. He had not forgotten the image of the woman that came to him last night, though she had lost a little of her strangeness. The others were soon ahead of him, and his breath came hard as his feet sank into the sand. It was easier once they were beyond the dunes, and he felt stronger, capable of anything that might be required of him. Now that he was on higher ground and had a better view of the island he was struck by its barrenness, which suggested it was all but impossible for anyone to survive there for very long. But his conviction that she was alive, that she had to be alive, overcame the testimony of his eyes, and he climbed on, trying to think of what it would be like afterward.

They found nothing on the first sweep. From the ridge it was possible to see the island from end to end. To the west, the sea was flecked with whitecaps. To the east, the mainland was little more than a dark line on the horizon. A group of sailors appeared at the southern end of the mesa, and one of them waved, seeming to indicate that they too had had no luck. A large stand of trees grew in the canyon separating them, and Harper pointed to it, saying, "We'll go back down there."

Not long after they began their descent Harper raised his left hand, stopping Fray Santos, who was walking beside him. "I'll be damned."

"What is it?"

There was a faint path, and when Fray Santos saw the outline of a bare foot he could only stare, crossing himself a moment later as an afterthought.

O'Reilly was breathing heavily when he reached them. "I'm perishing for lack of breath. What's the matter?"

"Look."

"Mother of God," O'Reilly said as he backed away.

Harper looked at him with disgust. "There's nothing to be afraid of."

O'Reilly confronted the footprint as if it were a snake, coiled and ready to strike. "Oh, that's fine for you to say, squire. As far as I'm concerned, that's a ghost mark as sure as there are saints in heaven."

"Do not blaspheme," Fray Santos warned. "This is the sign of a miracle and you have been its agent."

O'Reilly did not seem to be pleased with his exalted status as he stepped back a little farther.

"Is this where you saw her?" Harper asked.

"It could have been. I'd had a drop to drink."

"Come on," Harper said, and Fray Santos took hold of O'Reilly's sleeve, forcing the reluctant man down the path.

They came upon the village halfway down the canyon. When he first saw the huts through the stunted trees and heavy brush, Fray Santos remembered the excitement he had experienced years ago when he visited the settlements. This was something he recognized and understood. The circular shapes became more distinct as they went into the trees, but when they reached the open space where the huts were congregated, he realized that these dwellings were different from any he had seen. He stood in the middle of what had once undoubtedly been the center of the village, surrounded by whale bones embedded in the earth. A few of the structures bore the rotting remains of their seal-skin and woven-grass coverings.

O'Reilly looked around, appalled. "Saints preserve us. It's worse than I dreamed."

Fray Santos ignored him. Each bleached white shape seemed to have risen unaided from the ground, like a fantastic species of plant capable of blossoming into long clear bones. He vaguely remembered a drawing in a book of some heathen building, a Hindu or Moslem place of worship; but bare and stark as these skeletons were, they reminded him most of neither pagan temples nor whited sepulchers but of the mission's bell towers while they were being built by the neophytes.

"Devil's teeth."

"Over here," Harper called.

One hut at the far end of the village was in perfect condition. The skins were freshly cured, and the grasses still retained a green-ish tint. Harper looked inside and shook his head. The brothers squatted by the white ashes of the firepit, and Antonio motioned for him to come closer as he scooped a handful of ash to the side. Even before Fray Santos saw the embers glowing in the whiteness, he smelled smoke.

The hut was surrounded by a circle of bare earth that bore the marks of sweeping and footprints. A row of baskets was neatly arranged to the left of the entrance. Artifacts of the mainland tribes had always interested him, but these were more beautiful in shape and more subtle in design. Each was covered with a square of seal skin held in place by a fiber cord. He picked up a small one and found that it was woven to a tightness that made the individual rings feel smooth and continuous. Removing the cover, he found bone needles, knives, a rusted piece of iron hoop, and what appeared to be a piece of stone. He lifted it out and saw that a whale was carved into the upper portion as in a bas relief; lower down, two smaller ones followed in its wake. He found the blackened flesh of a cooked bird in the basket next to this one, and beyond it a larger one that contained water and a scoop fashioned from bone. The last two held dried nuts, fishing lines, and a length of cord Harper said was probably used for snaring seals. He demonstrated how the coiled end closed quickly on his wrist. Then he replaced it and stood up, his hands on his hips as he surveyed the village. "I was convinced it was a wild goose chase. You must be happy."

Fray Santos was too overcome by emotion to take any satisfaction in Harper's admission. She had appeared to him last night as in a vision, and now, with her things arrayed before him, her life was precisely drawn. The meagerness of her possessions filled him with renewed sympathy and he was more impatient than ever to see her. He wanted to hold out the smooth wooden crucifix he wore around his neck, wanted to hear Jesús address her in the lyrical language of the Chumash as he told her that the cross was the sign of her salvation.

"Do you want to rest, or go on? There's no telling how long this will take," Harper said.

"We must continue."

"At least let me have a drink," O'Reilly said. He dipped the scoop into the water basket and looked around, as if expecting her to appear at any moment.

They followed the path up to the mesa, Harper and O'Reilly walking on her footprints. Fray Santos was careful to step over them. He looked for others, hoping to see the smaller prints of her child. There were none, and he assumed that mother and child had set off in different directions, but the notion did not trouble him. He was certain that they would be found together.

It was windy when they reached the top, and Fray Santos thought wistfully of the heavy cloak he had left in the shelter. He pulled the hood of the cassock over his head and quickened his pace to keep up with Harper.

The mesa descended at a slight angle on the seaward side of the island. A few outcroppings of rock and scattered stands of bushes emphasized the barrenness of the land, which looked as inhospitable as the escarpment had when they approached the cove. They went down through the rocks and came out on a level place above a field of yellow flowers, and it was there, while they discussed whether to continue in that direction or turn back, that he noticed something in the distance, at the far end of the field. In that instant his heart beat against his chest, and he raised his hand and pointed.

"My God!" O'Reilly whispered incredulously. Although they were now sheltered from the wind, he closed his coat and held it with both hands at his neck. Harper wiped his forehead with the back of his hand as he looked down the slope.

"We must not frighten her," Fray Santos said. "Can you see the child?"

"No."

They went down the slope and approached slowly through the field. She was bent over, her back to them, apparently harvesting something from a bush. Suddenly two black dogs rose from the flowers, and as they barked and ran excitedly back and forth she stood up, putting her left hand to the small of her back as if easing the strain of her work. The commotion did not alarm her, and she was about to bend down again when she saw them. Fray Santos put his arm out and spoke to Harper without taking his eyes from her. "Slowly, very slowly."

The dogs came out a little way, barking and snarling, and when she called them, his picture came alive with the sound of her voice. The image he had contemplated was more lovely in the golden light of the yellow flowers. She stood motionless, and he could not tell whether it was from fear or surprise, though he was certain that she would not run.

She had nothing in common with the woman he had envisioned the previous night. Rather than seeing a weather-beaten face, he was looking into the smooth features of a woman not yet thirty. Raven-black hair fell around her face and shoulders, extending below her waist as it framed the strangest dress he had ever seen. At first he thought it was made of tiny pieces of brightly colored cloth, but then he saw that it was fashioned of feathers and would have suggested a chasuble were it not for the wildness of it.

When Harper fired his pistol into the air, the first shot made the dogs howl. The woman's eyes grew wide as she spoke quickly to the animals, who fell silent as she watched Harper stick the pistol in his belt and take hold of Jesús's sleeve. "Go," he said. "Tell her who we are."

O'Reilly laughed as Jesús shook his head. "He's afraid, squire, and smart for it. If he won't have nothing to do with his own kind there's reasons, mark my words. Tie her up and have done with it."

"Shut up."

O'Reilly glanced at Harper, gauging his seriousness. Then, shrugging his shoulders, he stepped back and made a hex sign.

"I'll leave you to the dogs if you don't talk to her," Harper said to the Indian.

"There's nothing to be afraid," Fray Santos said. "Now go on, do as you're told."

Jesús took a step, looked back uneasily at Fray Santos, and went to her, drawing the others forward until they formed a semicircle around him and the woman. As he spoke to her in Chumash, the woman's eyes darted like birds from his mouth to his eyes. Her lips parted. She said something, and then added four more words, pausing between each of them. Jesús turned around. "I do not understand."

"Try again. Tell her about the mission."

He gestured toward the mainland, but she shook her head slowly and repeated the words, and this time there was an urgency in her voice, which rose at the end of each word, as if she were posing questions. When it was clear that Jesús had failed, Fray Santos stepped forward and held his arms close to his chest while he made a rocking motion intended to suggest a child. The excitement that had animated her face drained away, leaving her mouth expressionless but still eloquent as she raised her arms in imitation before opening them and pointing to the earth.

"The child is dead," Fray Santos said.

She looked behind him, and he could hear the excited voices of the crew as they descended the ridge. She stepped backward as she watched and he turned quickly toward the men, putting his finger to his lips. "Be quiet. Do not frighten her."

"She'll have to get used to it," Harper said, looking at her in a peculiar way. "Do you think she'll come?"

"Of course. But tell your men to be careful and keep their distance."

He motioned to her in a courtly, old-fashioned way, sweeping his right arm up and away in the direction of the ridge. "Come, my child. Come."

She repeated the four words with a new inflection that made them sound more exotic and mysterious.

"Yes, yes," he said, as he nodded and turned his attention to the climb.

Surprised as he was that Jesús had been unable to find any common words, he was not disappointed, though the language barrier meant that her conversion would take longer than he had thought. During the short time they had spent together his hopes had come alive in a rush of possibilities, and he realized that her ignorance would act as a shield against anything the neophytes might try to teach her. The cult of María was still fresh in his mind; one never knew how far such influences might have gone. It was better for her to be ignorant, he decided, and as they continued up the slope it seemed that he was climbing toward her soul, on which he would inscribe the doctrine of his faith with all the skill of a sculptor deftly chiseling a shape from a virgin piece of stone. Chips of the hard but brittle carapace surrounding her soul were already falling to the ground, and he kicked them aside with the stones he came upon on the way up to the mesa.

By the time they reached the village Harper was impatient and wanted to go straight down to the beach, but Fray Santos begged him to wait. "She may want some of her things," he argued. When Harper relented, the friar led her to the hut and pointed to the baskets, using sign language to indicate that she should take whatever she wanted. She watched his hands and shook her head. The schooner was visible from where they stood, and she pointed excitedly to it, repeating the four words he had heard earlier.

"Grab her," O'Reilly said. "She'll run away."

"No. Look."

She waited at the edge of the village until they caught up, and then she moved on, glancing back from time to time to make certain they were following. When the path entered a grove above the dunes, she stopped by an old tree whose gnarled trunk bent at an angle away from the sea. Fray Santos saw what appeared to be a dead bird lashed in the crotch between two branches, and he was puzzled as she carefully untied the frayed cord holding it in place.

"What do you make of it?" he asked Harper.

"Who knows? Maybe it's a way to preserve meat."

"Bloody savage," O'Reilly said.

It was not a bird, but an effigy in the form of a ship whose hull was made of thin branches bound together by cords and covered with the same colorful feathers as were in her dress. Two masts were supported by rigging, and the sails seemed to be fashioned from bark, still faintly purple. She pointed to Harper's ship and then her own, repeating the four words. That was enough for Fray Santos. "No. You may not take it," he said sternly, shaking his head.

"What's the harm?" Harper asked.

"Can't you see? It's an idol, an abomination in the sight of God and every Christian. She must begin her new life fresh and clean."

He imagined María speaking to gods in a scatter of corn, or perhaps chanting. "My task is to rid her mind of graven images. Who knows what this represents?"

Harper smiled indulgently, but when he spoke his voice had an edge to it. "It's my ship. I say she takes it."

It was abundantly clear to Fray Santos that Harper would not be persuaded otherwise. "I understand," he said. "I thought better of you."

Harper laughed. "It's only a charm. Do you think she'll catch your soul?"

Before he could say anything, Harper called to the crew and went off in the direction of the sand dunes.

The three sails went up one by one, their wrinkles giving way to smoothness as they bellied out on the midday wind, and the *Elizabeth's Delight* began turning away from the island of San Nicolás, following the invisible track made ten years earlier by the *Enterprise*. While Harper threaded the ship between the black rocks, O'Reilly sat on the deck with his back against the cabin, sipping whiskey from a flask. Fray Santos stood near the mainmast and watched the woman move around the deck, touching davits and lines as if to reassure herself that they were real. She looked at him once and went on, clearly uninterested in his attention. The confusion and anxiety that had marked her face only an hour ago was gone, and it seemed that she had reached an understanding of some kind that manifested itself in an expectant, hopeful expression and a brightness in her eyes that was not tears. She passed him once more while the schooner turned, but when they were headed toward the mainland she went forward to the bow, compensating for the rise and fall of the deck like someone who had spent a lifetime walking to the rhythms of the sea. She had cradled the spirit ship like a baby as she explored the deck. Now, bracing her feet, she held it out at arm's length as she began to sing, and the sound of her voice was borne on the wind to Fray Santos, who could not deny its sweetness.

# 3

◆ ◆ ◆

In those days Santa Bárbara was little more than an outpost inhabited by friars, soldiers, Chumash, tradespeople, ranchers, gamblers, prostitutes, and riffraff. False-fronted wooden stores and warehouses lined Main Street for two blocks, and then the town, such as it was, gave way to fields and pastures, where shacks, houses, and a few buildings large enough in size and grand enough in style to be called mansions were scattered across the foothills. A fledgling prosperity could be detected in this array, a sense of coming civilization that kicked and fretted like an impatient child in the womb, but there was no birth yet, no elegance, no decadent wealth in the woods of Montecito. You could still look in any direction and see the end of things.

The few citizens whose business took them to Los Angeles, or north to San Francisco, left gladly and returned full of stories about those places. But the excitement soon wore off, and even the most optimistic travelers had to admit that a sense of isolation hung like wood smoke over the beauty of Santa Bárbara. To encourage the illusion that home was more expansive, they insisted on a vigorous community, and one of its most important features was gossip. When facts were scarce, people happily spread rumors, and little of substance escaped public knowledge. Servants in the large houses were prized sources of information, offering what they overheard and saw to the rumor mills, which ground fact and fiction together to feed the inexhaustible curiosity of the town.

The Harpers' housekeeper and cook, a young Mexican woman named Angelita, achieved considerable status because her master was well known for his capacious house and disliked for his success, which depended on sharp business tactics. Angelita enjoyed nothing better than meeting other young women after Mass on Sundays and exchanging stories with them about what had happened during the last six days; the gentry gathered in groups along the curving driveway and did the same. When the weather was good, the women sometimes went on walks in the fields or into the canyon, but they always left enough time to promenade along the driveway and beside the fences separating the stables and Chumash village from the mission in order to be seen by young bachelors who had come in from the ranches where they worked. It was a custom they had brought from Mexico and adapted to the configuration of the mission, which served the purpose as well as any square in a sun-baked Sonoran town. They wore their best dresses for this morning of prayer and gossip, and those who owned necklaces and bracelets and rings wore them too, so groups of three or four young women passed the bachelors like bright bouquets as they told their stories and glanced shyly at the men in front of the fountain and *lavandería*. The bachelors assumed that nonchalance provided an unmistakable air of confidence, and they leaned against the fences with their boot heels hooked over the lowest rungs, looking on appreciatively from beneath the brims of sombreros as they exchanged fantasies about the most beautiful women.

So it was that on the Sunday after Harper left, on the wild-goose chase made palatable by the mission's pesos, Angelita walked arm in arm with Graciela and María Elena, her best friends in the world, saying in a voice just above a whisper that the fat friar, Fray Santos, had gone with Harper on a voyage to the islands.

"No!" María Elena said.

"Yes. I heard Señor Harper talking about it at the party for Señor Ludlow, and he said that he wanted his reward as soon as they returned."

"Why did they go?"

Angelita knew the value of delay in storytelling, and she glanced at Graciela, telling her that the young man who worked for the Ludlows was eyeing her.

"Angelita," Graciela said angrily, "tell us!"

"What do you want to know?"

"Everything!" María Elena implored.

"They went for the ghost woman."

By the end of the day the story had spread from Graciela and María Elena to their households and then into town, where it enlivened what had been listless conversations at the livery stable and the waterfront saloon called Esteban's, on the ground floor of the St. Charles Hotel. O'Reilly could often be found nursing a whiskey there while he watched the card players and tried to cadge drinks from the winners. He had spent the day before the *Elizabeth's Delight* sailed bragging that he had allowed Fray Santos to persuade him to act as a guide on the voyage and implying some mystery he was not at liberty to discuss; he intended to convert the details of the adventure into a few days of free drinks when he returned. But his plan had been undercut by several of Harper's crew, who had freely admitted that they were going after the woman on the island.

By the time the news reached the gamblers and drunks, it was already old and had given way to many versions of the woman's fate; these passed back and forth as rapidly as the soiled cards being dealt by practiced hands. A man who worked in the tannery claimed, on what he insisted was good authority, that she had taken a pistol from one of the sailors on the *Enterprise* and shot herself in the temple. A soldier from the Presidio argued that she had climbed the mainmast and hanged herself from the crow's nest. There was even a suggestion that she was not an Indian at all, but a white woman from a good family in Paso Robles who voluntarily lived in exile because of some terrible secret. One of Harper's friends was convinced that the search was nothing but a ruse to disguise a remarkable adventure, perhaps the recovery of Juan Cabrillo's treasure. A sea chandler who disliked Harper because of his quick temper and devious business practices said he hoped that whatever had taken Harper to the islands would fail, and, barring the unlikely possibility that he would stove in his hull and be stranded, that he would at least return empty-handed and a laughingstock.

An hour earlier Elizabeth Harper had seen the sails while she was sitting in the gazebo her husband had built for her not long ago. Although the ship was too far away to identify, she had no doubt that it was Henry's. Schooners trading along the coast rarely made the passage so far out to sea, and even if one had strayed, it would not be coming from the direction of San Nicolás. So it was he, and though she felt wretched, her curiosity about the Indians rose up and held for a moment like a hummingbird above a flower before her thoughts returned to a more pressing matter and she leaned back in the wicker chair, giving in to the weight of her body.

Most of her friends cried or ranted in a crisis. She became heavy. For two days the weight of her pain had increased until she could hardly move her arms, walk, or think. She had spent most of the day outside after she had awakened in the dark and listened to the clock ticking on the nightstand for a long time before the first rooster crowed. The dry sound testified to the silence of the house, and she had been unable to decide whether she liked or detested the silence. All she knew was that her ambivalence came as no surprise. For two days it had been impossible to choose between simple things like a white dress or a blue one, or whether it would be better to see her friend Susan Ludlow or stay at home. She was still numb from what had happened the night before Henry left with Fray Santos.

The Harpers had given a party to celebrate Mathew Ludlow's fortieth birthday. In addition to Mathew and Susan, they had invited the trader Timothy Harrington, the Tallents and McHenrys from Goleta Valley, and other friends and acquaintances. A Mexican violinist named Juan Romero had brought three other musicians, and they played all of Mathew's favorite songs in the patio. It was a warm summer night and the windows were left open, so the dining room was filled with music while they ate. After dinner Henry presented Mathew with a pair of fine Mexican spurs as well as a case of wine. Later some of the guests went outside to listen to the musicians while she, Henry, the Ludlows, and Harringtons remained at the table drinking wine that Henry had brought back from San Francisco. Henry was pleased with himself, and it was not long before he began talking about his coming trip to San Nicolás. No one at the table believed that the woman and child could have survived.

"A brother put you up to this?" Ludlow asked incredulously.

"For three hundred pesos. His money is as good as any."

She had not liked it when the men laughed at Fray Santos, but that bothered her less than the thought that Henry was providing his ship because it was important to her. So there had been a subtle deception all along, she realized, and it was made worse when he told Mathew he was pleased to have pulled the wool over the friar's eyes.

"What if they have?" she said.

Ludlow's eyes were red from wine and laughter. "Have what, Elizabeth?"

"Survived."

"Then Henry can damned well civilize them."

"Fray Santos believes the Irishman," she said heatedly. "We should not belittle him."

"No disrespect intended," Henry said.

But he did intend it. He always looked for opportunities to disparage religion. She had enjoyed herself up to then, but the rest of the evening was tainted by Henry's cynicism, and she had gone about her duties as hostess with little enthusiasm and developed a headache behind her eyes.

Half an hour after the guests left, while she was sitting at her dresser, he came into her room. There was no question about what he wanted. She felt resentful and distant, but when she said that she preferred to be alone, he only smiled and sat down on the foot of her bed, where he began to remove his coat and braces. As soon as he pulled his shirt over his head she saw the scratches on his back in the dresser mirror. She wanted to believe they were only a trick of the light, shadows caused by the lamps, the impression of his braces.

She was even willing for them to be a memory of what she had seen a year ago, but when he bent down to pull off his boots, the scratches moved with him and the truth made a fool of her. "You've been with her again!" she whispered. "You promised!" He looked at her frankly but without speaking, without finding it necessary to lie. Then he sighed and stood up slowly, and a few moments later he was going toward the door carrying his coat and shirt, as if he wanted her to have a good look.

She frowned as she remembered, not certain whether the bitterness rose from anger or defeat or self-reproach for her own willed naïveté. All she knew was that it was bitter, and neither the stillness of the mountains nor the placid sea she looked on now could ease her pain.

As she rode to town the scratches patterned everything. They lay among the branches of the trees, divided tilled and virgin fields, cross-hatched the mission's façade, marked the sky, framed the ship coming into the bay; and she peered into this labyrinth, wondering what the woman looked like who had twice raked her nails down her husband's back. She could not imagine her, but she understood what had urged her fingers. In the early days of marriage she had felt the same thing, and the memory made things worse. She swung the riding crop against the horse's flank and bent to speed and wind so that she was breathing hard and her body was tense when she reached the town, applied a steady pressure to the reins, eased back, and let the horse walk off its sweat.

A hundred people were congregated at the water's edge. After she had tethered the horse to a rail at the end of the wharf, a boy riding bareback galloped by, and the heavy presence of the animal startled her, for she had not seen it coming or attended to the soft drumbeat of its hooves. A man she did not know tipped his hat. Two women smiled from beneath their parasols, greeting the famous captain's wife, who had come only because she was afraid that Henry and Mathew might have been right. If that were the case, Fray Santos would be mortified. She intended to console him in a way that Henry could not ignore, though she cared less about offering Fray Santos comfort than showing Henry where her allegiance lay. It was petty, vindictive, but she needed to assert herself, even though Henry might not care.

The shadows of the wharf's pilings ran out toward the *Elizabeth's Delight*. Two other ships lay at anchor nearby, partly blocking her view, and she moved to the right until she saw a boat being lowered over the side and people descending the ladder. Gustav Hansen adjusted his telescope and said, "There's a voman like a bird in that there boat!" Light gleamed on the oar's blades, gleamed on the metal oarlocks now that the boat was free from the schooner's shadow. She *was* there. In that moment of surprise Elizabeth's need to redeem her dignity was forgotten, and she watched, amazed. Two sailors rowed while Henry stood behind, manning the tiller and looking down on Fray Santos and the woman beside him in a multicolored dress. There was no sign of a child.

It seemed to Elizabeth that she was alone on the beach, and it made no difference that people talked or a man shouted "Hallo!" or that the boy rode through the shallow water and splashed people standing nearby. The crowd remained spread across the beach, clustered here and there in knots of kinship, friendship, men with men, women with women, woven together by the play of children. The boat rose on a swell, showed its sleek triangular bow, then raced down the face of the wave as the sailors took in their oars and the boat sped to shore like a cormorant with folded wings diving to its prey. It slowed, glided, and the sailors jumped out and took hold of the sides, guiding it until its keel struck sand. The congregation broke ranks and moved, like grains of sand pouring through the narrow waist of an hourglass. The boy who had been racing up and down dismounted, letting his horse wander off while he went in among the hats and parasols to have a closer look.

Much as she wanted to see the woman, Elizabeth held back, trying to think of some way to let Henry know that this time she would not forgive him. As the crowd closed around the boat, Fray Santos stepped into water deep enough to wet his cassock up to the knees and then, in a courtly manner, extended his hand to the woman. She took it and paused with one foot on the gunnel as she surveyed the crowd, looking first at those close by, then those farther back. From the way she studied the crowd, and the calmness of her demeanor, it seemed that she was prepared for the moment, that something complex was going on with her. Elizabeth's need to confront Henry no longer seemed as important as going to the woman and seeing for herself, close up, what in her face or eyes might attest to the life she had led.

The woman, Henry, and Fray Santos were surrounded by people asking questions. Where did they find her? Where had she lived? Where was the child? Could she speak? Was she insane? Did she fight? From time to time Henry and Fray Santos glanced at her or inclined their heads, and Elizabeth was angry; it was clear that her husband and the friar were exhibiting the woman and did not care what was going through her mind. Anyone could see that she was apprehensive, and that was why Elizabeth took advantage of her position as the famous captain's wife to move in among the on-lookers, the questioners, so that she could help. Henry saw her coming, and she met his eyes. Then Fray Santos smiled as the people stepped back and let her into the circle.

The woman was about her own age. Her hair was black and severely fashioned. The straight line of her bangs made her eyes seem large and luminous. The dress was fashioned of feathers. Black, white, and brown feathers overlapped, and there was a rich-ness to it, a beauty. It had no sleeves, and her bare dark arms hung at her sides, narrow as a girl's, unmarked, graceful. People stopped talking when Elizabeth came forward, but they began again with new questions, rephrased old ones; then, without a signal, everyone began moving up the beach and Elizabeth fell in beside the woman, who looked at her for the first time. She was waiting for something to happen. Never in her life had Elizabeth seen anything so clearly in another person's eyes. Without knowing that she was going to do it, she reached out with her left hand and touched the woman's shoulder, proffering the comfort planned for Fray Santos. The woman gazed at her frankly, said four words that might have been questions, and reciprocated with two slender fingers, which lightly grazed Elizabeth's cheek.

When Fray Santos saw it happen he said a little prayer of thanks.

While the *Elizabeth's Delight* crossed the channel he had savored his success, sucking out its sweetness as if it were a fresh honeycomb. Only when the mainland rose perceptibly on the horizon, asserting itself in the curve of mountains and the sheer face of sand cliffs, had Fray Santos forced himself to think of the future once again, but no solution came until he saw Elizabeth's hand on the Indian's shoulder, the Indian's fingers on Elizabeth's cheek.

In the interim between his second meeting with Harper and their departure some weeks later, he had thought of nothing but the woman and her child. His daily routine, the few pleasant hours he spent in the foundry, even the unpleasant business with the witch María could not distract him from his imagined success. His picture daily became more complex, radiating its promise in proportion to the growth of his conviction that something extraordinary was about to happen. But Fray Sandoval had interrupted his seamless vision of the future by the simple act of sitting down beside him one day while he was meditating in the Sacred Garden and saying that he wished to be a part of the great adventure. He reminded Fray Santos that he had experienced problems similar to those which would be posed by the woman and child during his service in a mission deep in the jungles of South America.

Fray Santos had listened politely and thanked Fray Sandoval for his charitable offer, sending him off with the promise that he would think about ways he might be useful. Earlier, he had given himself up to the slow rhythm of the summer day, content to absorb its warmth and light. The sweet perfume of blossoming flowers had been a tonic to the mildew of the mission's rooms and the acrid fumes of the foundry. He had been content, and in five minutes his pleasure had been taken from him. The warmth of the day seemed to intensify, but he could not bring himself to leave the bench, and he sat there, heavy and inert, sweating into his heavy cassock as he wondered what to do.

From the moment his superior agreed to fund the expedition, Fray Santos believed that he would have a free hand in everything concerning the Indians, and that the responsibility for their conversion would be his alone. By the time Fray Sandoval arrived in the

Sacred Garden his vision extended far beyond the confines of his picture, which was now only one of several scenes that lay before him like stained glass windows in an enormous cathedral. The void of the lost souls swirled in a black and violet turbulence of glass so thick and deep in color that only the vaguest outlines of the sky were visible. There was a portrait of himself and Fray Bernardino discoursing gravely beside the telescope. Beneath them, running the width of the window, a waving banner bore a Latin inscription attesting to the grace that comes upon those who search for light. Beside it was the portrait of himself and the woman and her child, and while its details remained unchanged, the colors had become richer, and there was a rising sun behind them, and a sky fired with yellow. Beyond it a new picture had begun to form, and while he had tried to ignore it because its subject and its composition suggested immodesty, it had taken hold of his imagination by showing his brothers from all the orders gathered around him as he presented the converts, dressed in white, to an eminence whose scarlet robes proclaimed a cardinal.

The back and underarms of his cassock were dark with sweat by the time he put his hands on his knees and pushed himself up. Then he made his way to the superior's room. Fortunately, Fray Velásquez was sympathetic when he explained that the rescue of the woman and child would present a problem he had not foreseen. After so many years alone they would undoubtedly be frightened by the bustle of mission life, and Fray Velásquez had immediately seen his point and suggested that a hut be built away from the others in the Indian village. Such a plan had occurred to him, Fray Santos said, but though a separate residence might be beneficial, he was not certain that it would address the problem fully.

"Well, then, Xavier, see what you can do."

No better solution presented itself before it was time to leave, and by sheer force of will he had put Fray Sandoval's threat behind him when he set foot on the *Elizabeth's Delight*, keeping it at bay during the two days that had led to the extraordinary moment when he looked down at the woman in the field of flowers.

Now, thank God, he had found the way. Harper, leading a

procession across the beach, was deep in conversation with two men Fray Santos did not know. Elizabeth and the Indian walked side by side, appraising each other with shy glances. As he quickened his pace to catch up with them, he realized that Elizabeth's attention was more intense than it had been the day he had spoken to her and Harper and put before them what he had learned from O'Reilly. She had believed him then, and he had no doubt that he could call once again on her good will. She would surely understand the necessity of what he was about to ask, and he was confident that she would be gracious.

"I must admit," he said, "that these two days have quite overwhelmed me."

"I knew it was true when you talked to us, though I had some doubts when I left the house."

"That is only natural, my child, but now we must do what we can to make ourselves worthy of this good fortune, wouldn't you agree? I believe that a remarkable trust has been placed upon our shoulders."

"Yes."

"A remarkable trust, and I must tell you that in preparation I may have spent too much time thinking about the spiritual significance of her rescue while ignoring its practical side."

"I'm not sure I understand," Elizabeth said.

"Nor did I, nor did I. The truth is that she has had a great shock. Only a few hours ago she was on the island. Now she is here."

"That is what we hoped for."

"Of course, but consider the consequences. She seems distressed, as is to be expected, and that is what I meant when I said that I have unfortunately ignored the practical side. You heard her say those four words?"

"Yes?"

"Neither Jesús nor the other Indians we took along could understand her," Fray Santos continued, "but I am certain they are names of relatives. Think how painful it will be for her to enter the village and learn that they are dead."

"You're sure?"

"I knew before we left, but that is not why I need to speak to you. The death of her family is only part of the problem. You see, her condition is not like that of the Indians who lived here; not at all. None suffered as she has suffered, none was deprived of companionship for ten long years. That is why I believe it would be prudent to arrange for a quiet place where she can slowly be introduced to civilization. Grace comes to us unexpectedly, and you would agree, wouldn't you, that it is a remarkable thing?"

"That goes without saying," Elizabeth acknowledged.

"Well, then, I must tell you that you were in my thoughts during the hours we were crossing from the island, and I will put it to you plainly. I believe that her welfare will be jeopardized if she goes to the village too soon. It is an imposition, I know, and I would not suggest this to anyone else, but I ask you to consider allowing her to stay a while with you and your husband."

They had reached the road at the head of the wharf by the time Fray Santos finished presenting his case. Henry was still talking to the men, but he had been watching Elizabeth, and when she saw him looking at her, she dreaded the thought of going home. She had forgotten about the scratches in her excitement about the woman. Now they floated into view again, precise and ugly. Fray Santos's proposal was the last thing she had expected, but she was grateful for it, grateful for the grace the priest had mentioned in a way Henry would never understand.

"I would be happy to, but we must ask Henry."

She had no idea what he would say, but she was willing to argue, and she was fairly certain that she would have the upper hand, because he was telling her with his eyes that he wanted to make amends, do something to restore harmony between them. It was always like that after they argued and he withdrew moodily into himself for a day or two. He had a need for tranquillity at home that almost made her laugh. Now she was going to take advantage of it.

He looked at her as Fray Santos offered him the idea, glanced at the woman, nodded. "I see no harm in it," he said.

Fray Santos thanked Harper for his generosity. He had been thinking of the difficulties the arrangement would present because of his other duties, but now that the Harpers had agreed to keep the woman, he felt confident that when he explained the solution to Fray Velásquez his superior would grant him permission to make daily visits to their house.

Word of the arrival of the *Elizabeth's Delight* had reached the mission while the schooner was still coming into the bay, and Fray Velásquez quickly ordered Fray Olivares to take the carriage down to the beach. The young friar waited impatiently for Fray Santos to finish his conversation with the Harpers, and he was happy when a drayman arrived with a wagon and told Harper that he would take his things back to the house for a modest fee. Otherwise they might have stayed there for hours. The crew had come ashore in a second boat with Harper's gear, and the two men who had carried his chest across the beach loaded it into the bed of the wagon. A third sailor put the model ship in with the other things, and when people saw it a fresh round of questions rose from the crowd. The sailor said that it was a totem of some kind, and did his best to joke about it until O'Reilly saw his chance and stepped forward. He was not about to lose an opportunity to establish himself as a spokesman for the adventure. "It's more than a toy," he said. "She'd tied it to a tree and worshiped it."

Fray Olivares pulled at the reins and made a soft clucking sound to the horses, who followed the pressure on their bits to the drive leading from the road to the Harpers' house. Harper had hired men to paint it white at the time he had the gazebo built, and during the day the house glowed bright as a flame, but now its whiteness had dulled to the color of pewter. Most of Santa Bárbara's houses were squat adobes, but the Harper place, as it had come to be known, was different in design and would not have been out of place on Cape Cod. There was clapboard siding, a shingle roof, and a widow's walk. Angelita had already lighted lamps upstairs and down, and the pale yellow light from the windows reached a little way into the blue evening. "This is our house," Elizabeth said, "where we live." She knew that the words would mean nothing, but perhaps the sound of her voice would be comforting.

As they pulled up, Angelita came out on the porch and made no attempt to conceal her surprise when she saw the woman. Elizabeth said she would talk to her shortly, and asked her to go back inside and prepare the guest room.

"For her?" Angelita asked, staring at the woman.

"Yes. Now, please." Turning to Fray Santos, she said, "It is a small room, but it will do nicely."

"I am certain of it. I will come tomorrow. Since she will be with you, we will try to teach her in English. Now you must be tired. Will ten o'clock be too early?"

"Not at all."

After the friars left she searched the road for signs of the wagon. There was a lone rider but no sign of Henry, and she assumed that he had stopped for a drink at Esteban's.

"Look," she said, pointing to the pale shape to the left of the house. "Gazebo. That is called a gazebo. Mountains," she added, gesturing into the dusk. "House, sea." And when the woman answered with her four words, the strangeness of the situation came home to Elizabeth. Like most people in town, she had never given the mission Indians a second thought. They were simply there, an aspect of the mission, like the bell towers or the portico. Strange as the woman looked in her plumage, odd as her language sounded, Elizabeth wished there were some way to know what she felt, what she thought; who this person was behind the barrier of language that separated them like a stone wall. She remembered struggling with Latin in the convent, where she had been educated at her mother's insistence, remembered nuns dictating stately sentences that she was supposed to write down and how the words had run together in a mass of syllables that confounded her understanding and left her feeling stupid and inadequate. She hoped Fray Santos would be a gentler teacher and the woman a more able pupil. In the meantime, before he set about his work in the morning, she could make herself useful by introducing her guest to common things, and she was about to take her inside when the woman tugged at her sleeve and pointed at the wagon coming up the road in the dusk.

"Husband," she said. "Henry." Then Elizabeth pointed to herself. "Wife. Elizabeth."

The words sounded hollow, and Elizabeth felt she was walking through their echo as she led the woman across the grass to the drive, where Henry and the drayman were unloading. When they came out after taking the heavy chest into the house, Henry paid the man and then approached, carrying what appeared to be a bundle of sticks. The woman spoke quickly, and Elizabeth was certain that it was not one of the words she had used before. Henry seemed amused as he held out something covered with feathers that resembled a ship. The woman took it and handed it to Elizabeth.

"She had it in a tree. Santos didn't like it, but she wanted to bring it along, so I told him that she could. As a matter of fact, I think it scared him."

Elizabeth did not rise to the bait. She had sworn that she would not let him upset her, and it felt good to have passed this first test. She wanted to know what had happened on the island, but she would not give him the satisfaction of asking. Fray Santos would tell her all she wanted to know.

"Elizabeth." He spoke softly. It was an overture.

"I don't want to talk about it," she said firmly.

"It meant nothing."

"I don't want to discuss it."

This time she would not listen to him. She did not have to listen, and she was even happier than she had been on the beach when Fray Santos made his proposition. The woman would shield her from Henry, at least for a while. When she was gone . . . She did not allow herself to go on with the thought.

"I'm going to take her inside now."

"Do what you want."

The woman was watching, listening. As Henry turned and went up the stairs, she looked at Elizabeth and said something, a quick phrase that might have been a question. Could she know? Elizabeth wondered. It was almost dark, but there was enough light from the windows to see her eyes. Elizabeth knew how her voice sounded. As she spoke to Henry her throat had felt as if he were gripping it, and it was all she could do to keep from crying. The woman would have to be deaf not to know that something was wrong. The knowledge cracked Elizabeth's reserve, releasing pent-up bitterness drop by acrid drop.

"I hope your husband was not like mine," she murmured.

The woman looked at her as if she were trying to understand. In that moment Elizabeth knew a stone had fallen, a breach had been made in the wall between them though they had no words in common. She herself had lived with a severed tongue for over a year. She had said nothing about Henry's betrayal to Susan Ludlow because it was too painful and humiliating. She did not mention it to Fray Santos in the privacy of the confessional because she knew what he would say. Endure. Pray. Set your mind on higher things. But now she could speak, and she moved close to the woman, talking rapidly about the night before Henry left to find her, and then what had happened a year ago. "He lay with another woman and she left her mark on him and he didn't care. Not this time, nor the time before."

It was better than confession, more purifying, and she did not care that there might be something sinful in her comparison. Nothing was as important as telling what she felt when she saw the scratches and remembered the others.

Afterward they went inside.

"Door," she said. "Window. Hall." She led the woman into the kitchen and named pots and pans, canisters, fruit, stove, table, and chairs. They went into the living room, the dining room, passed the closed door of Henry's office on the way to the stairs. She took her all the way upstairs and led her onto the widow's walk. The bells for evening prayer were ringing. "Those are for Fray Santos and his brothers," she said, and when she made a gesture with both hands to indicate the friar's girth, the woman smiled.

Downstairs, Angelita watched disapprovingly as they came into the dining room.

"The señor is having dinner in his office."

Henry always ate alone when he wanted to punish her, but tonight she was glad; tonight she did not have to sit at her end of the long table and pretend that nothing was wrong. She was happy to be with the woman and encouraged her to eat until it was clear that she had had enough.

Elizabeth took her to the upstairs hall and pushed open the door of the guest room with her elbow, standing with her back to the door as she motioned the woman to go inside. The woman looked around, stopped at the foot of the bed nearer the door, and went to the window, where she touched the glass, turned, and looked at Elizabeth questioningly.

"It is made of glass. In the morning you can see all the way to the islands."

The woman was still carrying the model ship, and Elizabeth gently reached for it. "May I?"

She handed it over, and Elizabeth propped it against the dresser mirror. "This is your room. You can leave it here, or put it wherever you like." Then she turned back the blankets. "Get in. Sleep. You'll feel better tomorrow."

Downstairs, a sliver of light showed at the bottom of the office door. Relieved that she would not have to see Henry until morning, she went to the kitchen and explained to Angelita that the woman was going to stay with them for a while because Fray Santos thought it would be better for her than going directly to the mission. Angelita seemed less resentful, and Elizabeth made sure that she praised her work before telling her that she had done enough for the day and was free to go to her quarters.

After Angelita left, Elizabeth went into the dining room and poured a glass of brandy from a decanter on the sideboard, welcoming its harshness as she drank quickly. She could not remember feeling so tired, and she went out to the porch and pulled up a chair to the edge. She looked across to the gazebo, whose pointed roof glowed beneath the moon. Beyond it a few lights marked the vicinity of the wharf and the length of Main Street. There was no peace in what she saw, no relief in the silence, though that was what she had hoped to find. Her mind was racing between the day's events as aimlessly as the boy who had run his horse up and down the beach. It was always like that when she was unhappy, and she would be a fool to think she could escape from a day so marked with upheaval. So she let it come, reliving the arc of her emotions from the morning's darkness, when she awoke feeling broken and seeing the scratches less as rents in Henry's flesh than fractures in her life, until the moment she saw the woman and felt the sympathy that passed between them. She was still surprised by the mutual touching, for she was reserved, even shy, but she was grateful, because it took her out of herself. Fray Santos's claim that the woman's rescue represented a kind of grace was more exact than he knew.

A gust of wind stirred the leaves and sent a branch sliding across the side of the house. She hoped the east wind would return and blow hard enough to polish the sky clean of the haze that had begun to settle at the end of the day, but it was a single gust and the evening regained its composure; in its stillness she found that she was able to choose between thinking of Henry and thinking of the woman. Now she remembered what had only been a feeling. She looked into his eyes and saw no sign of the man she had married five years earlier, looked into the woman's eyes and saw a complexity that she would never have suspected. Henry's eyes were known, set, hard; the woman's foreign, full of color in their darkness. She had been drawn into their darkness as if, by looking, she could see what made her who she was. Elizabeth thought she understood what it must have been like when the woman saw all those white faces and the town beyond, when she looked and failed to find the people who were summoned by the lyric names. The absence echoed in her own heart, reproduced her own distress.

Elizabeth remembered the words, and as she tried to say them she understood why there was still a slight distance between her and the woman. It had nothing to do with her guest's being an Indian. She had no name. Whatever it was had been abandoned on San Nicolás, and she imagined it floating there, unattached, like the names the woman spoke. Moonlight silvered the bay, but while the sea beyond was black and the islands were lost in darkness, she saw the islands in her mind's eye, saw the woman out there, a solitary figure moving against the sky. In that instant the word formed on her lips and she said "Soledad," and there was a rightness to it. The three syllables made the woman whole. Satisfied, she went off to bed. When she fell asleep, she dreamed of Soledad and of the little ship and of the two of them talking, telling each other everything.

# 4

◆ ◆ ◆

Mist rose and fell with a lazy rhythm, diffusing the first light so that sky and sea were indistinguishable one from the other. A hazy sickle moon held high up; because the mist moved, the moon moved too, and there was a magic to the faintness of the air. The land was purple, and the trees, and everything was still as dawn took hold, and the silver of the sea was the same color as the sky. The mountains behind the town and the silver wall of melded sky and sea held a stillness between them. Only gradually did it fill with the first cry of birds, a lone dog barking, a rooster's crow, a soft fluttering of wings as doves settled on the meadow and pecked for food in the grass beside the gazebo, their soft bodies only a suggestion of movement. The islands rose up dimly on the margin of the sea, and somewhere there was the thud of an ax cleaving wood. At the mission two sleepy friars went along the darkened halls to the towers, their full sleeves falling back upon bare arms as they pulled on bell ropes worn smooth from the grip of hands, and the rhythm of the sounds contributed to the shape of the coming day. The doves moved their soft roundness in circles of orderly attention, eating their fill, and then, suddenly, they rose and flew over the gazebo's roof. A little time passed before the source of their fear became visible in the shape of a lone rider coming up the road from town. At the juncture of the road and the Harpers' driveway he turned in, continuing at an unhurried pace to the corral, where he spoke quietly to the horse as he reined in. The soft padding of hooves went off in the silence and he rested his hands on the pommel and looked toward the house. Not until the ridge of the mountains glowed with the first light of the sun and the walls of canyons began to green did he take the reins into his hands and return to the road, where he continued north and soon vanished over a rise.

Later, when the sea was blue again and the islands took up their places, three riders came in from the north. A wagon, and then another appeared on the road, followed shortly by small groups of people walking. All went up the driveway, where they gathered by the corral. There was only a little talking as they looked expectantly at the house, whose front was now white in the sun and whose windows were gold with it so that they could not see the woman at the upstairs window nor Elizabeth watching them from the living room.

Elizabeth had not heard the first rider come or go, but she wakened to the sound of voices and the creaking of wagon wheels. The sounds were so unexpected that they could have been the language of a dream. When she understood what they meant, she dressed quickly and went downstairs. By the time she made tea more people had arrived; she stood by the living room window, looking through the curtains. She did not mind their curiosity, but she worried that they might frighten Soledad. She was relieved when the wagons left. Soon a horseman followed them, then the others, and only four men remained, lounging against the fence for a while before they too headed back to town. She heard them laughing as they crossed the fields.

Elizabeth went upstairs and brought Soledad down for breakfast, which Angelita served quietly. They went into the living room afterward and Elizabeth motioned for her to sit, saying, "I want to tell you something. I am going to give you a name. I am going to call you Soledad. Can you say it? Soledad?"

Three times she pointed and said her name, and she worried that Soledad would not understand. Then her face brightened.

"Dad."

"No. Soledad."

"Sol-dad," she said slowly, looking at Elizabeth.

"You," Elizabeth said. "You are Soledad." Then she put her forefinger to her chest and said her own name. "I am Elizabeth."

"Liza."

"Elizabeth."

She put her hands to her face, tapped her fingers on her cheeks. "Elizabeth. I am Elizabeth."

Soledad tried to form the last part of the word, but there was nothing like it in her language. "Liza," she said again.

Elizabeth pointed to the window, where they could see Harper working a new colt in the corral. "Henry, my husband. Henry."

Soledad tried to imitate Elizabeth. She carefully repeated, "Henry my husband."

Elizabeth shook her head. "*My* husband."

The words flew easily as birds from Elizabeth's mouth, but they seemed heavy as stones on Soledad's tongue. "Henry," she said slowly. "Henry."

"Yes. Good."

"Liza, Sol-dad, Henry," she said again, and Elizabeth smiled.

"Yes, that's it. Very good."

The brownrobe came on one of the animals with a large head.

"Horse," Liza said. "He rides a horse. His name is Fray Santos. He is a friar."

The brownrobe talked to Liza before he sat beside her and began saying different words.

"God," he said. "Jesus. Mary."

"Sol-dad Mary."

"No. Mary is the Mother of God."

"Other God," she said, and the brownrobe frowned.

Soledad had thought about her family all night, and she wanted to teach their names to Liza and the brownrobe. She said each one slowly, explaining that they were her mother and father, her brother and husband, but Liza and the brownrobe looked puzzled, and then the brownrobe said "God" again, and then the other words, and she did not understand why they refused to say her family's names. Henry came inside and listened as the brown-robe said more words and she tried to repeat them. There was something about Henry she did not like, and though she could not identify it beyond the way he looked at her, she sensed that something was wrong, and she was sorry because she was almost certain that he was Liza's husband.

She was in the living room with Liza when Henry appeared again with two large bags, went outside, put them in the back of the wagon, and drove away. Liza watched until the wagon was a tiny spot on the road, and Soledad did not understand why Liza seemed happy. When her own husband went hunting with other men, she had been sad every minute he was gone. That was why Liza's happiness was confusing, until she thought that Fray Santos might be her husband too. Later, when Fray Santos went into the kitchen, she tried to ask Liza if she had two husbands. She said Henry's name and pointed out the window in the direction he had gone. Then she made a circle with her arms and hugged the imaginary man. "Henry," she said, and then she said "Santos," and put her hands around the imaginary priest, making gentle, thrusting movements with her pelvis the way she used to do to hurry her husband's seed. Liza watched the slow, rhythmic movement of her hips, and as soon as she understood, her cheeks turned red.

"No!" she said quickly, looking in the direction of the kitchen.

# 5

◆ ◆ ◆

Much as he loved working with iron, Fray Santos's chief pleasure came from filling the pages of his journal. Until everyone in his family died, he had satisfied his need to write with long letters to his mother and aunts and cousins, writing one every day for a week until the seventh and last was finished and he had to wait for the beginning of the next month to start again. Over the years he compensated for their decreasing numbers by making the letters to the survivors longer; and when only his aunt Gabriela was left, he spent as many as three days filling page after page with the details of his life. He was more open and honest in those letters sent to Seville than he was with any of his brothers. Nothing was too trivial to record, and the recounting of the most mundane details gave him as much pleasure as descriptions of important events, which exhausted the black ink made by neophytes for the brothers' use. Except for the time devoted to his duties, he never felt more truly himself than when he wrote and his thought was synchronized with the rhythmical scraping of his pen.

When he learned that Gabriela had died of a fever, he found himself at loose ends. He vainly cast about for something to occupy the evening hours he had spent with his letters, but the best he could do was to set himself a course of reading. He chose the books carefully, with an eye to challenging himself, but no sooner did he begin a text than his mind wandered off. Except for the Scriptures, other men's words could not hold his attention. The idea of keeping a journal came as a blessing, and he soon discovered that its pleasures were greater than those of writing letters. He had not kept it long before it became a kind of commonplace book where he worked out ideas in his tiny script on the same page with lists of things to do, or passages copied from the Scriptures. Since O'Reilly's confession, he wrote only about the Indian; the notion that a special providence attached to her salvation ran like a colored thread throughout the pages. One evening he worked for two hours without stopping as he tried to account for the unsettling experience that had come upon him when he was saying Mass and had conflated her image with the Paraclete, finally concluding that the symbol of the Dove had joined in his memory with her feather dress.

Although he had contracted a bothersome congestion of the chest from sailing to San Nicolás, he went to the Harpers' house every day, squeezing in the visits between other duties and sometimes at the expense of meals. After conveying the news to Soledad of her family's fate, he stayed several hours every day because a crisis had come upon her, which was both profound and threatening. His health had made it impossible to write during the crisis, for he had scarcely enough energy to ride back to the mission and fall into his bed, coughing and clutching at his chest. Only when it was resolved did he give in to the illness and accept Fray Bernardino's medicines, which left him dizzy and vomitous.

Shortly after he had resumed his visits to the Harpers' he ate dinner quickly with the idea of spending an hour or two writing about all that had happened and at least beginning to sort out his troubles. He returned to his room with a steaming mug of tea liberally laced with brandy, placed it on his desk, and retrieved the journal from the bottom of his cupboard, where he kept it under clothing so that it would be safe from prying eyes. He removed his cloak from a hook on the wall and put it over his shoulders, for there was a chill in his blood despite the summer's warmth. The pages gave off a dry, pleasing sound as he smoothed them flat, and the warmth of the woolen cloak seeped into his bones. He was definitely improving; the knowledge made him eager as he sharpened a pen and peered into the inkwell, making sure that the neophyte had filled it. Someone passed in the hall, but the faint shuffle of sandals was soon gone. Then there was only silence. He stared at the blank page in the still light of lamp and candles. Sipping his tea, he debated whether to begin at the end of the crisis and try to resolve the problem that had come upon him that afternoon, or describe things as they had occurred, first to last. He pulled at the lobe of his ear, stroked his chin, and in a little while dipped the pen into the inkwell, allowing the excess to drip back into the cup.

*10 November*

Elizabeth has named her Soledad. It is a little mawkish to my tastes & for all I know may convey a sentiment the woman herself does not feel, for when we found her she was thin but in good health & seemed contented with her life. When I made these observations to Elizabeth and reminded her that the custom here is to name neophytes after saints, she remained quite firm, saying there was a rightness to it and since we would never know her true name, at least not for some time, this did a service for her. I did not press the matter, for a name is only a name except for Thine, Lord, & I wished to see no breach in our relations. Nor am I concerned with naming, only with other things.

After all my careful preparations, undertaken with the sole desire of defeating the evil one & bringing Soledad to an understanding of the one true God, something quite unforeseen occurred. It was my opinion that Soledad should be informed of her peoples' deaths as soon as possible, since keeping her ignorant would make the news more painful when it came. Accordingly, four weeks ago Elizabeth brought her into the spacious living room of her home, & by means of signs & the few words Elizabeth & I had taught her, I explained that her people had met their end some time ago. I was well aware that our conception of death is difficult for Indians to grasp, even those who have received instruction, but I did not anticipate a difficulty. There is an intelligence in Soledad despite her occasional confusion. So I penetrated her ignorance & no sooner did she understand than she uttered the four words I first heard on the island of San Nicolás. These, I was certain, were her family's names. Elizabeth put her arm around Soledad's shoulders, & I was touched by this further sign of the friendship that had sprung up between them & was about to remark about the spirit of *caritas* when Soledad moved away from her embrace & suddenly stood & began speaking to me in her native tongue. Her features were bereaved & the depth of her emotion most pronounced. For a moment I could not fathom what she intended, but then it came to me. She desired to return to the island. When I told her that she was now at home, she seemed to glimpse my meaning & would have none of it. Ignorant as she was of God's capacity to heal the wounded heart, I believed that my cassock, my rosary, & all the signs of my vocation that set me apart from other men would provide some solace from the agony of the news. A moment later she walked away with her arms hanging by her sides. I rose with the intention of following her, but Elizabeth put out her hand & said, in a way that suggested a deeper knowledge of Soledad than I was privy to, that I should let her go.

I accepted her adjuration & we remained in the living room while Soledad went outside & crossed the meadow to the gazebo, where she sat down in the middle of its floor. I asked Elizabeth whether she knew why Soledad had gone there & she replied that it had become a favored place since the evening she arrived. I remembered that the huts on the island were made of whale bones. There was a similarity between their structure & the gazebo's, and I feared she had invested it with some pagan meaning I would be obliged to rectify.

Then I was greeted with a shocking display. Until that moment Soledad had been most tractable to my ministrations, displaying a considerable eagerness to learn. I am of the opinion that then, only a few days after her rescue, she understood that there was one true God. Moreover she had learned to say His name along with those of the Son & His Mother. And so I was filled with chagrin when before my eyes she began indulging in rites like those I have seen in native villages after someone dies. She beat herself about the face & chest & pulled her hair, & these untoward gestures were accompanied by a keening that reached us across the meadow. The display saddened me, because it showed how deeply pagan beliefs were tangled in her mind. I realized how much instruction was left to be accomplished before I could bring her to the knowledge that would save her soul.

The acts I witnessed through the window were like pictures of all that I have dedicated my life to blotting from the minds of Indians. They pained me, & I was of the opinion that she knew I was watching & did not care. It was as if she were intent on affronting me & avenging herself on me & Elizabeth for our acts of charity. But as it happened they were nothing. They were insubstantial as chaff is to wheat, compared with what then followed. Even now the blood runs into my face when I think of the shame of it. Rising to her knees, she pulled down the bodice of her dress, & I was unable to avert my eyes before her breasts appeared. I quickly turned away, disgusted & angry because of the embarrassment her nakedness caused me in the presence of Mrs. Harper. I said so to Elizabeth, tho' I could not bring myself to meet her eyes. She on the other hand made a little cry & went out the door, & I watched her run across the meadow, mount the stairs, & kneel beside the naked woman & embrace her. This time Soledad did not shrug her off. I did not know whether I was more appalled by Soledad's savagery or Elizabeth's disregard for that modesty I had believed to form the very core of her being. To make matters worse, Angelita happened to appear in the hallway, stared at her mistress & the Indian, looked at me, & ran up the stairs. I waited, but the two women did not move. I left, not knowing what to expect & wondering what I had brought upon myself.

*11 November*
That afternoon marked the beginning of Soledad's decline, though I continued my visits & did my best to teach her. For two days she remained a dutiful student, listening to & repeating my words with much the same readiness she exhibited

before I told her of her family's death. But on the third day she made no effort whatsoever. She sat still as a stone on the chair facing me while I said words & pointed to objects, & she stared at me with a face as drawn as that of someone afflicted by a wasting illness.

She quickly grew thin & pale. Although that alone was cause for much concern, I detected a deeper blow to the work of her salvation, for her physical decline was accompanied by a mental one. I knew that Satan had gained the upper hand, sneaking like a worm into her soul & threatening to wrest away all the good that I had done. Others have turned away at the sight of such a thing, wringing their hands and praying for the best. I know of instances in this very mission, which charity forbids me to elaborate, though I will say this much: despite a certain brother's bragging of his conquests in the great land to the south, he has given up when faced with no more truculence than I met in Soledad. And so where others may have despaired, I vowed that I would bring her to the Light, & I set my mind on that task, challenged the evil one, & placed myself in front of Soledad.

With one thing & another I was not free to return until Tuesday of the following week. When I arrived, Elizabeth greeted me with the news that Soledad had worsened & now refused to eat. She was so weak that she had not come downstairs but preferred to lie in her bed. I know a thing a two about the way despair gnaws the heart & eats a gap wide enough for Beelzebub to enter, so I admonished her to go & bring Soledad. Not only was I worried about her wasting, but I believed that the sight of Elizabeth & me might help restore her spirits. That was not the case. There were dark circles beneath her eyes & an unsteadiness in her step as Elizabeth led her to her chair. Since it was noontime I told Elizabeth that we should try to feed her. To that end she spoke to Angelita, & shortly the girl appeared with a cup of soup & some small pieces of fowl dressed in the Mexican fashion. Elizabeth held out the cup, but Soledad declined. She cut up the fowl as one would do for a child, but Soledad shook her head, though in a toneless voice she identified the meat as chicken, no doubt in an effort to please Elizabeth. Then she turned sideways in her chair, resting her arms on the back as she looked out the window toward the sea.

I returned the next morning around ten o'clock only to learn that when Elizabeth had gone to wake Soledad, her room was empty. Elizabeth and Angelita searched the house, but she was nowhere to be found & they went outside & that was when they found her sleeping in the gazebo.

Elizabeth reported this in a frenzy & we immediately went to the gazebo, where Soledad lay on her side & acknowledged us with a sorry glance before turning away to stare again through the lattice. We remonstrated with her, but our efforts were to no avail. It was my opinion that she understood the gist of our words & signs, & this was proved some minutes later when she sat up & said "island" & "field," by which I determined her to mean that she missed her former life. Only a fool could not have understood the meaning of her being there. "She has taken up her station here to die," I said. I had hoped that her grief was like that of everyone I had ever ministered to; I believed that once her tears had dried, the grief would leave like a cloud & the rays of the sun would once more fall upon her life & I could resume my catechism. But I understood that the darkness had blinded her & she had settled upon a fast unto her death.

Captain Harper was still away at sea, so I was alone with the three women, & the Dark Angel was much upon my mind. The shadow of his wing was cast upon Soledad. As I watched her weaken, I believed that her time was not far off & soon I would have to watch her die. My teaching of the catechism had been curtailed, & hers would be a death without those rites which every Christian soul desires as the darkness is coming on. I prayed & studied texts on demonology in the hope of finding some means to break the hold of Satan. We did all we could to comfort Soledad, but nothing availed until Elizabeth out of desperation said that perhaps what was needed was the food that Soledad had eaten on the island. To my mind the problem lay far deeper. Soledad's appetite for life was gone, but I had exhausted all my thoughts & was near despair myself. Elizabeth argued that something as familiar as her former sustenance might awaken pleasant memories, so I put aside my doubts & agreed that it was possible.

With that faint hope in mind I rode to the wharf & commissioned a fisherman to catch & dress a seal. Later I went to the canyon & gathered berries & wild fruit. The next day I returned to the wharf, where the fisherman presented me with a flayed seal. With these provisions I returned to the Harpers' house. Elizabeth instructed Angelita to build a fire near the gazebo so that Soledad could see what we were doing & smell the odors. Elizabeth placed the seal meat in the ashes & while it cooked made a paste of the berries & fruits, following as well as she could instructions elicited from Soledad some time earlier about her means of preparing food. When this was done, *mirabile dictu* the dying woman allowed herself to be fed a little of the meat & a spoonful of the mixture Elizabeth had compounded. Never have I been filled with greater gratitude than I was as I watched her eat. Elizabeth wept with happiness, & a knowing look passed between them, a demonstration of the secret ways women have with each other. Although I could not condone Elizabeth's friendship with a soul still shrouded in darkness, I was happy too. I resolved to redouble my efforts even if it meant delegating some duties to my eager younger brothers.

All the rest of that day I tried to puzzle out the reason for Soledad's change of heart, & it was not long before I understood that she had responded to the generosity of Elizabeth's spirit & saw in the seal's flesh a concern with her well-being. I was moved by that knowledge, for it told me that my intuitions about this savage woman were correct.

That evening, quite overcome, I went to the chapel to give my thanks. Votive lights flickered by the altar, dispelling the darkness, & I savored the comfort of the beams & arches, taking in the beauty of the Holy Figures & the dull glow of silver. The pictures on the walls never seemed so rich with meaning, & the great scenes of Thy triumph surrounded me, & I felt myself becoming firm & strong as I saw Soledad brought into the embrace of the church & marveled once again that Harper and O'Reilly had been Thy instruments to rescue her.

He wrote for upward of three hours without stopping, and the effort cost him something. For the last half hour he had been coughing, and the warmth of the cloak was no longer enough to keep out the cold. He wanted to address the sudden and inexplicable change in conditions at the Harpers' house that occurred earlier in the day, but exhaustion lay its hands on him and he knew he could not go on. Perhaps in the morning. He was relieved to give up the work for a while, because he knew that when he returned to the journal he would have to deal with the event and his reaction to it, and that would take more energy than he had. A sip of tea was left in the mug, and he drank it off, pleased that some of the brandy remained in it. Then he put the tips of his fingers to his lips, pinched out the candle flames, turned down the lamp, and crossed to the bed, where he knelt and prayed. He felt drowsy as soon as he undressed and climbed in, pulling the blankets up to his chin. He wanted to think about what remained to be said, but soon what he had written and what he was going to write were mixed up in his mind with other times and places, and he fell asleep to the hooting of an owl.

The next morning he woke coughing, with a devilishly sore throat, and begged off his duties. He returned to his bed and lay thinking about all that Henry Harper had said to him following his return from five weeks of sailing along the coast. The more he considered it, the more frustrated he became, because he could not guess the reason for the change in Harper's attitude. He knew that Soledad had recovered by the time Harper returned, but he remained ignorant of Harper's feelings toward him. He would never know that Harper regarded his efforts to convert Soledad with detached amusement, and a long time would pass before he had any notion of what was happening between Harper and his wife.

Fray Santos did not know how much Harper loved the sea and the adventures that Europe and the Far East provided. Nor did he know how all that changed when Harper found himself in New York some years ago, where he was introduced to the daughter of Jeffrey Gallagher, who owned the ship he had captained for several years. Elizabeth was twelve years younger than Harper, an ethereal, naïve young woman who just missed being beautiful. At first Harper thought there was no chance with her for someone like him. He was content to drink with Gallagher, scarcely paying any attention to Elizabeth as she moved through the house and even when she joined them for dinner. But then he was given to understand that Gallagher had decided she should marry a sailor. More invitations to the stately old house in Dobbs Ferry followed and to Harper's surprise, they were married within a year. As a wedding present Gallagher gave him the deed to a schooner in San Francisco, and the newlyweds made the long journey overland. Some months later, Harper learned that a man could do very well for himself by moving down the coast, where vessels like his were constantly in demand.

Harper enjoyed married life more than he had expected to, and he was faithful for a year before going off on a voyage that took him to Vancouver, where too many temptations were put in his way. When he came back he continued to indulge himself, though he tried to be discreet; he had no wish to cause Elizabeth pain. The first time she discovered scratches on his back she fled to Dobbs Ferry, returning two months later because her family, staunchly Catholic, would not hear of her leaving him. She told him that she would stay but that she could never love him as she once had done. The marriage devolved to a hollow, ritualistic observance of the prescribed relations between husband and wife. She acquiesced to his desire whenever he visited her in her room, hoping that despite the trouble she had had conceiving, she would become pregnant. Months later, when she announced that she was carrying his child, he hired a man to build a gazebo, which he assured her would be a perfect place to sit on summer afternoons with children. He saw no reason to add that its real purpose was to encourage forgiveness.

After two stillbirths she begged him to leave her alone and he reasoned that her withdrawal allowed him his old freedom. It was during this period that he rediscovered the prostitute who had taken hold of his erotic imagination. He told Pepita to be careful as they embraced and she leaned back, laughing. "You are all like children with your wives, so afraid." Then she pulled him down, wrapped her legs around him, and in a little while she moaned and drew her nails across his back.

Early in the day that Fray Santos made his second journal entry, Elizabeth and Harper went outside to the gazebo. He wanted to talk to her, smooth things over. It took no great leap of the imagination to realize that he had been wrong in assuming that the Indian had made her more tractable. She was reserved, cold. He was still tired from long days at sea and could not abide the accusation in her eyes. It was worse than the first time she found out about Pepita. Then, she was injured, victimized. Now, a certain hardness had settled in, and he knew the unpleasantness could last indefinitely. So his anger blazed up. He said it was stupid to bear a grudge over something so inconsequential, and while he waited for her to respond, he happened to glance at Soledad wandering in the meadow. She did not seem in a bad way, even though Elizabeth told him that she almost died while he was gone. Her skin glowed, nut brown shading into cinnamon. Her hair had been lackluster when he left. Now it shone and reflected the light so that it was almost blue. She glanced at him and looked away all in the same movement, and the sorrow still apparent in her eyes only enhanced her beauty.

"She hasn't learned much English," Elizabeth said, "but she'll do better in a while."

"People are still coming to see her?"

"Not as many. I've tried to keep them away."

He sipped his coffee and put the cup down firmly. "I don't think it's a good idea to have her in the house."

He knew that he had struck a nerve when she tensed and the color drained from her face.

"What?"

"Ludlow said that people are talking. I have a position to maintain," he responded.

He was just trying it out, and at that point he did not know exactly what he was doing other than punishing her for her coldness.

"She can't go. She isn't ready. She almost died."

"We'll discuss it with Santos," he said. "She really belongs at the mission."

It was one of those moments when he recognized an advantage to be exploited. All the power lay with him. He allowed himself to savor it as if he were an emperor who, with the flick of the wrist, could dictate someone's fate. He was surprised by the fear in her eyes, and when she answered there was a tautness in her voice, as if she were trying to control its pleading tone, maintain her dignity.

"She is my only pleasure, Henry. Don't do this."

"Well," he said, standing up, "it won't hurt if we put off deciding until Santos gets here."

He left her, sure of his advantage, and gave no more thought to the matter after going to the stable and talking to his man Morales about a fine new colt. When he went into his office and began working on his accounts, the numbers bored him and he turned his thoughts to Soledad once again until he heard Elizabeth welcome Fray Santos. He joined them. Elizabeth looked frightened, and the pleading was plain in her eyes as he said to the friar, "I'll come right to the point. It's complicated, having the Indian here. I think the time has come for her to go with you."

For an hour he was treated to Fray Santos's arguments, which were so subtle and roundabout that he admired the man even while finding him pompous. He knew from the outset that the friar's interests were served by keeping Soledad at the house, though why that should be the case was not clear. Elizabeth was on the verge of crying, and Fray Santos spoke urgently about his fears for Soledad's well-being if she were moved too soon.

"I think I have a solution for the time being," Harper said at last. "We never use the bunkhouse. It can be fitted out for her."

That was why Fray Santos was so puzzled. He was ignorant of Elizabeth's distress and Harper's anger, and he had no way to know what happened when Harper saw Soledad in a new light. He was aware only of a threat to his plan and a sense that Harper knew how important it was to keep the Indian there, safe from interference.

And so he returned to his room the next morning after prayers and settled himself once again at his writing.

*12 November*

But those pleasures did not last, O Lord, & my thanksgiving soon lay like ashes on my tongue. Sick as I was, I went to the Harpers' house every day & made some progress with Soledad when her strength returned & her grieving was no longer so heavy on her heart. In the meantime I performed my duties, celebrated Mass when called, confessed the sinners of the town, & tried to work a little in the foundry, but the fumes set me to coughing & gagging, & I was obliged to let the fire grow cold & leave the metal half-bent & deformed beside the anvil.

There is no peace other than in Thine embrace nor is there gratitude beyond Thy capacious Heart, for in the midst of all my efforts troubles fell upon me from all sides. Diligent as I was despite my illness, caring as I was of Soledad & all our flock, I was accused of scanting my duties. I know that Fray Sandoval has borne me a grudge since I was chosen to oversee the Indian. He complained to Fray Velásquez, who summoned me to his room, where I endured his vigorous condemnations. I promised to attend more closely to my work and have done so to the best of my abilities. Yet, after promising to spend less time with Soledad, I was unable to forgo the daily visits. My work with her has been threatened because Henry Harper said that Soledad should be brought here to the mission to live among her own kind. After our meetings, during which Elizabeth tearfully begged that Soledad be allowed to stay, he acquiesced and made arrangements for her to be moved to a modest building some distance from the house. I do not understand. I know only that Harper is a difficult man. I have no idea how long the present arrangement will stand, but since the woman's conversion will be hampered if he sends her here, I see no choice other than to stretch my pledge to Fray Velásquez, though I will do my duties even though they may kill me.

I woefully miscalculated Harper's influence in these matters. If I could begin again, I would wait until Diego Madrigal or Marcus Whitby was available, but the past is past & spilled milk is spilled milk. As I recall our conversation, I remember that Harper quickly backed away from his idea, & I cannot forget the confusion that I felt when he said, "Since it's your idea, I suppose I should give in to it for the time being." I am no mind reader but I have learned enough of duplicity after years of confessing sinners to understand many things. I do not know why Harper suggested moving Soledad; she is quiet & well-behaved, & her presence is hardly noticeable. But I do know that Harper wants her to remain and sought my acquiescence. To achieve her conversion, to be able to bring her to the Light, calls for me to follow Harper's gambit, wherever it leads. If I am complicit it is surely harmless & merely the price of the game I must play with him.

# 6

◆ ◆ ◆

The bunkhouse, which was hidden by a stand of oak trees running up the hill, had been built after most of the money Elizabeth's father provided went into the house. It was a simple structure with board and batten walls and a flat, shingled roof. Two small windows that could not open flanked the door. Harper wanted a plank floor at the last minute, but the carpenters had run out of wood. He decided to leave it unfinished until he had realized his plan to breed horses when he retired from the sea and needed more hands. Since it had no practical function, he did not object when Morales began using it as a storehouse. Within a short span it became filled with discarded tack, broken tools, wagon wheels, panes of glass, and chipped dishes that Angelita stacked in the cupboard. It was a cast-off building for cast-off things long before Soledad moved in. While Elizabeth was aware of its forlorn aspect, she was relieved that Harper had backed away from his threat and did not argue with his plan. She consoled herself with the idea that the room could be made comfortable with a little work.

Angelita spent a day cleaning and neatly arranging the things that had piled up. Morales took apart a bed from one of the rooms in the main house and set it up in a corner of the bunkhouse. Elizabeth put good sheets on the bed and covered it with a new patchwork quilt. But the attempt to brighten the little place seemed a failure. It still smelled of dust as well as moldering leather, yet she knew that there was nothing more she could do.

After she managed to make Soledad understand that the bunk-house would be her home, they returned to the house, and Elizabeth encouraged her to take whatever she wanted from her old room. Soledad removed the spirit ship from the dresser. "Is that all?" Elizabeth asked, but Soledad was already out the door.

Elizabeth was consoled that Soledad accepted the news without complaint. She seemed to be able to accommodate herself to change, an ability Elizabeth sadly lacked. But she appreciated this without understanding that it was not a matter of choice.

Around six o'clock on Soledad's first night in the bunkhouse, Elizabeth brought a basket of food, and they ate together on the table beside the bed. It was dark by the time she lighted a lantern and started back to the house, and Soledad watched until the light disappeared. Then she surveyed the things piled along the walls, felt the narrowness of the room, and quickly removed the blankets from the bed, taking them to the edge of the clearing. There, she lay down beneath a moonless sky. The stars were as clear as they used to be on the island. Coyote burned bright. Eagle spread his wings. Fray Santos knew about them. She and the brownrobe shared enough words now for her to understand that much, though he did not know the real names of the gods. That morning he had talked about them and drawn dots on a paper that corresponded to their outlines in the stars. Then he told her again about his own gods who loved her and wanted her to live with them when she died. She was not disturbed by what he said; after all, the sky was large enough for many gods. But she was a little afraid of those whom Fray Santos worshiped, because he had made it clear that they would hate her if she did not find a thing called faith. He had used the word many times, yet she could not understand its meaning. All she knew was that if she did not have it, they would send her to Hell, and whenever Fray Santos used that word he talked of fires and pain and evil things his gods could do. She wished that she could see these gods, but no matter how hard she looked, the stars revealed only those she knew. It occurred to her that Coyote may have tricked him. If that was so, she felt sorry for Fray Santos. She wondered whether she should try to tell him that he had been tricked, that what happened to everyone was decided by the gamblers in the crystal house.

As time passed she learned to read Liza's face and understand a little of what she felt. When the sun came through the window, Liza's blue eyes were the color of the lagoon on the far side of the island and she could almost see inside Liza, where, deep down, there was something sad; it reminded Soledad of some of the young wives, those who could not bear children. She wondered whether that was what made Liza lonely. One day, when they were sitting on the bed, she removed her hand from Liza's and made a sign of a stomach ripe with child. Liza shook her head.

"Dead," she whispered. "Both died."

She wanted to tell Liza about her own daughter, but as she began searching for the words, there was a knock at the door and Fray Santos came in. Soon Liza and he were teaching her more about their words and the god called God.

By now a pattern was set upon her life. Liza came every morning with food; then they waited for Fray Santos, who always arrived out of breath and made her sit beside him at the table. He taught her something called the catechism that would prepare her to be a Christian. When her attention wandered, he became impatient and said, "Listen, my child. You must try very hard." Then he looked at her sternly.

"What is your only comfort in life and death? That is the question you must answer. The answer is that I, with body and soul, both in life and death, am not my own, but belong to my faithful Savior Jesus Christ. Now say it."

She knew that he would not go away and leave them alone until she said what he wanted to hear, but it was all vague to her, not clear like the old storyteller's teaching about the three worlds. After a while she learned to memorize most of the answers, repeating the words and feeling happy when he nodded and smiled.

"Good, my child. That is very good. Now, what do we know of God?"

She could not remember the answer.

"Soledad," he said impatiently, "what do we know of God?"

She looked at Liza, who was sitting behind Fray Santos, her lips slowly forming words. As she answered, she thought of the old storyteller, wondering what would have happened if she and Fray Santos had met. She would like to know what he would have said about the crystal house and the Nunasis.

That summer was hot and dry. More winds than usual blew from the east, and by October only trees and plants fed by the mission's aqueducts remained green and healthy. The chaparral withered under the sun, and when the winds dried the grasses into tinder there were wildfires in the upland meadows north of town. The mountains began to burn so that from dusk to dawn flames curled and leaped and made strange configurations in the night. During the day smoke stained the sky yellow; the sun was a pale disc, its light muted and diffuse. The smoke made people fractious and drove wildlife down the canyons. Deer roamed the fields, rattlesnakes lay coiled in the dusty roads, mountain lions loped across meadows where horses stood wide-eyed, their fear divided between the smoke and the tawny flashes of movement. Even when the fires burned down, a sultriness remained in the air and the distance was full of haze, which obscured the mountains, hiding the islands for many days.

Toward the end of the month clouds began building in the north, and at last it began to rain. Dry arroyos filled with roaring water that gouged streambeds into parched fields. Main Street became soggy, a place where wagons stalled and men were soaked to the skin as they pushed and pulled to free the wheels. Behind the mission water rose to the lip of the dam and spilled over in a waterfall that poured into the nearby fields. Roofs leaked everywhere, and there were buckets in the aisles of the church, where the drip of water made an odd counterpoint to the Latin of the friars. Outside, water cascaded over the arches of the portico and the neophytes returned to their huts, enduring the weather as best they could.

It was just after breakfast on the Wednesday following the storm that a young neophyte arrived at the Harpers' with a note from Fray Santos, apologizing to Elizabeth for business that would keep him at the mission all day. Elizabeth stayed in the living room for a while after the neophyte left. She was feeling restless and in need of a change of scene, so she was not unhappy with the news. She thought of taking Soledad down to the beach, or for a walk in the hills, but neither prospect seemed attractive. What she wanted was a little adventure, so she asked Morales to saddle her favorite mare. Then she thought of going to the painted cave. It would be a long ride, several hours each way, but that made it more appealing. After telling Angelita to make sandwiches and fill two canteens, she changed into a riding dress and took another to the bunkhouse, where she handed it to Soledad. When Soledad came out, she gave her a straw hat like her own. "We're going for a ride," she said, "all the way to the painted cave."

She had been there once before with Susan Ludlow, who had talked to her about the rock art. It was interesting, but as soon as the idea of going there with Soledad came to her, there was another kind of excitement. Elizabeth had no idea whether the images would be familiar, but at the least it would be good for Soledad to see something related to her people. Fray Santos would object, of course, and before she mounted she explained that the outing was for the two of them and that Soledad should not mention it to the friar. "This is our day, yours and mine."

Riding in tandem they set off down the drive, turned right on the road, and headed toward the pass that cleft the mountains north of town. It was just warm enough for her skin to feel supple beneath her riding dress, and even before they passed through town, where several people paused in their work to stare at the blond woman and the Indian, Elizabeth felt happy and free. The rain had cleaned the sky and everywhere new color defined the shape of things. She pointed to trees and wildflowers, told Soledad their names, and Soledad said the words in turn. By the time they began their ascent,

Soledad was telling Elizabeth the names of trees and plants in her own language, and although Elizabeth could not master the syllables sufficiently to repeat what she heard, she took pleasure in the lyric sounds.

For a while Elizabeth was afraid that she might have forgotten the way. The stage road meandered along the slopes and nothing looked familiar until an oddly shaped hill appeared and she remembered the faint trail, rising up the mountainside at a steep angle. They followed the trail along the southern face of the slope, cut back, rode past huge sandstone rocks. Then they were in among the trees, and she heard the rush of water from María Ygnacio Creek. When she saw the flash of sun on the water she wanted to tell Soledad that it flowed all the way to the plain far below and drained into a slough where cranes and egrets fed. But they had entered the forest and she no longer felt in the mood to talk. Besides, she had begun to wonder about her reason for coming. It was more than a desire to show Soledad the cave, or rather it grew from that impulse, but whatever it was lay off at the edge of thought, like a glow in the distance at night.

The cave was somewhere to the left of the trail. As they rode past a tall sandstone outcropping Soledad put her hand on Elizabeth's shoulder. She turned and saw the upper part of the entrance between four oaks. It seemed complicated to ask Soledad how she knew of it. A minute later they dismounted, and Elizabeth tied the reins to a scrub oak and led the way up a scatter of stone.

The entrance was at the bottom of the outcropping projecting from a ridge that formed a promontory above the canyon. It looked like a diving hawk, the top flaring off to the left corresponding to the outstretched right wing, the bottom to the left wing and tail. As Soledad went inside, her figure darkening in the shadows, Elizabeth recognized a beauty to the entrance that she had not noticed when she was there with Susan.

The smooth floor sloped upward to walls that surrounded them with a luminous dreamscape. Light pouring through the entrance seemed to impart motion to the images arrayed across the ceiling. Centipedes and suns divided with lines like a compass led the eye to a man whose hair stood on end and whose hands were lifted as if in supplication. Petaled images in red ochre suggested poinsettias. There was a graceful, leaping deer, birds that reminded Elizabeth of Maltese crosses. The sails of two invisible ships fixed to thick masts alternated bands of black and white squares topped by what appeared to be pennants waving in the stone wind.

At first the pictographs seemed jumbled, but Elizabeth soon understood that there was an order to the images sweeping across the stone, a rhythm aided by the light. She could discern a pattern now, and beneath it another, older one, for there had been overpainting here, revision. She imagined men at work, light just as it was now. Time seemed to leach out of the cave, and she found herself responding to this change, floating free of the present.

"*Antap*," Soledad said, making a gesture as if she were painting. The look of frustration Elizabeth had learned to recognize came into her eyes, and Soledad walked toward the back of the cave. When she moved, her left hand was outstretched and she brushed each of the images with her fingertips, tracing their shapes. She pressed the palm of her hand against the sails and held it there, as if she were blind, testing the contours of someone's face. "Old men," she said without looking at Elizabeth. "*Antap*."

Elizabeth did not know whether the vertigo that obliged her to sit down was from craning her neck, or the result of looking so intently at the concentric circles and swirling suns. Soledad came over and knelt beside her, and Elizabeth said, "I'm fine. I was just dizzy." She wanted to leave, but it was clear that Soledad was not ready. After standing up, Soledad again examined the images, and Elizabeth became aware that there was a recognition here, a connection to something beyond her own capacity to understand. She waited another twenty minutes as Soledad retraced her steps, and then suggested that they leave. Soledad was reluctant; she stood for a long time in the entrance looking back inside before she followed Elizabeth down the path of stones.

"What in hell do you think you're doing?"

They were at the foot of the porch, where Henry stood at the top of the steps. His vest was unbuttoned and his collar was open. His hands rested on his hips as he looked down at them.

"You have no right to speak to me like that."

"Apparently I need to. Tim Harrington saw the two of you going through town like a couple of squaws."

"We went for a ride."

"Wonderful. You went for a ride. In the middle of town."

"To the painted cave. Fray Santos couldn't come today, and I thought . . ."

"I don't give a damn what you thought. I won't have you making a fool of me."

One quick look at Soledad was all she needed to see that Henry had upset her. "At least lower your voice. She has no idea what's wrong."

He glanced at Soledad as if he barely saw her.

"If you show yourself in town again with her, that's it. *Comprende?*"

"I'll do as I please."

"You'll damn well do as you're told." He went through the door and slammed it behind him.

"He's been drinking. We'll be careful next time," Elizabeth said to Soledad.

She felt very tired, and when Soledad started across the drive toward the bunkhouse she was inclined to let her go. She could not explain Henry's anger, but she did not want to leave her like this, so she followed, caught her arm, and said, "Come, I know something that will make you feel better."

There was no tub in the house for the first year, and she had made do with sponge baths until the one Henry ordered arrived from San Francisco. The huge porcelain oval with clawed feet seemed like a pool the first time she used it. She would have preferred something smaller, but Henry had insisted on one long enough to stretch out in. She came to like it after a while, and had Morales build a shelf between the tub and the wall to hold her soaps and sponges and assortment of colored bath oils. Now she poured half a cup of the rose-scented oil into the hot water Angelita had carried up in pots. The room was suffused with the scent. The porcelain gleamed in the light as Angelita came in with towels and then brushed a wisp of hair from her eyes, looking at Soledad as if she could not believe Elizabeth was going to allow her in her tub.

"Do you need anything else?"

"No, thank you. You may go."

Elizabeth put her hands in the water and made washing motions. Soledad watched and laughed, shaking her head as if to indicate that she did not understand.

"Take off your clothes and get in," she said. "Bathe. You'll feel better."

She held out a towel and rubbed it on her arm.

"This is for later."

As she took a step toward the door, Soledad reached down and in one fluid movement pulled the riding dress over her head. Elizabeth was amazed that she wore nothing underneath. She had never seen another woman's naked body. She felt the color rising in her face and would have turned away if Soledad had showed a trace of self-consciousness. But she simply stood there, waiting. Her body was the color of cinnamon sprinkled on custard, her breasts small and well formed, tipped with areoles that were almost black. Elizabeth could not stop her eyes from straying down the woman's body, and was shocked that the cleavage of her sex showed clearly through a fine downy covering of pubic hair. There appeared to be a birthmark just above her pubis, but then she saw that it was a tattoo made of concentric circles, like the images at the painted cave.

Her hand remained on the doorknob as Soledad smiled and indicated that she too should take off her clothes. There was no other possible interpretation. Everything Elizabeth had been taught about modesty asserted itself: her mother's embarrassed hints, the nuns' warnings about the temple of the body, her own ambiguous feelings about the geography of her flesh. She was repelled by the thought of exposing herself, but as she shook her head Soledad stepped into the tub and held her arms out, and Elizabeth suddenly realized that communal bathing must have been part of Soledad's life. She imagined a shaded pool, women, the sound of laughter. She raised her left hand to the top of her dress, and as she undid the first button she caught the image of the two of them in the round mirror on the wall. The intimacy suggested by the picture made it possible to continue undressing until she was naked and stood there with one arm across her breasts, the other covering her sex. Their mutual nakedness neutralized the embarrassment she felt as she stepped into the tub, aware that she was crossing a boundary she had been ignorant of minutes earlier. She did not care; the connection she felt with Soledad was stronger than any she had known.

They faced each other from the opposite ends of the tub, each looking at the other a little shyly. Elizabeth took a bar of soap from the dish on the shelf and began laving her hands, but the soap slipped away beneath the bubbles. As she reached for it her hand closed on Soledad's foot and they both pulled back laughing. Stifling her giggles, she put her finger to her lips.

"Be quiet. Henry."

"Ban," Soledad said.

"What?"

"Ban."

"Yes. Husband. Good."

She took Soledad's left arm and soaped it, splashing water on her glistening cinnamon skin. Then she lathered her own hair, ducked under the surface, came up, and wiped the water from her eyes. Soledad imitated her, and afterward they leaned back against the smooth sides. Elizabeth was aware that something fundamental had changed in her life and wondered whether Soledad shared anything remotely akin to her feelings.

When the water became tepid she stood up and handed Soledad a towel, took another for herself, dried and wrapped her hair in the towel. She studied the faint tattoo whose edges were rough, almost serrated. The individual pinpricks were clearly visible. Soledad touched Elizabeth's stomach, said a word, asked a question.

"No. We do not have tattoos."

She wanted Soledad to repeat the word so that she could learn it, but she was afraid that Henry would come looking for her.

"We must dress. Put on clothes."

As they came out of the bathroom, Angelita appeared at the top of the stairs, stared at Elizabeth's wet hair, Soledad's, and then started down the hall.

"*Momento*," Elizabeth said. The girl stopped without turning around.

"I want to talk to you. Please wait in the living room."

"Yes, señora," she answered, and she retraced her steps. Elizabeth waited until she was at the bottom and going up the hall toward the living room before she took Soledad's arm and hurried her downstairs and through the kitchen.

"Good night," she said, and put her arm around her for a moment.

"Night."

She leaned against the open door as Soledad passed the gazebo. Light from the office door reached a little way across the darkened meadow. It took a precise form near the house, as defined as a candle flame. Then it became diffuse, and Soledad passed through it and disappeared into the trees. Closing the door, Elizabeth ran her fingers through her hair and fastened it in its usual knot with the pins from her pocket.

Angelita was standing between the windows and the fireplace; she looked quizzically at Elizabeth.

"Angelita, I should like you to say nothing to Mr. Harper about my gesture of friendship toward Soledad."

"Yes, señora."

"And you may take tomorrow for yourself. You've been working hard, and I value what you do."

"Thank you, señora."

"You may go home now. I'll see you the day after tomorrow."

She was tired from the ride but did not feel like sleeping. She was not happy with herself for bribing Angelita. It had been a superfluous gesture anyway, since the woman was a notorious gossip, but it was all she could think of at the moment. She spent longer than usual preparing for bed, and as she went through the rituals the day returned. The images from the cave were stark and beautiful and compelling. One stood out in her mind and she focused on it, wondering how it could have happened that Soledad's tattoo matched the rings in the cave. As she thought about it, the night seemed to take on a new dimension, and she settled back to see what it might bring.

# 7

◆ ◆ ◆

The next night was the first time Henry visited Soledad. She had been dreaming of her daughter playing in the village with other children while she sat outside the hut making a new dress. She wanted her to try it on, but the girl ran away and she followed her to the cliff, where a strong wind was blowing and people huddled together for protection. Torch flames leaped into the wind and she was afraid the fire would burn her eyes. When she sat up, still caught by the dream, she saw Henry lighting the wick of the lamp with a match. She smelled sulphur as he put the spent match down on the table, replaced the glass chimney, and the room filled with light. He looked very tall, standing over her. The lamplight flickered and shone like yellow water on his face; it made his shadow move on the ceiling. His expression surprised her, and she sat up, trying to shake off the remnants of her dream, but she was still confused.

"Liza?"

He blinked in response. As he turned up the wick and the flame brightened, he smiled, and the uneasiness she had begun to feel lessened.

"Good evening. Do you know 'Good evening'?"

He stood with his feet apart and his thumbs hooked in his suspenders.

"Good, Henry."

He smiled and she repeated the words, aware that she had got something wrong.

"Good, Henry."

He laughed then, his voice hardly more than a whisper.

She waited for him to say something else, but he only stood there, looking. He reached into his coat and removed a silver flask. Saying "This is what we need," he unscrewed the top, drank, then handed it to her. As she reached for it the blanket fell away from her breasts. She began to cover herself, but he sat on the edge of the bed and pushed the blanket down and touched her.

"Lovely breasts."

He put his finger to his tongue and as he slowly ran the tip of his moist finger over the nipple of her right breast she remembered the way he had stared at her when he first saw her on the island. There was the same appraisal, the way he had of examining her whenever they were together. There was no pleasure in his touch, but she was ignorant of the customs and afraid of what might happen if she turned away. She wondered whether this was part of being moved from the house. She knew that he wanted her for his wife, but there were ceremonies for such things; to take a woman without them was taboo. The men of her tribe were beaten and the women forced to live alone, out of sight of the village. She tried to think of a way to ask why he was doing this when he suddenly stood up, undid his braces, removed his shirt, and stepped out of his trousers. His flesh was swollen and its shadow was clear against his thigh before he sat down again and took her nipple in his mouth. She tried to twist away, but he reached up and grasped her shoulder. She wondered if the custom was for Liza to send Henry to her. She remembered asking whether Fray Santos was also Liza's husband and how Liza had grown angry; perhaps it was different with husbands. It must be, or Henry would not be doing these things. His hand slid down her stomach and she tried to keep her legs closed, but he was too strong.

"Liza?"

"She can't hear you."

"Liza says."

"Liza says nothing."

She did not want him to touch her any longer, but he was on top of her, and she cried out in pain.

In a while he rolled away and looked up at the ceiling. She felt ignorant. She wanted to know whether Liza had sent him and, if so, why she had not told her. His seed was wet between her legs; she was afraid that it might have found the place beneath the swirls on her stomach. An old woman once told her that she always knew if the seeds had taken hold, so Soledad tested her own sensations, tried to feel inside her body. If she swelled with child, would Liza and Henry live with her? Would she and the child be shunned?

"Soledad." He was still staring at the ceiling. "This is secret. Between you and me."

She knew the word *secret*. It was like Fray Santos's god she could not see.

"You," he said, pointing to her. Then he turned his finger to himself. "Me. No Elizabeth," he added, shaking his head.

"Liza."

"No Liza. You and me."

When she understood that Liza was not to know, she felt more lost than ever. Liza was like her people. They had bathed together in friendship, and when women did that there were no secrets between them.

"No Liza. No Santos, either. *Comprende?*"

She wondered why this was happening. She had not felt so unhappy since she learned that her family died.

"Though I think he knows," he added as he got up and put on his clothes. He smiled as he finished buttoning his trousers. Then he turned down the wick of the lamp and the room was black except for the pale squares of light from the windows.

"No Liza," he said, and then he was gone. She pulled the blankets up to her chin. Gradually her eyes became accustomed to the darkness and she touched the tattoo on her stomach.

Harper had intended to do nothing more than work on his ledgers that evening and perhaps look in on Elizabeth, who had stayed in bed all day. A few nights before, he had gone to her and she had turned her face away, endured him, and that was why he felt no remorse at going to Soledad. When he left the house an hour earlier, the knowledge that Elizabeth was in her bedroom heightened his anticipation. He had never accepted limits, but he liked the idea of testing himself against them, and that, he realized, had been part of it. His thinking ranged a little way into the future, toward the prospect of more nights with Soledad. Then he bent over the desk, running his finger down the ledger page. In a little while he was absorbed and the encounter faded from his mind.

At the end of the month Elizabeth spent a few days with Susan Ludlow, who had just miscarried. Before leaving, she told Angelita to take Soledad's meals to her and asked Harper to keep an eye on her too.

Susan was in a bad way when Elizabeth arrived. She did not feel like talking, so Elizabeth spent the day with Susan's two daughters, sending them into their mother's bedroom the next morning in their best dresses. After the children left, Susan said that she felt a little better, at least more resigned, adding that she knew that she should be grateful because she had the girls.

"It's God's will. They say that miscarriages have a reason and I believe it." She took Elizabeth's hand, adding, "I'm sure the next time everything will be fine. For both of us."

It was the perfect opportunity to tell Susan that she had missed her last period, but she did not because she had always been irregular, and she wanted to wait until she was certain. Yet she was convinced that she was pregnant, and she was willing to do anything to have the baby, even if it meant staying in bed the whole time.

Fray Santos spent several hours with Susan the next morning before taking Elizabeth out to the Ludlows' patio.

"How would you assess Soledad's progress?" he asked.

As soon as he spoke she was afraid he might be thinking of taking Soledad to the mission, and she must have looked worried, because he quickly shook his head.

"I'm sorry. I didn't make myself clear. She must stay with you a long time. This is something else entirely. Tell me what you think. She has done well, wouldn't you agree?"

"Yes, it seems that way."

"Exactly. I myself believe that the gift of understanding has finally come upon her, praise God. Now, in a month or two a member of the Los Angeles archdiocese will visit us on an administrative matter." He paused to emphasize the seriousness of what he was telling her. "It is my opinion that her competence in the catechism would make a considerable impression. With extra time she might be prepared to demonstrate her knowledge."

"It's possible, but you know she does well for a while and then something happens to set her back."

"That's why I'm asking you to make a special effort. She's always eager to please you. If you could impress upon her the importance of redoubling her efforts, it would be a special grace."

Susan was so much better by Friday evening that Elizabeth decided to go home rather than spend another night with the Ludlows. Her friend insisted that she stay for dinner, and with one thing and another she did not leave until nine o'clock.

She had a message for Henry from Mathew, so she looked for him as soon as she entered the house. In his office, ledgers were scattered on the oak desk and the air reeked of cigar smoke. Henry was a man of strict routine and she could not remember him leaving his papers about. He had an elaborate filing system to keep track of his business ventures and never left the office until he had put the leather volumes on the shelf behind his desk.

But she was determined not to waste her time worrying or to let anything interfere with her good mood. On the way home she had allowed herself to think about the future; she was certain that she was pregnant, and the knowledge held a promise of immense happiness. She knew that she should go to bed, but being alone in Henry's office was a new experience, and she wanted to stay a while. It was a masculine place of dark wood paneling he had ordered from San Francisco. She leaned back in the large black chair and surveyed the room, with its huge desk and two leather chairs separated by a table where a lamp burned warmly. There were paintings of the sea and ships, one of the *Elizabeth's Delight*, another of the ship her father sailed before he retired. A compass, a sextant, and a varnished piece of wood from a ship that had meant something to Henry in his youth were fixed to the walls. It was a sailor's room, and she supposed that its kind could be found in thousands of other homes around the world; but it was unique because his imprint was everywhere, and her feelings toward Henry softened a little. She tried to look past the night of Mathew's party to the man he was when they married, wondering whether she could find it in herself to forgive him. There were worse things, she told herself, and the baby might bring them together once again. She picked up a glass from the desk. The cognac was smooth and warm. She liked the idea that she was drinking from his glass. It was a gesture of good will, and she finished it, giving herself up to a new, tentative way of looking at things, determined to try to see whether she was capable of true forgiveness. She was making progress when the door opened and Angelita came in. When Angelita saw her, a change crossed her face. She looked confused, frightened.

"It's all right," Elizabeth said.

"I thought you were staying at the Ludlows', señora."

"Mrs. Ludlow is much better. Her husband and María are taking care of her."

Angelita nodded and turned to go. It was clear there was something on her mind.

"Angelita, what is it?"

"Nothing, señora," she said, keeping her eyes averted.

"Did you break something? I don't care. Just tell me."

"No," Angelita answered, "nothing's broken."

"Do you know where my husband is?"

Angelita stared at her hands.

"Angelita?"

"I have not seen him."

"He was here a little while ago."

"I haven't seen him. Please, señora, may I leave?"

"You're sure nothing's wrong?"

"Yes, señora. I just came to turn out the light."

When she left, Elizabeth stared at the closed door and reasoned that Henry had gone to Esteban's. She was not sleepy and decided that she would wait up so that she could see him; perhaps they would have a drink together. In the meantime she would go out to see whether Soledad was awake. Over the last few months Soledad had adjusted to the novelty of having light in the evening hours and had stopped going to bed at sundown. Elizabeth thought Soledad would be happy to hear how proud Fray Santos was of her achievements.

As she went outside her eyes were drawn to the lights of the town. There was a comforting familiarity in their brightness; Elizabeth realized that she was happier than she had been for a long time. Rather than continuing across the meadow, she went up into the gazebo and stood there, savoring the scent of jasmine and thinking of the possibility of new life within her and of a new life for herself. She hoped that Soledad was awake, because she wanted company, wanted to share her feeling.

At the bottom of the grove she entered a narrow lane between the trees. There was a clear view of the bunkhouse at the far end, where two yellow squares glowed in the darkness. Suddenly there were three. Since it was warm, she thought Soledad had opened the door for air, or perhaps she had gone to relieve herself. Then she saw a man outlined in the doorway. The possibility that Soledad had struck up a relationship with Morales or one of the other hands was hard to believe. If Soledad had a man, then she would have to tell her that such behavior was scandalous. Her sense of well-being evaporated as her curiosity about the visitor turned to resentment.

The third light disappeared and there were footsteps coming in her direction. If the man found her, it would be embarrassing, so she remained where she was. A moment later the footsteps veered off toward the edge of the grove in the direction of her house. Just when she had decided to wait until she no longer heard the footsteps, a match flared, and the glow of a cigar seared her heart.

Henry had stopped at the edge of the grove, probably to admire the view. Much as she wanted to scream, she neither spoke nor moved. In an instant everything that had happened from the day Fray Santos explained that Soledad might still be alive returned to her. She had gone about the business of living; committed herself to tending to Soledad. She had practiced forgiving Henry and had seen nothing of the truth. Now the scratches and the tattoo merged, mocking her for her ignorance. The open ledgers, the glass of liquor, the lingering scent of cigar smoke seemed to rise up before her as the glow began moving away toward the house. She had heard him in the hall several times late at night, and thought it was restlessness that had wakened him. Now she understood that he had been visiting Soledad. Suddenly her gorge rose and she vomited until her throat burned and her eyes streamed with tears. The knowledge that Henry had probably gotten her pregnant between visits to Soledad struck like a blow to her head as she rose from her knees.

The other lights went out when she was thirty feet away from the bunkhouse, but she continued without faltering, reached the door, and flung it open.

"Soledad!"

"Liza!"

"I saw him!"

"Liza!"

Soledad's voice came from the corner where the bed was. Elizabeth was afraid she might be sick again. She bumped into a chair, which toppled over and clattered on the floor.

"The lamp. Light the lamp!"

"Liza no Henry."

"Light it!" she yelled.

Elizabeth stared into darkness; a match flared and the wick caught. Soledad was standing naked beside the lamp. Elizabeth quickly stepped around the table and slapped her with all the strength she could bring to bear. Soledad staggered back and Elizabeth moved near the corner of the bed, where Soledad pressed herself against the wall, holding out her hands.

"Liza. Henry no husband. Henry no Jesus Mary Joseph!"

Elizabeth saw her descending from the boat, saw herself and

Soledad in the bathroom mirror, herself and Fray Santos patiently teaching the woman the words she was repeating now in a sickening perversion of her faith. Her heart had gone out to Soledad. She had been drawn by a mysterious sense of shared femaleness into the warm bath, had seen her own fertility in the blue tattoo, her own loneliness in Soledad's. She remembered the pity she had felt when she realized that Soledad's silence of ten years was made worse by her being brought to a place where she could not understand a word; how that in turn had given rise to Elizabeth's questions about what the friars were doing with the Indians at the mission. Now all she felt was disgust.

"Liza," Soledad whispered.

"No Liza!" Elizabeth shouted. "No Liza ever again. You are never to use my name again!"

"Henry no Jesus. Henry no Jesus."

As she listened to the singsong repetition, Soledad became all the women with whom Henry had betrayed her. She imagined them, a roomful of lasciviousness.

"Why didn't you die? Why am I not to have a chance for some happiness?"

Soledad came to the edge of the bed. Elizabeth raised her hand, expecting her to cower, but Soledad merely raised her face to accept the proffered blow.

"No," she said. "No."

Elizabeth's hand fell to her side. "It didn't happen? I saw him. Henry. Outside."

Elizabeth was certain that Soledad was trying to think of another lie. Her confusion grew more apparent by the moment. Now the eyes that Elizabeth had looked into so lovingly, that had taken in her own nakedness, seemed all pupil.

"I was your friend."

Soledad pointed her index finger at her own heart. "Me Henry," she said. "Me Henry." Then she pointed at Elizabeth. "You Soledad."

Elizabeth looked at her without the slightest comprehension. Her life seemed to be pointed backward, trapped in the neat lines of

the scratches she had seen in the mirror. Suddenly, with a movement so swift Elizabeth had no time to react, Soledad embraced
her, held her tight with her left arm and with her right hand cupped
Elizabeth's breast and squeezed until it hurt.

"You Soledad."

Elizabeth struggled, but Soledad held her fast and ran her fingers
over Elizabeth's nipple.

"No!" she screamed. "You filthy . . ."

"You Soledad."

She kissed Elizabeth's neck and forced her backward until she fell
on the bed. Then she descended with the full weight of her body.

"Dear Jesus!" Elizabeth cried and tried to squirm away, but
Soledad's strength was impossible to resist.

"Me Henry."

She felt Soledad's tears on her face as she thrust against her.

"Me Henry," Soledad said, grinding herself left and right. "You
Soledad."

Elizabeth had been pushing against Soledad's shoulders, horrified by the rhythmical movement. Now her arms felt heavy and
she let them fall as the knowledge came to her.

"Oh, God!" she whispered.

"Me Henry!" Soledad said insistently. "Me Henry! Me Henry!
Me Henry!"

Elizabeth wanted to curse, she wanted to cry, but all she could do
was raise her arms and circle Soledad's narrow back.

"Oh, my God, I am sorry."

Soledad's breath came in short gasps as she repeated the refrain.
"Me Henry. Me Henry."

"I understand," Elizabeth said, stroking her back. "I understand.
Forgive me. I understand. You Henry."

Soledad lay her face against Elizabeth's chest; Elizabeth knew
that the sensation would stay with her for the rest of her life. It was
one of the few moments when she had glimpsed the truth, and she
savored its sweetness. She had never felt closer to anyone in her life.

"Sisters," she whispered.

"Ters," Soledad answered as she eased herself down onto the

bed, turned on her side, and took Elizabeth's hand in her own. Elizabeth returned the pressure without taking her eyes from the ceiling. The lamplight thickened the shadows of the beams. Her love for Soledad and her anguish over Henry were pulling her apart, as if she were two people trapped in a single body. She could not imagine moving from the bed, but she had to. Somehow she had to rise and return to the grove, cross the meadow, re-enter her house.

"I must leave."

Soledad looked at her. "Henry no Jesus."

"No, Henry is no Jesus."

She brushed a strand of hair from Soledad's forehead. "I will come back tomorrow. We will learn with Fray Santos," Elizabeth said. "Sleep."

After Soledad drew up the blankets she turned down the lamp and went toward the moonlit windows. As she opened the door, Soledad said something so faintly that she could not hear.

"What?"

"Sisters."

The word filled the room.

"Yes. Sisters. Good night."

"Night," Soledad answered.

# 8

The door to his office at the far end of the hall was wide open, giving her a clear view of Henry bent over his desk. He was the only stable point in her vision. The floor was tilting left and right; the paintings on the walls moved up and down. It did no good to remember that she always felt dizzy in a crisis. Nothing was familiar. Not the hallway, not the paintings she had framed, not Henry. She had lived for over five years with this stranger, who calmly dipped his pen into the inkwell, oblivious of her presence. She wanted to shout his name, make him turn and look at her, but she had no confidence in her voice. He reached for his glass, and as he brought it to his lips he saw her; his eyes were perfectly familiar, as was his mildly startled expression.

"I thought you were at the Ludlows'," he said calmly.

"I know."

Her words sounded as hollow as they had in the painted cave. They were strange disturbances of the air with no connection to her.

"Susan hasn't taken a turn for the worse?"

"Where were you?"

"Esteban's."

She wanted to scream. "I saw Soledad."

His eyes narrowed as they always did when he sensed that something was wrong. The change in his expression was so slight that if she had not known him she would have missed it.

"She told me."

"Told you what?"

His brow arched. Then it was level. Had he shown even the slightest guilt, she could at least have pitied him, but he did not. His lie made her hatred rise as uncontrollably as the sickness had in the grove.

"Well?" he asked impatiently.

Always in the past when they reached a moment like this he attacked her, and she retreated into tears. But not tonight. For the first time in her married life she was going to stand up to him.

"Said what?"

"That you raped her!"

He laughed. "She's crazy."

"Liar! I was in the grove. I saw you!"

He looked away. When he turned back, his eyes were hard.

"You raped her."

"She's an Indian."

"She's a woman!"

"What does that mean?"

"You don't know?"

"She's an ignorant savage that Santos wants to confuse with his hocus-pocus."

"You're a damned soul, Henry."

"Enough!" he shouted.

"Not enough. I forgave you the first time. I tried the second. I've been trying tonight. I wish you knew what I was thinking when I was sitting in your chair. If you ever touch her again —"

"Stop it."

"No, not this time. I —"

"Stop, or she goes to the mission."

The momentum that had been building since she crossed the meadow collided with his words. She saw herself reflected in his eyes, diminished to a tiny figure. What she wanted to say was as useless as if she had dreamed the denunciation she carried across the meadow like a battle flag inscribed with heroic mottoes.

"You can't mean that," she said.

"Try me. Keep it up."

Her flag fluttered once and fell. Her last weapon, the secret of her almost certain pregnancy, was also useless. She was trapped, made defenseless by his threat. With one last glance she turned and ran down the hall.

She thought she would feel safe once she was in her bedroom, but as soon as she locked the door the sense of entrapment was magnified. The idea of the room as a sanctuary was an illusion. It was in the house they shared, and much as she wished that it was not so, her life was here, with him, sealed by her marriage vows. More than anything else at that moment, she wanted to be with her parents, wanted them to tell her that there were boundaries to marriage and that Henry had gone beyond them. She wanted them all to go to Fray Santos and lay it before him, wanted him to annul the marriage. Then, alone, she would feel less alone. But she also wanted to be with Soledad. Even as she imagined the comfort of Soledad's presence, she knew that Henry's threat was forcing her to confront her own selfishness. Much as she hated to admit it, Soledad would be better off at the mission, where she would at least be safe from him. The fantasy of annulment was a trick her mind had played to disguise the true source of her pain. Without Soledad, the house would be as barren as the islands. She imagined being alone with Henry in the dining room, each lost in silence at opposite ends of the table. She could not stand it. She was willing to sew her lips shut to keep Soledad there, but if in exchange for the pleasure of her company Soledad was raped again, she could not bear the guilt. The idea of giving up her friend hung suspended between her knowledge of what was best for Soledad and what she needed. She had to talk to Fray Santos, let him decide. She would have to find a way to raise the question in such a way that it would seem as if she were concerned only with Soledad's welfare. That way she could escape the trap of selfishness.

The following morning she went to the mission and caught up with Fray Santos as he was hurrying toward the chapel.

"Please, I must talk to you."

"What is it?"

"Not here."

"Very well," he said. "Meet me at noon."

To pass the time she walked slowly around the building. She wished there were some way she could stay there for a week, a month, long enough to get hold of herself.

She saw the Indians at their tasks and had a vivid image of Soledad pounding laundry on the stone escarpment, imagined her walking back to the huts of the village with a basket balanced on her head as dust rose around her feet. Whenever she came to the mission the Indians were bearing burdens, and she had never given them a thought. They had been part of the order of things that she would no more have questioned than she would have the conditions of her own life. But now she saw that they took no pleasure in the work. It was hard, she thought, but it was safe.

Fray Santos offered her a chair and stood before her.

"I'm grateful for your time," she said.

"I can stay only a little while, my child. What is it?"

Soledad's nakedness was imposed on her mind's eye, Henry's indifference, the scratches, the wreck of her marriage, all that was preface to what she had to say but could not tell him.

"I've been wondering whether Soledad might not be better off here, after all."

He smiled weakly as he pulled up a chair for himself, sitting forward with his elbows on the table, his fingers joined at their tips. As he looked at her the lens of his round glasses reflected the window, and she had to move to the left to see his eyes.

"Why have you changed your mind?" he asked.

"I think she might be happier with her own kind. She mourns for her family, you know."

"Yes, certainly. Yours is a Christian concern. You must have been thinking about this a long time, isn't that so? But we must be careful. The wrong decision is so easy to take and so long regretted."

"That's why I came. But if you're pressed for time . . ."

"Nothing that cannot wait. Now, then, let us examine the case." He began by turning down the forefinger of his left hand with his right thumb.

"What do we know of Soledad? That she suffered a great tragedy. What else? That she nearly died when she learned of her family's fate. Beyond that? That while she has recovered physically, she is still delicate. Is that a fair summary?"

"Very fair."

"If there were only one such consideration I would say, by all means, let her come. But there is more than one. As I said, I understand your concern. I too have thought of where she would best be served ever since our discussion with your husband, so you are not alone. We both want what is best for Soledad. Is that not so?"

"Of course."

He looked at her intently and his eyelids fluttered as slowly as a butterfly's wings. "Commendable, my child. I hope that one day she will understand how devoted you have been."

"Oh, I think she does already."

"I am happy to hear it. But that, as they say, is another matter. You wish my opinion and I will tell you. We must be selfless in this and set aside all personal considerations. The conditions of her salvation are of the utmost importance. What we know is that she still has only an incomplete understanding of the tenets of the faith. Bringing her to the point where she is ready for confirmation will be arduous; I make no claims otherwise, but it can be done. My opinion is this: we should consider only where she would learn most easily. I do not think this would be accomplished by uprooting her from familiar surroundings. Nothing has changed on this score since I spoke to your husband."

"You think she should remain with us."

He spread his hands.

"Under the circumstances. When we have the pleasure of seeing her confirmed, we will know the time has come for her to join her brothers and sisters."

Soon after Elizabeth left, Fray Santos was on his way up to the canyon when young Fray Olivares caught up with him and said that he was wanted by the superior. He reluctantly retraced his steps, genuflecting before the statue of Santa Bárbara as he crossed the garden. He remembered the admonition he had received from Fray Velásquez and, as he knocked and heard the superior's gravelly voice inviting him inside, was afraid that there might be more of the same. To his surprise the man's dour face lighted up with a beatific smile.

"Sit down a moment. There's good news I wish to share."

Fray Velásquez picked up a letter bearing an official seal and read a passage confirming the bishop's visit. "Wonderful news, don't you agree?"

"Splendid," Fray Santos said. "A blessing."

"I leave it to you to make arrangements, Xavier. Perhaps you can think of something special."

"Oh," he said, "I will try."

On the way to the canyon Fray Santos savored Fray Velásquez's words like a child sucking a piece of candy. He had thought incessantly about the visit. Until Fray Velásquez placed the arrangements in his lap it had seemed that the presentation of Soledad would be a minor part in the occasion, but now he moved his little scene to the fore. Compared with this opportunity, the unease Elizabeth had caused earlier seemed considerably less, and he took his place beneath the trumpet tree feeling better than he had since leaving her.

As soon as Elizabeth mentioned Soledad, he had feared that she would confirm some things Angelita had said the day before. "I have heard things," she told him, seeking counsel. "Seen things. One night he went out the back door and I paid no attention. When it happened again I watched and saw him cross the meadow past the gazebo. There is nothing on the other side except the bunkhouse."

"He could be restless. He could be out stretching his legs," the friar offered.

"I saw him twice when he came back. He did not look like a man who had been stretching his legs."

The evidence was either innocuous or compromising, depending on how one interpreted it. This was not the first time a servant had complained about her master. Sometimes the charges proved to be true, but just as often they were fabricated to avenge a real or imagined slight. He questioned Angelita gently, telling her that he would consider what she said and suggesting that things were often different from what they appeared to be. "A hawk in the distance is a sparrow close by. So it is with suppositions." Then he told her to speak of her suspicions to no one else and to remember that loyalty to those from whom we earn our daily bread was a virtue.

Afterward he had gone to the foundry and set to work. As he heated the iron and began bending it into shape, he was aware that if Angelita's claims were true, they would interfere with his plans. He knew about the devil in the flesh and had no doubt that Harper was capable of such behavior. Circumstantial as Angelita's evidence was, he had to consider the possibility that there was some truth in it. Soledad was comely in the way men might find tempting. There was, furthermore, the inescapable fact of her race, and the deplorable habits Indians had of fornicating outside marriage. He and his brothers were often at their wits' end to persuade the women to guard their chastity or remain faithful to their husbands. They had only recently been forced to build a dormitory for the younger women, where they were locked up at night for their own protection. If Angelita's charges were true, he thought, then he might have led Soledad through the catechism only hours after she had committed adultery. The idea repelled him, and he carefully went over everything she said and was relieved to find considerable room for doubt.

And yet as soon as Elizabeth mentioned Soledad's name, he was afraid that she was about to offer another version of Angelita's story. It even occurred to him that she might have sent Angelita to him in advance. As he joined her, he expected the familiar questions. How should she deal with her husband's weakness? How could she continue living with someone who had betrayed her? He had been ready to say that she should don the armor of her faith; emphasize that the ties that bound her to her husband were more important than her grief. The remembered pieties marshaled themselves on his tongue and he was ready to present them. The gap between his expectation and what she said was so wide that it was only with effort that he had calmed his nerves. Of course he could have asked questions that would have revealed whether Elizabeth also suspected Henry, but if Angelita had lied, what purpose would have been served in making Elizabeth suspicious of her husband?

The splash of water flowing into the aqueduct eased his mind, and he looked down the canyon, giving himself up to the sea and islands, the drone of bees, the rich scents of wildflowers, and the more subtle scent of dusty oaks. After a while he plucked a flower from an overhanging branch and held it by its stem. The shape resembled a bell more than a trumpet, he thought. He held it to his nose as he got up and set off toward the mission. The roofs of the Indian village glowed yellow in the late afternoon sun. He knew it would be foolish to alter Soledad's living conditions. He reminded himself that he was too prone to worry, always complicating things by mistaking smoke for fire.

By the time he reached the mission he decided that the flower was a trumpet after all. He imagined its notes, distinct and sweet, as he went along the portico.

# 9

◆ ◆ ◆

A month after Elizabeth's meeting with Fray Santos, Harper returned to Santa Bárbara from a three-day trip to San Luis Obispo, tired but pleased about a deal he had struck with a rancher for two blooded mares. The price demanded of him was too steep by half, even though they were good horses; afterward Ludlow congratulated him on his shrewdness in the bargaining.

As he rode up, Elizabeth was sewing in a rocking chair on the porch. He was not surprised when she refused to acknowledge his presence. Since discovering his treatment of Soledad, she had been silent at meals, and whenever they passed each other in the house or outside, she refused to look at him. Silence was her way of punishing him; while it was tiresome, he supposed that he ought to be grateful that she did not spend her time nagging at him whenever the servants weren't around. After all, he had only himself to blame. Even if Elizabeth had not found out, he would have stopped visiting Soledad; he had already satisfied his curiosity. But Henry was not about to tell Elizabeth this. In the first place, it would only bring everything to the surface. In the second, he'd be damned if he was going to ask for forgiveness. And in the third, he was angry enough to let her stew. If she acted true to form, her coldness would last for months, and he had no illusions that the thaw would ever be complete. If he gave rein to his anger, her silence could go on indefinitely.

By the time Morales came up to take his horse, Henry had decided to act as if everything were fine.

"I sold the mares for a price you won't believe."

It was obvious that she had no intention of responding. Her hands were shaking, but she persisted with her sewing. The tremor was so pronounced that she was obliged to insert the needle and pull it through the back of the cloth as slowly as an old woman.

"He had no idea what they were worth. It was like taking candy from a baby."

She looked at him with a quick, withering glance, and that was when he noticed the tears. Her hands remained nervously at work until she flinched from sticking herself with the needle. A drop of blood formed on her finger and spread on the cloth. She made no effort to stop the bleeding as she stared at the bloody material, and that was too much for him. He forgot his pledge about smoothing things over.

"Goddam it," he said irritably, "enough is enough."

"I have something to tell you."

"Good. At least you haven't forgotten how to talk."

"We're pregnant, Henry. Soledad and I are pregnant."

She put down her sewing long enough to wrap a piece of cloth around her finger. When she looked up, there were no more tears, though the brightness stayed in her eyes.

"Don't you have anything to say?" she asked bitterly. "Or is this too much even for you?"

"You're sure?" he said, ignoring her taunt.

"You're going to be the father of our children."

"It could have been one of the Mexicans," Harper said quickly.

Elizabeth stared at him. "Do you mean with me?"

"You know what I mean."

"It wasn't."

"How do you know?" he asked.

"I know. You should be happy. You wanted a child. Now you're going to have two." She paused and looked away. Then she turned back. "You'll be just like an emperor. A little white baby and a little brown baby."

"Stop it."

"A potentate," she added tearfully.

Her voice caught as he grabbed her hand. He had forgotten that she'd pierced her finger. "I didn't mean to hurt you."

"That's very kind."

Ignoring her sarcasm, he said, "We need to think about this."

"There's nothing to think about," she said, biting off the words. "Unless your conscience is bothering you. Do you have a conscience, Henry? I always thought you were one of those men who didn't, like that one-armed sailor, the one with a metal hook?"

As long as he stayed there she had the upper hand, so he did the only thing he could. He got up and went down the porch stairs, turning at the bottom.

"We'll discuss this when you're more reasonable."

"And what will you say then?"

Morales was coming up the path from the corral. Harper yelled at him to saddle the old roan, and the Mexican looked surprised.

"Do it!"

When Morales handed him the reins, Harper said that if he were this slow again he would be fired. Then Harper mounted and set off at a gallop with the idea of having a few drinks at Esteban's.

The news had shaken him more than he let on. He knew she was watching him ride off while she sat there wrapped in her virtue like a Chinese vase in excelsior. He would have to be careful not to upset her, though he knew that because of the trouble she had carrying a child she would soon be caught up in that and no longer be interested in harassing him.

After getting clear of the house he let the horse slow to a walk and was absently watching a ship tacking across the bay when he thought of Dr. Boyle. He jerked the reins so hard to the right that the roan shook its head in protest before taking him down Main Street in the opposite direction from Esteban's.

The doctor was standing behind a long table pouring a green mixture from a pitcher into wide-necked bottles lined up on a scarred table.

"What is it?" he said irritably. Then he pulled down the spectacles perched on his forehead and recognized Harper.

"Hang on. I'll be done in a minute," and he resumed filling the bottles.

This was the first time Harper had been in the office, and he was not impressed. Books were scattered everywhere. Tubes and instruments hung from nails on the walls and even at a distance he could see that they were dusty. The glass eyes of a phrenological head regarded him from the desk. A skeleton stared at the door. He went over to the window giving onto the street and stayed there until Dr. Boyle screwed the cap on the last of the elixir bottles and came out from behind the table.

"What can I do for you?"

"I have a problem."

The doctor looked at him blankly.

"You know that the Indian from the island is living with us?"

"Everyone does. Has she come down with something?"

"One of my Mexicans has got her pregnant. I want you to take care of it."

"I don't follow."

"Oh," Harper said, smiling slightly, "I think you do."

"You've come to the wrong person," the doctor said as he sat down behind the desk. "I run a respectable practice."

"That's what everyone says, and I'd be happy to spread the word."

"Meaning?"

"Pepita, for openers. Others she'd be happy to tell me about."

The doctor leaned back and wearily pushed his glasses up on his forehead. "How far along is she?"

"Not far," Harper answered, relieved that his threat had worked.

"Why not let it happen?"

"Because it would complicate my life."

A trace of a smile crept over the doctor's lips. "I might have something to spread myself."

Harper looked at him straight on. "That wouldn't be a good idea. Take my word for it."

"These consultations are expensive."

"I knew we'd see eye to eye." Harper took out his wallet and began laying bills on the desk beside the phrenology model.

"One more," the doctor said, "in the event of complications."

Harper dropped another bill on the desk and put his wallet back in his coat.

"When?" Boyle asked.

"Tomorrow. Come out to the ranch. I don't want her being seen here."

"There is a discreet place?"

"She lives out back. Follow the road past the turn for my house, and you'll come to a dead sycamore. There's a path you can take through the grove to the bunkhouse. I'll meet you at ten."

"Eleven." The doctor wanted to be in charge.

"All right."

Half a dozen men were drinking at the bar, but Harper was not in the mood for conversation. He only nodded to them as he ordered a whiskey and went to a table in the far corner, where he had a good view of the wharf. Although he was angry about having to pay Boyle such an outrageous price, it would be worth twice as much to take care of the problem. Now all he had to worry about was Elizabeth. On the way from the doctor's office he thought it might be a good idea to tell her when he got home so that she could get used to it, but he had no way of knowing what would happen if he tipped his hand, and he decided it would be easier to wait. She would be upset, but by then it would be too late. It was possible he might even be able to convince the Indian to say she'd miscarried.

"Are you wanting company?" O'Reilly was standing over him, bleary-eyed and determined.

"No," Harper said, but the man helped himself to a chair. They had run into each other occasionally since the voyage to the island, but Harper always managed to give him the slip. O'Reilly repelled him. Besides his cowardice, there was an unsteadiness about the man, an unsoundness of character manifested in his insinuating manner.

" 'A lonely man,' I said to myself when I saw you. 'He's needing a companion.' "

"I'm happy by myself."

"Maybe you'll warm up if I just sit here a while, Captain."

Harper looked out the window. O'Reilly coughed, then hummed a few bars of a shanty.

"Still living on your ranch, is she?"

Harper glanced at him contemptuously. "Santos and my wife are tending her," he said coldly. He wanted to toss down his drink and leave, but he was damned if O'Reilly was going to drive him away.

"No bad luck?"

"What do you mean?"

Harper wondered whether the news had somehow got around, but he dismissed the idea out of hand. O'Reilly shrugged and looked appraisingly at his drink. "Do you remember what I said when we found her?"

"I don't believe in your clap-trap."

"I wouldn't call damnation clap-trap, Captain. Some do, of course, them that don't know which way the wind blows. Don't take offense. Just remember me in case she cuts your throat in the dark. She's an unquiet spirit, mark my words. I knew it from the start, even before I seen her on that island."

O'Reilly licked his lips as Harper drank.

"You wouldn't see your way to buying one for an old shipmate, would you now?"

"No."

"I didn't think so." O'Reilly looked around not very hopefully as Harper pushed his chair back and stood up.

"Some would say it's a splendid thing, of course. But me, I'm not so certain."

"What are you talking about?" Harper asked sharply.

"Are you happy with the two of them is what I meant. I know men who'd envy you, two to have yer way with, but maybe that's one too many."

"Watch your tongue."

O'Reilly drew back in mock terror. "I've no wish to anger you,

Captain. It's just that I don't often hear of a hareem here on the south coast."

"Not that you'd be welcome in one."

"Me?" He laughed. "My mates, Captain, not O'Reilly. O'Reilly and men of God have nothing to do with women." He winked. "You know the old saying: 'Gash may be fine, but old one-eye for mine.'"

Harper headed for the door without a word. O'Reilly drained the leavings in the shot glass and watched Harper mount and ride off. Then, to no one in particular, but loud enough to be heard by the men at the bar, he said, "A fine horse, if I'm any judge, and a fine rider too, but mark my words, there goes a man of sorrows."

Harper did not see Elizabeth the next morning when he came down to breakfast. When he asked Angelita whether she had seen his wife, she shook her head and pretended to concentrate on cooking his eggs. He was not surprised by Elizabeth's absence; she had suffered from morning sickness at the outset of her other pregnancies. If that was the case now, he could make a favorable impression by going up and asking whether there was anything he could do; but subservience went against the grain, and he was not about to take the chance of having his knock unanswered or, worse yet, of her saying something cutting through the bedroom door. He had enough to worry about with Boyle, because he knew he had glossed over the effect the abortion would have on Elizabeth. There would be trouble when she found out. He wished there were some way to keep the Indian quiet. He did not think that she understood the value of money in exchange for silence, but it might be worth a try.

After breakfast he went out to the stables to work with Morales on the young colt. He wanted to be careful with the animal because it showed promise, and the prospect of another sale was on his mind after his success with the man in San Luis Obispo. He had just fitted the halter when he saw the doctor's carriage coming up the drive, and he swore quietly.

"Work on him by yourself," he said, handing Morales the halter. He had no idea why the idiot had not gone to the bunkhouse.

The only thing to do now was to send him back to the road before Elizabeth saw him.

He caught up with Boyle at the foot of the drive.

"I couldn't find it."

"You must be blind."

"I saw the oaks, but no path."

"I told you to go on to the dead sycamore. Move over. I'll drive."

Harper climbed in and snapped the reins. As the horse lunged against the traces, Elizabeth came out on the porch.

"This is why I told you to take the back way."

"I'm sorry."

"That doesn't mean a goddam thing. Wait a minute."

He got down and headed for the house. It was just possible that she had no idea that doctors had capacities like Boyle's.

Elizabeth watched the doctor until Harper reached the stairs, and then she looked down at him. "What is he doing here?"

"I want him to take a look at Soledad."

She had not looked well when she came out into the sun, but now her face was ashen. She put her hand to her mouth. "Oh, my God!"

"It's all right."

She glared at Boyle.

"There's nothing else to do," he said. "Be reasonable."

She cast one horrified glance at him before hurrying down the stairs. He caught her sleeve, and as she pulled away, the stitches ripped at the shoulder.

"Get out!" she screamed at the doctor.

Harper stepped between her and the carriage.

"She hasn't been well," he said over his shoulder.

"I don't want any trouble," the doctor muttered.

"Don't worry," Harper answered quickly. "Give me a minute."

He took Elizabeth by the arm with the intention of walking her a little way down the drive, but she twisted away and ran back to the porch, where Angelita stood watching them.

"What are you looking at?" Harper shouted. "Get back to work!"

As Angelita followed Elizabeth inside, Harper turned to Dr. Boyle. "Can you find it now?"

"Probably."

"Go on. I'll meet you in a few minutes."

Elizabeth came out the door with the little two-barreled der-ringer. She stopped at the top of the stairs and pointed the pistol at Boyle.

"Elizabeth, for Christ's sake, put that down."

The shot sounded very loud in the stillness. Harper turned to see that the bullet had penetrated Boyle's medicine bag. Liquid was already staining the scuffed leather. He did not even have time to speak to Boyle, because the doctor quickly snapped the reins, forc-ing him to step back to avoid the horse. Elizabeth was still holding the pistol in her outstretched hands as he went up the stairs to her.

"That was the stupidest thing you've ever done," he said. "Give it to me."

He stared at her until she handed him the pistol and went over to the railing, where she watched Boyle's carriage disappearing down the road.

"Elizabeth."

She tightened her grip on the railing.

"Are you listening to me? I won't have her here afterward."

# 10

◆ ◆ ◆

Early in February an old friend of Harper's in Los Angeles hired him to deliver a load of building materials to Mexico. After taking on the goods in San Pedro, he sailed south to the tip of the Baja peninsula and then across the Gulf of California to the settlement of Mazatlán, a tiny fishing village with a spectacular bay and the whitest beaches he had ever seen. No one appeared at the dock the first day, and the Mexicans there professed to know nothing about the shipment.

On the second morning a tall, thin man wearing expensive clothes appeared on the dock at the head of a procession of ten large wagons. He was about thirty, as far as Harper could tell, and sported an elegant if ostentatious mustache. He went by the euphonious name of Don José Avellanos. The honorific put Harper off because he considered himself a democrat and was always sensitive to his own modest beginnings. He did not like the Mexican's style. His clothes were all black; his fingernails were manicured. He had an ironic way of speaking in both English and Spanish that made Harper feel awkward and unfinished.

When all the papers were signed and the materials loaded into the wagons, Harper thought they would part ways, but Don José offered to buy him a drink in a cantina up the road. Within a few hours Harper discovered that behind the manners was a kindred spirit. That was not something he had found in another man for a long time. While he enjoyed Ludlow's company, there were considerable differences between them, the most obvious being Ludlow's thoroughly domestic nature, which bordered on the uxorious. There were times when Harper winced at the way he deferred to Susan. Ludlow was a good drinking companion, he was knowledgeable about horses, and he had been successful with his ranch, but his spirit was reined in; that, more than anything else, was what made Don José's companionship so pleasant. The Mexican had a way of putting things that Harper had often thought about but had never been able to articulate. Later that afternoon Harper returned to the *Elizabeth's Delight* and told the crew that they were staying a little longer in Mazatlán.

Don José offered Harper a room at his hacienda, which was far more comfortable than the run-down inn where he had stayed the night before, entertaining himself by stamping on cockroaches. The hacienda was a few miles out of town. Its rooms were filled with dark, handsome furniture and fine silver, which Don José said came from Oaxaca, where he had an interest in a mine.

The first two days they spent their time riding Don José's Arabians and doing a little bird shooting with the Mexican's custom-made rifles. When they returned, Don José dumped the game bags on the kitchen table; a few hours later a woman named Elena served the birds in a wonderfully spicy sauce.

They hunted again on the third day, and Harper was looking forward to a new variation for dinner when Don José poured them glasses of tequila and announced they would eat out; he had a surprise he thought Harper would enjoy.

Half an hour later they stopped in front of a dilapidated building with a badly tiled roof. Harper laughed and asked if it was some kind of joke.

"See for yourself, amigo." Don José smiled as they tied up their horses at a railing and went inside.

Los Murales was divided into two sections, with one wing set aside for the women's rooms and the other for the cantina. The rich scent of spiced meat and tortillas filled the air. As Harper's eyes adjusted to the muted light, Don José lighted a cigarillo and watched Harper survey the murals. Each wall, including the one behind the bar, was decorated with huge pictures showing every act of love he knew about and some he had not imagined. The figures in the pictures engaged in dazzling displays of athletic prowess, and their arms, legs, genitals, and mouths swirled in a kaleidoscopic sexuality that was both absurd and erotic.

Don José cupped his hand to make himself heard over the noise. "It is all the work of the fat man behind the bar. Roberto used to be a pimp in Mexico City. When he made enough money, he moved here because he wanted to be close to the sea. He painted all of them. I myself think they are very good."

Harper pointed to a whitewashed section to the left of the bar. The lines of an under drawing were barely visible, but he could make out the figures of three women who appeared to be swarming over the prostrate body of the owner. "It looks as if he hasn't finished."

"That is part of the charm of the place. Roberto is a man who believes only in the here and now. All the women in the paintings work here. When one leaves, Roberto cleans the wall and paints her replacement. Since the beginning of Los Murales, all the pictures have changed."

They had a splendid time that night, and because of the pleasures of Don José's company during the day, and some of the women depicted in the murals in the evening, Harper prolonged his stay for more than a week.

On the last night, as he and Don José were riding back to the hacienda, Harper confessed that he found Mexican women superior in their ability to excite passion, citing Pepita as an example and adding that his weakness for her had caused unpleasant confrontations with his wife.

"I understand," Don José said. "I am of the opinion that a man's emotions are always fed by love of the exotic. On the other hand, you do not need her to brand you with her nails."

Harper appreciated his friend's sympathy. He was also feeling the effects of Roberto's excellent tequila. When Don José began humming a song one of the guitarists had played, Harper became downcast at the thought of returning to his old life. The time he had spent with Don José seemed idyllic, whereas everything at home was enormously complicated. He felt compelled to tell his friend about Elizabeth's pregnancy.

"I have three sons myself who live in Oaxaca with their mother. It is good to have children. They give a man ballast."

"It's not so simple," Harper answered, explaining that Soledad was pregnant too.

"Have you denied it?"

"Elizabeth knows."

"What will you do?"

"Send her away afterward. Elizabeth would go crazy if I did it now."

"Well, don't worry, amigo. There are bastards everywhere."

The weather in the gulf was unsettled when Harper put in the first night at Cabo San Lucas. In the morning he woke to the sound of wind howling in the rigging, and the storm followed him all the way to San Diego. Another squall came up off Point Dume, and its winds intensified until he was obliged to heave to in the lee of San Nicolás.

Waves crashed against the rocks and wind blew the water in great gusts across the cove. The island's ridges were obscured by clouds, but the lowlands remained visible, though deprived of color by the driving rain. Normally Harper was not affected by the weather. Storms were part of his life, to be endured and then forgotten. But as the ship rolled back and forth, he became aware of a strange sensation; it seemed linked to the island, and soon he found himself thinking about what life must have been like there for Soledad. It was not empathy. To him, her life was an abstract example of the condition of loneliness. He imagined how the wind would howl on the island and the way the waves would look rolling into shore. A paradoxical silence lay behind the wind, and then it seemed that the blank face of loneliness was looking back, regarding him with large, unblinking eyes. Later, when he went below to his cabin, the face seemed to hover over the charts and maps. It did no good to tell himself that it was only the result of his imagination. The unease remained until the squall blew off and he gratefully ordered the crew to raise the sails.

# 11

◆ ◆ ◆

On the morning Harper had left for Mexico, Elizabeth asked Angelita to air out the guest room and put clean sheets and blankets on the bed.

"Is somebody coming, señora?" Angelita asked. She was always curious about the Harpers' guests; they often gave her small presents and sometimes money.

"Yes. Soledad."

Angelita's eyes widened. "What will the señor say?"

"I don't care. This is my house too," Elizabeth said firmly.

"He will be angry."

"I will deal with it. Now, will you pick some nice flowers?"

Soledad was sitting outside in the sun when Elizabeth arrived at the bunkhouse.

"Come, you're moving back to the big house. We are going to live together again."

Soledad made no effort to rise. "Henry say no."

"Henry is gone. He is sailing for many days."

Elizabeth followed her inside. When Soledad began putting her belongings in a blanket, Elizabeth touched her on the shoulder. "No," she said. "Angelita will do that." But Soledad insisted on taking the spirit ship from the windowsill.

Soledad was happy to be back in her room. The clean white walls with pictures pleased her, and she loved the softness of the comforter, whose deep blue was scattered with pink flowers. She liked being on the second story, because she could see the mission's towers and the northern thrust of the mountains. Most of all, she was pleased because she had been afraid that she might have to spend the rest of her life in the bunkhouse. Henry's face had said so when they moved her. Fray Santos's. Even Liza's. Or so she had thought. She would try to remember that things were different here, that she could never be sure of anything. Except that was not quite true. She was sure of Liza, though Henry had forced his seed into her. There was hardly any change in her body yet, but soon she would be big. She wondered whether the child would have her color or his, if one eye would be blue like his and the other black like her own. She did not like the idea of this particolored child, so she busied herself by putting away her things after Angelita brought them.

When the room was in order, she balanced the spirit ship on the windowsill. She liked looking at it there, outlined against the sea, though she felt sad when she remembered making it. Over the years, as its spars and masts had dried out and pieces of the hull decayed, she had come to fear that it had no more power. But it had brought Henry, Fray Santos, and the man who had been so afraid of her that he would look only at her feet. She had told Fray Santos about it, because she thought it might help his gods come to him from their place in the sky, but he did not like hearing about such things. He became very angry whenever she mentioned Coyote and the Sky People, and from then on she had kept the secret of the spirit ship to herself, except for telling Liza, who could not understand. She hoped that Liza had something like it for herself. The little stars that Liza and Fray Santos called crucifixes were like that, she supposed, and she decided to ask for one soon and put it in the spirit ship to increase its power.

Liza did not look well when she came in. Soledad was lying down and started to get up, but Liza said, "No, stay there," and looked at her for a long time before closing the door.

"May I?" Liza said, gesturing toward the bed. Soledad nodded, and Liza lay down beside her.

"There are so many words you have to learn. One is mother. I am going to be a mother too."

"Mother?"

"Mother."

She put her hands on her stomach and made a gesture indicating roundness. Then she put her hand on Soledad's. That was the first time Soledad knew that Henry's seed had taken hold in both of them. She wondered whether it was common among Liza's people for one man to do this.

"Always? This?"

"It is not our custom."

When she tried to answer, her words tumbled in her mind and Liza took her hand.

"There is nothing wrong with us," Liza said.

Soledad could not remember having to think about two important things at once. It was not that life on the island had been simple when she was with her people, only that it seemed ordered in a different way from what had happened ever since Henry and Fray Santos came for her. There would be one thing, then another, and always enough time to think about them. That was why Liza's news made it hard to think. Happy as it made her, she could not concentrate on Liza's good fortune; she had her own baby to think about. She was still not certain that she understood what Liza said in answer to her question about the customs of white people. She seemed to mean that what Henry had done was not a custom, but she still could not understand why there was such sadness in Liza's eyes. And what would happen when the babies came? As she tried to think about all these things, she consoled herself with the idea that as she learned more of Liza's words, she would be less confused. Until then she would be happy with her new life in the big house.

When Fray Santos appeared at the door the next day, Soledad was eager to start the lesson, hoping that they would go to the gazebo, as they sometimes did. It was easier to think outside; the answers she had to remember did not get lost as often when she could see the sky and ocean. But Liza told her to wait and took Fray Santos outside, where they sat in the chairs on the porch.

As soon as they began talking, Fray Santos smiled and took Liza's hand. Soledad knew that she had told him about her baby. He had a special feeling for Liza, which she expected would show now, and she was glad because she wanted Liza's sadness to go away. But her friend's smile quickly faded and Soledad knew that she was not talking about baby any longer. Fray Santos glanced inside and she turned away; she did not want him to think that she was spying. When she looked again, he was listening carefully to Liza. The color of his blood rose in his face. Once again he looked inside. This time their eyes met, and she knew that he was angry. Abruptly he went to the edge of the porch and put his hands on the railing and looked at the sea for a long time. He said something, but Liza did not answer. She held her hands in her lap and cried. That was when Soledad knew that Liza had told Fray Santos that they were both pregnant.

Fray Santos stared at Soledad's stomach when he and Liza came inside, but he would not look at her until they sat down on the sofa. Then she tried to tell him with her eyes that she had not asked for Henry's seed. She was sorry and tried hard to remember what she was supposed to say. He noticed how hard she was concentrating, and though he did not smile at her as he usually did when he was pleased, she was certain by the time he left that he was no longer so angry with her.

After that morning Fray Santos did not go into the kitchen first to have tea and cookies with Liza. He did not laugh. He came straight into the living room, or motioned Soledad to follow him outside to the gazebo. The first thing he did every day was to stare at her stomach. She felt bad when he looked at her, but she did not know what to do except try harder to find all the answers to the questions that he posed with greater urgency than before.

Liza said that there was time on Mother Earth but no time in Heaven. Until the day Liza told Fray Santos that they were pregnant, Soledad believed that the friar did not care about time. But she was wrong. Nothing else would explain why he made her hurry, or why he made his lessons longer than before. This urgency made her nervous; she feared that something bad might happen if she did not learn quickly enough. She wanted to please him, and even after he went away she thought about the things she was supposed to learn. While she preferred Coyote and the Sky People and her spirit ship to Fray Santos's God and Mother and Son and crucifix, she forced herself to think about them all the time and to memorize the answers. She thought about the things he called sins and then she realized that there might be another reason for the man's impatience. If she did not learn quickly enough, she might have to go to Hell. He had made it sound so terrible that sometimes she cried at night when she thought of the great fire that was said to rage there. Then she prayed to Coyote to save her. Sometimes she mixed up her answers, or could not pronounce the words; when this happened, Fray Santos was not as patient as he used to be. He scolded her, making her do it again and again until it was the way he wanted.

One day after he left Liza took her to the kitchen and gave her cake and milk. Liza seemed happier than she had in a long time, and after she dusted the crumbs off her hands she pointed out the window.

"Gazebo," Soledad said.

"No, the mission. We're going there tomorrow. You will be presented to a great man, a bishop. Fray Santos is very proud of you, very happy with what you have learned."

It did not occur to her to ask why she had to see the bishop. Liza said that Fray Santos was happy with her, and that must mean he had forgiven her for being pregnant. She wanted to please him, but that was not the only reason she was interested in what Liza said. Ever since she learned that her family was dead, she had wanted to see where they had been buried and make certain that all the rites had been observed. The pain that had made her want to die, that had been so strong she could not breathe, had dulled, but that night it burned the way embers do in a dying fire. She imagined all of them. The picture of her husband made her think of the child behind the circles of her tattoo, and she wished her husband's seed had put it there.

She was surprised by the size of the mission. It was many times larger than her village, and the great lodge seemed to rise forever into the sky. People were in the fields, and men dressed like Fray Santos watched them carrying things, overseeing the work.

"My people."

"Yes," Liza said, "there are many of them."

That was not what she meant. "Family. Where they are?"

"We will ask Fray Santos," Liza said and there was sadness in her eyes.

The ceiling of the great room was so high that the little torches burning along the walls could not dispel the shadows. There were many pictures and the Jesus she had seen on the crucifix Fray Santos wore was larger than any man she had ever seen. He looked very sad and in pain, and she felt sorry for Him as they passed through a door and Fray Santos greeted them hurriedly before he took her away from Liza. He told her how good she was and once again said that all she had to do was repeat the words he had taught her.

"This bishop is a very holy man. He is eager to see you."

She heard the bishop before she saw him. A dry, racking cough came from behind the door, and when Fray Santos opened it she saw an old man sitting at the head of a table, his body shaking as he coughed again until he finally managed to clear his throat. He had a large nose, watery brown eyes, and a loose, supple mouth that moved a little as Soledad and Fray Santos crossed the room. Wisps of gray hair showed beneath his skullcap, fringing a narrow, seamed face. He acknowledged Fray Santos with a quick glance and then shifted his eyes to Soledad, regarding her skeptically. The tip of his tongue appeared between his lips as he leaned back and raised one hand to the arm of the chair. Light gleamed on the bright stone in his ring. Soledad understood why Fray Santos was nervous; the old man had power. As they reached the table his hand rose from the arm of the chair and he held it out, the way animals do when they have injured a paw, motioning first to the chair on his right, then to the one on his left. Fray Santos went around the table and as he pulled the chair out she saw that his hands were trembling.

"Sit down, my child," the bishop said. He turned to Fray Santos. She could not understand all the words they used, but it was clear that the bishop was asking about her. Fray Santos murmured, keeping his hands below the table, explaining her life to the bishop, who seemed to have forgotten she was there. No longer under his scrutiny, she felt a little better, thinking that perhaps this was all that was going to happen. She relaxed and looked at the paintings on the walls. Jesus was in some of them but they did not interest her as much as two that hung behind the bishop. One showed a man whose clothes were torn and bloody from many arrows that pierced his flesh. His face was full of pain, but his eyes looked up to the sky as if he were searching for something. She was shocked and wondered what he had done to deserve this, who his enemies were. In the one beside it a man was being cooked over a fire. She could not take her eyes off him for a long time. When she did, she wondered why they had brought her to this room filled with so much pain.

"Now, Soledad," Fray Santos said, and the sound of her name surprised her. He was smiling and nodded at the bishop.

"You must answer the bishop's questions."

"What they do?"

"What?"

She pointed at the pictures.

"Why?"

Fray Santos glanced over his shoulder, and when he looked at her again she could tell that he was unhappy.

"She has never been here," he explained to the bishop apologetically. "They are saints," he said to her. "Remember the saints?"

She nodded.

"Saint Lawrence was a holy man."

"Who eats him?"

There was a dry, snorting sound and the bishop's mouth turned up at the corners in a wry smile.

"No one," Fray Santos said angrily. "That is his agony."

"Agony?"

"Perhaps she is not ready," the bishop said.

"It is only distraction. Soledad, listen to the bishop. This is why we are here. Listen and answer."

The bishop bent forward. "What is your only comfort in life and death?"

It was the question Fray Santos had posed many times, but although she remembered the answer, she was not ready to tell it; she was upset by the man being cooked.

"Soledad. Come now. There is nothing to fear."

The bishop looked at Fray Santos, and she could tell that he was angry.

"You know the answer, Soledad. Speak."

She was sorry that she had made him unhappy, so she answered quickly because she wanted him to feel better. Many of the words she had memorized still did not make sense and it felt strange to say things she did not understand. Fray Santos began smiling, folding his fingers together in his lap when she answered the second question. With the third, his hands stopped trembling and she saw that he was very happy.

She forgot nothing. The bishop asked the questions, and as she answered his eyes filled with pleasure. After her last response the bishop said he was very pleased with her. He took Fray Santos's hand and smiled. "Your lost soul is a little miracle."

The men got up and stood by the painting of the body pierced with arrows, talking in low voices. After a while a brother came in, and Fray Santos led her back to the place where Liza waited. Soledad was tired, but she knew that she had done well. She was happy that Liza and Fray Santos were happy, but when Liza got up and said that they should leave, Soledad shook her head.

"My family," she said. "Where they are?"

Fray Santos listened as Elizabeth explained what Soledad wanted.

"The graves are unmarked. They died in great numbers."

"I think she'd like to see anyway."

"Very well, but hurry. I can't keep the bishop waiting."

When they reached the door with a stone skull above the lintel, Soledad thought it must be an evil omen. She stopped abruptly.

"What's wrong?" Fray Santos asked.

"Soledad?" Elizabeth said.

She pointed to the skull, and Fray Santos laughed. "It's only a memento mori. Come now," and he pushed the door open to the graveyard. Square flat stones stuck out of the earth. There were no graves such as her people made. They continued through the rows of stones until they were in a field between the graveyard and the church.

"There," he said, pointing to a barren place. She saw nothing but weeds. Her family had not been buried in the right way. She did not even know where they were.

"What's wrong?" Fray Santos asked.

"I don't know. I think she expected something else," Elizabeth replied.

"Where they are?" Soledad asked.

She wanted to tell Liza and Fray Santos that this was not the way it should be, but the words for it were trapped in her mind, so she spoke her own language, knowing they would not understand yet hoping that she could somehow convey how terrible this was for her family. She did not know how her people would be able to find their way to the Afterworld.

"No!" she said.

"Take her home. Talk to her," Fray Santos said.

"Where they are?" she called after him, but he went through the door, quickly closing it behind him.

"Soledad, listen to me."

Liza took hold of her arm, but Soledad did not care that she was trying to comfort her.

"No!" she said again, pulling away and walking a little farther into the field. It was covered with brown grass. Ahead there were depressions in the ground, each as long as a person's body. She had imagined their belongings suspended from grave poles, but nothing was there. In the distance only a brownrobe watched one of her people plowing. The sound of men's voices came to her on the still air, though she could not make out what they said. She did not know what to do. She had come because Liza wanted it, because she hoped to make Fray Santos happy. Now as she thought about the old man and Fray Santos, the feeling that had been with her all morning, the excitement of being close to her family, vanished in the dry air. Nothing connected her to the fields or Liza. The mission blocked her view of the sea.

She knew that she was supposed to pray, but she could not help opening her eyes a little to look at the girls kneeling beside her in their white dresses. "The color of purity," Liza had said when she gave her the dress she was now wearing. Liza had made her put it on and take it off many times while she stood on a stool in the living room. Liza had walked around it with pins in her mouth, tugging here, adjusting there, and then telling her to get undressed so that she could sew the sides and hem and sleeves until it fitted like a second skin.

When they reached the mission that morning Soledad had been surprised by the number of people there. She had not seen so many whites since she arrived on the beach and those first mornings when they had gathered at dawn outside the house. On both occasions they had looked at her with amazement, but now they regarded her differently. Some of the women's eyes were softer; as she and Liza went up the stairs they smiled. Others looked at her coldly and she knew they did not like her, though she had no idea why.

Soon the smell of sweet smoke perfumed the air as Fray Santos approached the altar wearing clothes she had never seen. They were elaborate and beautiful and there were tiny images on a narrow cloth around his neck. His expression was more solemn than she could have imagined. He seemed withdrawn, concentrated upon himself, like the shaman before he went off to seek the Sky People. There was the same intensity of purpose, a gathering in of strength, but the shaman had ignored everyone while it seemed as if each of Fray Santos's gestures was meant to be observed. He gazed at the huge Jesus behind the altar. When he glanced toward her, she smiled; then he looked ahead once again. In that instant she knew he was transformed, that all the time she had known him, from the day he came to her through the field of flowers until their meeting with the bishop, had been preparation for this rite.

Liza had told her that he would speak Latin, a language he had never used with her. As she listened to the words she wondered whether he would teach them to her. She tried to remember the ones she liked, saying *Dei* to herself, and *Gloriam*, as she and the girls did what they were supposed to. After she allowed the wafer to dissolve on her tongue, after she drank the wine that was the blood of Jesus, she and the others took their seats, and Fray Santos looked at her. He said her name, talked about her, called her the Lost Woman who had been found. He was telling her story to the people just as he had done a few weeks ago to the bishop. He said that his God had sent him to the island to save her, that he knew she was alive, waiting for God to come. She wanted to say that it had not been like that at all, that it was the power of her spirit ship. He spoke for a long time, and his voice sounded deeper and stronger than ever. There was a kind of music in his words, and when he reached the end, his eyes glistened in the light as he made the sign of the cross.

# 12

◆ ◆ ◆

The noon hour chimed on the mantel clock. A little later there was a commotion on the drive, and they both looked up to see Harper sitting in a wagon.

"Don't worry," Elizabeth said, "it will be all right."

There was something in her voice, an unfamiliar firmness, that made Soledad believe it might. As soon as Elizabeth went out to meet him, Soledad got up and stood beside the curtains, where she had a clear view of two men carrying chests up to the porch. Harper paid them, and the wagon went off. It was a still, peaceful spring day with land and sea layered and distinct. She saw Harper against the distant façade of the mission watching Elizabeth descend the stairs. Her stomach was so big now that she had to put her hand to her lower back to ease the baby's weight. Harper was brown from the sun; he had let his beard grow. He appeared fit and strong as Liza approached him on the drive. Soledad could see, from the way he pointed to the house, that Liza was telling him she had come in from the place among the trees. Liza shook her head before coming inside, leaving Harper distraught and angry.

"Keep out of his way," Elizabeth said. "I think you should stay in your room until he gets used to your being here."

Soledad was happy to go up and close her door, content to stay there for days if only Harper would not send her back to the bunkhouse. She had mastered solitude a long time ago, learning that time could be made to pass simply by observing, listening.

There was a good view of the mission from her window. As it grew dark the mission faded in the violet light until it disappeared into the solid mass of the mountains. She attended to the sounds of evening. A horse neighed and there was the muted thud of hooves as it ran in the pasture. She heard the squeak of a rocking chair on the porch, an owl calling, the scream of a small animal. Liza's voice came to her from the living room, sharp and distinct; soon her words were followed by Harper's harsher ones. For a little while the voices were pitched against each other, rising in a crescendo that ended with the slamming of a door.

A woman Soledad had never seen was telling her to lift her dress. The midwife stared with great surprise at the circles before she touched her stomach and the pain turned to fire. Soledad cried out. When Elizabeth asked the midwife what was wrong, Mrs. Hawthorne only shook her head and said the baby would be a long time coming.

They stayed long into the night. When the pain became too great to bear, Elizabeth held Soledad's hand while Mrs. Hawthorne racked her brains for some clue to what was wrong. Elizabeth bathed her face with a cool cloth as Soledad dozed on and off, always waking to find Elizabeth looking at her, trying to smile.

Soledad could not tell if it was daylight or if lamps were lit, but there was light in the room. After a while she could see Elizabeth talking to Mrs. Hawthorne and Angelita. A large basin on the dresser and a stack of towels hid her spirit ship. She wanted Elizabeth to bathe her face, but as she asked pain flared in Elizabeth's eyes and she put her hands to her stomach, whispering to Mrs. Hawthorne. Soledad did not hear what Elizabeth said but she knew that what she had thought of many times was happening now.

"You're sure?" Mrs. Hawthorne asked.

"Yes." Elizabeth gasped, and the word hissed through her teeth.

"Where's your room, dear?"

Elizabeth shook her head. "I won't leave Soledad."

Mrs. Hawthorne could not believe her ears. "Nonsense! You have to lie down."

"I'm staying. You can see to both of us."

The other bed was narrow and sagged in the middle. Mrs. Hawthorne took one look and said that it would never do.

"Listen to reason, Mrs. Harper."

"I'll lie down here, but I won't leave."

Mrs. Hawthorne rushed out the door. Moments later she had Harper in the hallway, talking excitedly to him and pointing first to Soledad, then to Elizabeth. As soon as she dismissed Harper, she ordered Angelita to fetch more steaming water.

Elizabeth's contractions were coming more quickly by the time Harper and Dr. Boyle arrived. The moment Elizabeth saw the doctor, she screamed, "Get him out of here!" but the men stayed and Boyle examined first Soledad, then Elizabeth, who tried to hold the sheet over her body.

Soledad wanted to speak to her friend, but Elizabeth's face was pale, and Soledad knew she was trying to deal with the pain. A moment later the men went to Elizabeth and lifted her by the arms. By the time they reached the door she doubled over.

"Sisters," Soledad whispered as they took her away.

Elizabeth was led down the hall, Harper on one side, the doctor on the other. Though she was in too much pain to resist, she begged them to let her stay with Soledad. Dr. Boyle had never seen anything like it and hoped that Harper would explain what was going on with the women, but it was clear that all Harper wanted was to get Elizabeth to her room.

Harper left quickly after they helped her into bed, feeling a great sense of relief sweep over him as he went downstairs. Now that the time had come, the situation struck him more forcibly than ever; as he waited, his emotions went back and forth between a sense of guilt and a kind of pride in his virility. He heard Elizabeth cry, then Soledad, the quick movement of feet from room to room. He soon learned to distinguish between the doctor's heavier steps and those of Mrs. Hawthorne and Angelita. Finally it was too much. Taking a bottle from the sideboard, he went looking for Morales so that they could drink and talk at a safe distance from the struggles going on upstairs.

When they finally heard a baby's cry, they did not know which woman had delivered. Harper did not move until Angelita came out on the porch looking harried and exhausted as she called that he had a son. He asked how Elizabeth was; when Angelita said she was fine, he went up to the room where his son was wrapped in blankets. After looking at him a moment, Elizabeth whispered something he could not hear. He bent over the bed, asking her to repeat it.

"Soledad. How is Soledad?"

"Fine," he said. "She's fine."

He said that he would be back soon, but he stayed longer than he planned at Esteban's, returning so drunk that he fell asleep on the sofa in the parlor. He did not waken until the sun was well up. Angelita brought coffee and said that Soledad had not yet delivered. Mrs. Hawthorne came downstairs, looking distraught and frightened. She told him that, in her opinion, Soledad's life was in danger and she had sent for Fray Santos. Boyle was nowhere to be seen.

Soledad dreamed that she was in church, where Fray Santos kissed a satin cloth and draped it around his neck. He began speaking in Latin; the steady march of syllables was as soothing as his fingers on her forehead. There was the taste of stones in her mouth, sea water, fire. Coyote danced among the stars as she went off to the hills, where she placed her daughter's possessions on the pole above her grave.

Everything was dark; then there was light. Mrs. Hawthorne pulled her down to the end of the bed and pushed her legs apart and soon there was a different pain and a baby's cry but she could not see. She fought the darkness and then she saw Mrs. Hawthorne holding the baby, saw the gleaming purple cord and the tiny cleavage between its legs. She wanted to touch her daughter, but Mrs. Hawthorne quickly wrapped her in a blanket and took her from the room.

Mrs. Hawthorne and Fray Santos were standing beside the bed.

"Baby?" Soledad asked.

"She is at the mission," Mrs. Hawthorne whispered.

"With your people," Fray Santos added.

"Heaven?"

"No, my child. With a woman. A mother." He turned to Mrs. Hawthorne. "Do you think she knows what a wet nurse is?"

"Baby?" Soledad repeated.

"You will see her as soon as you are better," Fray Santos explained.

"When you are well," Mrs. Hawthorne said.

Soledad remembered the women in the mission. They had given her child to one of them.

"Baby!" she shouted.

"Rest," Mrs. Hawthorne said. "You are weak."

"My baby."

Mrs. Hawthorne squeezed out a cloth in the basin and started to cool her forehead, but Soledad struck her hand away. "No! Give baby!"

She hated the fat old woman. She hated Fray Santos. But she hated Harper most of all. She struggled to sit up, and when she began the song of lamentation a terrible expression came over Fray Santos's face. He told her to stop, but she did not care that he was upset, nor did she care when he said that his god would be angry. She sang, and she would not look at either of them.

All that day Soledad sang the songs that had driven Fray Santos back to the mission, disheartened by her backsliding but consoled a little by the thought that the child would grow up in the bosom of the church. The day moved to the measure of her voice. Soledad's songs were slow. The words came in a stately rhythm until it seemed to Elizabeth that the house had never been without them, to Angelita that the air was shaped by song, to Harper that he would never find silence again. Exasperated by the sound, he went out the back door and felt a great relief as he mounted his horse and rode off to town. The singing died on the wind behind him, but it lived on in the house. Elizabeth and Angelita would not look at each other until they heard the first crack in Soledad's voice, then another, and at last the pure sound was corrupted by hoarseness. There were pauses, resurgences of melody, longer pauses, and then silence as night came on and Elizabeth retired to bed with Daniel, determined that in the morning she would go to Soledad and see what could be done to ease her grief.

Much later the moon came up, lighting the far corners of the south-facing rooms as it rose. When the moon was high and her room was bathed in light, Soledad turned back the comforter and crossed the room to the cupboard, whose doors she opened, carefully muffling the sound. Elizabeth had given her a dozen dresses and she ran her fingers over them until she touched her own. After slipping it over her head, she ran her hands along the feathers, as much to feel their shapes as to smooth them down. She was unsteady on her feet; her head spun so that she was obliged to stand still until her balance returned enough for her to make her way to the window, where she removed the spirit ship. Then she went out into the hall, down the stairs, and, seeing light at the bottom of Harper's office door, went outside as silent as a ghost.

The slanted roof of the stables shone like silver, and silver light ran along the top of the fences as she crossed the driveway. The coolness of the earth soothed her feet. She moved soundlessly to the gate; unlatched the leather thong. When she was inside the enclosure, two horses raised their heads, the whites of their eyes gleaming for a moment before they understood that she was no threat. They moved close to her and she stroked their muzzles, feeling the softness of their breath.

The tack room was dark. She moved slowly along the walls, feeling her way, lightly touching the halters, the bridles, until she felt the coil of rope. The horses watched her come out, followed her with their liquid eyes as she went through the gate. In the meadow the grass was wet. As she crossed to the gazebo her feet left black prints in the dew; the outline of her feet was imprinted on the steps. She saw the moon through the lattice as she looked up and threw the rope once, then a second time, and then a third, before it curled round the stout beam and the end came down close enough for her to grasp. She placed the spirit ship on the railing against a supporting beam. She threw the long end of the rope into the moonlight, and it arced once again over the beam; she repeated this until she felt resistance. Stepping up on the railing, she coiled the rope, opened it, slipped it over her head, and launched herself into the patterned air. In the stables the horses watched her swing. An owl nestled in the oaks nearby fell silent, frightened by a movement it had never seen. A night bird veered in its flight. In the house Elizabeth stirred to the sound of wood stressed into creaking. The sound came to Daniel in his crib and he fretted; two miles away Soledad's daughter cried out in her sleep.

At dawn there were clouds behind the islands; gusts of wind blew at the weather's edge, roughening the sea into whitecaps. The trees in town moved with the wind, were still, moved again. The chiming of the mission bells was borne on the wind to the Harpers' house. Angelita approached slowly because she was still terrified by what she had seen two days ago. She had resolved never to have children if that was the price she would have to pay. As she neared the house, she remembered the cries and the blood; to calm herself she began humming a song she had learned in Mexico, breaking off when she realized that it was a lullaby.

Morales watched her. After feeding the horses, he had gone into the stables for a bridle. As soon as he stepped inside he knew someone had been there. He checked to see that all the saddles were there; it was only as he was about to leave that he noticed the empty place on the wall where the rope had hung. The theft bothered him less than the idea that his domain had been invaded. It seemed unlikely that Angelita had taken the rope, but he wanted to speak to her.

Elizabeth woke to Daniel crying and sleepily put him to her breast. After he had drunk his fill, they dozed together until a door closed with a bang and she heard Angelita's voice raised in anger. Beyond it was the sound of the wind, and beyond the wind a sound she did not recognize which was like the creaking of the house but less distinct. She glanced out the window as she dressed. The clouds had drifted south and the sea was blown clear of mist. She thought of Soledad as she looked at the islands, deciding that she would bring her tea and bread and try to make her understand that she would be with her baby soon.

Harper was sitting on the edge of his bed, pulling on his boots, when the scream startled him. It began as a moan, scarcely distinguishable from the sound of the wind. Then it rose to a note that should have been beyond the capacity of a woman's voice; it held that note, prolonging it until there was no air left in Elizabeth's lungs. A silence followed as she caught her breath and screamed again. Daniel began wailing down the hall as Harper opened the drawer of the nightstand and grabbed the Colt. He went down the stairs with one hand on the bannister, the other holding the pistol up in the air, thumbing back the hammer as he rushed into the kitchen, where he found Elizabeth and Angelita in each other's arms, staring out the window. He was on edge, and when he found no antagonist his excitement turned to anger.

"What the hell's wrong?"

Angelita glanced at him quickly, but Elizabeth continued staring out the window, and as she moaned Harper looked. Soledad was swaying a little in the wind. As Morales burst through the door, Harper pointed. Morales whispered, "*Dios mio!*" crossed himself, and grabbed a knife from the table before racing out the door. As they watched him go, Daniel's crying peaked, caught, went on.

"I'll take care of him," Angelita said.

"Please help," Elizabeth said to Harper. "Please." There was a necessity in her voice he could not ignore; it touched both the pity in him for what she felt and his need to stop the swinging. The pistol made a hollow sound when he put it down. As he went out the door Elizabeth staggered but held on to the edge of the table as if it were a crutch, and she watched him stride across the meadow. Soledad was too high for Morales to reach the rope with his knife. Harper took hold of Soledad's legs while Morales climbed up on the railing, holding on to one of the posts supporting the roof as he began to saw with the knife. One strand snapped and curled away. Then another. The rope held for one long moment before Morales severed the remaining strand and Soledad came down, falling over Harper's shoulder. Elizabeth heard the breath go out of him as he took the weight and staggered back. He was kept from falling only by the railing, which he stumbled against, sending the spirit ship flying into the grass.

# 13

◆ ◆ ◆

*June 3*

Five days have passed since this headache came upon me & still I have no respite whatsoever. When Morales came into the foundry & told me, we rode like madmen to the house. I was sick at heart when Harper said she had died a suicide, & Elizabeth's despair only worsened when I told her that Soledad could not be buried in holy ground because of mortal sin.

The next day they buried her in the cemetery north of town & that was when the pain began as a throbbing at the temples. Soon the dome of my skull was squeezed as tight as if some devil had it in a vise. That evening it was an agony & I took the nostrum that leaves the taste of metal in my mouth, hoping that when I woke the pain would be gone. But it was there with the dawn. I crawled under the blanket because the light was like knives in my eyes & I gave myself up to it, for there was nothing more that I could do.

This morning I dragged myself to Mass & Fray Sandoval's words ached in my ears. The incense made me sick until I thought I should vomit. Afterward I begged Fray Velásquez to let me stay in bed. This he granted because there is kindness in him, but Mariano accosted me on the way back to my room, saying that Soledad's child was a trial to Margarita, the woman we gave her to. She cried day & night & neither Margarita nor any of the other women could stop the sobbing. I told Mariano I was ignorant of such things & came back to be alone & endure this wretchedness, only to hear the braying of Humberto's orchestra. I went out & asked him to please stop, which he did, but he grumbled & the Indians threw hateful glances at me.

I am bearing up as well as possible. I know that Soledad's death goes hand in hand with the pain in my head. It does no good to remember that I knew from the beginning the battle for her soul would not be easy, but how was I to know how deeply the pagan gods were lodged within her mind? She learned; she was confirmed. There was no reason to suspect I had not led her through the wilderness. But Satan's hand is everywhere; I see that now. Everywhere there is deceit & treachery. Satan has made lies of truth & truth of lies so that nothing is as it seemed. Moreover, there is all that led to Soledad's death & in that too I was deceived. What I learned came too late. Besides, I could have done nothing to prevent what happened. By the time Angelita came to me, Harper had already lain with Soledad & doubtless she had conceived. Even if I had believed Angelita, what purpose would have been served in bringing Soledad here? It would only have delayed her conversion, for I have no doubt that Fray Sandoval would have been compelled to meddle. Besides, she would have been a curiosity to the Indians, & those who still practice secret rites might well have had an influence upon her mind.

But now the course is forged. A soul is lost but another awaits redemption. Tomorrow Soledad's daughter will be baptized & christened Constancia at Elizabeth's request. I pray that this fair-skinned, blue-eyed bastard will not be shunned & will grow strong & be an example to her kind. May all be well.

*Two*

# THE
# MISSION

◆ ◆ ◆

# 14

—◆ ◆ ◆—

After Constancia's baptism, Elizabeth became an insomniac. During the day she helped Angelita with Daniel, went for walks, rode a docile mare into the hills with the intention of wearing herself out so that exhaustion might let her rest. She stayed up long past her usual bedtime, drank cognac though she took no pleasure in it, climbed the stairs, lay down, but her eyes would not stay closed. She stared into the darkness as the clock downstairs chimed the hours.

One day she took up the drawing pad she had not touched in years and spent three hours making pictures of Soledad. It did not matter that her talent was indifferent. They were intended as aids to memory, and she slipped them into the frame around the dressing table mirror with the idea that she might find some relief by looking at them. But memory only made things worse, and when she understood that, she set about forgetting. She took the drawings down and put them in a folder. After that she banished the images whenever they entered her mind, attended to Daniel as if he were the only child born in the house that night, lived with Henry as if he were a stranger who had certain inexplicable rights to lodging and to food.

The rules she chose to live by then seemed no less stringent than those which guided Fray Santos through the Franciscan day. She would not look east where the gazebo stood. She wanted the long rows of windows on that side of the house to close upon themselves like anemones in tide pools. She blinded herself to the meadow, the oak grove, the mountains, wished that the world existed only in the west and that everything in the direction of the sunrise would be gathered up in darkness. Yet though she became a connoisseur of forgetfulness, there were times when the geometrical intricacies of the gazebo returned, and Soledad would suddenly be swinging, swinging, swinging in the morning light, the feathers of her dress shining brightly as she fell into the arms of Henry, who tilted his head back so that he could gaze into her eyes.

Two months passed in this way, then three more, but it was not until the end of the year that she admitted to the futility of what she had tried to do. Day by day she allowed her eyes to stray a little farther. The boards came down that she had so carefully imagined nailing over the eastern windows. Doors and curtains opened. As she looked out toward the meadow, where bluebirds pecked busily at the grass, she confronted the grief she had been afraid of.

That week dark circles appeared beneath her eyes and her hands began to shake. Sometimes she was obliged to give Daniel to Angelita and retreat to a chair in the corner, where the long black shadows of interdicted mourning fell in thick lines across the room and she would confront scenes from her life with Soledad that were so intense they hardly seemed like memories. She thought they were the price she had to pay for trying to forget, and she waited for them to fade, hoping they were the final assertions of the past. Instead, they became clearer, and as they paraded through her mind, moving with a stately precision all their own, she saw that a change had come upon her friend. Every movement was different from before. This Soledad was neither the person she had sketched wading ashore with Henry and Fray Santos nor the one with whom she bathed; neither Henry's woman nor the swaying figure in the morning light. There was an authority to her now that she had lacked in life, a bearing full of grief and dignity. Moreover, Elizabeth had the impression that this new Soledad was making demands, that everything about her was cast in the imperative mood. Yet it seemed as if she herself were deaf, as if she were watching Soledad's mouth moving and heard nothing, not the faintest sound.

She searched for clues. She went to the gazebo and studied the place where the rope had rubbed away the crossbeam's paint. She sat in the airy parlor, in the kitchen redolent of food. She spent hours on the porch trying to hear, but her efforts did no good; Soledad's silence would not give way to sound.

That was why Elizabeth turned to Susan Ludlow one sunny afternoon when her friend came to visit with her daughters. They were watching the girls playing in the gazebo.

"A strange thing is happening to me," Elizabeth said. "I see Soledad everywhere. She wants something and I don't know what it is."

"You've had a terrible shock."

"No, more than that. She's asking me to do something," Elizabeth insisted. Because it seemed perfectly natural to say these things, she was surprised when Susan looked at her oddly.

"You should get hold of yourself, Elizabeth. If I didn't know you better, I'd think you were talking about a ghost."

"I don't believe in ghosts."

"What, then?"

She did not know, but shortly after Susan's visit she asked Angelita to arrange a meeting with the *bruja*.

She had learned about her months earlier when Angelita began neglecting her duties to such an extent that she felt obliged to call her aside and tell her that her work had to improve. Angelita broke into tears, and after confessing that the young man she wanted to marry had betrayed her, she said that she and other girls consulted an old woman about such things. She sniffed, wiping her nose on her sleeve. "The señora gave me a potion."

"To increase his love?"

"No. To make his life a tragedy."

"Revenge is wrong, Angelita."

"I believe in the *bruja*," she insisted.

"Perhaps you should talk to Fray Santos," Elizabeth said. "He is very understanding."

"I do not talk to him, I do not confess to him, no more," she said angrily.

"But why?" Elizabeth asked.

"He knows things," she said petulantly.

"What do you mean?"

"I mean he is not your friend, señora. Please. Don't ask me any more."

She wondered what Angelita meant, finally putting down her anger to her disturbed state of mind. Elizabeth had all but forgotten about the incident until her conversation with Susan. It was frightening to think of visiting the *bruja*, but Soledad would not leave her alone.

Early on the day the old woman had agreed to see her, Elizabeth rode north for an hour. The road was scarcely more than a rutted path paralleling the sea, where haze shrouded the islands. When she came to the stand of trees Angelita had told her to watch for, she saw a wisp of smoke rising straight into the sky. The shack was nestled between two oaks. Its slanted roof of curled and rotting shingles jutted like a brow over the single dusty window looking unblinkingly toward the sea. Rain and wind had weathered the boards to the color of granite. Had there been no smoke from the chimney, she might easily have gone by, thinking the shack only a huge stone beneath the sheltering oaks.

She stopped short of the clearing before the door and rested her hands on the pommel. The look of the place made her uneasy, though there was no single object, color, or scent that she could trace her feeling to. At last Elizabeth dismounted, tethered the mare to one of the oaks, and turned to see the dim outline of a face in the center of the window. She could not make out the features, only the oval shape veiled with dust. The face disappeared, and before she could consider what to do, the door opened on a woman much older than she had imagined. The *bruja* shuffled toward her with a gnarled cane that looked like an extension of her bony hand. Mottled light ran over the faded flowers of her dress and the black cloth wrapped around her head. She was intent on the ground in front of her, making her way across the clearing as if she were reading the leaf-strewn earth. When she reached Elizabeth, her dark watery eyes seemed to pinion her like an arrow through a rabbit's heart. Suddenly the *bruja* raised the walking stick and Elizabeth took a step backward.

"No, don't be afraid." The cane touched Elizabeth's shoulders, explored the length of her arm, her side, her flank before the *bruja* leaned on it again. "*Venga aqui,*" she said, motioning with the cane toward the house.

Odd figures made of sticks and wool adorned the walls. The *bruja* motioned to a chair and pulled another close as she asked Elizabeth why she had come.

"I need help."

"Everyone does," she said. Reaching out, she ran one calloused finger over the backs of Elizabeth's hands and then turned them over. Satisfied, she looked up at Elizabeth. "What is wrong?"

"A woman died," she answered quietly.

"From what?"

"Grief."

"Sadness?"

"Yes."

"Over love?"

"Yes."

"Of a man?"

"A child."

"Hers?"

"And my husband's."

The *bruja*'s eyes widened. "Tell me."

"I can't."

"You want help," the old woman said, suddenly impatient. "Then you tell me."

She did, haltingly. When she finished, she looked pleadingly at the old woman, making an inconclusive gesture with her hand. "She is always there, day and night."

"I understand," the *bruja* answered. "It is not so hard. She wants her child."

"But she's dead," Elizabeth said, not understanding. "What can I do?"

"Be her mother."

"But the child lives at the mission."

"Find a way," the woman said. "Make Soledad easy in her grave."

On the way back she was not sure what to make of the old woman. She had felt guilty in the shack when she thought of what Fray Santos would say if he knew she was there. But the old woman possessed no magic. She had merely listened. Anyone, Elizabeth thought, anyone at all could have done the same.

The next day she told Fray Santos what she wanted. He advised against it, saying, "It would be better to leave her alone."

"I am her godmother," she insisted. "I have the right."

A split wood fence enclosed the Indian village where narrow lanes separated long rows of adobe huts stretching north to the fields and south to the Sacred Garden. No trees, no bushes, nothing green. The adobe was only slightly different in color from the dusty lanes. Elizabeth had the impression that the earth had simply risen up and shaken itself, and when the shaking was done, the broken surface had settled into these rows of hovels where children played. Smoke rose through holes in the roofs; there was the heavy scent of oil and fried corn. When she reached the hut, she looked into the darkness and called hello. A moment later Margarita came to the door with Constancia at her breast.

"I want to talk," Elizabeth said in Spanish. "I want to tell you something."

Elizabeth was not sure that Margarita remembered her from the day of the baby's baptism until she stepped aside and let her enter. Light came into the room from the doorway and the smoke hole. There were no chairs. She gathered her skirts in one hand and sat on the floor, smoothing them across her legs.

"I want to help with Constancia, be with her."

Margarita stared. "They gave her to me," she said suspiciously.

"You know about her mother?" Elizabeth asked, speaking barely louder than a whisper.

"Yes."

"It was not my fault, what happened." She reached out and touched Constancia. "She and my son were born the same night, in the same place." Elizabeth spoke softly. She added, "I want to know her."

"Why?"

"Because her mother was my friend. We were like sisters."

Margarita looked at her skeptically. Elizabeth was afraid Margarita would say no. She had decided against asking Fray Santos to intervene, but now she was not so sure.

"Like sisters?" Margarita asked. Elizabeth nodded.

"What do you want?"

"Just to see her sometimes."

"She will still be mine?"

"Yes," Elizabeth said.

Margarita eased the baby from her nipple. "You have your own baby? You will not take her?"

"I only want to see her from time to time."

"Well, come when you want."

Her secret life was difficult at first, but Elizabeth never questioned her decision to keep what she was doing to herself. After a while she no longer thought of her visits to Constancia as a lie but as a parallel life. She grew strong in the pursuit of it as three years passed, then five, and then eight. She brought news of a different world to the mission with the hope that Constancia would understand it and one day be at ease among her father's people. She assumed the duties of a language teacher, and by the time Constancia was ten they conversed in a patois of their own, weaving Spanish and Chumash phrases like garlands around their English speech. Most of the time Constancia was attentive, but occasionally she withdrew into herself and a puzzled look would come upon her, as if she had heard something, or her mind had wandered. She would simply not be present for a moment. It was very odd, but Elizabeth never questioned her because it was at such times that Constancia seemed most herself. It was as if she were holding still, allowing Elizabeth to study her almond-shaped eyes and strong cheekbones, which were replicas of Soledad's. Henry's features were there, too, clearly apparent in her mouth and deep blue eyes. Sometimes Elizabeth wondered whether anyone else was aware of this doubling of Constancia's features, and whether the color of her eyes and light skin might trouble the Chumash in the village. There was no evidence of this, but the idea nagged at her, and one day, as she was riding home, she found herself imagining that she had washed Henry off Constancia's face, darkened her eyes, and reshaped her mouth so that her face bore no resemblance to her father's.

Pleased as she was by the intimacy with Constancia, Elizabeth could not savor it completely. As she and the girl became closer she was aware that a change was coming upon her life with Daniel. Until he was ten the boy had been little more than an irritating presence in Henry's life. But things had taken a different turn recently. Henry was spending hours with him, telling him sea stories and taking him for long rides in the mountains. Sometimes they went to the Presidio to watch the soldiers drill. Only a few weeks ago Henry had bought a fine sailboat and was teaching Daniel the tricks of winds and tides. And he was making plans. One day he told her that he had decided Daniel would go to college, and soon afterward hired a tutor to supplement the education offered at the school. He even encouraged Morales to teach the boy what he knew.

She did not fully understand the meaning of this attention until they took Daniel to see a traveling show that came to town. After wandering through the tents for half an hour Daniel had grown bored and asked Henry whether they could go down to the harbor to see the ships. It was clear that he wanted to be alone with his father. Henry put his arm around the boy's shoulders, and as Elizabeth watched them, it seemed as if they were not so much walking along the road as leaving her. At that moment she realized that Daniel was no longer exclusively her son.

She talked about what had happened with some friends, who assured her that it was only natural. They too could cite such moments, and while it hurt to know the parting had begun, it was necessary. Otherwise, how would boys grow into men? In time the longing faded and to her surprise she found that she had gained a certain peace of mind. She even permitted herself to think that theirs might not be such a tragic family, after all.

On his thirteenth birthday, Daniel's party began with an elaborate lunch. The night before, Elizabeth and Angelita had decorated the living room with paper streamers and stayed up past midnight baking cakes and sweets. She had invited all his friends; after lunch the children went out to the stables, where Henry presented Daniel with a fine colt that he had already broken to saddle. Daniel allowed several of his friends to ride before he took off for a gallop around the house. There were more presents when they went inside, and it was not until three o'clock that the children went home and Daniel and Henry left for a ride in the foothills.

For years Elizabeth had carefully divided the day. The morning was Daniel's, the afternoon Constancia's. As soon as Daniel and Henry rode off, she went upstairs and removed the presents from her closet. She had hired a woman to make a fine wool sweater and had also bought an illustrated breviary. Both were wrapped in expensive paper carefully decorated with ribbons.

She was happy as she drove out to the village in the carriage. Daniel loved the colt and the presents from his friends, especially the diary Marion Whitby had given him, though when Elizabeth recalled the way he looked at the girl, she felt somewhat wistful. It had not been quite the look of children that passed between them.

She was just nearing the gate when Fray Sandoval rushed down the path from the mission.

"What is it?" she asked.

"Smallpox."

Shortly after she and Henry had arrived in Santa Bárbara, an outbreak of diphtheria had killed hundreds of Indians. It was common knowledge that plagues regularly struck the populations of the missions, and although she knew nothing about the disease, the word had an ugly ring.

"How is Constancia?"

"Who?" Sandoval answered.

"The blue-eyed girl who lives with Margarita and Emilio."

"I don't know. So many are sick."

She quickly got down from the carriage and started for the gate.

"Don't!" he shouted. "It's dangerous!"

She looked back and saw that he had not moved. "They'll need help."

"Don't," he said again, and she hurried away, too upset to wonder why he stayed behind.

There was no one in sight. Smoke rose from many of the huts, which seemed strange, since the day was hot. Dogs roamed the narrow streets, their barks emphasizing the absence of footsteps, voices, the creak of cart wheels. But she was wrong about the silence. As she paused, sounds came to her: faint, muted voices escaping from the huts. A boy not much younger than Constancia lay in the entrance of one to her left. His face was bloated; sweat glistened on his forehead. When she spoke to him he groaned without opening his eyes. Now that she was closer she saw that his face was fiery red; small pustules deformed his forehead, clustered about his neck and the backs of his hands. An old man appeared in the door and knelt beside him, shaking his head.

As she went along the street she saw other people huddled together, looking at her fearfully. Now she knew why there were fires. It was because of fever.

By the time she reached Margarita's hut, the ribbons of Constancia's presents hung loose and the bows she had so carefully tied were flattened and bedraggled.

"Margarita!" she called. "Constancia!"

Margarita's husband, Emilio, appeared. "Water," he said. "Bring water. They are burning up."

He disappeared inside and quickly came out with an earthen pot. She hurried back down the street to the well, lowered the bucket, and hauled up water. When she entered the hut the heat was like a blast from the bread ovens. The hole in the thatched roof vented some of the smoke from the mesquite fire, but a blue haze veiled the room. Margarita and Constancia lay on the far side of the fire, and Elizabeth watched Emilio help them sit up long enough to drink.

Their illness was conveyed more by their postures, by their coughs and moans, than by any marks of disease. Elizabeth knelt beside the girl. Her eyes were closed and her face was filmed with sweat. It was worse with her than it had been with the boy. Large blisters ran from her forehead across her face. They seemed to move in the firelight.

"Constancia," she said softly, "it's Elizabeth."

The girl opened her eyes slowly, then closed them. Elizabeth did not know whether she recognized her.

"Presents, for your birthday." She opened the package with the sweater and spread it across the girl's chest. Constancia's hands closed over it, smoothing the wool.

"How long have they been sick?" Elizabeth asked over her shoulder.

"Five days, six," Emilio answered in an agonized voice. "The brownrobes say they can do nothing."

"And you?"

"Not yet."

"Give them more water. I'll be back."

"Where are you going?"

"To Fray Santos."

A breeze ruffled the deserted fields and whistled in her ears. As she ran, the happiness of the day trailed away behind her. She remembered Daniel riding in the hills, the parlor festooned with colored streamers, Constancia's feverish face. In the Sacred Garden she startled an old friar sitting in the sun. Two other men walked on the portico, hands behind their backs. Fray Sandoval appeared at the far end and vanished into the chapel. She passed a room where friars were writing, another where one was weaving white rope for belting cassocks. At last she came out on the far side of the chapel near the foundry, where she heard the rhythmical *tap, tap, tap* of a hammer on iron patterning the air. Inside, sweating over a red-hot piece of iron, Fray Santos raised his hammer to strike again.

"Why didn't you tell me?"

The hammer fell. *Tap, tap, tap.* He put it down beside the anvil and wiped his hands on a rag. "I'm sorry. I didn't hear you."

"The smallpox. Why didn't you tell me?" Elizabeth demanded.

"What good would it have done?"

"I could have taken care of her!"

"There is nothing to do in these cases. We consulted Dr. Boyle. He said it will run its course. We pray for the dead."

"He had no advice?"

"Plagues strike them down. It is God's will."

"They are feverish, thirsty," she said. "They need comfort."

"Fray García is very brave. He goes to them in the morning."

It was inconceivable to her that they had no plan.

"This is life, Elizabeth. The vale of sorrow. Pray to the Virgin. What else can we do?"

"Help them."

"Prayers will help."

She saw the eruptions on Constancia's face. "There is no time for prayers."

His eyebrows rose. "You cannot cure Constancia."

"I can be with her," Elizabeth insisted.

"You might carry the contagion to your house."

"But you said it is their disease."

"The doctor did, but he also warned us to stay away." He looked at her sadly. "You must think of Daniel."

So it was fear. She understood that. And she could imagine Daniel covered with eruptions. The picture was complete, down to the last horrible detail. She wanted to ignore Fray Santos's advice, return to the hut, and put her arms around Constancia. She had never wanted anything more than that. But as she looked out the foundry doorway toward the village and the columns of smoke, she knew that the friar's fear had infected her. That was what made the picture of Daniel in her mind. Much as she wanted to nurse Constancia, she could not risk it. She glanced at Fray Santos, then back to the lane. Without another word she left and walked to the carriage, filled with anguish and guilt, for she knew that she would not turn toward the village.

She could not tell anyone. Trapped by secrecy, she went through the ritual of the birthday dinner with Daniel and Henry as if she were sleepwalking. When Daniel asked whether anything was wrong, she said that she did not feel well. She went upstairs as soon as she could, and that night she thought for the first time of telling him that he had a sister.

By morning word of the epidemic had spread to town. A meeting was held at Esteban's and there was much questioning of the wisdom of bringing savages to the mission. O'Reilly drank better than he had in years as he recounted his experiences with the ghost woman, traced a recent earthquake to her, the dying off of fish. "The pox," he said, tossing off a whiskey. "I lay it at her feet." Afterward Harper returned home and told Elizabeth that people had threatened to burn the village if any whites were taken ill. In the meantime soldiers from the Presidio would be posted at the mission to prevent the Indians from escaping.

After Mass the following Sunday, people gathered around Fray Velásquez, asking for news of the plague. It had spread, he told them, and it was his opinion that it was the hand of God come to chasten the unrighteous. The Lord worked in mysterious ways, but He had made His purpose known in the disease. Was it not the lamentable truth that some of the neophytes still practiced pagan rites in secret, worshiping idols and all manner of filth? Since only the Indians were affected, was that not proof that this was punishment? Fray Velásquez waited for his words to sink in. Then he added, "But take no comfort in this visitation upon the neophytes. This is a warning to everyone."

That afternoon a yellow haze blanketed the mountains. Even with all the windows open, the house was stifling. Elizabeth retreated to the gazebo, where she tried to read, but she could concentrate on nothing besides Fray Velásquez's sermon. The idea that the disease was a punishment for the Indians seemed cruel and unjust. She watched the columns of smoke rising from the village, and the smoke seemed to mock her cowardice. Then she knew that she could stay away no longer.

As she rode past the curving drive leading to the portico, she saw half a dozen friars standing together. She saw that all of them were masked and one was waving her away. But she was determined to have news of Constancia and rode on. She stopped the carriage when she saw a friar approaching.

"Don't be alarmed," Fray Sandoval said. He explained that the superior had ordered them to wear masks after a message arrived from their brothers in the Santa Ynez mission that such a measure might protect them. He handed her a piece of cloth.

"You should wear it even this far away. They say that the sickness travels on the air."

She insisted on speaking to Fray García. When they found him in the chapel he said that nothing had changed with Constancia, though Margarita seemed better. She watched his mouth moving behind the mask, and that only made things worse.

"The blisters?"

"Covered with them. They all are. The blisters have hardened now, crusted over. It is a terrible sight."

For two weeks she went to the mission every day, and Fray García told her how things stood. Then one morning she arrived to see that none of the friars wore a mask.

"It has abated," Fray Santos told her. "There is no new sickness."

"Is it safe to see her now?"

"I think so," Fray García said.

"Perhaps you should wait a little longer," Fray Santos added. "One never knows about such things."

"I've waited too long," she answered softly, and with that she headed for the gate, the friars following.

On the way up the narrow lane she saw Indians sitting in the doorways and she was horrified by the scars. When they reached Margarita's hut, Elizabeth touched Fray García's arm. "I want to see her alone."

"As you wish, but prepare yourself, my child."

There was no smoke. The sun coming through the hole in the roof fell on Constancia lying on a mat, resting her weight on her left arm. Margarita and Emilio looked at Elizabeth with great sadness in their eyes. The girl shifted her position, and when Elizabeth saw the unblemished skin on her left cheek she sighed with relief. But then Constancia sat up and the right side of her face became visible. The scars began at her hairline and traveled uninterrupted to her jaw. Elizabeth bit her lip to keep from crying. She wondered whether Constancia knew and quickly looked around, relieved that there were no mirrors.

The birthday sweater lay in a heap with the blankets. Elizabeth picked it up and shook it out, brushing the dirt off the front.

"Are you warm enough? Do you want this?"

Constancia nodded slightly and Elizabeth put the sweater around her shoulders.

"Where did it come from?" the girl asked.

"Don't you remember?" Elizabeth said. "I brought it for your birthday. And the breviary."

"I remember nothing," she answered, "but my dreams. They helped me when I felt on fire."

Elizabeth glanced at Emilio, who shrugged his shoulders.

"Do you want to tell me?"

"They were very strange."

Constancia put her hand to her cheek, barely touching the scars, and there was a look in her eyes that made Elizabeth understand that the girl needed no mirror.

"I dreamed of them," Constancia said. "Once I dreamed that I took them off one after the other and put them on the floor. But they sprouted legs and crawled back onto my face."

She said that she had dreamed of moonlight piercing the windows of a house she had never seen. It had crawled along the walls toward a mantel, where it touched a tiny ship. One after another dust motes rose from the masts, fanning out as the ship floated off into a shaft of sparkling light. She had dreamed of sweating and shivering as she floated along a street, her body trailing flames like the mane of a running horse. She had crossed meadows where wildflowers burst into flames. Then a cool breeze touched her face, caressed her burning arms and legs as she plunged into the sea, and the flames hissed and she felt the cold water kill the burning on her skin.

"The flames floated away in the darkness and I saw the ship again. Its sails curved like the wings of birds and then I was on the ship and the wind had the sound of a voice I had heard before."

She looked at Elizabeth then, clearly puzzled. "Do you know what it means?"

Elizabeth put her arm around her. "It was only a dream," she said. She needed to gather herself. As Constancia spoke, she had remembered Soledad's presence and how that had sent her to see the *bruja*.

"You're tired," she said. "Rest. I'll come tomorrow."

"Will I be all right?"

"You'll be fine."

Outside the sun was so bright that she had to squint. The friars had wandered off and were standing near the gate, engrossed in conversation. She wanted to consider Constancia's dream and her own intimation of Soledad, but that could wait. Since she first learned of the plague she had been too distraught to think of anything but Constancia's welfare. Now she could let her anger out and she walked quickly toward the friars.

As she approached, Fray García turned, his face full of compassion. "So now you know," he said. "It is sad, but you should be relieved. She is alive, after all."

She looked at Fray Santos, ignoring his brother. "I will never forgive you for allowing her to come here."

# 15

◆ ◆ ◆

One spring morning six years after Constancia began spending her nights in the women's dormitory in the village, Fray Santos was walking up the canyon, anticipating a pleasant hour beneath the trumpet tree, when he heard an unfamiliar sound. He paused; there was nothing but the call of a mockingbird. Assuming that his imagination had played a trick, he was about to continue when the sound returned. This time he recognized voices. Curious about who would be there at that time of the morning, he stepped off the path and quietly made his way through the trees. The voices grew more urgent, and he became alarmed as the male voice alternated between words and groans, the female's sounded short, urgent cries such as he had never heard. Then he understood. There was no question but that he had stumbled upon Indians engaged in a pagan rite. Such violations would have infuriated him no matter where they happened, but he considered the clearing around the trumpet tree his private domain, and he felt as if he had opened the door of his room to find a thief going through his possessions. Giving up all pretense to stealth, he went crashing through the chaparral.

The voices came from beneath low-hanging branches of a pine which he quickly pushed aside. Fully expecting to find Indians on their knees, praying to a totem or a casting of bones, he found, instead, a gigantic brown beetle slowly moving up and down. The shape of a woman's naked legs protruded from the carapace of Fray Olivares's cassock. Fray Santos had a general idea of what procreation entailed, but the actual sight of copulation surprised him so completely that he could neither move nor speak. He watched, stunned, as the woman turned her head from side to side. When she saw him, her cries became a shriek.

"Yes," Fray Olivares said breathlessly. "Oh, yes!" and in his excitement he raised himself higher, until the cassock revealed his pale buttocks framed by Rosita's thighs. She shrieked again, beat on his shoulders, and when Fray Olivares turned around, there was a look of total disbelief on his flushed and sweating face.

"Oh, you sinner!" Fray Santos shouted. He broke a branch from the pine tree and began lashing at the pale buttocks as if he were striking the devil. Fray Olivares rolled away, and as soon as she was free Rosita disappeared into the woods.

"Come back!" Fray Santos yelled, but she was gone.

"Forgive me, please!" Fray Olivares whispered as he pulled down his cassock, but Fray Santos grabbed him by the sleeve.

"You are finished."

Fray Olivares began to cry.

"You are doomed," Fray Santos pronounced.

Twenty minutes later he pushed the distraught friar into Fray Velásquez's study. After he described what he had witnessed, the superior ordered Fray Olivares to his room. One of Mariano's men was sent to find Rosita, and soon after she was dragged to Fray Velásquez's study, she admitted to meeting Fray Olivares in the canyon. When she cited the many times he had said he loved her, Fray Velásquez boxed her ears and ordered the *mayordomo* to lock her in the barn until a punishment could be settled on.

Fray Velásquez was sensitive to the effects of scandal and determined that the friar be dealt with quickly. That afternoon he spent two hours questioning the penitent. As soon as he was satisfied that he had learned everything, Fray Velásquez announced his decision, and the next morning Fray Olivares departed on a mule without so much as looking over his shoulder. In a leather bag slung over the saddle was the superior's letter to a priest in a poor church at the edge of the Mexican desert. Fray Olivares's sin was described in great detail, and the suggested penance would keep him among the cactuses for the rest of his life.

Constancia tried to intervene when Rosita was tied to the whipping post the following afternoon, but Mariano pushed her away so violently that she fell. When she got up, she ran into the fields and crawled under an overturned wagon far enough away so that she could not hear the whistling of the whip and Rosita's screams. She knew what the Scriptures said about the temple of the body. Like all the other young women, she had been forced to listen to the brownrobes' warnings about the devil in the flesh, but there was no justice in Rosita's whipping, because everyone knew that she had been encouraged by the brownrobe. Rosita was very simple in her mind and went with Fray Olivares because he gave her worthless trinkets, which she kept in a box beneath her bed.

The next morning inside the dormitory, Constancia stood impatiently beside the door, waiting for Mariano to unlock it. Except for its size, the building at the southern edge of the Indian village was identical in design with the family huts; it had the same thatched roof and crude adobe bricks. What distinguished it, what made it notorious among the Chumash, was its purpose. As soon as girls reached the age of puberty they were forced to leave their families and live in the dormitory along with widows and a few married women whose husbands were sometimes permitted to leave the grounds. During the day they enjoyed the company of friends and family. But at dusk Mariano's men herded them inside, and then the *mayordomo* produced a huge padlock that had been manufactured in Mexico City. He placed it on the door as if he were fitting a chastity belt to the body of his beloved. The key, which Mariano wore on a chain around his neck in partnership with his crucifix, was ten inches long. Its head bore a complex design that would not have been out of place in a stained glass window. Setting the tumblers of the Mexican lock required a complete turn, and when they fell into place with a satisfyingly dull thud, Mariano and the friars who had given him this task were certain that they had interdicted lust.

There was much frustrated love in the village until one young woman inspected the barred window and discovered that the nails holding it to the frame could be removed. Soon afterward soft but urgent voices could be heard in the night, and from time to time a woman without a husband grew big with child. The lovers' window was never discovered, but there were those who could not wait until the night, and they found ways to be together. Most often they succeeded in their secret love, but chance prevailed in these matters, and when they were discovered severe punishment quickly followed. Sometimes the woman was shackled to her bed or placed in the stocks just outside the door. For the most flagrant transgressions, there were public floggings.

As soon as the key turned in the padlock Constancia took a pitcher of water from the table by the entrance and hurried outside. Rosita was slumped against the stocks, her back covered with dried blood. Although it was early, flies crawled on her shredded dress. Constancia helped Rosita drink. Then she moistened the hem of her dress to bathe her forehead. Grateful as Rosita was for her attention, her tongue was too swollen for her to speak; when she tried, she croaked like a blackbird.

Although Constancia's education had lagged behind her brother's, she was fluent in English and Spanish as well as the tag ends of Chumash, which was rapidly dying out in the village. Over the years Elizabeth had brought her books, especially histories, and from time to time they read a little poetry together, as well as some of Shakespeare. What she learned from Elizabeth interested her, but she had also begun to listen to the elders, who spoke both wistfully and in anger of the old gods and the old ways. By the time she was nineteen the routine of village life, the strictures of the dormitory, the public floggings had all coalesced in her mind, giving rise to a question that seemed more insistent whenever she asked it: Why was she there? People ran away from time to time. The soldiers killed them or brought them back in ropes, except for two young men who had escaped last year and had never been heard of again. Little by little their absence filled her with the idea of freedom. She knew that she could live with her scars, but she was no longer certain that she was willing to live with the brownrobes.

She was thinking about this when Elizabeth arrived the day after the flogging and proposed a walk up the canyon. Constancia did not want to be reminded of Rosita and suggested that they cross the fields to a place beneath an oak tree where they could see the mission and the sea. Elizabeth had rehearsed what she would say, but now that the time had come she did not know whether she was strong enough to tell Constancia what was on her mind. She had the habit of stroking her cheek whenever she was upset, and her fingers brushed against her face as soon as they sat down.

"What's wrong, Elizabeth? You don't seem like yourself."

"Nothing."

"You've always told me to say what's on my mind."

"I know. I suppose I should set an example." Elizabeth looked at her hands, convinced that she should have considered this more carefully, but knowing that retreat would be worse than going forward. "I haven't been honest."

"What do you mean?" Constancia looked confused.

"Do you remember when we talked about your mother a long time ago?"

"Yes."

"I didn't tell you the truth, not about her or your father."

Constancia had been thinking about Rosita's back, wondering what pattern the scars would take. Sometimes the cuts healed in thin lines; sometimes they were broad as a man's thumb, cross-hatched, like parched earth. She had been attentive and distracted at the same time, but Elizabeth's words penetrated the images of the scars.

"Why?"

"Because I couldn't; because I wasn't ready."

"What changed your mind?"

Elizabeth tried to laugh. "I've begun to feel my age — it happened all at once, on my birthday."

There was a tightness in her voice as she began telling Soledad's story. Fascinated as she was, Constancia had to look away, let her gaze drift off toward the sea, because it was too painful to watch Elizabeth. She listened to what had happened with the *Enterprise*, her mother's exile, her rescue. Sometimes Elizabeth faltered and had to force herself to go on. Sometimes Constancia did not know whether she could stand to listen anymore, but she had no choice. Her breath caught when Elizabeth said that her mother had hanged herself. It seemed like a dream to Constancia. There was only darkness, and then images began to appear; the island and the ship filled in her history. She tried to imagine Soledad's feather dress, the way she would have looked in it. Then she thought about her father.

"My father. Who is he?"

"A man in town," Elizabeth said, flatly.

"You know him? Tell me about him."

"I don't know if I can. Maybe I shouldn't have told you anything."

"I have the right to know."

When Elizabeth looked at her, Constancia thought her eyes held the purest sorrow she had ever seen.

"You won't hate me?"

"Why should I?"

"My husband," Elizabeth whispered.

Constancia thought she had misheard. Then she wished that were so. Everything Elizabeth had told her was spinning around in her head, and wild as it was, there was another meaning to it, another sense, a complication she could not deal with.

"What?" she asked. It was the only word that occurred to her, a single burst of incredulity. "What?"

"My husband. He refused to recognize you."

"Like the brownrobes."

"He is no friar," Elizabeth said, remembering the way Soledad had said "Henry no Jesus."

"How did it happen?" Constancia added resentfully.

"He went to her when she lived out back."

"Why didn't you keep me?"

Elizabeth had been waiting for that question, dreading it. Of all the things she knew she had to tell Constancia, it was the most difficult. "It's very complicated," she said, trying to find the courage to explain.

Angry as she was, Constancia could see the guilt in Elizabeth's eyes. And pain that was the equal of her own.

"I trust you," she said, "but I want to know why you didn't take care of me."

Elizabeth looked at her, and when she began to speak, the words came slowly, as if she had to force them from herself, push them out into the air.

"As soon as he knew Soledad was pregnant he said that you couldn't stay. I honestly don't know whether I believed him. If I did, I put it in the back of my mind. When you were born, it was too late. I . . . wasn't well. By the time I could get up you were gone."

Elizabeth leaned back against the tree. Her eyes were bright and distant, and Constancia knew there was more. It seemed impossible, but it was there, in her eyes.

"You weren't the only one born in the house that night. You have a brother. Your mother and I gave birth within a few hours of each other. It was very hard for both of us."

"What is his name, this brother?" Constancia said softly.

"Daniel."

"Do we look alike?"

"He looks like your father. He has blue eyes, like yours. We sent him to college a year ago, a place called Yale, far away from here."

"College?"

"A place where there are people who know things they teach to young men."

"Like here?"

"It is not religious."

"I'm glad."

"Why?"

"Many reasons. Two days ago they whipped my friend Rosita, the one with the simple mind. She went with a brownrobe, Fray Olivares. But that is not the only reason I hate them."

She was sorry she had told Elizabeth that she had turned against the brownrobes, but there was too much to think about and she could not control her mind.

"Have you told my brother?"

"I will, soon. It has been so hard keeping you apart, Constancia."

"But you changed your mind."

"The time had come. I think you'd like each other," she said softly, trying to brighten her voice.

"Maybe we would."

"Do you want to meet him?"

"No," Constancia answered forcefully.

"It doesn't have to be right away."

"I'm not thinking about time."

For a moment Elizabeth did not understand. Then it came to her. "Constancia, he won't care."

"How do you know?" Constancia snapped. "You don't see how people look at me, even those I have grown up with. Even the brownrobes."

"Because I know him."

Constancia looked at her for a moment and then pointed toward the village, where women were gathering in front of the dormitory. "I have to go," she said wearily. "It's time to be locked up. I need to think about what you've said."

There was just enough time for Constancia to take a cup of water to Rosita and feed her a piece of bread saved from the noon meal before Mariano shouted at her to go inside. She ate a bowl of watery pozole and then went to bed, waiting for the *maestra* to tell them to pinch out the candles, waiting for darkness, when the voices would begin to whisper and fade. The story Elizabeth had told allowed her to see beyond the darkness to Soledad, whom she imagined walking on the beach in her feather dress. Her father was a shadow and so was Daniel, but she saw the bunkhouse, and knew it was no different from the dormitory. She saw the friars and Mariano and Rosita's eyes rolling backward in her head. But what she saw most clearly was the story of her secret life.

For the next five days she spent every spare minute with Rosita. In the morning the stocks were protected by the shade of an overhanging roof, but by noon the shade shrank back to the adobe walls, and Rosita took the full force of the sun. Constancia brought her water, begged Mariano to allow Rosita to relieve herself, helped her sit when her arms and neck were once again locked in the wooden jaws. When she was released, Constancia made a fresh bed for her friend, brought her food, bathed her, helped her change into a clean dress.

That night she waited for everyone to fall asleep. After the lamps were put out there was talk in the darkness. Two young girls spending their first night away from their families were being comforted by older girls. The murmur of voices rose and fell along the row of beds until midnight. When it was quiet, Constancia dressed quickly, took a bag from beneath her bed, and tiptoed to the far end of the dormitory, where she easily slid the nails out of the lovers' window. Outside, she carefully lowered the window, shouldered her bag, and went to the corral, where she was surrounded by the warm muzzles of horses. They seemed huge in the darkness; she whispered to them, ran her hands over their muzzles, patting their necks as she coaxed the old mare to the barn and quickly fitted her with a bridle.

A full moon covered the mountains with blue frost, and she searched their blueness for the peak the old men said lay near the southern end, where the ridges began their slow glide to the sea. It was there, a faint presence against the sky. The painted cave lay somewhere in its shadows. She gently nudged the mare's flanks with her heels, clicked her tongue, whispered to the horse. As she rode away she thought of her mother's spirit ship floating off the mantel in the house she had seen only in the distance, sailing like an arrow that was guiding her to the place where she was going.

At dawn she saw the shape of a flying bird hollowed out of the stone. The ships in the cave were like the one she had imagined when she had dreamed of running into the sea. They sailed across the sandstone past red deer running beside black centipedes with graceful legs. Another sun shone here, another moon, stars configuring the shapes of gods. These were the images the brownrobes had tried to erase from memory, but she possessed them now. She felt a sense of peace, as if she had found the center of the world.

\*     \*     \*

At the Presidio the soldiers grumbled when Captain Ortiz entered the *casa de armas* on the afternoon of Constancia's escape and told them that they had to find another runaway. Once it had been amusing to track them down, a break from the routine of drilling in the dusty quadrangle and lounging in the barracks. Except for the captain, who was a member of the Catalonian volunteers, they were unhappy conscripts whose families had been too poor to buy them out of the Mexican draft. Their wives and lovers were back in desert villages, and they had hardened in the time they had been away from home. In the beginning they had ridden out to the villages and lassoed women for their pleasure, but Captain Ortiz had been chastised by the friars and had been hard on them in turn. Now it was nothing but duty and boredom. They all hated the runaways. The captain's order meant at least a day of combing the foothills and, if they were not successful, God only knew how many more in the mountains. But like all soldiers they had no choice; so they cursed Captain Ortiz under their breath, imagined loathsome diseases striking him, wished that his penis would fall off in the middle of the night, as they put on their stiff leather jackets and helmets reeking of old sweat, armed themselves, and within the hour set off in a single column. As they left the Presidio six boys and two dogs fell in behind and followed for a quarter of a mile.

Captain Ortiz had gone after enough runaways to know that this one had probably followed the same route north to the pass. He was riding at the front of the column with two Chumash trackers when they reached the coastal road and the Indians went ahead, breaking into a canter. He knew that if the runaways were unfamiliar with the country, they were usually found within a few miles of town. If they had lived in any of the nearby villages, they knew where to hide.

Two hours later there was still no sight of the trackers, and the soldiers looked at each other knowingly, rolled their eyes, wondered how many days would have to pass. But then Captain Ortiz pointed toward a hill where the Indians waited on their horses; when the column reached them the Chumash said they had picked up a trail, and the captain ordered his soldiers up the pass.

*      *      *

Constancia woke when the mare neighed. For a moment she did not know where she was. She had been sleeping on her side, and she rolled over quickly. The ships on the roof of the cave appeared larger than they had the day before, and she felt good when she saw them. It did not bother her that the mare neighed again. She was content to lie there, trying to decipher the strange images, when she heard footsteps on the path leading to the entrance. There was only time for her to be afraid before two soldiers were outlined against the morning light.

"*Hija de puta!*" one shouted, and then they were on her. When she tried to break free, a soldier struck her in the mouth with the back of his hand. She tasted blood even before they knelt down and wrestled her arms behind her, tying her hands with a length of coarse rope that first burned and then made her hands numb.

A few minutes before noon the day after Constancia escaped through the lovers' window, a plume of dust rose over El Camino Real. When the column turned off the road and crossed the lowlands, word spread in the village. Soon people gathered in the yard in front of the dormitory. An old woman whose vision had been affected by smallpox could see nothing beyond the corral except faint gray shapes.

"Do they have her?" she asked.

"They're still too far away."

Sunlight reflected off the hafts of swords, buckles, buttons. Rosita said there were only soldiers.

"I don't see her," someone else said. "Maybe she got away."

A young man climbed the fence surrounding the corral, shading his eyes against the sun.

"No, she's there. Near the end of the line."

The soldiers came through the gate in single file. Constancia rode near the end of the column between two soldiers. She spoke to friends, nodded to others. Rosita called to her, but when she answered one of the sergeants told her to shut up. The soldiers helped her dismount in front of the portico, where Fray Velásquez stood, glaring at her. Constancia returned his gaze, unashamed. They watched the soldiers ride away and there was no sound other than the rhythmic fall of the horses' hooves and the creak of leather. When the column reached the road, Fray Velásquez turned to her.

"You know what will happen?"

She looked at him quickly and turned away.

"Well?"

"I do not care."

They locked her up in a cell in the back of the barn that served as the mission's jail. Her shoulders ached from riding so long with her arms tied behind her. She was tired and thirsty, but she forced herself not to think about water because she knew they would give her neither food nor drink until after she was whipped. She was not afraid. Ever since the plague she had become used to fear and pain. The brownrobes would order her placed in the stocks and Mariano would whip her. Afterward they would watch her the way hawks followed prey in corn fields.

The smell of old leather, horses, cattle now defined her life. She could see people through cracks in the boards, and it seemed to her that life outside was only another version of the one here in the shadows. She watched this mirror of her life until the street was empty and the slits between the boards framed nothing but the color of twilight. Then she lay down and slept. Soon waves rose all around the spirit ship. Wind tore at the masts, but Constancia slept peacefully on the deck, which was dry and smelled of the earth.

Mariano's face was immobile as a mask, but his men were ashamed and would not look at her. As she walked between them she held on to their shame. She had done nothing wrong. When they bound her to the post, she heard brownrobes talking behind her and the soft patter of sandals in the dust as people gathered. Fray Velásquez said it was necessary to make examples of those who transgressed. He seemed to go on forever. When there was silence, she knew he was signaling to Mariano. A moment later she heard the whip hissing through the air and a line of pain parted her shoulders with great precision. Each stroke was clearer than the previous one. After a long time there was no more hissing and she knew that the five lessons in humility, the five lessons in clarity had been given.

Through slitted eyes Constancia saw Fray Velásquez in front of her. He nodded to Mariano's men, who led her to the stocks. There, her head and arms were fitted between two large timbers. He looked at her with what seemed like pity.

"We do this because we love you, child. Pray that your soul will be cleansed."

A week later Constancia and Elizabeth walked down the path behind the church. Constancia held herself very straight because it lessened the pain.

"What possessed you? Why did you do it?" Elizabeth asked.

"Because of what you see out there," Constancia answered, pointing to the fields where a friar walked beside a line of men. "Because of what they did to Rosita. Because of what happened to my mother. Out there is why I ran away. We were not always that way. The old men and women told me we were not always behind plows, not always bearers of laundry. Look at them. We were not born on our knees with those expressions. The brownrobes tried to make the old ones forget our gods, the young ones never to believe in any but their own. But I will tell you something. At night we pray to Coyote."

After leaving Constancia, Elizabeth went to the foundry. The coals were cold; the bellows lay on the ground like a dried manta ray. In the garden the statue of Santa Bárbara basked in the sun. Elizabeth was thinking about the day Fray Santos had sent word to her about Constancia's escape. She had rushed to the mission, and he assured her that everything would be fine. They would bring her back, and that would be an end to it.

She spotted him coming up the path behind the church talking to Fray Velásquez, who turned into the garden. She watched Fray Santos approach.

"Elizabeth."

"You lied."

"What?" Fray Santos said, surprised.

"You lied! Why did you let them whip her?"

"It was decided —"

"They *whipped* her! I saw the cuts. Now she's marked on her face and back. You promised!" she shouted, close to tears.

"It was the superior's decision, not mine," he said defensively.

"And you did nothing," she said angrily.

"His word is absolute."

"Regardless of what you think?" she asked incredulously.

"I think what he thinks," he said, as if that would satisfy her. "Come, let us go into the garden where we can sit. You are distraught."

When they passed through the gate the friar guided her to a bench near the statue of Santa Bárbara.

"There must be rules," he said, trying to mollify her. "Otherwise life in the village would be chaos."

She was adamant. "You whipped a nineteen-year-old woman who wanted nothing more than to be free."

"We have a duty —"

"You said that you would protect her!"

"The superior decided it was too serious. We are bound to uphold the laws."

"And lock up young women," she said bitterly.

"For their own good." He was angry now.

"And make a prison of these grounds."

"Elizabeth!" he said, clearly shocked. "That is sacrilege."

"You should weep for Constancia."

"She is misfortune's child."

"She is Soledad's child!" she shouted. "And my husband's! You called us here. You paid Henry."

"Soledad came to God because of it. We brought the lost soul home."

She remembered the phrase from his sermons.

"You should have brought Soledad here immediately, as soon as she recovered from her illness."

"But your husband —" Fray Santos's voice trailed off; his memory was hazy. Vivid as the episode had been at the time, his mind had skimmed it, leaving only his personal triumph. He had forgotten the arrangement he made with Harper.

"What about him?"

"Nothing," she replied. "It was so long ago."

She had a sudden vision of Soledad's tattoo, remembered the friar and Henry talking, remembered Angelita saying, "He is not your friend." And suddenly it made sense to her. As she stood up, his left hand inched the white rope belt into a coil on his lap.

"You *knew!* You lied!"

"Elizabeth! Think of what you say."

"You knew, all along."

The end of the belt disappeared into his hand. He was trying to follow what she said, and for a moment there was only confusion on his face. Then he blushed and searched the garden for an answer.

"I have never told him that you come here to see the girl."

"Constancia!" she shouted. "Her name is Constancia!"

She looked at him as if he were a stranger. Then she got up and left without another word.

He watched her pass through the statue's shadow into the sun, and then she was on the path, hurrying away. "I kept your secret!" he called after her, but she did not acknowledge him. She had already reached the stairs of the portico and he knew that he could not catch her. All he could think of was to go back to his room. He was so distressed that he failed to look where he was going and ran into an old man carrying a load of branches.

"Idiot!" he said irritably. "Watch where you're going!"

It was cool inside and he leaned against the thick door to catch his breath before crossing to the writing table, where he turned the pages to the back of his journal. Before long he would have to cut new ones, but there were enough for what he wanted to say.

> How quickly Thy people forget, O Lord. How short are their memories of kindness. I have heard bitter forgetfulness in a woman I have attended as closely as any of my flock since the day I lay prostrate in the nave of Our Lady of Seville & took the awful holy orders of Thy priesthood. Elizabeth, whom I have succored like a newborn lamb, a weak sister of Eve, for whom Thy humble servant Xavier Santos labored long & hard, now abuses me with foul accusations. She does not

understand the necessity that forced me to agree with her husband in order to make certain that the woman Soledad was saved. How was I to know that Harper's was any other than an innocent accommodation of my need, or that he would betray his wife with the Indian? This I would have told her if she had stayed, but no. Wrapped in her righteousness, she stamped off, going who knows where, no doubt with some tale of intrigue to tell her friends & even my brothers. I am sick at heart at this deception & seek Thy blessing, because lies will be spread. I know it.

Elizabeth confronted Angelita in the kitchen. Angelita denied that she remembered anything, but Elizabeth insisted, and in a while the maid began to cry and told her everything.

"Come," Elizabeth said, pushing open the door.

"Where are we going?"

"To see Fray Velásquez."

While Fray Santos lay on his bed, thinking of what he had written, the two women faced Fray Velásquez across his desk. As Elizabeth told the story, Fray Velásquez leaned back, his head turned slightly to the left in order to hear with his good ear. He looked skeptical until she described what had happened between Soledad and Henry and told him about Fray Santos's role.

"He approved of what my husband did, aided and encouraged him by saying nothing. He allowed it to happen. He was complicit."

Fray Velásquez leaned forward, his face red with anger.

"What proof do you have? A man's reputation is at stake. We must have proof."

"Talk to Angelita. Ask her what she told Fray Santos."

Angelita glanced at Elizabeth and shook her head. "I can't."

"You must."

"If you have something to say, my child, tell me," the priest said in a kindly voice. "I know you have done nothing wrong."

"He told me I had imagined it," she said tentatively, "but I didn't; it was the truth."

The blood drained from Fray Velásquez's face long before she finished.

"Now," Elizabeth said, "a proposition. I will say nothing about this, nor will Angelita. You have had one scandal with Fray Olivares. I ask for only one thing."

"You are attempting to bribe me."

"Call it what you like. My silence in exchange for Constancia's freedom."

# 16

◆ ◆ ◆

Fray Santos had never seen Rome, but he had devoured drawings of the Holy City from the moment he entered the seminary on his sixteenth birthday. Since then, he pestered his more fortunate brothers who had been there for details of the Sistine Chapel and every other famous site, adding their descriptions to his imaginary picture of the place, to which he hoped to be called one day. He had thought of the prospect from time to time over the last nineteen years, ever since he sent Soledad's feather dress to the Vatican. After carefully folding and tying it, he had written a note explaining its origin, saying that he believed it to be an artifact of a remarkable conversion worth preserving. But the brevity of the note did not do justice to its subject. Perhaps it was his habit of writing at length in his journal, or his secret desire for recognition of the part he had played in Soledad's conversion that led him to tear it up and write a lengthy letter incorporating his ideas about the Lost Woman. The letter and dress were, no doubt, moldering in some forgotten cupboard, but sometimes Fray Santos permitted himself to dream a little about the fate of his letter and to remember the care and craft that had gone into it. Whenever he indulged in this reverie he reminded himself that Rome ground exceedingly fine. Nineteen years was no more than a moment in the life of the church. Perhaps one day some scholarly soul would put his hand on the letter, shake off the dust, and discover that the text was worthy not only of preservation but also of recognition, particularly for the light it shed on the strange artifact to which it had been affixed.

He was in his room, musing a little about the prospect, when Fray García knocked on the door and told him that he was wanted in the superior's office on a matter of the utmost urgency. Since he knew of no crisis at the mission or in the town, he allowed himself the pleasure of speculating that a letter had arrived from Rome in a leather bag covered with the dust of continents, the stains of sea spray, of oil from the hands of many brothers charged with delivering this call to the Holy City. He thought of what he might say if it had actually happened and Fray Velásquez looked at him with tear-filled eyes, exclaiming that this hour had been long in coming and richly deserved. He even gave some thought to what he might write in his journal afterward, something pious and memorable. Making his way to the superior's office, he shook his head merrily at the mysterious and yet beautifully just ways of God.

In the anteroom Fray Sandoval stood scowling beside the door leading to the superior's office. Fray Santos smiled at his old adversary, thinking that the time had come for them to heal the rift that had sprung up years ago. If the call to Rome had actually come, he was prepared to accept it humbly, admitting that his writings had been inspired as much by the example of his brothers as by any special light vouchsafed him. He made a comment about how the wind was coming up, but Fray Sandoval ignored him and simply opened the door. The light from two windows reflected on a large crucifix behind Fray Velásquez's desk. The old friar sat rigidly in his chair, hands balled into fists so tight that his knuckles showed white. His face was as red as if he had been working in the sun. There was no battered leather bag on his desk. Nothing but an inkwell and a pen.

"Sit!" Fray Velásquez commanded. Then he leaned forward. "You have committed a grievous sin, brother."

The vague prospect of being called to Rome was still alive in

Fray Santos's mind, and he looked at the superior with a startled expression.

"I don't understand," he answered.

"Liar!" Fray Velásquez growled, apparently unable to go on for a moment. Then he continued. "Are you so far gone that you can no longer tell the truth?"

"About what? There must be some mistake."

"No mistake! I have learned that you abetted the seduction of that Indian from the island. You were in league with Henry Harper. I know everything."

Fray Santos could not meet his superior's eyes. He looked away from the crucifix.

"I-I-I," Fray Santos said, repeating the word several times as he tried to find a verb to give it some direction. But all that came from his startled lips was repetition as rapid and hopeless as a chronic stutterer's who knows beforehand that he will never complete his sentence.

"Be a man, Xavier, or is that beyond you?"

"It was for her," he stammered. "For her salvation. Nothing more."

"It was for *you!*"

Fray Santos remembered Angelita's warning, his own careful deliberations, Harper's vague threats. What had happened was very clear to him now, but when he tried to explain, nothing came out right. Even though the superior listened, Fray Santos knew he was losing ground with every word. When he finished, Fray Velásquez stared at him. The candlelight seemed caught in his eyes.

"The moment I learned what you did I said to myself, 'This stinks in the nose of Heaven.' I called you here to say that I have turned that stink into words in this letter to the archbishop. I grant you the right to know what I have said."

Fray Velásquez removed a closely written page from a drawer in the desk. He began reading immediately and it was worse than Fray Santos thought.

"I have no doubt that its contents will find their way to Rome," Fray Velásquez concluded, "where you will be dealt with as you deserved. Until I hear from the authorities, you may stay in your room, but you may not say Mass or perform any offices. Go and pray for your soul, brother."

Fray Santos pressed his face against the nave's cold stones. His dream was like the aftertaste of wine, a lingering flavor on the palate which he tasted one last time before it turned to the bitterness of anguish. Lying on his stomach, he caressed the smooth stones with his cheek while his eyes filled with tears. Flames of votive candles ate delicately of the darkness he had sought after the unspeakable agony of his interview with Fray Velásquez. His superior's outraged words still wound through his mind, circling his prayers like the vines that threatened to choke his beloved trumpet tree. The stones against which he pressed his face were wet with the saliva of his prayers. He put his mouth against their hardness until his teeth cut into the soft tissue of his lips. Fray Velásquez's shouts seemed to echo in the empty church. But even though the explosive sounds reverberated in the farthest corners, he could not believe that the future held nothing but disgrace, through which he would have to wander until his days had ended.

Prostrate in the nave, motionless except for the heaving of his chest, Fray Santos intoned his prayers. Only when the remembered ones and those he invented began to run together and his mind seemed a maze did he rise to his knees, grasp the side of a pew, and stand. Slack-eyed and disheveled, he shuffled toward the large carved doors, bent his weight against them, passed through. He went along the portico on legs stiff from the stones' coldness. As he reached the corridor leading to his room, two brothers stopped along the dark passage. By now, he thought, everyone must know. He felt naked in front of them and was glad when they scurried away.

He walked on, head bent, eyes fixed on the tiles worn smooth by his and his brothers' sandals. Before his audience with Fray Velásquez, each detail of the mission, each arch, window, and grille had been a talisman of all that was noble and enduring. Now everything seemed alien. He had the impression that the arches of the portico were moving away from him, and he was almost afraid that if he turned around, he would see the church itself retreating. He repeated a string of Ave Marias until he reached the end of the portico, where he peered into the brightness of the day with eyes still accustomed to the church's darkness.

His brothers stood like crows in the distant fields. The Indians' plows moved slowly. Nearer, the waters of the *lavandería* broke into faceted light as women pounded clothes on rocks and spread their work to dry on the smooth flat surface. They were all very dark. Their hair shone blue-black in the sun as their breasts swung rhythmically to the work. It seemed that the effort of all his long years of service was being pounded and flattened by their indifferent hands, as if he himself were in those clothes and felt the beat of the strong, flat hands on his face and chest. Then one of the women looked up, squinting against the brightness as she fixed him with her gaze. Her round flat face bore not the slightest resemblance to the features of Spaniards or *gente de razon*. It was the face of a savage, as wildly foreign as Soledad's had been that day on the island when he made the sign of the cross and bestowed the blessing he had dreamed of giving since he first heard her story. The woman's face was wrinkled with age. He was suddenly, violently repulsed. When he reached the carefully raked earth of the Sacred Garden he passed through the gate without looking up at the statue of Santa Bárbara.

By late afternoon the light had softened to a pastel yellow. High up in the mountains trees swayed as the wind whistled and moaned in the woods sheltering the painted cave. Soon after Fray Santos had gone back to his room it began to gust down the canyons, flattening grasses and swooping upon the chaparral where birds sought shelter. Leaves, pine needles, and dust rose swirling into the sky as the wind gathered strength, the canyons funneling its energy so that it struck the town in one great rush that tore fronds from the palm trees and sent leaves and small branches flying against the houses and the mission.

Fray Santos had taken refuge in his bed with a raging headache, and now he lay still, hoping the wind would die. Instead, it wrenched apart the wooden shutters of his room so that they banged against the thick adobe walls. As the shutters blew open, the wind invaded the room, sweeping his porcelain basin and pitcher to the floor, where they shattered. He went to the window, grasped the shutters, and drew them inward, forcing the cast-iron hook into the round latch with a sense of relief. But the closed shutters made an instrument of themselves, giving off a high-pitched, keening sound that was almost worse than that of the wind.

With shaking hands he lit two candles and placed them on his table. Shards of the basin and pitcher were scattered across the floor, along with leaves and twigs. His picture of the Virgin and Child hung askew on the wall, as did his crucifix, but he did not have the energy to right them.

Returning to bed, he pulled the blankets up to his chin. He hated the wind. Whenever it screamed through the town, an undefinable sensation came upon him. There was something malicious in its voice that made him feel helpless and alone. Tonight it was worse than ever. He clutched the coarse blankets tight in his hands as he listened to the rushing palms.

An hour before matins there was a lull. Then, as suddenly as it had assaulted the town, the wind died. Fray Santos opened his eyes. The candles had guttered out in the night and silence lay upon the mission. He rose and went out to the terrace fronting the church. Branches and palm fronds littered the steps; trees were motionless.

Something small and viscous had entered his body in the night, eating greedily of his dream. Now he was empty of everything but a sorrowful rage. He felt the hollowness as he went up the canyon to the leaf-strewn bench. Brushing away the leaves, he sat down heavily. Not one bird called, and even when a breeze sprang up, the sound in the branches of the trumpet tree barely disturbed the quiet. At the height of the gust three flowers were torn from their stems and floated down, making bright yellow patches against the brown decay at his feet. The breeze subsided, then rose again, and he heard Fray Velásquez's pronouncement as it blew. Looking through the falling flowers, he seemed to see the island of San Nicolás, Soledad, Harper; and as they loomed up before his startled eyes he spoke so softly that not even a bird could have heard him: "God damn their souls!"

*Three*

# HARPER'S CHILDREN

◆ ◆ ◆

# 17

◆ ◆ ◆

Daniel was not prepared for the hazing of upperclassmen when he arrived in New Haven. It seemed childish and stupid, but he endured it until two seniors, Henderson and Wiggins, began harassing him about his manners and his clothes. He put up with them for two weeks out of deference to tradition before inviting Henderson outside one evening, saying, "Let's settle this."

They crossed the cobblestone quadrangle and stripped to the waist when they reached a grassy square. Henderson was a large man, but he moved slowly and seemed to think that what Daniel had in mind was a wrestling match as he crouched and began moving his hands slowly from side to side. Daniel waited for his rush, and when he came forward he set his left foot firmly and threw a punch that caught Henderson below the heart. The man's breath exploded, and as he staggered Daniel struck him in the mouth with a left hook and Henderson went down to his knees. He slowly put his hand to his bloody mouth and fished out a tooth, which he looked at with disbelief. "All right," he said thickly. Then he got to his feet unsteadily and his backers helped him across the quadrangle to the dormitory.

The status that came to Daniel as a result of the fight immediately increased his standing, and as his classmates got to know him, they listened with growing respect to experiences they had only dreamed of. He had already begun to excel in the natural sciences; that also impressed his friends. He explained that it was owing largely to his having grown up under the eye of Juan Morales, who had taught him to hunt and fish, as well as instructing him in the secrets of the mountains and the sea. Daniel told them that from the time he was ten he had sailed on his father's schooner and learned what high seas could do. His skill in mathematics had the advantage of being learned from maps and the complexities of deep sea navigation.

By the time the first snows fell, he had happily settled in, learning from men who were wildly different from those at home. His father's crudeness fitted him like a second skin, and so did that of Harper's friends. Anything not practical had no place in their lives, and while Daniel understood why, they began to seem limited and provincial. It made no difference that his professors were as unworldly as Fray Santos; their knowledge excited him, though some spoke in monotones and made no secret that they regarded students as little more than savages. Their attitude did not matter, because they filled his mind with ideas. By the end of the year he could look back on who he was when he arrived and see a boy who had become a scholar. He felt a new confidence in himself, believing that he was capable of almost anything.

When he returned home in May he was afraid that the sophisticated worlds of New Haven and Boston might make it impossible for him to live happily again on the quiet central coast. But the notion died as soon as he got off the stagecoach and hired a drayman to take him home. The east, he realized, had starved his life of color. Poppies and lilacs flowed over the foothills in great swaths of orange and lavender; the yellow blossoms of acacias hummed with bumble bees. The dusty scent of oaks, the flowered hills, the long curved beaches claimed him once again, and it seemed as if they had always been imprinted on his heart.

That afternoon Angelita spent three hours in the kitchen. At dinner her enchiladas burned his tongue, and he was grateful that his father kept pouring beer.

Afterward he and his parents went out to the porch. Harper poured two more glasses of beer and handed one to Daniel.

"So tell me what my money bought," Harper said cheerfully.

"Where do you want to start? Caesar's campaigns? Algebra?"

"Who have you met?" Harper answered. This time his tone was serious.

Before Daniel left the previous fall his father had advised him to cultivate people who were likely to be useful. "That way," Harper had said, "you won't have to scramble, the way I did." Daniel had nothing against bettering himself; what he objected to was the crassness of his father's suggestion. He had taken his friends as he found them, but he did not intend to tell Harper.

"There's a man in the room next to mine whose family owns half the shipping interests in Boston, and McClure's father is in law."

Harper looked interested. "You get on?"

"As well as with anyone."

"Good," Harper said, nodding. "Spend as much time as you can with them. It'll pay off in the end."

His mother had been listening quietly, but when Harper finished she said, "No, that's not the most important thing."

Harper glanced at her irritably. "You don't understand, Elizabeth."

Daniel would not have been surprised if his father added that she never had. Harper usually dismissed anything she said about the ways of the world. His father's habitual rudeness had always upset him; while he enjoyed his company when they hunted or sailed, it was years since he had looked at Harper uncritically, and now this insult to his mother diminished him even further in Daniel's eyes. Elizabeth looked sharply at Harper, then retreated into her customary silence. He had hoped that this time she would hold her ground; now he was disappointed, though he knew it was her nature. His father ignored her, poured more beer, asked about his plans for the early part of the summer before they left for Mexico.

"I want to see my friends," he answered in a subdued voice. "And I'd like to spend some time with Morales."

If he weren't angry, he would have told the truth. He wanted to see Marion Whitby more than anyone else, but he was in no mood to listen to his father tease him about her. A little later he asked as casually as possible whether they had run into her recently. His father smiled a little oddly, he thought, and his mother looked uneasy.

"I'm too busy to pay attention to the neighbors," Harper said.

As he spoke Elizabeth got up, saying that she was tired and promising that Angelita would prepare all Daniel's favorite things the next day. Harper watched her go inside. Then he turned and told Daniel that his old friend Don José Avellanos had written to insist that they stay with him at his hacienda. "He'll give us some of the best bird shooting you can imagine."

While Harper went on about what was in store for them in Mexico, Daniel thought about his mother. Something that was said had hurt her and he wanted to track it down. It wasn't the insult; that much was clear. He saw her standing by the window in the parlor, looking out at the darkness. He knew that something was not quite right as soon as he got home that afternoon, but since she often seemed a little distant, he had not thought of it again until now. He decided that if nothing changed over the next few days, he would ask her what was wrong.

That spring Marion's letters had been filled with affection, and he remembered every word as he rode out to see her the next morning. She was resplendent in a blue dress, beautiful as only an eighteen-year-old can be. It was clear that she had missed him, and it appeared that his rivals, two young men from the northern part of the valley, had lost credibility in her lovely eyes.

The year away had changed him. He found that he could speak to her more intimately, as if he suddenly had access to his emotions. Last summer she had occasionally allowed him a kiss, though it was always perfunctory and she remained passive in his arms. But now, when they found a place to be alone in one of the barns, she was more responsive than he had hoped, and he realized that a change had come upon her, too.

After meeting there for several weeks she led him to the ladder that reached the hayloft. He had a vague idea that something was going to happen as he followed her with all the eagerness of a young man who knows that the most unimaginable luck has come his way. The light coming through the loft window seemed to embrace her as she slipped her dress over her head and removed in slow succession her delicate white underclothes before drawing him down onto the petticoat she spread out with amazing delicacy. Suddenly the world was reduced to the circumference of her body. His family, hers, the town, his life at Yale, no longer existed. Afterward, lying by her side with pieces of hay clinging to his glistening body, he thought that he would be content to die.

His summer plans vanished like smoke. Books were impenetrable. Riding, talking to Morales, walking in fields with childhood friends, anything that was not Marion seemed the incarnation of triviality.

They devised complex strategies in order to be alone, left notes in a gnarled oak tree or between two loose bricks in the mission's outer walls. Once Fray Sandoval came around the corner just as Daniel was about to slip a note into the niche asking her to meet him the next day in the canyon. He had to stuff it into his pocket and spend an hour with the friar, who insisted on taking him by the arm and walking him into the very canyon where he hoped that he and Marion could commit glorious fornication. When the friar tried to elicit a promise that he would come to Mass more regularly, Daniel wanted to tell him that the dreary pictures in the church had been replaced by Marion's nakedness, that the songs of the choir were dissonant compared with her cries of love. The friar had always seemed a decent man, but that day he joined the long list of people and entertainments overwhelmed by Daniel's lust.

No conscript ever stepped aboard a ship more sorrowfully than Daniel did the morning after he and Marion said goodbye. No shanghaied sailor drugged in a Hong Kong brothel ever woke to deeper anguish than he did the following morning in Los Angeles, where the ship lay to as loads of merchandise were laboriously stored in the hold. While his father worked the crew like galley slaves from dawn to dusk, Daniel, carrying boxes from the pier up the gangway to the ship, thought of Marion's sumptuous body. The ideas introduced by his education were no more relevant to his life as a budding sensualist than the moldy records of the mission Fray Santos had once shown him or the account of Juan Cabrillo's voyage that the friar had given him on his eighteenth birthday. It made no difference that at the end of the summer he would return to the east and be separated from her for another year; all he could think of was that the long days of backbreaking labor were sapping strength that could have been expended in the hectic pursuit of love.

On the evening of the third day, exhausted and nursing blisters he was determined not to complain about, Daniel realized that he felt less miserable. In fact, he was actually looking forward to the ship's departure. Marion had not ceased to obsess him, but the old hold of the sea, which preceded her by many years, had reasserted itself. He gave in to it, aware that he would be a fool if he did not try to enjoy the adventure.

The *Elizabeth's Delight* was battened down, the decks scrubbed clean, the ropes coiled neat as snail shells. Most of the crew had gone ashore, leaving only Daniel, Harper, and two other men on board. A bottle made the rounds, and before long the whiskey had his father talking about hurricanes and exotic ports. "I almost drowned a dozen times," he said. But those narrow escapes were less frightening than the prospect of being stranded on some god-forsaken island where a man could spend the rest of his life without seeing another human face. "That's the fear I've never beaten, if you want to know."

Long after Harper got drunk and went below, Daniel sat up under the bright stars, listening to the creaking ship. The man he knew at home was nothing like the one who talked so enthusiastically about the sea. Daniel was struck by the notion that the company of men composed his father's true element more completely than he had ever guessed. Certainly he had never heard such candor when his parents were together. Their conversations were seldom more than perfunctory, as if each wanted to finish as quickly as possible and go about his and her business. He realized that his father had a secret life, just as his mother did. He had known about hers since he was eleven or twelve, when he discovered that she had a special connection with the mission that went beyond her friendship with Fray Santos. Whenever he asked why she went there so often, she said it was for spiritual reasons. He had believed her for a long time. But as he grew older he became aware of a strain in her voice and noticed that she seemed uneasy whenever he mentioned the mission, though her reaction was so subtle that anyone who did not know her would have missed it. He was not sure whether she was lying or merely telling a half truth, only that there was more to it than she was willing to talk about. Harper's unusual frankness about his passion for sailing and the fear he had expressed sharpened Daniel's sense of his mother's secret, and he decided that it might be worthwhile paying more attention when he returned to Santa Bárbara.

He pulled out his watch and saw that it was almost one o'clock. Harper insisted that they rise before dawn. Since he would be tired if he stayed up any longer, he went below to the crew's quarters and crawled into his narrow bed; he drifted off to sleep with an image of his and Marion's tangled bodies haloed by golden light.

The Mexican riding across the beach toward the wharf was Don José, his father said. When he was a little closer, Daniel knew why his father liked him. It had to do with the way the Mexican sat on the stallion with a kind of assurance that was only slightly different from his father's. After the men embraced, Harper clapped his hand on Daniel's shoulder. "My son," he said, introducing him with obvious pleasure.

"I'm pleased to meet you," Don José said. "I hear of my friends' children, but since the men always come alone, I never see what they boast of."

The Mexican was a little taller than his father, and his black clothes seemed like an affectation, but he had an infectious grin that put Daniel at ease. The hand he offered was firm and thin-fingered. Daniel saw that it was manicured.

"You've had a little journey, no?"

"I enjoyed it."

"You like sailing?"

"Very much."

"Of course. You would not be your father's son otherwise."

"This is a vacation," Harper said. "He's cut out for other things. He's a university man. Yale."

"I know of it." Then, looking at Daniel, Don José added, "And what do you study in this university?"

"Natural philosophy."

Don José raised his eyebrows. "A broad subject."

"He's inclined that way," Harper said affectionately. "Always has been."

"Well, perhaps you will see things here that you can take back, no? A little adventure to tell your classmates." With that, he winked at Harper and motioned for them to follow.

That evening they rode back into town from Don José's hacienda and had dinner at Los Murales. Afterward they went into an adjoining room, where there were a dozen scantily dressed women, and Daniel realized that the place was a whorehouse. The murals were amazing. He looked at them quickly, then glanced at his father and Don José. They were smiling, waiting for a reaction. He was upset that they hadn't warned him, and he had no idea what to say when one of the women came over and spoke to Don José.

"This is Elena," he said. "She is very — what do you call it — athletic."

She wore a transparent dress through which he could see her breasts and the triangle of pubic hair. He wanted to continue looking, but he was embarrassed because his father was there. When a man came up behind her and circled her waist with his arm, saying, "She's mine tonight," Daniel was intensely grateful.

It occurred to him that his father must have assumed he was still a virgin. He had come across something in his reading about fathers introducing their sons to manhood, but he did not remember anything about whorehouses. His pride was injured and he thought of telling Harper about Marion, but then he felt terrible, as if he had violated her trust. There was no relationship between her and these women. At the same time, he admitted to himself that some of the things he saw on the walls were very interesting, and realized that he would like to try them with Marion.

"Don't do anything you don't want to," Harper said.

The remark was intended to put him at ease, but the effect was just the opposite, and his embarrassment returned; he felt acutely uncomfortable being with his father in this place.

"I think we'll play cards for a while," Harper said.

"I'll watch," he answered quickly, noticing that Don José was trying hard not to laugh.

"Whatever you want," Harper said. "Maybe you'll learn something."

Three men at the table nodded curtly when they sat down. Then the cards were dealt. Daniel had never liked card games, but he paid attention in an effort to get hold of himself.

The third hand was just being dealt when a group of musicians started playing and the atmosphere became electrified. Daniel had drunk two glasses of tequila by then, refusing the mescal with the worm in the bottom. He knew that he was getting a little drunk when the room suddenly seemed very close. Harper was studying his hand; he only nodded when Daniel got up and made his way past the musicians to the door.

The air outside was filled with the scent of flowers, a definite improvement over the rank odor of cigars in the cantina. He had tried to see the humorous side of the situation, but he could not rid himself of the resentment he felt toward his father and Don José. They had pulled a rotten trick on him. It would serve his father right if he went back inside and took off with one of the women. If it weren't for Marion, he thought, he just might. Instead, he decided to walk a little way down the road.

There were four windows on the seaward side of Los Murales, and on the way back he could see his father and Don José. He was passing by the windows when the musicians stopped playing and he heard his father's voice: ". . . he takes after his mother."

"It's not such a bad thing, amigo."

"It would be easier if we got along."

"You and Daniel?"

"His mother and me."

A peal of laughter from the table next to Harper's obliterated his voice. Then he said, "After the first year it was impossible to love her."

"A pity."

"When I'm not in town, there's no problem. I have what you call a 'regular' in San Francisco, but in Santa Bárbara . . ."

"You languish?"

"I have to be careful. She went crazy the last time she found out. Did I ever tell you?"

Laughter broke out again, and when Daniel backed away it seemed to follow him down the road. As he walked toward the bay he tried to hear nothing but the slap of his feet on the ground, see nothing but stars. The lights of Mazatlán sparkled and a faint phosphorescence marked the place where waves broke and rolled to shore. He concentrated on the pinpoints and the coruscating line of the surf, hoping that he could forget.

When he was too tired to walk any farther he sat down on a rock, aware that he was acting like a child. His father had probably qualified his words in the next sentence. Men always joked when they talked about marriage. But he knew that he was lying to himself. The truth was that Harper had probably said even more disgusting things after he left. His father's words rang in his ears, thrusting the past before his eyes in remembered scenes of his parents together. Their faces were masks and the house he had so happily returned to was rotten with lies. He tried to think of Marion. But even as he saw her in that holy hayloft, his father's words broke the image. He had to go back to the whorehouse, and he had no idea what he would do.

They were still at the table; Harper was studying his cards. Daniel quickly walked to the bar and asked the fat man for a bottle of tequila.

"Not a drink?"

"A bottle."

He sat at the table, letting the music wash over him, grateful that it was loud and jarring. The tequila had a faintly medicinal taste, but he drank two glasses in a row. The musicians smiled at him. A whore younger than Marion sat down, caressed his thigh. She left when he ignored her. There was a time when the musicians seemed to have gone. Then they were back; he was surrounded by music once again.

His father and Don José were laughing as they helped him get on his horse. A hand steadied him from time to time as they rode through the darkness, and the stars spun crazily. His father's words were disordered and made no more sense than the song Don José was singing.

He was violently ill the first day at sea, vomiting until there was nothing left. The second morning he felt weak and shaky, but he ignored Harper's offer to let him spend the day below. He found things to do that kept him away from his father. For once, Daniel was glad that Harper did not see pain in other people. He hauled sails, adjusted ropes on the cargo, and asked for more to do, but the ship shrank day by day until he felt like a prisoner. Then all he could do was endure the tiny space and try not to think of Harper.

Long before the islands appeared on the horizon, Daniel was aware that a change had come upon him. For the first time in his life he was cynical. He laughed at his naïveté when he remembered how his home had seemed such a warm and stable place. Days later, when the towers of the mission rose out of the distant greenness, they mocked him with an illusion of solidarity. There were two versions of everything, he realized: what he saw and what lay behind it. He remembered the time when he was a child and had seen the friars in the distorting mirror of the traveling show. That was what everything was like, even home. Home was a book written in a language he did not yet know, and now he would have to translate it, word by word.

Daniel was trying to make sense of Euripides a week later when his father came into his room with a letter from a Spanish merchant in Monterey offering a commission to ship some goods to San Francisco.

"Why don't you come along?" Harper offered. "We'll be back in time for you to rest up before you have to leave."

From the day they returned from Mexico, Daniel had tried to avoid him by staying in his room or going for aimless walks on the beach. He was still too confused to know whether he hated his father — a definite possibility — or merely felt disgust. Probably a little of each, he thought. Whatever it was, the idea of being confined with the older man on the schooner was inconceivable. The Euripides had begun to seem tedious before Harper came in, but now he was grateful that he had it.

"I have to get through this," he said, holding up the book and then reinforcing his lie with a comment about the demands of his Greek professor. His voice sounded as if he were being strangled, but his father did not seem to notice. Harper seemed to be disappointed as he glanced at the book. Then he shrugged and said there would be other chances next summer.

In the morning Daniel was awakened by Harper and Morales carrying sea chests downstairs. He stayed in bed, pretending to be asleep in the event his father looked in. Fortunately, there was only the clatter of the front door closing and a little later the padding of horses on the drive. As the sound grew fainter he realized that this was the first time since coming back from Mexico that he could look forward to the day; he wanted to fall into Marion's arms, wanted his world to be as it was before he left, before his father had thrown a shadow on his once bright passion. But much as he wanted to be with her, he knew that he was not ready yet. He was still uneasy about Harper's confession. Absurd as it was, he felt that by virtue of being Harper's son he too was somehow tainted. The notion persisted throughout the morning, lodging itself at the front of his consciousness. Reading was impossible, so he spent the rest of the day at the beach walking and exploring tidepools for hermit crabs and starfish.

He did not feel any better the next day and debated whether to put off seeing her indefinitely. It was probably the best thing to do, but he was feeling lonely and vulnerable. His thinking became only more confused, and by midday he had convinced himself that it would be all right if he went out to the Whitbys' place. This would not be the first time Marion's presence had helped him through a rough spot.

Marion ran down the stairs while he was coming up the road skirting the pasture. As soon as he dismounted he saw the anger in her eyes.

"I heard you came back last week," she said accusingly. "Why did you wait?"

"You know how Father is," he lied. "You wouldn't believe what you have to do after a trip like that. With the ship, I mean."

She stared at him incredulously.

"It was a mess, honestly. Can we get away?"

"We can walk a while."

He embraced her when they reached the barn and thought everything was going to be the way it had been. There was the same clean smell to her hair, the crisp scent of her clothes, the still unbelievable softness of her lips. But there was resistance, too. In a moment she pulled back, slowly disengaging herself from his arms. She was clearly upset, and she had a right to be. It was a mistake not to have seen her right away.

"I'm sorry," he said. "I really couldn't come."

"It's all right. Tell me about it."

He tried to, but as he spoke there was an odd formality in his voice; the more he attempted to make the trip sound interesting, the more distance he felt between them. And then he understood; *he* had been resisting *her*; she was waiting for him to come out from behind the place he had gone. He could not. It was as if they were not sitting side by side, but were looking at each other from the opposite banks of an arroyo.

She asked a few more questions before falling silent. She would not look at him.

"What is it?" he asked.

"Nothing," she whispered.

"Then why don't you say something? Are you still angry?"

"You're the one who went away."

"Marion, I had to. Believe me, I'd rather have stayed."

She wrapped a strand of hair around her finger and stared at it. It was something she did whenever she was moody; he would have been angry had he not felt so guilty.

Finally she looked at him, searching his eyes as if she had lost something.

"Marion?"

"You're different, Daniel."

"That's silly. I'm the same."

"Then why are you talking to me like this?"

He wished he knew. He could have asked himself the same question.

"Like what?"

"As if I'm a stranger and you'd never seen me before. You never kissed me like that."

"I'm tired," he answered softly. "That's all." He meant it to be an objective statement, a fact, but even he heard the tinge of sarcasm, and there was no way to explain that it had nothing to do with her.

"Something happened," she said coldly. "You owe me the truth, Daniel."

He had been waiting for her to say that, dreading it and wanting it at the same time. Whom could he tell if not her? Not Angelita. Not Morales. Certainly not his mother.

"I've told you everything."

He thought: If you can't speak about something, haven't you told everything? Even if the truth hasn't come out? His tortured logic disgusted him, but he had to believe in it and that made him only more miserable, that and the knowledge that he knew she would be sympathetic. If he told her, she would cry and put her arms around him; they would make love. That was another reason he could not tell her.

"Honestly," he added. "There's nothing else."

She had not expected him to answer; that much was clear from the hurt in her eyes, the way she seemed to draw away from him, though she did not actually move for a few seconds.

"I'm going back," she said flatly.

"No. Wait."

But she was already walking to the barn door. He followed, and when he tried to put his arms around her, she pulled away. "It isn't the same."

This time he was the one who felt like a stranger. "Sure it is."

"I have to go."

"May I see you tomorrow?"

"No."

"When?"

"I don't know."

Then she set off across the fields. He was sure that she would stop before going into the house, but she rushed up the stairs, where her mother was holding the door open. Mrs. Whitby had never been very friendly. For some reason she disapproved of him. When Marion went inside, her mother looked at him sternly before following her daughter.

Rather than go home he went to the beach not far from Marion's house. It was easier to think by the ocean. As the horse plodded along he passed a few other riders, some people walking. He gave himself up to the familiar shape of the half-moon bay, continuing until he reached the southernmost end of the beach. After making certain that no one was headed in his direction, he undressed, walked into the water, and dived into an oncoming wave, swimming under water until his lungs felt as if they would burst. Surfacing, he gasped for air and tossed his hair out of his eyes. The mission's towers were clear against the mountains. When he lay back and floated, the world was reduced to a circle of sky. His face was rimmed with water as he said Marion's name, and it had a muffled, distant sound, as if he were speaking in a cave.

He kicked and turned, intending to swim parallel to shore, when he saw the shadow. The hull of the schooner bearing down on him groaned, the spars creaked, the sails snapped. He heard a sailor shout and then he dived, scissor-kicking down and down, going as deep as he could, ignoring the pain in ears and lungs. As the ship passed overhead, its long shadow cut through the glistening surface of the sea. Only when he surfaced and saw the schooner tacking westward toward the islands did he feel afraid.

Back on the beach, he dried off with his shirt, then sat down on a rock. He had hoped that swimming would allow him to see things in perspective, but it had changed nothing.

In a while he mounted and rode along the coastal road. While he knew that the meeting had been a disaster, he was as confused by his own responses as he was by Marion's. On the way out to her house the countryside had seemed benign and familiar, as if promising the comfort he had hoped to find with her. Now everything looked different. There was a coldness to the mountains, and a flat sluggish color lay upon the sea. When things went badly for him the world always became strange and distant. With any luck that would change; he would ride out this way again and things would be fine. He was making too much of it, he reasoned. Marion was famous for her quick temper; he remembered many times when anger had flashed in her eyes and an hour later she was the same as ever. There was no reason to believe that she would stay upset for long.

He spoke authoritatively to himself, like a schoolteacher admonishing an inattentive pupil. But there was another voice behind the teacher's telling him that nothing was going to change unless he told her what had happened. All he had to do was to go back, insist that she listen, and everything would be fine. Then it came to him with a terrible lucidity: *he could not go back.* He had chosen his father over Marion not because he was afraid of what she would say but because of what he would feel if he admitted that a bond had been severed by his father's words in Mazatlán. That was the truth of the matter, and it showed more and more brightly as he rode, flashing like a sail in the sun. He invented excuses, argued that it was only a matter of time before he could tell her. But by the time the house came into view he knew that he could never admit to Marion what had happened. It was inconceivable to think of going with her to the hayloft. He left his horse in the stable; as he crossed the pasture toward the house he knew that he and Marion were dead.

The next day his mother left shortly after breakfast. She returned late in the afternoon and seemed distracted throughout the evening, begging off when he asked whether she would like to sit with him for a while in the gazebo. He was disappointed, because he wanted to talk. He could not tell her that he had lain awake most of the night thinking about his father's confession and hating him as much for the casual way he had related it to Don José as for the fact itself. Nor could he tell her that he had wept over the loss of Marion. He would have talked only about the most trivial of things, but that would have been enough. There would have been voices and distraction. Instead, he retired to his room to read, trying unsuccessfully to avoid thinking of the way Marion looked when she knew that he had lied.

On Friday Fray Sandoval appeared at nine o'clock and retired with his mother behind the closed doors of the parlor. Half an hour later Susan Ludlow arrived. The three of them spent a long time together before the friar left. During lunch, the women seemed uncomfortable with his presence; as soon as Angelita cleared the table, his mother said that she and Susan had things to discuss. They spent the rest of the afternoon in the gazebo.

When the truth hit him he felt like a fool for not seeing it sooner. The events of the last few days had all the appearance of a crisis, especially since his father was away. The only conceivable reason for his mother's behavior was that a new liaison of his father's had been discovered. The more he thought about it, the clearer it became. The knowledge brought with it a sense of disgust; Harper was capable of anything. He wanted to tell his mother that he knew, tell her that the trip to Mexico had opened his eyes.

The only mystery that remained was his mother's attachment to the mission, which seemed irrelevant, so he dismissed it. He would let her have that secret, gladly allow her to keep it in the hope that it would provide some solace. He did not have to imagine what she was thinking. It was there before him, vivid and continuous. What his father's betrayals had cost her sailed into his mind unbidden; he felt the pain and humiliation, felt the sorrow that she must feel. She would welcome his knowledge and sympathy. Together, they would open the doors of this now unfamiliar house and there would at least be an understanding, a pact. Perhaps, he thought, the emptiness he had felt since that night in Mexico would be filled. He would say, I know what happened. We will go through it together, you and I; we will leave him behind us, where he deserves to be. And if she said that she had not wished this on him, he would tell her that it did not matter, that they were on the way to something new.

He was awakened by a knock and his mother's voice calling his name. When she came in, there was neither the usual morning smile nor cheery words, only an intent, serious expression. He took her in with a quick glance and knew that she had come to tell him. He wanted to say, Wait, I know. But there was something about her that rendered him silent. She sat on the foot of his bed and clasped her hands primly in her lap as he set himself to receive the news.

"I wanted to wait until you were up, but I couldn't. Would you like some coffee? I can tell Angelita."

She looked terrible now that she was nearer, as if she hadn't slept. Still, her voice was firm and resolute, as it always was when she had something on her mind. He felt like a child, not because she was sitting there as she used to do years ago, but because he was going to allow her to suffer the indignity and humiliation he had imagined. In an instant he changed his mind. He would take it on himself. "Mother —"

She put her finger to his lips very gently. "No, wait. There's something I have to say. If I don't, I may not have the courage later. All right?"

He nodded, saying, "What is it?" in a pinched, hypocritical voice.

"It has to do with our family."

He wanted to say that he knew. He also wanted to tell her how clear and pure her voice sounded, how opposite it was from the one that had come to him in the Mexican night.

"Things are not the way they seem, and it's my fault." She paused and took a deep breath, but before he could interrupt she went on. "Our family is larger than you know. You have a sister. Her name is Constancia."

His mind went blank. The things he had been planning to tell her, the consolation he intended to offer, the denunciation of his father that had been building up since yesterday, which even as she came into his room had become more insistent and demanding, flew off like startled birds, and over the whir of their disconsolate wings he could only say, "What?"

"A sister. You have a half sister. I told her about you not long ago."

The comment could not have been more nonsensical than if she had said, "You are made of stone," or, "I am God."

"What do you mean?" There was an angry edge to his voice born out of this nonsense and his frustration at not telling her what he knew.

"Constancia is your father's daughter. Since both of you were born, she's lived at the Indian village. Certain things have happened," she added. "I've arranged for her to live with Mrs. Ludlow."

It was still a shock, but it was no longer nonsense.

"That's why you've gone there all these years."

"Yes."

"Why is she there?"

"It was your father's wish. It's very complicated. Her mother was Chumash."

For a moment the past was a blank. Then he looked at her, and he knew that she knew what he was going to ask, and he did not care enough about her pain to stop. "Soledad?"

"Yes."

He knew that Soledad had lived for a while in the bunkhouse before she died. As a child he and his friends called her the ghost woman, after a name they had heard from an old drunken sailor. Her spirit was said to live in the painted cave, and she was supposed to be responsible for all sorts of strange happenings. She had never seemed real, but now his mother was telling him that this legend was his sister's mother.

"Tell me," he said.

A question rose and died in her eyes. Then she began. He sat there, transfixed. The degrading truth that had come to him on the jasmine-scented air of Mexico seemed to have grown two heads and spoke now with two voices, one his father's, one his mother's, joined as if in a recitativo he had heard not long ago at Yale. The two voices told him that he was right when he had seen the masks, but they told him more, and as he listened it seemed as if he were watching his life being taken apart year by year, emotion by emotion, idea by idea, until he had returned to the time of his birth. As his mother spoke, his life was being reconstructed, but everything he had assumed about himself and his family was different, and he was different too. He listened with new ears, thought with a new mind. He was certain that if it had been within his power to get up and take the mirror from his dresser, his face would appear changed too. His fascination with that idea stayed with him as his mother went on in a voice that had now consumed his father's, rising and falling with grief and anger and frustration until she had no more to say. She had remade him, and now that they were back in the present, nothing would ever be the same again.

"This is terrible for you," she said.

"And for you."

"Yes, but I feel better. You don't know what it's been like having this hanging over my head all these years."

"Maybe I do," he said, thinking: It is like what I have felt since that night, only it has gone on for nineteen years. I have taken on that burden because I still have my father's secret, which I can never tell her.

"Try not to judge him. He was young, Daniel; he had spent his life with sailors. Afterward things were better. Acceptable. I had you."

He let it go. There was nothing else to do. "He doesn't know you've been seeing her?" Daniel asked.

"No."

"What if he finds out?"

"There's no reason, unless you tell him."

"I'd rather die," he said. "And I want to meet her. What did she say when you told her about me?"

"She was shocked, as you are. I don't think she's ready. Maybe things will be different when I tell her that we've talked." She paused. "There's one more thing. She's very sensitive about her scars. They are . . . pronounced."

"Tell her I don't care."

"I will."

"Does she look like him?"

"She has blue eyes, but you can see Soledad in her face."

"That doesn't help."

"I made some drawings not long after Soledad died. I thought they'd help me remember her. Would you like to see them?"

He nodded and she left, returning a minute later with a brown folder bound by a faded red ribbon. She handed him the folder and said, "You can keep them, or give them back when you're done."

"Is there anything else you want to say?" he asked.

"I've told you everything. And you?"

Yes, he thought, but nothing I can ever say. She was searching his eyes and he added, "You were right, Mother," trying to bring it to a close.

"You aren't angry?"

"I'm grateful. When does she go to Mrs. Ludlow's?"

"Soon."

"I want to meet her before then."

"I'll tell her."


The ribbon broke when he untied it, and he knew that his mother had not looked at the drawings since she made them. For some reason they seemed more precious that way, more intimate and secret. He sat there a while without opening the folder out of respect for what they meant to her and also because he was a little fearful of what he would see. The past, *his* past, lay behind the faded cover. His sister's mother. His father's . . .

Soledad was sitting on the porch steps, her back straight, her legs crossed beneath a flowered dress he vaguely remembered his mother wearing. He had imagined a congeries of women's faces: his mother's, Angelita's, Marion's, Indians he had seen at the mission but who had never fully emerged from their background. Soledad was like none of them. His mother was not good at perspective, and Soledad's face and body were distorted. She was younger than he had expected, and the heavy shading that his mother had given to her skin emphasized her otherness, her darkness. The darkness and strong cheekbones and almond eyes held him off for a while, and then he felt the power of the sketch and his connection to it. His sister's mother. Therefore, a kind of mother to him, too.

His eyes were drawn away to the islands framed by the window of his room. Although he could not see San Nicolás, he remembered the way it had looked from the *Elizabeth's Delight*. It was out on the horizon, twenty or thirty miles away; it seemed inconceivable that anyone had lived there. He remembered his father's fear that last night in Los Angeles. Like everything else about Harper, that too had undergone a change. He had believed in the fear, but no longer. His father could not begin to imagine what it would really be like out there, nor could he.

He glanced at the sketch again before putting it aside.

Now Soledad was wearing the feather dress. There was an agony in her eyes, a sense of hopelessness that appeared absolute.

She was standing against the southern side of the house.

The next showed her in the parlor, sitting on the sofa with the spirit ship in her lap.

She sat between his father and the friar in a longboat.

She lay sleeping, and there were dark circles beneath her eyes.

A design of concentric circles.

His father was surrounded by thick angry lines, as if his mother had tried to cancel him out. And there was a hand reaching out of the corner, palm out, as if to fend him off.

Daniel carefully gathered the sheets together and replaced them in the folder. He had seen his mother's love for Soledad in each of them. As he tied the folder with what remained of the ribbon, he imagined her bent over the drawing pad and looking up briefly before going back to work. He had been right about what the pictures would do to him. The folder was closed again, but it was as if he had the power to see through the thick brown cover, because the sketches were all there before him, discrete and connected at the same time, the latest additions to the summer's images. He saw the unbelievable beauty of Marion's nakedness, his father framed by the windows of Los Murales, an undefined image of the sister he had not seen, her features a vague combination of his father's and Soledad's, and they all seemed to assault his innocence. It was impossible to decide what was most important.

The idea of Constancia that was held in his imprecise picture of her was no less harrowing than his first glimpse of Marion's splendid body in the hayloft's golden light. His father's confession struck with a force equal to that which came when he imagined Constancia framed by the arches of the mission's portico. The only difference in their effect was that while he had been the passive recipient of his father's words and Constancia's existence, he had taken the active part with Marion, seducing her after three long years of guile that he had not been ashamed to use to rid himself of the stigma of virginity. They were all important, all bound together in ways that made him dizzy to think about; and together, he knew, they had altered his life as surely as a natural disaster, or a sudden loss of faith would do. He had to sort them out, rearrange them in some order that was still beyond his understanding.

The day he was finally to meet Constancia he rose early, bathed, and was so distracted that he cut himself shaving. No narcissist had ever contemplated himself in a mirror more carefully, yet it was not self-love that encouraged attention to the planes of his cheeks and forehead, the folds of his eyes, the arch of his brow. He was trying to imagine his own face softened into a young woman's, but at the moment it seemed he might succeed the image disintegrated, leaving an empty oval. When he searched for her in vain, his anger at their father rose with a fine insistence, as if a hammer had struck a piece of steel.

He nervously descended the stairs half an hour later and followed his mother into the parlor, where they waited while Morales brought the carriage around in front. He had felt uneasy with her ever since he had seen the drawings, whose naked emotions had opened a new view of his mother. There was no reason why she should not have expressed her feelings so intensely, but her drawings contradicted his sense of her, making her more complex at a time when he had too many other conflicting emotions and ideas to think about her properly.

"How do you feel?" she asked.

"Excited. Afraid."

"It's the same for her."

"No," he answered, making a leap of understanding. "It's worse for her."

Fray Sandoval was standing on the portico. When they joined him, the friar said quietly to Daniel, "Your mother has told you about her . . . infirmity?"

He nodded.

"It's a pity. Such a lovely girl, but there seems to be a weakness in her race, an inability to withstand disease."

From the moment his mother told him about Fray Santos's role in keeping Soledad at their house, his feelings about the friars had changed. Until then they had seemed decent men, and while he knew that Fray Sandoval had not shared in the deception, he could not think about him separately. In his eyes all the friars were tainted.

"That was a stupid thing to say," he responded.

Fray Sandoval looked surprised. He was obviously not used to being questioned. "I didn't mean to offend you, my son."

"You offend my sister."

The friar drew himself up, as if ready to argue the point, and he probably would have if Elizabeth had not joined them.

"Is she here?" she asked.

"No, in the dormitory. I thought it best if you and Daniel arrived first. I'll go for her now."

Fray Sandoval was halfway down the corridor when Fray Santos appeared from a doorway and nodded curtly at his brother. When he noticed Elizabeth and Daniel, he blanched and backed into the doorway like a turtle retreating in its shell. It was the first time Daniel had seen him since his mother told him about Constancia. Instinctively, he started after him, but Elizabeth said, "No, please don't. There's nothing you can do."

"I can tell him what I think."

"He knows. Didn't you see his face?"

He had. The friar's eyes had widened behind the tiny lenses; his mouth had opened, either to say something in his own defense or merely to utter a surprised cry. But it was not enough to see him humiliated. Daniel had relished his mother's description of what happened when she told the superior about Fray Santos. Nothing had followed from that meeting so far as he could see. Fray Santos was still here, and he did not seem to be suffering from anything other than acute discomfort, apparently untouched by what had happened. That was intolerable to Daniel, who had begun to think of justice lately and who had realized that there was very little of it.

"He deserves to hear what I have to tell him," he insisted.

"It will only hurt you."

"What do you mean by that?"

"Revenge isn't a worthy emotion. I know what I'm talking about, Daniel." She appeared very much convinced of what she had said, but he was not in the mood to accept it.

"That depends."

Had this been any other time, he would have ignored her and gone after the friar. He had only the most general notion of what he would have said, but for a moment he allowed himself to imagine Fray Santos cornered and forced to listen. The friars always spoke eloquently about hypocrisy; that would have been his subject too, that and the way he had ignored Soledad's well-being. Despite what his mother said, he believed that there were times when revenge was important, necessary, honorable. But he realized that this was not one of them, not the day he was going to meet his sister. She was somewhere out there, in that maze of dilapidated huts beyond the neat flower beds of the Sacred Garden. He knew why she was there, why she had spent her life there, but he was struck by amazement. The longer he looked, the more upset he became. He wanted to stay there and study this place he was truly seeing for the first time, but he did not want to see Constancia coming up the road, nor did he want her to look up and see him standing there as if he were spying on her.

"Let's go inside," he said, and his mother looked relieved when he held open a door from the portico.

It was impossible to sit on the stiff chairs at hand, so he circled the room, trying to concentrate on the dreary pictures. Fray Sandoval seemed to have been gone for hours.

"Where do you suppose they are?" he asked irritably.

As Elizabeth made a little gesture indicating that she did not know, he heard footsteps in the portico. He wanted to draw himself up, clear his throat, assume one of the expressions he had practiced in front of the mirror, decide on one of the greetings he had prepared. But he was helpless in the face of the moment, flat-footed and stupid. He saw the ornate handle turn, heard the tongue released in the catch with a dry sound. The door swung open and Constancia stopped just inside the room, glancing quickly at Elizabeth before looking at him. She held her head a little to the side, the way birds do when they are intent upon something. She was smaller than he had supposed. He recognized her muslin dress as one of his mother's. She stood quite still, hands to her side, her bronze arms set off by the white dress, which glowed in the sun coming through the windows. The almond shape of her blue eyes was infinitely appealing, but then he glanced away, suddenly unsure of himself. The friar was fingering his beads.

When Daniel looked at her again he knew that she had not taken her eyes off him. He wanted to say something, but their silence was important to her and he knew why a moment later, when she turned to show him her right cheek, deliberately averting her eyes so that he could see the scars without embarrassment. A family of tiny opaque spiders clung to the right side of her face, beginning at her temple and extending to her jaw. He knew she was testing him, that this moment was as intimate as the one in the hayloft when Marion had first slipped out of her underclothes and raised her eyes. Constancia was asking whether he could look at her in spite of her tragedy. For a moment he did not know if he could. She was the first person he had ever seen who bore the scars of smallpox, whose cheek looked as if it had been annealed in fire. She was telling him that she knew all that and wanted to know how strong he was, whether he could look back into her history, their history. So he crossed the room, aware of what she was thinking, and held out his hands. She paused and then she took them.

"Hello," he said shakily.

"Hello," she answered.

He did not know until she spoke that he had expected a voice to match her scars, that he had imagined, without being aware of it, a timbre that would be fragile, cracked. Her voice surprised him. Its register was deeper than his mother's or Marion's, not harder but firm, knowing. Somewhere in it, like the overtones of music, there was an intimation of anger or resentment that lingered in his mind after she released his hands and he did not know what to do with them.

"We'll leave you alone for a while," his mother said. He watched her and Fray Sandoval go out the door, knowing that it had to be this way but regretting it, because he felt awkward and unsure of himself. The feeling surprised him. He had expected that she would be shy and withdrawn.

When he asked if she wanted to sit down, she made an impatient gesture with her head, then changed her mind, and he was glad, because his legs felt weak.

"She said she told you everything," his sister said.

"Yes," he answered. "I don't know what to say."

She laughed. "There's nothing to say about it."

"I agree. The past is past."

"Yes." But there was something in her voice telling him he did not understand.

"It's not our fault," he added.

"No."

"We have to look forward."

"That's easy for you to say," she answered bitterly.

"What do you mean?"

"I'm sorry. You wouldn't understand."

"I'll try."

She looked at him critically. "It's different for you. I told Elizabeth that."

"I don't understand."

"You should. A few months ago I knew nothing about you, or our father. Now I know he sent me here, his daughter. That is what is different."

"I had nothing to do with it."

"That changes nothing, Daniel. What good is this? We meet, and what then? You go on with your life, I go on with mine. Elizabeth told you that I will live with Mrs. Ludlow?"

"We'll be able to see each other, get to know each other."

Constancia shook her head as she answered, "I think it's too late for that. I think maybe that was impossible when our father sent me here."

"But why?"

Things were not going the way he expected, and he had the impression that he could not change them.

"For many reasons. The only one that makes a difference is that I am going to Mrs. Ludlow."

"You don't like Mrs. Ludlow?"

"It is not whether I like her. What is important is that I have lived *here*. There is no forward from here, not if you think about it."

"What do you mean?" He did not understand.

"You need to see something, Daniel."

She got up and waited for him to follow her to the window.

"What do you see?" she said, pointing outside.

"The village. People."

She indicated the *lavandería*, where women pounded and scrubbed. "Do you think it will be any different at Mrs. Ludlow's?"

"You won't have to work like that," he protested.

"But I will work," she said, "for her. What will you do, Daniel?"

"I'll work too," he said defensively. "Go back —"

"To your college," she said mockingly.

"Constancia —"

"It's not your fault," she said, "but that's not what I'm trying to tell you. We have different lives. I think it would be best to live them that way, alone."

"We're brother and sister," he said seriously.

"The world does not care."

"I do! I'll make it. Mother will." Then, hopefully, he added, "Maybe things will change. Maybe you can live with us."

"Our father? He would agree?"

"I detest him," Daniel said contemptuously.

"That isn't what I'm asking."

"What can we do?"

"Nothing. I told Elizabeth that I thought nothing could be done. It's too late. I did this only because she wanted it, because I love her."

"Try for her sake . . . mine."

"I didn't say I would not try," she said quietly.

Elizabeth and Fray Sandoval wandered into view.

"This has been very hard on her," he said. "I want to make it up to her, to you." He paused a moment, then added, "And to Soledad."

She was staring out the window and seemed far away.

"Did she ever show you the drawings?" he asked.

Constancia nodded.

"I wish you could have known her. Maybe it would have been easier."

"I know her."

"Yes, but I mean —"

"I know her," Constancia insisted.

"So do I. The pictures —"

"Not from the pictures."

He looked at her, and she softened a little for the first time. "We do not understand the same things, Daniel."

"I don't know what you mean about Soledad."

"Do you want to hear?"

"Yes. Everything."

"She has come to me all my life at different times. When I was sick. The first was at my baptism."

"But . . ." Daniel said uncertainly.

"Listen. I remember crying as Margarita handed me to Elizabeth, who carried me inside the church and held me while Fray

Santos performed the rite. I cried because it was cold and dark and because he frightened me. It made no difference that Elizabeth rocked me and stroked me. I went on until I heard another voice over his Latin and I searched the figures on the ceiling and saw nothing, but I heard her talking. She said, 'My body would not give you up. For three whole days I held you inside me. When I could keep you no longer you came forth in one great bloody rush of life, and I saw you as the woman raised you in the air, glistening and nut-colored, still connected to me by the cord, which she cut and tied before she left with you in her arms. That was how your father wanted it, though I did not know it then. You left untouched, unkissed, went through that door into the hall's faint light and out of my life forever. That is why I come to you now, to make you strong enough to do what you must. It will be as if you had always known that what will happen must happen, that it cannot be otherwise.'

"I heard her, and even though I understood the words no more than I did the brownrobe's, they lodged in my mind and they waited until knowledge came to me."

Much later that afternoon, hours after he had ridden home silently with his mother under lowering clouds, still too surprised and disheartened to speak, he removed an oilskin and hat from the entry to the kitchen. He went outside just as the first drops of rain splattered on the drive. He had to raise his eyes and look straight in front of him, because the rough little circles in the dust reminded him of Constancia's pockmarked face. The scents of dust and water followed him across the meadow, past the gazebo he could no longer look at to the bunkhouse, where, minutes later, the storm arrived. Thunder broke and rain swirled out across the meadow. Soon the sea disappeared.

He sat on the bare frame of the bed whose mattress, blankets, and down comforter had long ago been removed, sat with the door open so that he could see out over the town to the lip of sea still not obscured by the storm.

Constancia had looked at him a long time after telling her story.

Daniel had been able to do nothing but return her gaze; he was trying to understand something that was beyond his capacity but which nevertheless he knew to be true. Then she slowly turned away, and he understood that the conversation was over, the meeting ended, even before she pointed to his mother and the friar and said, "Now, go to your mother."

"May I see you again?" he had asked.

"Do you want to?"

"Yes."

"Well, come then, but remember who I am."

She did not intend, he knew, to make him feel like a child, but he did, and he had obeyed because she had demonstrated her superiority over him, her access to something that was stronger and more powerful than a dream. There was something remarkable about Constancia.

As the rain covered the pockmarked dust with a thin layer of water he remembered her ravaged face, her anger, the way her voice had changed when she repeated Soledad's words. Most of all he remembered what she said about her life at the mission. Her anger had surprised him, he realized, only because of his ignorance, and now he felt ashamed. He had grown up almost in the shadow of the mission's walls, and while he had never liked what he saw there, the servitude had seemed in the nature of things. Now he understood, and the anger he had focused on Fray Santos spread out to encompass all the brothers. That she would be freed and go into service with the Ludlows offended him almost as much as that she had had to spend her life in the village. He watched the rain for a long time, and though no solution came to him, he felt better just addressing the problem; less helpless, but no less guilty over their separate lives.

# 18

◆ ◆ ◆

Harper and Ludlow had been out since sunrise, having ridden north to the El Capitan foothills, where they left their horses in an oak grove and set off on foot with the dogs for a morning's shooting. They had hunted together as long as they had been friends. Mathew Ludlow was indisputably the better shot, rarely missing any bird, rabbit, or deer with the bad luck to cross his sights. It was a matter of patience, he told Harper, but his advice did no good.

The dogs followed them along the bed of a dry arroyo leading to an upland rise of wild grass and chaparral, quivering excitedly when the men moved into the field and the sky filled with quail. Ludlow tracked a bird flying low to the left, fired, and watched with satisfaction as the quail's wings folded in midflight and it sailed to the grass. He fired the second barrel, picked up a single-barrel shotgun already loaded with scattershot. A second bird fell from his gun. A third from Harper's. Then the covey was out of range and Ludlow spoke to the eager dogs, who exploded into the fields. The black hound named Satan returned with a plump bird fanning its wings slowly against his muzzle.

"Come," Ludlow said gently, and when Satan gave up the bird, Ludlow banged its head against the rifle butt.

They returned to Ludlow's place late in the afternoon, leaving their bloodstained game bags on a table in the patio before going inside to celebrate their good luck with whiskey. As usual, Ludlow had taken the most birds. He had learned long ago that Harper was sensitive to the differences in their skills. Now he led the conversation away from hunting to horses in the hope that Harper would feel better talking about something he knew. Ludlow was interested in a Tennessee walker owned by a man in Ventura, and he wanted Harper's opinion of the breed.

"Pretty but skittish," Harper said as he downed a drink. "The gait does something to their brains."

He was trying to convince Ludlow that he did not need anything besides a common breed when the girl came into the parlor from the kitchen. The Ludlows did not have much luck keeping help, because Mathew had a short temper when he drank and took it out on whoever happened to be around at the time. As a result, Susan always seemed to be showing some new girl the ropes, and casting murderous glances at her husband when things went wrong.

"There's birds outside that need cleaning," Ludlow said.

Harper normally paid little attention to Indians, but this one was slim and graceful, and he watched appreciatively as she passed through the room. Something was wrong with the right side of her face, but he could not see what it was because of the bad light. As soon as she went outside, he asked who she was. Ludlow smiled partly because of Harper's chronic interest in young women and partly at his own weakness for having given in to Susan's insistence that they add the girl to their household.

"Name's Constancia. Sue wouldn't say where she came from and got mad when I asked. She's been skittish lately, so I thought what the hell. You know how women are."

Harper nodded sympathetically.

"I think Sue feels sorry for her. She's got some nasty pox marks, did you notice? Give me the creeps."

Harper watched the girl through the open door. She approached the work with clear distaste, gingerly picking up a bird by the tip of its wing and looking away as she pulled ineffectually at the feathers. Her delicacy amused him, but when Ludlow noticed how slow she was, he said, "Goddam! We'll never get dinner this way. Hold on a minute." And he went outside.

"Give it here," Harper heard him say. "Now look. This is how you do it."

Ludlow put the bird down on the table and began vigorously plucking the gray feathers. The girl watched for a moment and then averted her eyes, but Ludlow was too busy to notice. Once the bird was clean, he picked up the knife and in one quick movement cut off the head, which he tossed into a large bowl.

"Now you clean them, take the guts out, understand?"

She nodded without saying anything. As Ludlow made an incision through the chest and stomach, he glanced up and caught her looking away.

"Goddam it, girl, how are you going to learn if you don't watch?"

He finished the cutting and then shucked the guts into the same bowl with the head. The girl blanched at the sight of the blue and red offal.

"Give it to the dogs, but not here. Out in the barn. You know what to do now?"

"Yes," she said, looking at the pile of birds on the table. "All of them?"

"Every one, just like that. Now get a move on. They rot fast in the sun."

A breeze came up as Ludlow left, and sent feathers and downy undercoat swirling; the girl fanned her hands trying to keep the feathers off. Harper kept stealing glances at her while he and Ludlow argued about horses. Whenever she dropped one of the limp white bodies on the table, she had to turn. He could see the scars. They appeared severe and disfiguring in the sunlight, but they also made her interesting, gave her a history.

Half an hour later she brought in the wooden platter piled with bodies, stopping beside the sofa, apparently not sure what Ludlow wanted her to do with them. A few feathers had caught in her hair and some of the downy undercoat stuck to the front of her dress. When Harper reached up and carefully removed a feather from her sleeve, she glanced at him quickly and he saw that she was surprised and irritated. He liked her response. Her blue eyes pleased him too. They were very clear against her nut-colored skin, the sign of some white man's pleasure with her mother. The scars, he thought, were not as bad as they had seemed.

"Take them to the kitchen," Ludlow said impatiently. He shouted after her, "And tell María to cook them right now. We're starving. Make sure she uses that wine sauce." He shook his head, adding, "I don't know about her. Susan says she's all right, but she doesn't seem to cotton to work. Moody all the time."

Harper had planned to have dinner at Esteban's and spend the evening gambling, but it seemed like a fine idea to stay. He watched the girl disappear into the kitchen hall; when he turned back, Ludlow was smiling, his eyes narrowed in mock disapproval. They laughed and had another drink before going outside to have a look at a new mare.

Susan had not been around when they returned from hunting but she was in the parlor when they came back from the corral, and she looked irritated when she saw Harper.

"Add another plate," Ludlow said. "Henry's staying."

Her eyes flickered but she put on a forced smile. Harper did not know what to make of it. She had always been pleasant when the four of them were together, but after he returned to town six weeks ago she had seemed cold, and spoke to him in a way that suggested it was costing her something to be civil. He had supposed that she and Mathew were having trouble again over his drinking. But now he was almost sure that her displeasure was directed at him, and he decided to be conciliatory for Ludlow's sake.

"How are you, Susan? What do you hear from the girls?"

"We're fine," she said, glancing at her husband busily filling his glass. "I didn't know you were staying for dinner."

"After shooting the way he did, Mathew owes me a few quail." Harper laughed. "I hope María got all the shot. I don't feel like breaking a tooth."

They moved to the dining room, and the girl came in with bottles of wine. While she struggled to remove the corks, Harper tried to catch her eye. He noticed Susan looking at him even more severely than before and realized that she was being protective. It angered him a little, and as soon as the girl left he said, "She doesn't seem to know very much."

Susan glared, caught herself, smiled weakly. "She hasn't been in service before."

"I told you," Mathew said, biting into a tiny drumstick.

"Constancia . . . she's learning. In a few months you'll be glad I found her."

"Was she lost?" Harper laughed.

Susan sipped her wine deliberately and looked at the food on her plate as if she were trying to hold her temper. "She has had a difficult life."

"No wonder, with that face," Ludlow said. "Looks like somebody pounded nails into it."

"I will not hear that kind of talk. It wasn't her fault. What's the matter with you?"

"Just talking, Sue. Nothing to get all worked up about. She *is* hard to look at."

Harper knew a fight was coming. It amazed him that Ludlow was docile around Susan when he was sober and then needled her unmercifully after a few drinks.

"I won't listen to any more of this," Susan said.

"Suits me." Ludlow shrugged. "Henry, pass the birds, and help yourself to some wine."

Susan cut a piece of meat and then suddenly stood up and left without speaking.

"I told you she's been edgy," Ludlow said.

"You were nagging her."

"Well, I *know* that. All the same, something's gotten in her craw."

In the living room after dinner Ludlow poured two cognacs. "Sue hasn't been the same since the girls married," he said.

"Maybe that's why she brought in Constancia," Harper answered. "As a substitute. Elizabeth was jumpy all last year after Dan left. She went back east with him a few days ago, did I tell you? It's hard on the women. No more birds in the nest."

"Never thought about it that way."

The question of their wives' dissatisfaction, or maybe the wine and cognac, had put Harper in a thoughtful mood. "We aren't that much different from them."

Ludlow raised his eyebrows.

"That's not what I meant. Look. Here they are, past forty. They've made their lives around their babies, and now they've flown the coop. What do they think about?"

"God only knows, Henry. Wish I did."

"They wonder if that's all there is. As if it's the end of their lives."

Ludlow nodded appreciatively. "Can't say I care much about it, being that there's nothing I can do. Now tell me some more about why I don't want that walker."

"Wait a minute."

"You can't figure 'em out," Ludlow said impatiently. "I thought you knew that."

"I'm talking about us."

"What's that supposed to mean?"

"That's what I was getting at when I said maybe there isn't that much difference. Doesn't anything ever nag at you? Are you satisfied? Have you got what you want?"

Ludlow had never heard Harper go on like this. He looked around the room and made a sweeping gesture with his hand. "Seems pretty good to me."

"I've never felt that way."

Harper watched the fire crackling in the hearth. His mind had opened to a sense of dissatisfaction he wanted to get hold of. It was connected to his feelings about the girl, but it would not do to let Ludlow know, at least not yet.

"It's like hunting. You know how you felt when we got out there this morning? Excited? The anticipation? What if there hadn't been any birds in the field?" Harper asked.

"We'd have gone where there were."

"Goddam it, Matt, I'm serious."

"Well, say what's on your mind. I've never seen you beat around the bush like this. Maybe you need another drink. Here."

"I'm talking about the best birds you've ever seen, the biggest, juiciest ones. The ten-point buck you know's out there in the woods but always gets away and you have to settle for the four-pointer, but you aren't satisfied."

"I don't need any ten pointers."

"Neither do I, but I want one, just once."

"What difference would it make?"

"I'd put it over the mantel and look at it when I was old and gray. I've never denied myself, not one thing that I could get. Saw no reason to. I've done better than I had any right to expect. Cabin boy at thirteen, captain at twenty-one. My own ship, thanks to Elizabeth's father. I thought that'd be enough. A ship and a wife and money. Some recreation on the way. But you get on the sea and you never have the weather you want. There's always better wine. Better horses, bigger houses. Women."

"You're getting to be a romantic."

"I've been this way all my life."

Harper had always been idealistic in matters of the heart. After he drank a certain amount, he would feel that he had entered more deeply into himself and that anything he said was not intended to enlighten the person he was talking to as much as it was to clarify his ideas to himself. Constancia weighed heavily on his mind, spoke to him of what he had always wanted but never found. Her blue eyes and dark skin reminded him of exotic women he had known, but it was her youth that excited him. It reminded him of Elizabeth's utter innocence when they met. For the last few years he had felt no transcendent pleasure with any of the women he seduced or bought, no happier frame of mind. That was why this girl held out promises. She might be his El Dorado.

These were not things he could say to Ludlow, but they were all he wanted to think about. Mathew's talk about horses was boring him; as soon as he could, he said that he had to leave. He stood in front of the fire for a minute and, when Ludlow was not looking, quickly put his pipe on the mantel and felt pleased that he now had an excuse to return.

On the way home he let the horse go at its own pace. A three-quarter moon burned above the islands and a cool breeze sobered him and gave a fine edge to his emotions. Beyond the moon the constellations that had guided him across the seas beckoned familiarly. Pegasus. Cygnus. And it did not surprise him that he imagined Constancia among them.

Although it was well past midnight when he got home, he did not feel sleepy. The empty house suited his reflective mood, so he stayed in the parlor while he drank another cognac. The moon cast a pale, watery light over the furniture, glistened faintly on the demijohn in front of him. He could not remember feeling so at ease in a long time.

Later, he went into his office, lighted a lamp, and spread out a sheet of paper for a letter to Don José. The Mexican would appreciate the poignant pleasures of the night that was drawing to a close.

*12 September*

Amigo,
Past midnight and only a little the worse for wear, so thought I'd take the opportunity to write. There hasn't been time since I saw you last, what with another commission that came my way only a few days after I got back from Mexico. It was good to see you, though the effect on Dan wasn't what I'd planned. From what I've been able to piece together, he's gotten himself mixed up with a girl and I'm pretty sure he didn't enjoy the trip because of her. Soon as I figured it out, there were some uneasy days, because I had had a fling with her mother and worried about what the daughter might know. Stupid, but I did. I know for a fact that Irene keeps a diary, and the first thing I thought was could she have left it lying around. That would have been too much for the young and tender to resist. Wondered whether Marion would tell him if she found out, say something coy like, "We're closer than you think"; that sort of thing. Don't know why it took me like that.

Anyway, the summer didn't turn out the way I thought it would. As far as I can see there have been three rifts. The first was when we left for Mexico and I think had to do with disrupting whatever was going on with Marion. The second happened the last night we were all together. The best I can figure is that I offended Dan by suggesting that he indulge himself with the whores. I keep forgetting that he's delicate in his nature. The third I have no clue about. It happened three days before he left for Yale last week. I came back one afternoon, and he just walked away when I tried to talk to him. Later on I gave him a silver watch and he mumbled so I could barely hear the words. I asked Elizabeth if she had noticed anything, and she got huffy and said she didn't have the slightest idea.

I've become a little sentimental about him and have started thinking about trying to get him involved in the business after he finishes school, though that wasn't my intention when I sent him there. He blows hot and cold about the idea, but he likes the sea.

Interesting development today, though, and totally unexpected. My friend Ludlow's wife has taken a new girl under her wing. Close to Dan's age, if I'm any judge. Yes, very young, with the kind of body they can only have at that age. She's shy, a little on the haughty side, something you don't often find in help up this way. You might say she was downright cold, but I don't mind. Makes the prospects all the more pleasant to think about. She's pretty, but one side of her face is scarred by pox. Can't figure it out, but instead of putting me off they add to her interest. Has blue eyes, the color you Mexicans use in pottery. Untouched, amigo. There's something about that you can't ignore. And luck is on my side. Elizabeth decided to go east with Dan and then on to New York to see her family, so I'm here alone for a few months. Will let you know how things turn out. I've been looking for a commission that will take me your way, but no luck so far. If something develops, I'll write. I fancy some good shooting with you. Ludlow and I had fair luck with quail today. You and I might also see what we can do with the ladies. Are there any new faces on the walls?

The next morning Ludlow was about to leave with his foreman to ride the fences when Harper arrived with the excuse of retrieving his pipe. Harper had gotten up late that morning after a restless night and had planned to spend the day on board the *Elizabeth's Delight* doing some repairs, but he realized that he would be irritable if he went down to the wharf before trying to capitalize on yesterday's contact with the girl.

"Long way to come for a pipe."

"My favorite. You know how I am."

Ludlow said nothing as they went inside.

"There," Harper said, pointing to the mantel. "Stupid of me."

Ludlow was impatient to leave, but Harper forced him to stay for another ten minutes while he described the virtues of a good stallion that might be just the thing for his friend. He hoped for at least a glimpse of Constancia, but the only woman to appear was an old Mexican who had been with the Ludlows for years.

Harper spent the next few days on board the schooner trying to distract himself by helping a carpenter lay some new planking. During this time he weighed and discarded half a dozen plans before settling on one that seemed to offer the maximum advantage and at the same time provide some cover for Ludlow. He was so pleased with himself that he went to Esteban's and passed the night over cards, winning nearly fifty dollars, which he took to be a good omen.

He showed up at the Ludlows' in time for lunch the next day. Susan was away. While Constancia served Mathew and him out on the patio, there was plenty of time to confirm his initial impression. Her shapeless dress concealed the outlines of her body, but Harper's imagination was acute enough to supply vivid images of the grace that lay beneath the loose folds of material smelling of soap.

When they finished eating, Ludlow leaned forward on his elbows. "You're acting like a schoolboy."

"That obvious?" Harper smiled.

"Yes."

"You don't have any plans yourself?"

"Absolutely not," Ludlow said, rolling his eyes. "Susan would gut me."

"You don't mind?"

"What you do is your business. But Susan's got a bee in her bonnet about Constancia. Be careful."

Just then the girl appeared at the far end of the house carrying a load of laundry to the lines strung between the eaves and a sycamore tree. She had removed the bandana she had worn earlier, and the fall of her hair over her shoulders when she reached down for the clothes was very beautiful. Her bodice pulled tight across her breasts as she stretched. Every curve confirmed Harper's ideas about the shape of her body, and he allowed himself the pleasure of savoring the purity of his desire. It was always the same when he set his sights on a woman but had not begun the intricate dance of words and gestures and touching. If his love of the sea was excepted, this was as close as he ever came to an esthetic experience, and he wanted to hold on to the feeling for as long as he could.

To keep it pure he looked past her to the upland meadows rising to the mountains crowned by the painted cave. He maintained no illusions about what might happen. He was prepared for something as brief as a single joyous encounter, drawing on the experience of many years, which had taught him that nothing could be taken for granted other than passion itself. There was no contradiction between his notion of making an El Dorado of her and the very real possibility that he would glimpse the fountain of youth and see the glint of sunlight on its golden streets only once. Duration had nothing to do with the place he had made for her in his heart. For him the first act of love was always the only one, its successors being little more than echoes.

"Well," Ludlow said, "what do you have in mind?"

"Angelita's gone and the house is a mess. Couldn't Susan spare her for a day or two?"

"She's got something against you, Henry. I don't know why, but I know she'd refuse."

"Then tell her it's Madrigal's place. That should give you an out."

Harper arranged the sale of a horse and looked into the prospects of two commissions, deciding on the second, even though it was less lucrative, because it would take him to Mexico. He wrote to Don José that he could expect to see him later in the fall; he hoped to be able to share the details of his latest adventure, which was proceeding nicely. Then he wrote a long letter to Daniel about the boy's succession to his business and how his education could only increase their standing in the trade. He was, he realized, becoming even more sentimental about his son than he had indicated to Don José, and he liked the feeling so much that he added a postscript: if Dan wanted to, they could take a trip on the sailboat next summer, maybe explore the islands.

The letters put him in a fine frame of mind, but after mailing them his sole occupation became waiting, and that created a problem because silence affronted Harper. That was why he was happiest when he was around sailors. Men shouting, wind screaming through rigging, the steady hiss of a ship's bow somehow guaranteed that the world would go on. He needed human voices the way other men needed love or religion.

When two days passed without a word from Ludlow, he decided to take the sailboat out. He packed food and a bottle of wine in a wicker hamper and left on a light breeze, congratulating himself once again on having chosen this little boat, which handled so beautifully. He planned to sail up the coast, but as soon as he left the harbor he thought it might be pleasant to go farther out into the channel.

By noon he had reached the halfway point between the mainland and San Nicolás Island. The wind held and he continued for another half hour, long enough for the island to become a solid presence on the horizon. While he ate and drank a little of the wine, the wind died and soon there was barely enough to fill the sails. With only the faint hissing of the boat and the cries of gulls for company, he was forced to remember his discomfort with silence. Whenever he met a deaf person he always gave generously and left as fast as possible, as if mere proximity might infect him with the person's tragedy. The same feeling surfaced when he thought of the desert dwellers Don José had told him about, people whose lives were unimaginable in the soundless creosote basins of the Sonoran Desert. The only time he had ever pitied Soledad was when they were returning from San Nicolás, and he suddenly imagined what it had been like to hear no other human voice for all those years. The memory made him vow never again to go out this far alone as he nursed the sailboat on the weakened wind back to Santa Bárbara.

A message from Ludlow was stuck in the door: WEDNESDAY.

The unpleasant thoughts that came to him in the channel were replaced by anticipation as he imagined the sweet tone of Constancia's voice, conjuring her up more by that melodious sound than by his vivid memories of her body or her half-scarred face. Stuffing the note into his pocket, he went outside and found Morales grooming one of the horses and told him that he could take the next day off.

"I have work," Morales said.

"It'll keep. I won't need you till the day after tomorrow."

By the time he went to bed his whole being was attuned to the music of her voice, as if he were a lanky cougar stretched along a branch, waiting for the crack of a dried leaf to draw his yellow eyes in her direction.

He was drinking a cup of coffee in the kitchen when he heard footsteps on the porch. A second later Constancia knocked. He had bathed as soon as he rose, trimmed his beard, carefully combed his hair, but he was still wearing his dressing gown. He wondered for a moment about going upstairs for his coat, but then it pleased him to think about greeting her in the silk gown. He knew he cut a handsome figure in it.

She wore the same dress she had on the last time he saw her, and her hair was tied back with a piece of blue cloth that set off the color of her eyes very nicely. She took in his dressing gown with a quick glance before meeting his eyes.

"Mr. Ludlow sent me to clean," she said flatly.

"Yes. Thank you for coming."

He held the door open. Clothes were draped over furniture; dirty dishes were piled high on the kitchen sideboard; empty bottles sat on tables.

"What do you want me to do?"

"You might as well start in the kitchen; then do the dining room."

She looked at him with the same flat stare, nodded, and asked where the kitchen was. He pointed to the door, and when she turned to look the scars were pronounced in the morning light. He touched her shoulder casually, and she drew back.

"I'll be in my office," he said, "down the hall. When you're done, come in and I'll tell you what else I want."

He worked on his accounts for an hour, though his excitement made the usually pleasing tasks more difficult. He heard her in the kitchen and a little later in the dining room. When he could stand it no longer, he went in.

"Time for lunch," he announced.

"What do you want?" she asked.

"Soup. I'll fix it."

They ate together in the kitchen, and he was disappointed that he did not have much luck drawing her into conversation. She answered his questions without volunteering anything of her own. Her voice was as musical as ever, but there was something in it he had not heard before, a trace of sullenness he chose to ignore. When they finished eating, he thought of kissing her as she stood up, but the kitchen was not the right place, and he let the impulse go, knowing that its belated flowering would be all the sweeter when it came.

She was in the guest room polishing a table and did not look up until he closed the door.

"Please, leave it open. It's getting dark."

"It's all right."

He waited a moment before crossing to the bed, where he sat down, cutting off the way to the door.

"You're very beautiful."

He had hoped the unusual arrangement with Ludlow might have given her a clue, and he searched her eyes, looking for tacit agreement. Finding none, he decided to move slowly, though she might prefer it if he were demanding. He did not know which it would be, and hesitated a little longer in order to draw the last bit of pleasure from his anticipation.

"I thought you were beautiful the first time I saw you."

She glanced at the door. He stretched his leg, barring her way.

"You must feel bad about the scars, but you shouldn't. I don't see them."

"I do not want this." She was apprehensive now, and the sullenness had brightened into anger. "I want to go."

She started toward the door, and when he did not move his leg she took hold of it just below the knee, digging her fingers in. He stroked her arm.

"Don't!" she yelled.

"Take it easy." He stood, and without taking his eyes off her, unbuckled his belt and in a quick movement pulled his shirt over his head.

"I do not do this." She looked at his bare chest, then backed up to the wall. "Please."

In two steps he was beside her, holding her head between his hands, but she pulled away when he tried to kiss her and her eyes moved rapidly around the room. He came to her again and in one quick movement drew her down on the bed.

"No!"

He felt the tension in her body as he started to unbutton the top of her dress. When she turned away, his patience broke and he tore it open in one swift movement; as he pinioned her with his body, her struggling stopped. Her eyes were full of contempt, as if once she knew it was impossible to stop him she had abjured her body, and by doing so denied him the pleasure of the struggle.

Afterward he went up to his room and lay with his hands clasped behind his head, satisfied enough not to be disappointed that she had failed as his El Dorado. The opportunity had come and gone, its duration bracketed by his first sight of her at Ludlow's and the moment when he paused in the doorway of the guest room ten minutes earlier, looking at her motionless body faintly lighted by the lamp in the hall. He could not tell whether she returned his gaze, and he left the door open, knowing that she would soon escape, knowing too that there would be times over the next few months when his desire would return. But this was an end to it. What he felt now was its elegy. He was confident that she would accede to silence because she would know that scandal always led to the dismissal of girls like her, and the prospect of losing her livelihood would stop her voice.

In a while he drifted off, aware of no loss other than of his pristine desire, of no consequences besides the sadness that attended the aftertime of passion. The faint sound of the front door closing passed unnoticed, and he did not hear the owl screech, or the faint scream of a cougar, crouched beside a pool in the mountains, that sent smaller animals scurrying for cover. When the moon came up and bathed the tangled bedding in the guest room, the timbers of the house sighed and creaked minutely. An oak branch scraped against the roof. A gust of wind sang faintly through the eaves.

As Constancia crossed the fields she heard the owl shriek, the faint cry of the cougar, the persistent wind. When she reached El Camino Real she might have heard the ghostly sound of soldiers and friars were it not for one sound that stayed in her mind, repeating itself like the refrain of a song: his breath in her ear, that hard indrawn gasp, the groan that followed. That was the sound that mattered, and she was willing to do anything to make it stop, to forget the cause of it. The body that carried her along no longer seemed like her own but rather a thing as separate from her as a wagon or a horse or a stick of wood. But though it no longer belonged to her, her body was faithful to its past. Every inch of flesh remembered the touch of his hands. She knew that if she tore off her dress and looked, her body would bear the images of his hands as a basket does designs, that she would be circled by the imprint of palms and fingers.

She tried to live only in her eyes, to see nothing but the stars swept clean by the wind. But her body insisted on talking to her. As she turned north toward the Ludlows' ranch every muscle, nerve, artery, and vein echoed the voices of girls and women in the dormitory talking about their secret loves and the pleasures of the flesh, the ecstasy they took and gave. And her hatred of Harper grew as she realized how complete, final, and pervasive the theft had been. She hated her body because it had betrayed her, given her up when she was not ready, offered itself to be marked with the design of Harper's hands.

Constancia went up the road dry-eyed, because what had happened to her was filled with tears but still beyond them. Yet she wished that she could cry; then she would not have to look at the sea that offered itself in a faint silver glow, would not have to think about how useless it was to increase her pace, to break into a run and plunge into its coldness because nothing would wash this away. The sea could not cleanse her mind of what had been done to her. Nothing could do that, not bathing, not Elizabeth, not Daniel. Long before the lights of the ranch came into view, she knew that this night had made her one with her mother, that the wind was her mother calling, offering comfort. That was what she clung to as she walked, sober-eyed and cold, wondering whether Susan and Mathew Ludlow had conspired, whether words had passed between them and the man whose name Mathew had not even given her when he sent her to his house that morning.

The front door was locked. She beat on it, but no one answered. Thinking that she could rouse them by tapping at their bedroom window, she started across the patio but stopped when she saw a match flare inside. The soft widening glow of a lamp brightened the living room. Susan's voice was muffled by the thick adobe walls but clear enough for her to hear its fear. She also heard Mathew telling her to stay inside. When he called, "Who is it?" she tried to answer, but something checked her voice, and she watched silently until the lock clicked and the door swung open, revealing Mathew in his nightgown, gun in hand.

"Constancia! What the hell?"

Susan pushed by him and came out the door. Then she stopped and stared. Constancia had not cared about how she looked as she made her way across the fields and up the road. Now she looked down and saw her breasts and the scratches left from the sudden, violent tearing. She looked at Susan, then Mathew, searching for the answer to the question she was going to ask in the hope that she could see it in their faces and not have to speak, avoid having to find the strength to put it into words, because all she wanted was the answer and sleep. What she saw was shock and disbelief. The knowledge of what had happened to her was there in Susan's eyes. Susan groaned and came to her, tried to put her arms around her, but Constancia pushed her away, not sure she could bear the touching until she knew that Susan had not played a part in this.

"What happened?" Susan asked.

"You can see," Constancia said. "Did you know what he wanted?"

"What?"

"Did you know?"

Ludlow seemed to become more immobile as he stood there, looking from her to Susan and back again.

"Mathew? Do you know what she's talking about?"

"No. Jesus, I can't stand this." And with that, he turned and went inside. Constancia watched him, almost certain, but there was still a doubt. There had to be.

"Constancia?"

Susan was crying and then Constancia knew it was all right and she felt the tension ease in her shoulders and neck, in her jaw and mouth, because she had been ready to shout, ready to tell Susan what they had sent her to.

"Come inside," Susan said, putting her arm around her, and this time she did not pull away.

Susan roused María and told her to fill the tub. When they went into the bathroom, the windows were fogged with steam and Constancia stood there like a child while Susan helped her out of her dress. She stepped into the tub, and when her body was immersed in the hot, sweet-smelling water she began to cry. Susan washed her back and neck.

"Where did it happen?" Susan asked. "Do you want to tell me?"

"In a house." Her voice was flat, characterless.

"How did you get there?" Susan asked. "Were you taken?"

Constancia was quiet for a moment. "No, I was sent."

"By whom?"

"By Mr. Ludlow."

Susan did not understand. She did not want to understand but she had no choice. "Did you know him?"

"Yes."

"Who was it?"

"His friend."

"Madrigal?"

Constancia shook her head.

"Who?"

"The tall one," she said angrily; "the one with blue eyes."

Susan held the warm sponge to Constancia's neck, and her fingers felt the water running from it, coursing down the girl's narrow back. She did not know if she could move her hand. She had to speak, but she could not trust her voice. The only thing she seemed certain of was that Constancia did not know. Otherwise, she would not have spoken as she had.

"I see," she said, and her voice sounded rough and hoarse. "I understand."

They went to Constancia's room, and Susan was afraid to look at her, convinced that her own eyes would betray what she knew. Constancia turned away and faced the wall as soon as she got into bed.

"Do you want me to stay? Just tell me," Susan said.

"I want to sleep. That's all." Her voice was hardly more than a whisper.

Susan touched her arm. "If you need me, come to my room. Wake me up. If not, we can talk in the morning."

Mathew was pouring a glass of whiskey when she came into the room and he held the bottle up, silently offering her a drink. She hated whiskey, but she needed courage, so she took the bottle and ignored the glass he held out, tipping it up and wincing at the heat as she swallowed.

"Take it easy," he said, laughing a little.

She looked at him but was not ready to speak. She saw Constancia in her bed, her legs pulled up like a child. While the girl was in the tub she had been on the verge of asking whether she knew how to protect herself, but she could not when she learned that it was Harper, even though that made it all the more important. She could not ask tonight, though she would in the morning. Susan felt stupid. The little that she knew about such things would not fill a thimble.

"Tell me the truth, Mathew."

He looked at her balefully before glancing away.

"You said she was going to Madrigal's."

"Yes."

"But she went to Henry."

"I know. It's complicated."

"You fool!" she shouted. "You idiot!"

"There's no need — "

"Shut up! Mathew, you have no idea what you've done. Why?"

"I didn't see any harm. Henry was taken by her. I didn't think —"

"You didn't think and you didn't know."

"What are you talking about?"

She wanted to scream it out in the hope that the energy demanded of her would calm the revulsion she was feeling more intensely every second, but all she could manage was a whisper.

"Something terrible has happened." She wanted to cry, because the plan that had seemed so right was even more torn and tattered than Constancia's dress. She should have told him. If she had, this would not have happened.

"I couldn't tell you about Constancia because Elizabeth didn't want me to."

"What does she have to do with it?" Mathew said hesitantly.

"Everything."

"You don't have to say anything."

She was disgusted with him for having lied, but that was nothing new, and she could not avoid her own guilt. If she had told him, it would not have happened.

"It's terrible," she whispered.

"You said that."

"Constancia's his daughter. Soledad's child."

Since then Susan had been in her room, staring at the blue stationery on the table beneath the window, robin's egg, her favorite color. The tea she had brought in remained untouched. *"Dear Elizabeth,"* she had written. Then it seemed as if she could not put down another word. But there was no choice. Whether she wrote now or waited for her to return was the only issue, and that was what settled it. She could imagine Elizabeth rushing into her arms with a horrified expression, but she could not imagine her smiling, saying that she had missed her, saying that so many things had happened while she was in the east that she did not know where to begin. It was the coward's way she chose as she sat there, but the only one available to her, so she picked up the pen again. *"You must prepare yourself,"* she wrote. *"There is something terrible I have to tell you."*

Susan found Constancia in the kitchen. The girl looked at her with suspicion.

"I didn't know, Constancia. Please believe me. I'll see to it that he never comes here again. What can I do?"

"Nothing."

"Would you like to go to church?"

Constancia looked at her bitterly. "I never want to see that place again."

"Do you want to be alone?"

Constancia shrugged. "It doesn't matter."

"We could go for a walk," Susan said hopefully.

Constancia looked out the window toward the mountains. She had thought unceasingly of Soledad from the moment Harper left her alone in the guest room. There was only one place she wanted to go.

"You can take me to the mountains."

"If that's what you want. Where?"

"High up. To the painted cave."

It was early afternoon when they passed through the flying bird. Constancia pointed to the images.

"They are older than any of the pictures at the mission, and they are holy."

"The ships?"

"They were made by the *'altomolich.*"

Constancia did not want to say any more, and she was grateful that Susan did not press her for explanations. All she wanted was to sit there and look. This was the one place that could offer some relief from the dirtiness that had not come off when she bathed. She still felt his hands on her and wondered how long it would be before her body forgot, wondered if it ever would.

Much later Susan said that they should start back; Constancia did not mind. She had found a little peace. The pressure of his hands was less distinct, the sound of his breathing less apparent. The painted cave had strengthened her for whatever was coming. She had seen the suns and moons, the spirit ships, and they would guide her.

When they mounted the horses the animals seemed grateful that they were heading down the mountain, following the almost invisible trail that Constancia had found a few years earlier more by instinct than by the directions that had been given her by the old men in the village. From time to time fires raged in the mountains; one of the miracles of the place was that hillsides burned to reddish blackness sprouted new growth. There were places where burned trees stood gaunt against the afternoon sky, black sentinels reminding the women of the catastrophes of only a few years ago. But these shapes were exceptions, and they gave themselves up to the lushness, to the far shapes of the canyons below, the sea, which spread out like a plate of gray glass imprinted with the shapes of the islands.

Halfway down they entered a shallow canyon known to be one of the sites where the old shamans came at night to listen to voices on the wind. Susan and Constancia went that way only because the trail passed through it. Neither of them would have thought to pause; Susan was consumed with worry about Constancia, and Constancia was intent upon the memory of Harper's hands. As they rode on, a monarch butterfly sailed past, the sun glinting on the orange markings of its wings. A little farther down the trail another butterfly appeared, then another and another. They were close enough to a grove to hear the down-canyon winds in the trees.

Then they saw that one of the trees was glowing. It took a moment for Constancia to understand that it was not on fire but was covered with thousands of orange-and-black butterflies, that the shimmering was not the flames of a single tree but the vibrant movement of their bodies and their wings. She had never seen anything like it, and because she wanted to watch, needed to watch, she held out her hand, signaling Susan to stop. In that instant the tree exploded into movement and the colony rose en masse so that the sky above the grove was filled with the rich orange of their wings. In their flight Constancia thought she saw the contours of the spirit ships that sailed on the granite ceiling of the painted cave. Then, in a movement so fast that the eye had no time to follow it, they changed into the shape of a woman's face with trailing hair. She stared, amazed, as the colony rose and the face was scattered in a thousand directions.

# *Four*
# MASKS

# 19

◆ ◆ ◆

The boy who delivered provisions and mail to the Gallaghers heard the hum of voices on his way through the maze of carriages and tethered horses toward the fine old house. Its gables always reminded him of eyes perpetually staring toward the western end of the valley; he was glad when he reached the porch and did not have to look at them anymore. The oblong pane of beveled glass set into the front door framed a crush of people. Tables set up in the middle of the long room were filled with platters of food and tubs of ice that held bottles of champagne. He did not think anyone would hear him knock, but he did anyway, hoping that Mr. or Mrs. Gallagher would see him; he was shy and did not want to go in where he was uninvited.

When no one noticed him, he knocked one more time so hard that his knuckles hurt. He would have turned around and gone back to town if the letter had not been marked *Urgent* with a line underneath to emphasize the word. Since he had no idea what kind of trouble he would be in if he waited until tomorrow, he reluctantly turned the handle and stepped inside. The laughter and scents of food wrapped around him and made him feel good after the cold. Two men sized him up with unfriendly looks, and he decided that if he did not find Mrs. Gallagher soon he would leave the letter on top of the presents piled on a table beside the entry. One of the men was approaching when he saw her across the room; he held the letter over his head, waving it back and forth, and was relieved when she excused herself and came through the crowd.

"I'm sorry, Mrs. Gallagher. I wouldn't of come in except for what it says on this letter."

"That's all right, James," she said as she glanced at the inscription. It was addressed to Elizabeth. The envelope was crumpled on one side, and there was a small tear, as if it had had rough handling. "Goodness knows, you could have stayed out there till you froze before someone heard you. Is there anything else?"

"No, ma'am."

"Well, have some cake before you go. And there's hot cider on the table."

The underscored word made her nervous. For all she knew, something might have happened to Henry or to the house. She looked around for Elizabeth with the idea of giving it to her right away, but some people had come up as she was talking to James, and she was obliged to accept what seemed like the thousandth congratulation on her fiftieth wedding anniversary. As soon as there was a lull in the conversation she craned her neck and saw Elizabeth and Daniel in the far corner of the parlor with a group of people listening to Thomas holding forth from his favorite armchair in the corner. Excusing herself, she squeezed through the crowd. As old Dr. McDermott made room for her, she heard her husband regaling the guests with sea stories. That meant he had been drinking, even though she had pleaded with him to stay sober for her sake as well as the doctor's orders. She glanced at McDermott, whose bushy eyebrows went up and down, as if to say that there was nothing either of them could do.

"How long has he been like this?"

"About half an hour."

When Thomas started drinking, he bored people half out of their minds with stories about narrow scrapes at sea, and then, regularly as clockwork, after a second whiskey he started in on filthy stories about foreign places that made her cheeks burn with embarrassment.

" . . . Marseilles," he said. "Three ladies of the night and a one-armed mate off a French coaster. Even with two hands he'd have been in trouble, but —"

"Thomas!" She would not allow this to go on, not on her anniversary, certainly not in front of people from the church. "You promised!"

He looked up a little bleary-eyed but happy as a lark. His white beard framed a beet-red face, showing that he had had more than two drinks. He winked and smiled at his audience.

"You heard Florence. I guess you'll just have to wait till she's not around. That's a pity, because once he got 'em back to the ship —"

"Thomas Gallagher!"

Daniel circled her with his arm. "It's just getting interesting, Grandma."

"There shouldn't be anything interesting to you, young man!"

He bent down and kissed her on the cheek.

"In case you haven't noticed, I'm grown up. Besides, you know he'll be in a snit if you don't let him finish."

"Now don't start siding with him. He doesn't need any encouragement."

Daniel looked at her affectionately. "It's a good story, Grandma."

"Well," Florence said, "you'll just have to wait until the two of you are alone." Then she caught Elizabeth's eye across the room. When her daughter joined them, she said, "There's something for you, dear. A letter. It says urgent. I hope nothing's wrong with Henry, for heaven's sake."

Elizabeth recognized Susan's handwriting.

"Who's it from?" Daniel asked.

"Susan. She must be bored. She's already written twice."

It did not seem odd to her that *Urgent* was scrawled on the envelope. Susan was always given to dramatic gestures.

"Shouldn't you read it?" Florence inquired.

Elizabeth had asked Susan to keep her abreast of news about Constancia. That, more than the word on the envelope, piqued her interest, but it would be rude to leave the party and find a place quiet enough to concentrate, so she slipped it into her pocket.

"I'll save it for a treat after everybody's gone."

At six o'clock Martha announced that dinner was ready, and everyone lined up for the buffet. Afterward they gathered in the parlor, where Daniel handed each present to his mother, who read the tag and gave the package to her parents. Thomas had sobered up and took it all in stride, but Florence was teary by the time all the presents had been opened and gushed over. Martha served dessert then, and it was well after ten when the last guests offered their final congratulations and went outside to face the first cold night of winter. Thomas had sneaked a cognac or two with his cake, making him unsteady enough to need Florence to help him negotiate the stairs. When Elizabeth volunteered to help, her mother laughed. "I can handle the old reprobate myself. I've been doing it for half a century and I see no reason to stop now."

"Rubbish," Thomas said. "I'm fine." But he missed a step, catching the bannister just in time to keep from falling. "Almost." He laughed. "Well, come on, woman, give me a hand." And he lurched up the stairs beside his wife.

Elizabeth was pleased when Daniel asked her to go into the library for a nightcap. Since he arrived two days earlier, he had seemed a little abstracted. She wanted to talk to him, but her mother had been in a state over the party and there simply had not been a minute for them to be alone. Although she was tired, she thought they could have an hour together before she had to go to bed.

A cheery fire was blazing in the library. After they pulled the maroon wing chairs close to the hearth, she unfastened her shoes and put her feet on the warm footstool.

"This was my favorite place when I was a girl," she said. "I'd curl up here and spend whole afternoons lost in a book, contented as a cat."

"Just like now."

"Yes."

She looked at him affectionately, and he smiled. Then he got up suddenly and took the poker to prod logs that were doing perfectly fine by themselves. Something was bothering him, and she knew immediately that it must have to do with Constancia. Too much had happened at the end of the summer for either of them to absorb. She had expected him to be shocked by the news that he had a sister, but his reaction had been stronger than she had imagined. On the journey east he had begged off discussing it, saying that he needed time to think. As he gave the logs one last poke, she remembered the letter. "Maybe there's some good news from Susan," she said brightly. "Shall I read it?"

He looked quickly at her; then glanced away. "What could be good?"

It was not a question she had anticipated, and nothing came to mind. "Why, any number of things."

"Like she's become an excellent cook?"

"Daniel . . ."

"Or a perfect laundress?"

"What's the matter with you?"

He sat down, moved his feet toward the fire, then pulled them back.

"The situation with the Ludlows is temporary," she said hopefully. "There may be other things."

"Like what?" he said.

She heard the skepticism in his voice, but he seemed willing to listen. "Well, marriage," she answered tentatively. "She's — "

"With her scars?"

"The right man wouldn't care." She spoke defensively, as if to prove a point.

"You aren't being realistic, Mother. Think about it."

The truth of the matter was that she had not thought seriously about what Constancia might do; she was too relieved that she was safe with Susan and Mathew to worry about the future. Besides, she thought, there was progress, regardless of what Daniel said. But her conviction seemed a little tattered around the edges.

"Listen, Mother. There's something I have to get off my chest. I wanted to be here for the party, but I really came to talk to you."

"What in the world about?"

"Remember what I told you Constancia said when we met? That we have unequal lives? I've been thinking about it for the last two months and feeling more guilty every day. I go to my lectures like a good little student and get my brain filled up with Greek and botany and math. By the time I get back to my room, I've forgotten everything. You know what I see when I think about her? A common servant. My sister."

"The Ludlows are wonderful people."

"It wouldn't matter if they were saints. I can't stand it."

"It's better than what she had," Elizabeth said deliberately.

"That's a useless comparison."

When she looked down at her hands he said, "I'm sorry," and got up, standing with his back to the fire. "It's not right." He looked up at her. "He wrote to me."

"Your father?"

"He wants me to consider being his partner after I graduate. I was thinking about leaving Yale and taking him up on his offer so that I could spend time with Constancia. But I've had a better idea."

He paused for a moment, partly to let her prepare herself, partly out of sheer excitement. She studied him with a mixture of surprise and expectation.

"Well?" she asked.

"What would you think of having her come here to stay with Grandma and Grandpa? There are opportunities in the east. People are more broad-minded. I could come to see her. Maybe she could even go to school."

It was the last thing she thought he would say. The idea seemed improbable but not impossible. She had never told him how anguished she had been over Constancia's life, not completely. Now, in the face of his suggestion, her attempt a few minutes ago to put the situation with the Ludlows in the best light seemed pathetic. There was no way to deny that the circumstances of Constancia's life were unpleasant even though she was no longer in the village. She had no idea how the plan could be accomplished practically, no more than she could guess her parents' reaction. It would mean opening her secret life to them. But they were good, decent people. She was, she realized, optimistic.

"I have no idea what they'd say."

Daniel looked relieved. "But you think it might work?"

She thought of Constancia at the Ludlows'. Susan had promised to take care of her. Still . . .

"It just might," she said.

"Well, let me tell you what else I have in mind."

She put out her hand, laughing. "Tomorrow. We can talk about it tomorrow. I'm exhausted."

"Do you want another drink?"

"I should go to bed."

"Well, I'm going to stay up a while," he said. "Maybe we can go for a walk in the morning, if it isn't too cold."

"Yes, I'd like that. Good night."

"Good night, Mother."

Her bedroom on the second floor had remained unchanged from the day she had left on her honeymoon. The framed etchings of English country scenes, the mahogany furniture, the white-skirted dressing table were still there. She imagined Constancia in the room. There was something right about it, appropriate, and that seemed more important than the complexities involved in getting her here. If Constancia came to live in her old room, it would be as if the girl were beginning over again. A new life, Elizabeth thought.

Then she remembered Susan's letter. A late, unseasonal fly buzzed at the window, and she wondered vaguely where it came from. She watched it crawl up the windowpane, making angry sounds before settling on the embroidered loop of the curtain, where it began to wash. Reaching into her pocket, she remembered something about multiple eyes. Confident that there was something in the letter to cheer her, Elizabeth brought the lamp over to the nightstand, plumped the pillows, and settled back. She was looking forward to Susan's gossipy irreverence. As the fly rose from the loop and circled the room, buzzing loudly, she removed the pages and flattened them on her lap with the palm of her hand.

> Please prepare yourself. There's something terrible I have to say. I've thought about it all morning, tried to find the right place to begin, but there's no right place. Now that I've started, I don't know how I can go on. I don't know if I should, if I have the right. In other circumstances I'd ask Mathew for advice, or Fray Sandoval. But — I hardly know how to say it — Mathew is part of it. And after all that happened at the mission, I couldn't bring myself to see the friar, not about this. There isn't time. Either I tell you now, or wait till you come home, and I can't wait. This can't wait. Trust me. I'd want to know. I know I would.

Looking up, Elizabeth saw her reflection in the dressing table mirror. She wondered whether she should put the pages back in the envelope and save them for tomorrow. If Susan was in trouble, she'd need to concentrate. But the warning could be a prelude to more terrible news than she could imagine about Susan or Constancia, even Henry. If she did not read it now, she would worry all night. She reminded herself that Susan always exaggerated; told herself that she was being silly. The fly buzzed around the room and settled again on the loop of the curtain, where it sat motionless, noiseless.

*A few days later she told me everything. She left early one morning. I thought she was going to Madrigal's.*

There was a long paragraph explaining how Mathew had told her about Madrigal needing someone to help around his house for a day, how Susan had resisted and given in only after Constancia said that she was willing to go.

*She said that the change of scene would do her good. She hadn't left the house since we brought her from the village, and I thought it was a good idea. How could I know?*

She read slowly, as if she were walking at night, afraid of stumbling over an unseen obstacle. But then she saw Henry's name, saw Constancia on the driveway leading to the house, and her pace quickened and it was as if she were on a sled going down a slope, feeling the terrible unchecked speed taking her into the house, throwing open doors and windows, leading her to something so horrible that her mind refused to take hold of it. Now Susan's words alternated with Constancia's, which were set off with bold dashes, as if Susan needed to show Elizabeth that she could not have invented this, as if the dashes separating Constancia's words from her own would absolve her of the unspeakable thing that had happened, that was happening again, now, as she read.

Elizabeth uttered a sound that seemed no more connected to who she was than the fly's buzzing, a sound somewhere near a croak. She cut it off; to let it out would be to acknowledge the truth she was vainly trying to banish, as if it were a sick dream that at any moment would let go of her. In one quick movement she threw the pages toward the window. She wanted to scream to make it stop, but she was sobbing now. Her gorge rose, and the sickness came up before she could reach for the chamber pot. Wrenching spasms came and came and came until nothing was left, and she lay back, gasping for air. The fly settled on her lip; when she weakly brushed it away it returned to the loop and that was when she remembered that it had thousands of eyes.

She had no idea how long she lay there before she found the strength to get up and walk unsteadily to the dressing table. She poured a glass of water and drank slowly, focusing on the soothing coolness that dampened the burning of her throat. She looked dumbly at the pages strewn on the floor, at the chair beside the window. Then she sat down heavily, turned the latch, and pushed open the window, welcoming the cold air. The fly buzzed once and flew out the window. For a moment she heard it in the darkness and then there was nothing but silence and the cold. She wanted to run in the hills until she was surrounded by trees and white meadows, but she could not move. All she could do was repeat the terrible sentences, moaning when she realized that she had memorized the words on the blue pages, the rhythms of Susan's voice, Constancia's. She had no volition. She was reduced to two seeing eyes.

When the first light of dawn came upon the sky, she was still there, staring blankly at the violet snow and the black leafless trees striding from the darkness like spectral men marching in a column. It seemed as if she had been forced to see and see again every detail of the letter, as if Henry had sewn her eyelids open so that she could not turn away.

That was how Daniel found her later in the morning after being sent upstairs by his grandmother, who was worried because Elizabeth had not come down for breakfast. She did not answer when he knocked, and then he began to worry. Calling "Mother?" he opened the door and saw her in the chair looking out the window. Only when he asked whether she was all right did she turn and stare at him with wild eyes. Her lips were dry, her skin pale, almost translucent in the morning light. Her hands shook; her whole body was vibrating. He knelt down beside the chair, but when he tried to take her hand she withdrew it slowly, like an old woman.

"What is it? Do you have a fever?"

She closed her eyes, kept them closed for a moment, and her eyelids fluttered when she opened them. Looking over his head, she said, "Leave me alone." Her voice sounded dead.

"But you're sick."

"Please, leave me alone."

He saw the pages strewn on the floor, the bed that had not been slept in.

"Was there something in the letter? Is Constancia all right?"

As he leaned down to retrieve the pages, she made a strange sound deep in her throat.

"What?"

"Don't!" she shouted. "It will ruin you!" She shouted again as he picked up the pages, a sound, not a word. But she knew she could not shelter him, and as he began to read she sank back into the chair, watching, unable to protect him or herself from what was coming.

# 20

◆ ◆ ◆

Elizabeth and Daniel talked quietly beside a scarred table in the station, paying no attention to the gaunt farmer and his wife on the far side of the room and only vaguely aware of the balding drummer leaning against the wall, picking his teeth. When they arrived, the others could not help wondering what had caused the mother's anguish or why they spoke in muted voices, the mother shaking her head slowly, the son looking down at his hands. By the time the coach arrived half an hour later, the drummer had invented a girl in trouble, a quick flight from responsibility. Pushing himself away from the wall, he discarded the toothpick, convinced that the boy was being sent away for his own good. The farmer imagined a crime, his wife a breach between mother and son, none of the three able to conceive of the true source of the pain that had descended three days earlier, after Daniel put down Susan's letter and said in a faltering voice, "We have to go home."

Elizabeth had watched him read, attentive to every nuance in his face. There was an unfamiliar gravity in the way he held himself, as if he were closed off, sealed inside his thoughts like a butterfly in a chrysalis. When he said they had to go back, she shook her head; the thought of entering the house made her feel exposed and vulnerable. But it was not merely dread at the prospect of seeing Henry that had caused her response. During the night she had realized that her house was no longer home. It was only a place where she had lived. She did not want to tell Daniel, but she had to.

"I can't," she said, "not after this. I'd have to see your father. I can't see him, not ever again."

Sickened as Daniel was by what he had read, overwhelmed with disgust and a desire for revenge, it was impossible to imagine confronting Harper alone. It did no good when he realized that pressing her to go would be selfish, that he wanted her there as much for himself as for any comfort she could give Constancia.

"It's your house too," he said tentatively. "You have rights."

"None that I want," she answered wearily.

"She'll need you."

She would. He could sympathize with Constancia, comfort her, but she would need a woman. It was true, he knew, but he had said it to goad her into giving way, said it to protect himself.

"I can't," she repeated. "It would kill me to see him."

She looked helplessly around the room. He felt ashamed. He also was afraid, because she meant what she said. There was absolute conviction in her voice, though she spoke barely loud enough for him to hear. Now the horror of the letter was compounded by a responsibility that seemed impossibly heavy. There were words for his condition, he thought, something he had read in the fall, but he could not remember except that it was in Shakespeare.

"Promise me something," she said.

She was looking at him again; her eyes appeared lusterless and very old. He knew it was settled. There would be no bargaining. He would have to go alone.

"What?" he asked.

"That you will bring her back, get her away from him."

As the coach left the station Daniel hoped that a course of action would present itself during the journey, something that would resolve the rage he felt toward Harper and clarify his own emotions. Once before he had been confronted by a stunning, elemental fact: his father's confession to Don José. He had fled from it, lived with his secret as well as he could. But this was more primal;

this time he could not hide his emotions. It was as if the event in Mexico had been a preparation. It made no difference that he did not want the role, or that he would have to act alone. The disgusting, outrageous truth of what Harper had done to his daughter had changed Daniel's life. Nothing, he thought, nothing will ever be the same again.

When the farmer and his wife tried to engage him in conversation, he smiled weakly and looked out the window. When the drummer began telling jokes, the laughter of the others rang obscenely in his ears. In a while they no longer tried to speak to him, but his presence in the coach was troubling. Obsessed as he was with his father's crime, Daniel was unaware of his effect on his fellow passengers, unaware that at every station where he ate tasteless food and slept in vermin-infested beds, his silence forced people to invent explanations for his anguish. He had no idea how intolerable it was for others to be confronted by his eyes, the wooden stiffness of his body. If a stationmaster had drawn him aside one night, saying, *We cannot endure your misery, tell us what has happened,* Daniel could only have listened, for no words could calibrate feelings such as his, or ease the disquiet of those he traveled with and others who tended him along the way.

By the fifth day, drivers and stationmasters had woven a tapestry of stories compounded of blighted love, loss of faith, an illness in the bones. In Cheyenne, while a blizzard raged, an old man served him whiskey before putting on his mackinaw and going outside, choosing to endure the freezing cold a while rather than look again at the young man whose eyes registered knowledge that should not come to anyone of such a tender age. It was his eyes that caused the stationmaster's wife in Laramie to herd her children into the family quarters when he came inside, keeping them there until the stage was out of sight.

The story that forced such responses came to Daniel day and night, and neither the steady fall of horses' hooves nor the creak of wood was loud enough to drown it out or stop him from imagining himself before Constancia, begging her forgiveness. Hours went by during which he thought of nothing but the moment when he would see his father. His impatience grew day by day, but his desire for the journey to be over did not speed the endless travel, did not alter the slightest breeze, did nothing to open roads made impassable by snowdrifts or mend shattered tongues and axles. Weeks had to pass before the coach's wheels spun across the mountains to Santa Fe, where the sun was setting behind the Sangre de Cristo range, and the valley turning purple in the dusk offered an intimation of the sea. He dreamed of its blueness that night, saw it in his mind's eye as the coach sped south the next morning past San Ildefonso until there was only the road again, straight and smooth as an arrow pointing toward the plains of Albuquerque and beyond them to the sea.

Until it happened, Constancia had reveled in her newfound privacy and was almost content. In the Ludlows' house there were no bickering girls, no women who talked in their sleep, no disconsolate widows crying out in their nightmares. Instead of bunk beds, the matron's stern face, and the door slammed shut by Mariano, there was a single bed covered with a pretty blanket, her own decision about what to do, a door to whose lock she possessed the only key. Small as the room was at the southern end of the rambling house, it seemed like a kingdom.

Afterward she was in an agony waiting to discover whether she was pregnant. When her blood came and washed away the fear, there was still an inescapable feeling that he had stolen her will, and she was not certain that she would ever feel strong again.

Afterward she dreamed of how he stole her strength, of the way he had unfastened his belt, torn her dress, descended, the look of the windows when she stopped struggling and pleading that she did not want this.

Before it happened she was one thing, afterward another. In some fundamental way the person she was had ceased to exist. When she dreamed, she was this other woman who rose from the bed in the house where it happened, this other woman who hurried through the dark unfamiliar hall, down the stairs, and started across the open fields. There was no sensation of the earth beneath her feet, no feeling of grass and stones. Nothing at all. When she looked down, her dress moved like a ghost across the fields, its hem advancing, curving around her absent ankles, the sleeves moving rhythmically to the swinging of her invisible arms, her torn bodice flapping back and forth, revealing only space, only empty air where her breasts should have been.

Before it happened she wakened only after the sun came through the window whose curtain was never drawn because the view of the sea was a novelty to someone who had slept in a closed room for so many years.

Afterward she woke in the dark, afraid to move for fear that she had no body. She lay still for a long time, looking out the window at the sea, telling herself that it was only a dream, that he could not make her disappear, saying it over and over until her panic began to fade and she slowly filled her skin with bones and muscles. When her body returned, she began work in the silent house. She had to do things, had to be in constant motion; otherwise, she would think about her dreams.

On the morning after she had gone with Susan to the painted cave, she was polishing the cherrywood table in the parlor, trying to concentrate on the look of the furniture because it was not human, bore no relationship to him. Susan came in; Constancia glanced up and continued working. Although she wanted to talk, vent her feelings, she knew that she would cry and that would only make things worse. Her rage was voiceless, it seemed, her humiliation hollow as the empty dress. "Good morning," she said quietly as Susan crossed the room.

"Is there anything I can do?" Susan asked.

Constancia shook her head.

"It will be better in time," Susan said reassuringly.

Constancia continued rubbing the shiny surface of the table, turning her head a little so that Susan did not have to see the scars.

"I've been thinking," Susan went on. "Henry —" She laughed, cutting the word off quickly. "Mathew, I mean Mathew —" Susan made the shift casually, and when Constancia continued rubbing the table she believed that it had been successful. "Mathew suggested —"

She did not complete the sentence, because Constancia looked up, leaning on her hands. Though there was only a faint uncertainty in Constancia's eyes, not even suspicion yet, Susan could not carry off the deception. She felt herself blush; she looked away, but it was too late.

"Henry?" Constancia pronounced the name hesitantly, for her mind had not quite caught up with her emotions. "Elizabeth's *husband?*"

Susan tried to smile, but her mouth was like a cut across her face.

"Mathew," she said stiffly. "I meant Mathew. I don't know what's wrong with me this morning."

"Henry?" Constancia repeated incredulously.

Susan's eyes welled with tears. "God forgive me."

"You know who he is?" Constancia asked.

Susan refused to look at her as she slowly nodded.

"My *father?*"

The word sounded ugly. He was not a real father, she told herself, not truly, but that did not lessen the shock or the revulsion. She was not afraid of the taboo; she was afraid of the absence of rules, decency.

"Did he know?" she asked quickly.

Susan reached for her hand, but Constancia pulled it away. "Did he?"

"He couldn't have," Susan whispered. "Nobody . . ."

Constancia closed her eyes. Her heart was beating the way it had when he trapped her. It was worse now. It made no difference that he was ignorant of who she was. She threw the cloth on the table and started out the door.

"Where are you going?"

She did not answer as she headed toward the patio. For a moment she thought of running into the fields, but she felt sick when she got outside and sat down heavily on the bench. Susan appeared in the doorway, and Constancia turned away, saying, "Leave me alone." She remembered the first time he came, when Mathew had made her clean the birds, remembered the way he looked at her, the way he acted, as if she belonged to him. She had never thought of revenge after Mariano whipped her. There were too many of them, and she had eaten her hatred silently. But this was different, this was worse. She would not be still anymore. She looked out to the fields, thinking about herself and her mother and Henry.

A few days later there was a festival at the mission. Booths festooned with colored ribbons lined the curving driveway; women sold sweets and handiworks while Fray Humberto's orchestra played in the portico. On the access road behind the fields men challenged each other to horseraces. Friars wandered among the booths, or watched the races, but Fray Santos did not join them, having been ill for some time. Lights had been flashing in his eyes since dawn. They had been bright and vivid during Mass and continued afterward, when he prostrated himself in the nave, as had been his daily custom since his interview with Fray Velásquez. As he lay there praying a numbness crept into his legs and arms; he was unable to move for a while. When his strength returned, he made his way to the path behind the church, ignoring the racers. The walk up the canyon was painful, and several times a darkness came upon his left eye.

For a week now he had been troubled by the lights and numbness, but as he rested on the bench the tingling eased and soon the brightness went away, and he could watch the blossoms coming down on a gentle breeze. Clouds showed through the branches of the trumpet tree, and the double flight of clouds and flowers was a balm to the grief and humiliation that had become his lot. The flowers broke from their stems, and each time one parted from a branch it seemed to make a tiny metallic sound, a single note that joined in a melody as it fell with the others in a rain of petals that brushed his face and formed a garland on his shoulders. They came down without a pause, a steady stream of flowers floating to him as gently as butterflies. In a while it seemed that he too was falling, not through the air but through the lies that had been told, the slanders, the misunderstanding of his desire. The flashing lights returned;

numbness crept along his arms. As his body began to shake he saw the picture once again, saw learned men discoursing in a Roman archive that held the feather dress, heard voices reciting the sentences of his letter. A coyote barked far up the canyon. Looking up through the lights and falling flowers, Fray Santos thought he saw Soledad standing in the bow of Harper's ship, arms outstretched as if in greeting. He made a strange guttural sound, all that was left of speech, to signify the horror of confusing her with the Paraclete.

At eleven o'clock two lovers met behind the church and hurried up the path leading to the canyon, the girl running ahead, stopping long enough for the young man to catch up before going on with the intention of teasing him into a fine agony. Once they reached the woods above the dam, she disappeared into the trees and the young man followed her into the shade, where he kissed her hair and cupped his hands over her breasts, expecting her to sigh. Instead, she screamed and pointed to the clearing. Fray Santos was slumped against the bench, hands folded, his rosary dangling from one limp finger. She did not scream because of his posture, or even because he was dead. She screamed because the agony of having conflated his Savior with Soledad still registered in his eyes. For a moment the lovers stood there, pinioned by what they saw. Then they ran all the way back to the mission, reporting what they had seen to everyone they knew.

Harper listened impassively when the news reached Esteban's. Later O'Reilly came in drunk and with a wicked gleam in his eyes. The Irishman stopped a few feet away, but Harper ignored him, concentrating on his cards.

"So that's it, is it? Too good to drink with me? Aye, that's it in a nutshell," he said as his voice trailed off in a whine. "Too good for old O'Reilly."

"Go back to your hole," Harper snapped.

"Oh, yes, treat me like a mangy cur. Too good to drink with me," O'Reilly repeated, looking for support among the others. Finding none, he went on, "But he wasn't too good to sail with. No, nor once to listen to." He waited for an answer, and when Harper refused the bait he drew himself up in injured dignity. "You got that squaw from me, squire, you and the friar what's dead. If that ain't worth gratitude, what is?"

Harper stood up, hoping that he would not have to hit him, but prepared to if it was necessary. He flexed his hands, waited.

"You should heed signs when they come, squire. It was the ghost woman killed your priest, sucked his heart out while it was still rattling, like savages will do." He paused, measuring the effect of his words. "Like she sucked the marrow out of you, I'll wager."

Harper grabbed him by the collar, tightening his grip as he pushed him toward the door.

"Leave," Harper said through his teeth, "or you'll get hurt."

"Oh, I'll leave, all right. O'Reilly never asks for pain. But mark my words. She's cursed. She damned him, and she'll damn you too."

Shoving O'Reilly outside, Harper waited in case he tried to come back, but the swinging doors slowed and stopped. When Harper returned to the table Whitby said, "You should have belted him, Henry."

"With a head like that? I'd have broken my hand, and then how could I fleece your lambs?"

# 21

───◆◆◆───

Late in the afternoon of the thirty-fifth day of Daniel's journey, the coach crested San Ysidro ridge. He could scarcely believe that no more immeasurable distances lay ahead, that he had finally reached the end of the road plummeting to the west. But it was true. The mission's towers showed bright in the setting sun; there was a clear view of the familiar streets, the curve of the bay, the fall of the mountains. The sun's last light still held in the sky above the town, transforming a few stray clouds to the iridescent pink of abalone shells in firelight. Daniel's view of the sunset was restricted by the confines of the coach, but people who happened to be outside that evening talked for days afterward about the extraordinary play of light that made a mirror of the sky, reflecting town and bay and then briefly but vividly the shape of a ship that seemed almost too precise to be an illusion.

His body still moved forward with phantom motion when he descended from the coach and hired the drayman to take him home. On the way through town the man tried to strike up a conversation, but Daniel pleaded fatigue. His kidneys ached from the jarring ride. He had slept fitfully, if at all, in the stations along the way. As he crossed the country he had considered what he might do, considered and rejected possibility after possibility until he was thoroughly confused by the time he had reached Los Angeles. But his thought had sharpened as the coach went north, and by the time he reached Point Dume and saw the sea, a new idea had taken hold of his imagination, one that chilled his soul. He tried to ignore it, deliberately looking away from the sea at the rolling brown hills to the east, but he still saw the sea and the idea would not let go.

Now, as the wagon turned north off Main Street, his home appeared in the distance, a vague white presence in the dusk. The house was like a talisman for his idea. He resisted letting it form into words, expand into a plan, because it frightened him, made him feel as if he were crossing a boundary, had, perhaps, already crossed it. He thought: Something else will occur to me, something less dangerous. Besides, he reasoned, there were more immediate things to attend to. He did not know whether to rejoice or despair over the darkness that greeted him; the reprieve only put off the moment when he and his father would meet, the moment he had anticipated and dreaded for over a month. As soon as the drayman unloaded his things, Daniel paid and went up the stairs.

Entering the house, it occurred to him that he might wait in the darkness and spring on Harper when he came in, beating him within an inch of his life. He had imagined a fight on the way west, remembering his victory over Henderson a year ago. He stood in the hall for a minute. The prospect pleased him; he imagined the satisfaction of the blows, the quick sounds of pain, the things he might say as he struck him. "This is for Constancia. And this." But he knew that a fight would be futile; there was more at stake than could be settled by a brawl. Bruises would heal; a broken jaw would mend. There would be no justice in bruises and fractures. He was tense from thinking about fighting, and as he forced himself to relax, to conserve his energy, the idea that had come to him earlier reasserted itself. He began to consider it when a sound came from the direction of the road. Anxious and belligerent, he waited, but the beat of hooves diminished. Whoever it was passed to the north.

He sat down in the dark parlor determined to stay awake, but fatigue reached into his bones. The next thing he knew the clock was striking three. Groggy as he was, he realized that his father was spending the night elsewhere. He was surprised that he had not thought of the possibility earlier. Harper frequently gambled all night at Esteban's, returning bleary-eyed and drunk while he and his mother were having breakfast.

His room was at the back of the house, its windows looking away from the road. He lighted the lamp and removed the folder from his desk, spreading the sketches on its surface. As he brought one after the other into the pooled lamplight, coyotes called in the distance, their voices brought from the canyons on a faint wind. His mother's talent was even more rudimentary than he remembered, but the sketches could have been as crude as those of a child, and they would still have enlivened his imagination. He studied them for a long time, seeing Constancia and his father as well as Soledad. His stomach tightened with anger as he put the sketches back in the folder and returned it to the drawer.

Constancia was carrying a basket of laundry to the far end of the Ludlows' house when a horse appeared on the road. Putting three clothespins between her teeth, she began to hang the sheets, watching over the top of the line. When she recognized Daniel she could not believe it. She had thought Elizabeth might return because of Susan's letter. It had never occurred to her that Daniel would. He had to know; there was no other explanation. She placed the last pin on the line, ducked under the sheets, and waited, her feelings edged with suspicion, her face set in a hard, protective mask. She felt the scars pull tight as he approached, but when he waved she relaxed a little. She felt like crying when he dismounted and came to her slowly, not knowing quite what to do. He looked terrible, as if he had not slept in days.

"You know?" she asked.

He nodded. "I'm so sorry. I started as soon as I found out. How are you?"

"I'm all right." She was in control again. Happy as she was to see him, her anger took a fresh turn; she had forgotten how much he resembled Harper. Before she could say anything else, Susan rushed out of the house.

"When did you get back?" Susan asked.

"Last night."

"Did your mother come too?"

"No. She couldn't." He glanced quickly at Constancia. "It had nothing to do with you."

"I had to tell her," Susan said. "Is she all right?"

"No. It was a shock. It will take time."

"Oh, God," Susan said, pressing her hands together.

"It was the right thing to do," Daniel said reassuringly. "We're grateful."

Susan looked at them. "Go inside," she said softly. "I'll leave you alone."

On the way to the ranch Daniel had thought of a dozen things to say. He had imagined tears, even hysteria, a suffering victim. But with Constancia sitting quietly at the other end of the sofa, he felt tongue-tied, almost shy. He had miscalculated her strength — that much was clear — though the rape was there in her eyes, bright as a bird against the sky.

"I want to help," he said tentatively, "to take care of you. Mother and I decided . . ."

"How?" Constancia said suddenly. "What can you do?"

"Protect you."

She laughed. She couldn't help it. She had never heard anything so silly in her life.

Daniel looked at her questioningly.

"You don't understand?" she asked, her voice tightening. "Remember what I said when we met?"

"That's all I've been thinking about since I went back to school."

She started to say something but he put up his hand. "Let me finish. Mother and I want you out of here; we want you to come back east. My grandparents . . . ours . . . have a big house."

Her eyes softened. "Thank you," she said. The formality of her answer sounded ludicrous. "I belong here. This is were I live. I want to be near my mother." Then, "Is that the only reason you came?"

He wanted to know what she meant about Soledad, and he would have asked if her voice had not been so insistent.

"I intend to deal with Father."

"Good," she said. "Tell me how."

"There are ways. Something occurred to me this morning."

The idea was clear as an object in sunlight. But now that he was on the verge of telling her, his fear returned. Regardless of what he had done, Harper was still his father. He looked away. "I'm not sure . . ."

She watched his lips, waiting for him to go on.

"This isn't easy," he said.

"So nothing will come of it?"

"Constancia . . ."

"He can do this?" she said incredulously.

"No, damn it, but he's my father. Yours," he added quietly.

"I'm your sister! I was a virgin, Daniel. No man had ever touched me."

It made him sick to think of his father and Constancia.

"This is for you to decide," he said wearily. "What do you want?"

"Revenge!" she cried. "I want him to suffer." Then she paused. "Remember, he did the same to my mother."

He did not need to be reminded.

They crossed the fields to a grassy bluff shaded by oaks. The curve of the land was visible all the way to town. The sea was calm and glassy. Haze obscured the islands. As the afternoon wore on, the tree's shadow moved left to right, the sea brightened, and later the haze lifted to reveal the islands. Sometimes Constancia looked at the sea, but most often she watched Daniel as he talked. He had seemed much younger than she when they first met, unfinished in a boyish way. As the plan unfolded she understood why he had been reluctant to tell her about it, why it had been necessary to goad him. There was a sorrow in his eyes and it lay upon his voice, affecting every syllable. What their father had done to her had affected him far more than she expected. She had been too angry when he arrived to judge the depth of his response. But she saw it now and realized that she could trust him.

It was still light outside when Daniel had heard the front door open and went down the upstairs hall to the head of the stairs. Harper looked up, as startled as if he had seen a ghost.

"Well, I'll be damned!" Harper said. "What are you doing here?"

Daniel was prepared to say anything that would sustain the illusion that he was happy to be home. But there was no suspicion on Harper's part, only the searching look of a man who has come upon something unexpected.

"I wanted to surprise you," Daniel answered. "Mother told me to write, but I said no." Then he took a deep breath and descended the stairs. "I've decided to take you up on your offer."

After that the lies came easily. His reasons for abandoning his studies marshaled themselves, explanation giving rise to explanation until it was clear that Harper believed that the pull of the sea had brought him home, that the sea had a greater purchase on his imagination than books or teachers.

When they had eaten dinner and discussed the business, Harper said that they would have some time to themselves, since the schooner was not commissioned until the end of the month.

"That gives us a few weeks to go over things. Not that there's much you don't know. Is there anything you want to do?"

"Remember your offer to take me sailing?"

Harper smiled. "I've been thinking of something along those lines myself. Where do you want to go? We could head up to Moro Bay."

"Maybe later. If it's all right, I'd like to see the islands, maybe go out to San Nicolás."

# 22

◆ ◆ ◆

There was no haze that morning, no low-lying banks of fog; the islands were perfectly outlined against the sky. After storing their provisions Harper took the tiller, but Daniel insisted on doing the sailing, and his father gladly acquiesced. It was not often that he had an opportunity to enjoy the sea without having to reckon with it, so he took a seat in the bow as Daniel slipped the painter, and they set off in a light southwesterly breeze. Settling back to enjoy the first leg of the voyage, Harper succumbed to the pleasure of thinking about what they would name their enterprise, narrowing the possibilities to Harper and Son and Harper and Harper, favoring the latter because it sounded more professional.

An hour passed before they skirted the southern tip of Anacapa and San Nicolás asserted itself against the sky, another before its cliffs became defined. Harper had sailed by many islands, had passed the Faralons off San Francisco a dozen times, negotiated the tricky currents off the wooden isles of the San Juan de Fuca Strait, but none affected him like this outrider in the chain. He did not know whether it was the rusty color of the cliffs or their peculiar shapes that retrieved the past, but his experiences there came back in a rush. He remembered the silence when he first caught sight of Soledad in the field of wildflowers, the incessant wind, visiting his memories the way archeologists explore ancient sites, with a blend of fascination and nostalgia. To his surprise, he found that he regretted what had happened with Soledad; he should have left her alone. He shook his head as he recalled his visits to the bunkhouse, excusing them as the inescapable need of a young man's flesh. When he thought of the child a twinge of regret came on him. Although sending her away had been necessary, he did not consider himself to be a heartless man.

Until Daniel felt the current strengthen and was obliged to concentrate on keeping the boat on course, he had been free to study his father; he hoped that he could penetrate his mind, bore into it as a miner cuts through rock. He was desperate to know what Harper was thinking. What he wanted more than anything in the world was a sign of guilt, some trace of remorse that might allow him to turn the boat into the wind and sail for home. He would welcome Harper's startled expression, his question about what had got into him, confident that he could invent a dozen explanations. But his father's skull was obdurate as stone; Harper watched the island without a word and without a gesture.

As they drew closer to the island the current seemed to grasp the keel with pale green hands. It took all of Daniel's skill to guide them past the bay where sea elephants basked in the sun, regarding the boat's passage. A great male rose up, then another. Daniel thought they would enter the water, but they only watched before slowly sinking back, their flesh melting into the sand.

While they were crossing the channel, the island had seemed dormant, almost an object of contemplation, but it asserted itself as they ran parallel to the cliffs and entered a great shadow cast upon the water. Strange plants clung to the sheer face of the iron-stained cliffs. The scent of the sea was different from any he had known; harsher, more pungent, old. The air came alive with the cries of gulls when they passed into the sun. Cormorants and a species of sea bird he did not recognize joined in the jubilation, their bright treble notes forming a counterpoint to the waves crashing against the rocks: a polyphonic music one never heard on land. Daniel had spent the last three nights studying charts, memorizing depths and positions of rocks and shoals. When they entered the mouth of the cove he was sure of himself, confident of his seamanship. But he had overlooked one thing. He had made no accommodation for his feelings, had not suspected that there would be a reservoir of filial regard, a sudden, acute awareness that he was Harper's son. Compared with navigating *that* boundary, the challenge presented by the rocks was child's play. He had miscalculated the price that would be exacted for his plan; it made no difference that Harper had brought it on himself.

"Nicely done," Harper said as he turned and smiled approvingly. With a vague gesture to the south, he added, "That's where she jumped from the ship. Crazy, but she did it."

Daniel imagined Soledad flying through the air. "She had no choice," he answered.

Harper looked at him closely, then turned away, presenting his profile against the sky. He had assumed an uncharacteristic pose, lips slightly pursed, thumb and forefinger pulling at the corners of his mouth.

"It cost her ten years." He shook his head as if in emphasis. "There's something about this place . . ."

Daniel wanted his father to go on, hoping that he would add something crude, make a joke, say anything that was more in character, because that simple phrase, spoken guilelessly, had touched him, brought back a faint memory of what Harper had said the night before they left for Mexico and in doing so provided an unwanted glimpse of Harper's humanity. It made no difference that he knew his sentimental response was a final gesture to deflect himself from his purpose; Harper's words had touched his conscience. To counter his guilt he forced himself to remember the sketch of the rope descending from the gazebo's roof, to hear again what Constancia said his father had done. Her words were clear and bitter as the boat struck sand.

"Hand me those bags," Harper said, standing knee-deep in the water. Daniel lifted them from the bottom, passed them to his father, and stepped out. Then he reached for the others.

"We'll only be here a night," Harper said.

"I might need something," Daniel answered flatly.

On the beach Daniel dropped his bags. Harper removed a flask, took a long drink, and handed it to Daniel, who accepted without a word.

"We camped up there," Harper said, pointing to the grassy bluff.

"What were you thinking?"

"When we got here?" Harper asked.

Daniel nodded hopefully.

"That they were dead. After I saw the place, I hoped they were."

"And when you found her?"

Harper regarded him with amusement. "You're full of questions."

"I'm interested in what happened."

"Well, nothing much, so far as I remember. We knew she was alive from the prints we'd seen. She looked like the Indians at home, except for her dress." He laughed a little. "She insisted on taking that totem your mother keeps in her room, but Santos made a fuss. I told her to do it anyway, just to irritate him. He'd got on my nerves. If you want, I'll show you the village after a while."

Daniel's heart was racing, trying to escape his chest.

"Why not now?" he said, aware that he was a coward, looking for an excuse to put off what he had to do, what he had promised Constancia. But his promise was an abstract thing, a meaningless idea compared with his father's innocence, his ignorance. "I'd like to see it while there's still good light," he added.

"In a while," Harper said. "Let's set up camp first."

Daniel tried to control himself. He was close to panicking. "If that's what you want," he answered, hearing the edge in his voice and aware that Harper had noticed too.

"Are you all right?" his father asked.

"A little tired," he lied. "It's a long way out here."

"Well, let's get started. You can rest afterward."

"Go on," Daniel said. "I'll catch up. There's something in the boat."

"Up there," Harper said, pointing toward the bluff as he slung two bags over his shoulder.

Daniel watched his father until he was halfway up the slope.

Then he took one step backward, and another, walking backward for ten or fifteen paces before he turned quickly and ran down the beach, his eyes burning, scarcely knowing whether his tears were for himself or Harper, for Constancia or his mother or Soledad. Stumbling through the shallow water, he pushed until the boat came loose from the bottom. He climbed in and quickly raised the sail. The tiller was smooth and polished from years of handling; he could not bring himself to touch it. He did not want to look back, either, but he had to. Harper was watching, his face blank with surprise. A swell rocked the boat and Daniel reached for the tiller, moving it to the right so that he could run parallel to shore. Harper was coming down now, yelling at him.

"What the hell are you doing?" Harper called.

Daniel watched him across the water, his emotions divided between outrage and dismay. Harper stood there, clearly baffled. There had been something almost jocular in his question, but as Daniel waited he saw a flicker in his father's eyes. Apprehension, he thought, not knowledge. "What does it look like?" Daniel answered evenly. He wished that he could prolong the uncertainty, make him suffer, but his anger was rising now, demanding. "I'm leaving, you bastard!"

Shocked, Harper's head went back as if recoiling from the insult. Then his eyes narrowed, taking on an expression Daniel recognized. "Now hold on," Harper said authoritatively. It was the voice of a father about to admonish an errant son, but Daniel cut him off. "I know what happened with Soledad!" he yelled. "And with my sister!"

Harper stared.

"That's right," Daniel said, his voice breaking. "Ludlow's girl! Constancia!"

There was total confusion in Harper's face. "But . . ." he said. Daniel waited, willing for a moment to let his father speak. Instead of going on, Harper glanced away. His eyes were full of anger when he turned back, and perhaps a glimmer of fear.

"This is for both of them," Daniel said. "I'll come back when you understand."

"Now wait a minute," Harper shouted, but he spoke too late. Afraid that his resolve might give way if he looked at Harper any longer, Daniel let the wind fill the sail. It blew from the east, carrying faint scents of trees and flowers, but as the boat headed into the channel the island's scents were left behind, and soon there was only the sound of the bow hissing through the water.

The wharf was already casting long shadows across the bay when Constancia reached town. Two hours later, as the sun was sinking to the horizon and the water was turning pink, she saw the sail. Gripping the railing, she waited for the boat to reach the bay. She heard the hollow sound of footsteps as Daniel climbed the ladder fixed to a piling. He reached the top rung and accepted her hand and stepped unsteadily onto the wharf.

"Now he knows," he said.

His face was agonized. When she saw that he was shaking, she took off her *rebozo* and wrapped it around his shoulders. She took his arm and they headed toward the beach.

They rode through the town, looking straight ahead, ignoring people on the sidewalk, the lights in the doctor's office, Pepita standing in the alley and casting a quick glance at them before searching the street for the night's first customer. They said nothing until they reached the house and crossed the meadow to the gazebo. Constancia knew that it had cost him more than he had expected. Much as she hated the idea, she was willing to give him a chance to change his mind.

"You could go back in a few days," she offered tentatively.

"No," he answered. "He stays. There are provisions for two months; more if he's careful."

# 23

◆ ◆ ◆

When Daniel climbed into the boat and raised the sail, Harper thought it was some kind of joke, but as he descended the embankment and shouted, he began to feel uneasy. Harper could see the anger in his son's eyes and something else, an inexplicable pain. He still believed it was a joke; then he heard "sister" and "Constancia."

He became aware of a singular sensation, as if an insect were crawling on his heart. The meaning of the words hovered before him as the boat moved to the mouth of the cove. A moment later it struck. His heart thudded against his chest. He breathed from the top of his lungs, taking short, rapid gasps as he saw the boat reach the invisible line connecting the points of the cove.

*Ludlow's girl.*

*Constancia.*

*This is for both of them.*

The words held in the air. Harper could neither ignore their sound nor shut his eyes against the pictures they made. He stood there watching, listening. *I would not have touched her if I had known.*

"How did you know?" he shouted after his son, though there was no way the boy could hear.

Daniel sailed into the sun; boy and boat were silhouetted as they neared the bright track of light on the sea. Harper averted his eyes from the blinding light. Taking in the shape of the cove, the rise of the island, circling gulls, he grasped for the idea that had come to him only moments ago as if it were a buoy that would keep him from sinking.

*I did not know.*

He tested his ignorance against the first time he saw her, against Ludlow's answers to his questions and the way she looked cleaning the birds. He remembered her standing at his door weeks later, her expression when he entered the guest room.

*I did not know. I could not have known.*

His ignorance would save him, pulling him from danger as surely as if he were in the water and someone had reached down and taken hold of him with strong hands.

*I would not have touched her.*

He saw himself and Constancia as if he were looking through a peephole in one of the rooms at Los Murales, saw the two of them depicted in a mural. The images were extraordinarily clear. There was no protection in ignorance. He had crossed an unspeakable boundary.

Retreating up the beach, he asked himself how Daniel knew. He wondered how Constancia had got to the Ludlows, whether they knew who she was. It occurred to him that Elizabeth might have had something to do with it, but he dismissed the idea. He would have known. Her mind had always been transparent to him.

The only plausible explanation was that Constancia had talked. She had ignored her own self-interest and talked to Susan Ludlow. *That* was how Daniel knew. When the boy returned he would tell him that he had never set eyes on Constancia after she was born. There was no way he could have known who she was. Any minute now Daniel would tire of his little game and tack for shore.

But the boat did not turn. It ran to sea, gathering speed on the freshening wind. Harper cursed. He was angry but unafraid. There was enough food for weeks. That was why Daniel insisted on bringing everything ashore. He had thought it all out in advance! Daniel's lies were something to take hold of, counterweights to his own guilt. He tried matching the two acts in his mind, his own mistake and Daniel's subterfuge, assigning values to them, but he could not escape the sting of remorse. He tried to focus on the distinction as he watched a flight of pelicans skimming the cove on motionless wings.

The path to the village was obliterated by tenacious plants, but he remembered the way. As he carried the bags of provisions he imagined Soledad in her feather dress. He could not help glancing at the fork of the tree where she had lashed the totem.

Sage shimmered in the mottled sun lighting the common. He had expected to find the village in a final stage of decay. The other huts had been consumed by rot, but Soledad's was almost intact, tilted a little to one side, like a child's drawing of a house. As he stepped through the entrance of the hut a snake slithered past; there was a rustling of mice. He had planned to stay there. Now the idea gave him the shudders. He could not abide the thought of creatures running across his chest while he slept. Stepping outside, he set to work clearing a patch of ground. He cursed Daniel again and began mulling over what he would say when the boy returned.

After eating some jerky and hardtack, he unrolled blankets, built a fire, and lay back. It had grown cold and he was pleased by the warmth. He was confident that the bags of provisions had been a rhetorical gesture. Daniel would return in a day or two. Until then, he would make the best of it, pretend that he was on a hunting trip.

Stars showed through the branches of the trees. The underside of their branches glowed pale yellow, reflecting the fire. He had never seen so many stars, nor had they ever seemed so far away. Uneasiness seemed to descend from their erratic pulse and glow as he tried to remember whether anything might have given him a clue to who Constancia was. He wanted to believe that her scars had masked any resemblance to Soledad, but that was not quite true. He saw the girl and her mother, penumbral presences in the night, clear enough for him to recognize the shape of their eyes and the roundness of their faces. There was, he realized, an unmistakable similarity, and as he wondered why he had failed to notice it, he told himself that it was the passage of all those years after he and Morales cut her down. He refused to blame himself for his desire. Besides, in some part of the girl's mind she had to know what might happen. It was commonplace. Convincing as the argument seemed, there was no lessening of his discomfort, no dilution of either shame or disgust as he watched the fire burn down to embers.

Darkness settled in. The rhythm of the surf came to him, and indeterminate sounds from the woods. Soon he was dreaming of sailing through the sky. Planks groaned and wind whistled in the rigging, but there was no water, only black air and the ship falling through it, plummeting. Soledad was standing in the prow, her hair flowing on the wind. Her dress was made of thin black snakes coiled around each other in a strange design. I have waited for you, she said. We will live here forever. He sat up with a start, unaware of where he was. When he remembered, he decided that first thing in the morning he would go to the cove and wait.

Daniel did not return that day, nor the next, nor the day after.

Each morning Harper spent hours on the beach. Each afternoon, discouraged and frustrated, he wandered off to explore the island. Once he paused on the ridge, certain that he saw a sail in the distance. When it became a gull he thought of revenge, imagined beating Daniel, disinheriting him, driving him from the house. As for Constancia, there were other punishments that seemed appropriate, and he let them play out in his mind, unashamed. It was she who had brought this on him, after all.

Near the end of the first week strange noises came from the margins of the woods, followed by the barking of wild dogs. He felt the ground beside his blankets for a stone and threw it in the direction of the sound. Satisfied that he had frightened them away, he got up and lashed the food bags in the crotch of a nearby tree. The precaution made him feel in control, but when he lay down again he could not stop thinking about the surprising lightness of the bags. He tried to cheer himself up with the thought that he would not be there long. Daniel had said he would come back.

In the morning he crouched beside the fire, inspecting the dogs' tracks; he scratched his scalp, ran his fingers through his beard. The dogs watched on the far side of the clearing; he stared back. They looked at one another for a long time before the larger one whined and they both disappeared into the woods.

During the days that followed he began thinking about the arbitrariness of time. Hours, days, and weeks were at odds with island time, which was only a continuum of darkness and light, light and darkness. At home he had worked from dawn to dusk. There was an orderly routine of accomplishment, pleasure, sleep, a progression marked by clocks. Now that his occupation was reduced to waiting, there seemed to be no distinction between one day and the next.

He watched the tide wash rhythmically onto the sand, recede, wash up again. It seemed as if he were losing something of himself whenever the spent waves returned to the sea. He picked up a piece of driftwood and began to make a calendar in the sand of the days since Daniel left. He inscribed six lines, drew a cross through them, and then dropped the stick. It seemed that he had lost count. He watched the waves roll into shore, wash up, wash up again, and with each wave his fear increased. What if Daniel did not return? The froth formed lacy patterns on the sand; the bubbles broke and disappeared. Standing up, he scuffed his foot across the calendar and set out briskly down the beach.

That night he dreamed that the island was a great chronometer encased in a crystal bell. He walked among the parts, admiring the precision of the wheels and springs and counterweights, the bright white face haloed by Roman numerals. Whirling wheels and ratcheting levers turned an axle in the center of the dial, but there were no hands, only a steady ticking, a mute whir and click of metal parts.

Until the dream he had been able to fall asleep immediately, sometimes not waking until the sun was overhead. Afterward he became an insomniac, waking with a start soon after lying down and staring into darkness. He tried to believe that he was too sensitive to the sounds of the island, but he knew it was a lie. The empty sea had banished sleep. When he looked at himself in the pool where he gathered fresh water, he saw a haggard man.

One night, frustrated and a little drunk, he put on his heavy jacket and left the village for the beach. The moon was up. He would walk until he was tired. Then he would be able to sleep.

Since the tide was out, he skirted the promontory, and in a little while he reached the western coast. The cliffs were gentler here; the moon was very beautiful and the beauty drew him on. He walked for half an hour before noticing that the beach in the distance glowed more brightly than the strands he had passed along the way. It was not the color or the brightness so much as the strange shapes that held his interest. The beach was studded with them, and though he was far away he could tell that no two were alike. The shapes disturbed him, but he went on out of curiosity. By the time he had gone another hundred yards he saw that he had come upon a marvelous thing, a vast graveyard of white memorials. He went forward slowly, sober now, apprehensive, certain that he had found a grove of granite stones, tablets, columns carved into unearthly totemic shapes. Only when he was ten feet from the nearest one, an outrider set apart from the others, did he realize that it was not a cemetery. The shapes were natural, a petrified forest that extended for a quarter of a mile to the north.

There was no way for him to know that they were the lime skeletons of sea creatures that had encased living vegetation, which decayed and left these huge fossils whose whiteness mirrored the moon's. He went in among the white shapes, touching them one by one. The wind rose and a vague keening became audible as it blew across the sharpened edges of the forms. The sound was uncertain in its pitch, intermittent as the notes of a violin being tuned. Recognizing the wind as the source of this strange music did not lessen his apprehension that the ghost forest somehow mirrored his own condition. No sound had ever filled him with such anguish. Putting his hands to his ears, he quickly retraced his route until he reached the empty beach, hurried past the promontory, and returned to the Nicoleños' village.

Compared with the whistling he had heard, the decayed huts seemed raucous and full of life. He built a fire to dispel the shapes, ate a piece of jerky, wolfed down the berries that would have been his breakfast. He needed strength because Daniel would return soon, perhaps tomorrow. It was stupid to think otherwise. When he returned he would tell him what it had been like, tell him about the ghost forest, tell him that tonight, for a little while, he had feared for his sanity, ask if that was what he had wanted, if that was payment enough.

Many days later, while he was picking berries, he stood up to ease the strain on his back and saw the triple sails of a schooner beating south. Quickly wrapping the fruit in a stained shirt he used for foraging, he ran downhill with the agility of a mountain goat, jumping fearlessly from rock to rock, intent on reaching the pyre of wood he had erected on the upper end of the beach beyond the cove. He ran through bushes and brambles, stumbled, fell, got up, shouting for the sheer joy of hearing his voice, and as if in practice for the moment the ship drew near.

He always carried matches wrapped in an oilcloth, and he patted his pocket for reassurance, congratulating himself on his foresight. What if he had left them at the village?

The match was in his hands even before he reached the pyre. When he scratched it against a stone its sulphur smelled sweet as jasmine. Touching the match to the kindling, he exulted at the speed with which the fire roared to life. There was a wonderful scent of smoke. Standing back, he admired the black plume rising into the sky, calculated the direction of the ship, its speed. Any moment now they would see his signal. The captain would nudge his mate, an order would be shouted, the helmsman would spin the wheel. In an hour the ship would drop anchor and a longboat would be lowered.

In his excitement he ignored what he knew to be true about the way his signal might be interpreted, refusing to recognize that everyone who sailed the channel knew that wildfires burned on the islands throughout the year. Even when the schooner had passed well to the south he continued to hope that one of the sailors was not a blockhead and would realize that the smoke came from the beach and not the hills.

As the three sails merged into one white shape he shouted, "Idiots! Fools!" The wind shifted, blowing smoke level with the beach and into his lungs. He staggered back from the pyre coughing and cursing, eyes streaming with tears.

He returned to the village and spent the better part of the afternoon cleaning Soledad's hut. He would not sleep outside again, even for one more night. He pinioned a snake just behind its head with the heel of his boot and killed it with a stone. He stamped on mice, fed them to the dogs, swept the earthen floor with a leafy branch, made barriers of earth around the base of walls. He made a place for everything. The order pleased him. Only then did he allow himself to think of the pyre that had failed to summon the ship. He was contemptuous of his work. The fire had been too small to command attention.

For the next few days he laboriously hauled wood to the beach and began a new pyre beside the other's cinders, devising a ladder so that he could build this one higher. It rose in the shape of a pyramid, beautiful to see. When the next ship appeared on the horizon he would light the pyre carefully, according to an elaborate plan. It would explode at once in a ball of fire. The flames would be immense. They would sear the sky. The plume would rise all the way to the clouds; the flames would be so bright that if his eyes were strong enough he could see them reflected in the windows of the town. As he worked, he lost track of time, but he did not care. He lived in a continuum of wind and sea and imaginings. He became a devotee of fire.

He dreamed of fire, saw embers punctuate the sky with the intensity of stars at midnight. Their light fell and hissed on the dew as he made his way to the woman swaying on the wind. The feathers of her dress rustled as he crossed the meadow; when he reached the gazebo her eyes mirrored the stars. She stared, and spoke in Chumash before flying to the woods.

It was dark beneath the trees. When he reached the cove, a full moon made the sea silver, the beach silver, made silver scrolls of waves brightened at their crests with phosphorus. He went down to the sea elephants' cave, retraced his route, feeling strong and capable as he went along the beach, searching for footsteps. He climbed the embankment nimbly, exulting in his strength as he looked into every ravine and crevice where she could hide. He climbed the bare back of a ridge that led up balconies of stones to the island's highest point. Ahead was the place on the verge of the cliffs where weathered totems stood. He closed in slowly, savoring each step, eyes moving warily. Moonlight crept up the ravines, pushing him on. She could not escape, not now. The totems cast thick shadows as he called her name, dared her to appear, ready to launch himself into the air if that was how he had to reach her. Her name echoed from the cliffs, from the shadows, from the moonlit rocks.

He was still calling her name when he woke and threw the blankets back in such a frenzy that the dogs who had been sleeping with him rushed out the entrance into the darkness of the woods. He followed, but when he called they refused to come; their reluctant eyes made four iridescent circles in the night.

The dream about Soledad terrorized his heart. He had dreamed little, or not at all, when he was home. Now he was afraid of dreams because they followed him into the day, tracked him, gave him no rest. It was only a weakness, he told himself, a weakness that sapped him because he had nothing to occupy his mind. The solution was activity. A vigorous routine would banish the dreams and fill the time until Daniel came.

One morning after breakfasting on berries and dried fish, he went down to the sea elephants' cave, watched the animals a while, went on. He came on an old canoe that had belonged to the Nicoleños. It was swamped with drifted sand, probably rotted through. He passed on, discovered a rookery, stole three eggs while a cormorant screamed and another dived to scare him off. While he walked he thought of places he had been, recalled details of ships he had commanded, remembered old companions, relived the pleasures of Melbourne, Hong Kong, Singapore.

One afternoon he made crude chess pieces and drew a board in the earth outside the hut. At home, when he and Ludlow played every week, he always won. It was compensation for Ludlow's pre-eminence at shooting. He had perfected his game over long years at sea, played men he had had to teach, and men who had showed their superiority in three moves, after which he had struggled futilely to find an advantage that never came.

For two days the game was a pleasure to him. On the third he moved a white pawn, then a black. After that he moved no more because he could no longer imagine an opponent. It was impossible to conjure Ludlow, Don José, tavernkeepers, mates. What he missed was conversation, the endless repartee of men. He would have given anything for one moment of conversation, a single word, but the only voices were those of birds, the wind, and the rhythmic chanting of the sea. He listened immobile as a monk, but without a faith to enliven the silence of his mind. Out of desperation, he recalled the last voice he had heard, repeated out loud what Daniel had said, and he was repelled by the hard, unpracticed syllables. He remembered Daniel's voice growing fainter as the boat drifted away. A moment later he laughed with pleasure, got up, and hurried inside. He had remembered that on the morning of their departure Daniel stopped to take some books.

His fingers trembled while he loosened the knot. Pulling open the mouth of the bag, he found them piled on top and plucked them out with all the excitement of a miner discovering gold flecks in the gravel of his pan. But his enthusiasm faded as he opened the first book and saw the incomprehensible letters of Attic Greek arrayed mutely across the page. He would not even look at the second volume for a time. When he finally did, he expected more elegant but indecipherable shapes, and when his own language spoke to him he almost cried. It was a book of natural history; he thumbed its pages greedily, delighted by the sound the words made inside his head.

The third was a slim volume bound in scuffed leather. He immediately recognized it as the story of Juan Cabrillo's voyage that Fray Santos had given Daniel on his eighteenth birthday. It was in Spanish, but he had learned the language long ago as an indispensable part of business. There was an inscription to the boy on the frontispiece.

"Historians think he was Portuguese. There is evidence that he served as a crossbowman when Cortez conquered the Aztecs, and lived a while in Guatemala before embarking on his voyage that led to the discovery of the channel. He died on San Miguel. Many years later a man named Juan Páez, who was a member of Cabrillo's crew, summarized their adventure. Since you are interested in history, I thought this would be appropriate."

The first page was stained but legible, and the stately language drew him on.

I, Juan Páez, an old man crippled in his joints, did sail with Juan Cabrillo on the 27th day of June, in the year of Our Lord 1542, from the port of Navidad. All these many years that voyage has lain like an itch within me as age crept its way along my bones. Words have never been my friend, but I seek acquaintance with them now in hope of giving some account of what befell us in New Spain. Perhaps then, God willing, I may cast forever from my mind the image of that wind-swept island where we buried poor Cabrillo. I begin with that, and then work back to all the other things that came to pass.

Juan Cabrillo sent us north, but winter was soon upon us, and some leagues beyond a bay where fogs rolled in like smoke he bade us turn about and make our way along the coast whence we had come. Many days passed before we reached the bay of Santa Bárbara and there, in the lee of an island he christened San Miguel, we sheltered the *San Salvadore* and *Victoria* off a sandy beach. The next day, while climbing with a party on the island, Juan Cabrillo lost his footing and tumbled into a dark ravine. I was the first to reach him and see the whiteness of the bone sticking through his tunic below his shoulder. We carried him to the *San Salvadore*, where the surgeon splinted the shattered bone as well as any man could do, but that very night a raging fever came upon him and two days later the scent of corruption filled the cabin.

Day and night Juan Cabrillo tossed upon his bed, throwing off wet cloths the surgeon placed upon his brow. Moans rose and fell like waves, and soon his mind drifted off from reason. As Padre Romero prayed, the captain shouted that he heard a curse. That night, with eyes rolling like a madman's, he screamed, asking if I did not hear it too. I turned away, for I

could no more look upon him. As I gazed through the port-
hole I heard the priest. *Pater noster,* he said, *qui es in coelis:
sanctificetur nomen tuum. Adveniat regnum tuum. Fiat voluntas
tua, sicut in coelo, et in terra.*

Late that evening, the 3rd of January 1543, Juan Cabrillo
died. In the morning sailors dressed him in his richest tunic
and trousers and then put his armor on. His sword, sheathed
in a scabbard embedded with fine jewels, was laid upon his
chest. Then his lieutenants bore the stretcher down the gangway onto the rocky island soil. A hard wind blew the grass
against the ground, and the company of both ships bent their
heads into the wind as we climbed to the island's ridge. There
we buried Juan Cabrillo, where his grave would always look
upon the sea.

None of his dreams had left him with the sudden chill that came
upon him as he read. The crew of the *San Salvadore* and *Victoria* had
wintered off San Miguel, a place no more hospitable than San
Nicolás, but they at least had had the shelter of the galleons, one
another's company, the certainty that when the weather cleared
they could continue on their journey north. No matter how hard
the wind blew, they were safe together in their little world, observing the hierarchies of command, whereas he had already begun to
forget the habits of civilization. He was the man with shaggy hair
reflected in the pool, the man who talked to himself and talked to
dogs. Instead of offering comfort, the mellifluous voice of Juan
Páez had betrayed him. He saw Cabrillo's feverish face, his wild and
rolling eyes. In one quick movement he threw the book into the
underbrush, and the dogs raced to where it fell. The larger one
reached it first and shook it back and forth. The smaller fixed its
teeth into the spine. They fought, snarling and gasping, until the
shredded pages blew about the village, and the words of Juan Páez
festooned the trees and settled on the bushes. Circling, tongues
lolling, the dogs sniffed the confetti.

The idea of escape blossomed from the shredded book. Harper
saw how naïve he had been to believe that all he had to do was wait,
endure solitude, prepare for his son's return. Now he understood

that he had been stupid to believe that the duplicity which left him on the island would not be repeated by the boy. It was inconceivable that he would not return, yes, but it was just as conceivable that he would not.

Two choices were open to him. The old canoe might still be seaworthy. He could make a sail of the bags, an oar and tiller from deadfall in the woods. If it was beyond repair, he would have to wait with the knowledge that the boy might never come. He had spent long hours sitting absolutely still, thinking of nothing. That habit would increase with despair. Soon, he knew, all action, all movement, would seem useless, volition would flake off like the dried paint of a ship, and one day, one day he would be nothing but a husk, an emptiness, and the death that lay in wait for him then would make Cabrillo's seem one of gilded ease. It was either the canoe or loss of will, a deterioration, a long, dry dying. He rose, shaking the confetti from his tattered shirt, and hurried down the beach.

So much sand had drifted into the canoe that the prow jutted into the air, as if it were sinking. He scooped out the sand a handful at a time, growing apprehensive as he neared the bottom. If moisture had been trapped there, if he discovered a hole too large to repair . . . But the last handfuls were as dry as the first, and he sighed when his fingers scraped against the hardness of the hull. Freed from the sand's weight, the canoe tipped forward. The movement puzzled him until he dug around the outside of the hull and found three decaying logs. The Indians must have intended to move it. Their failure gave him his solution.

It took the better part of a day to find logs, trim their branches, and haul them to the beach. The next morning he dragged the last two logs into place, making a terrace leading from the canoe to the shore. He gathered seaweed and lay the long, rank-smelling strands across the logs. Until then he had not dared push the canoe for fear its weight would be discouraging. Now he grasped the sides and rocked it back and forth. At first it hardly moved, but he kept the motion up, and it came loose. Setting his feet, doubling his body into a spring, he forced the canoe another inch, then another. As it slid forward, the prow rose and there was a beautiful sound as the hull ground over the logs. He shouted with pleasure as he pushed it within ten feet of the high-water mark.

After cutting the bags down one side, he lay them on the sand and made a pattern for a triangular sail. It was smaller than he wished, but he had no doubt that it would work. There were needles in Daniel's mending kit. He removed the stitching from the bags, using the coarse thread to sew the pieces into a sail, made a second row of stitches so that the seams would not tear. By the time he finished, his fingers were raw and bleeding. He rested a day, and spent the next fashioning an oar, which could double as a tiller.

After lashing the sail to the mast and the mast to a crossbeam in the prow, he moved his provisions, blankets, and water jug to the beach. He would launch the canoe in the morning. By the end of the day, with any luck, he should reach the mainland. He allowed himself to imagine the house, his bedroom, soft sheets and warm blankets. He drank a little whiskey and lay down, thinking, *This time tomorrow I will be home.*

At sunset the whole sky turned red and yellow. He was content to lie there, propped up on his elbows, watching the colors changing. The canoe resting on the logs reminded him of the spirit ship. It was an imprecise correspondence, but close enough to dull his pleasure in the sky. My mistake, he thought, was in waiting.

The colors faded until the canoe was barely visible against the darkened sea. The sense of pleasure that had come with the sunset, the feeling of accomplishment, the relief that tonight would be the last he had to spend there were replaced by a steady glow of anger, a need to contemplate revenge. He would not hurry it. He would let it come slowly, allow himself time to find exactly the right way to proceed. He lay back, closed his eyes, savored possibilities.

He woke to the sound of wind. The surf was heavy and irregular, impossible to cross. Whitecaps checked the sea. It began raining, and he retreated to the shelter of two trees some distance from the beach. It rained into the night, and he shivered in his sleep, dreamed of the ghost forest, of a dance of strange white shapes.

In the morning the sea was calm. Fog hovered in the distance, but he was certain that it would blow away to the north. He laughed at how easily the canoe slid over the last two logs. With one final shove, he launched it.

Several miles off shore the sky changed from blue to gray. Fog rose up, absorbing the wind. Sunlight poured down bright shafts to the sea, patterning it with silver pools, which quickly dulled to a deep dead gray. An hour passed, then another. He was almost becalmed, but as long as he moved at all he was not worried. At day's end he might find himself miles off course, but even if he landed far south of town, he could find someone to take him home.

Two days later Esteban's sons were gathering shells at the water's edge when Ernesto pointed to the breakers.

"Manuelito, look."

His little brother squinted.

"A seal."

"Have you ever seen one floating like that?"

"Maybe it's taking a siesta."

"They don't take siestas; everybody knows that."

"Well, come on. It's a seal, anyway."

His brother was probably right. The dark shape really didn't look much different from the other seals dotting the bay. He caught up with Manuel and forgot about it as they wandered down the beach.

On the way back half an hour later they saw it again. Just before it disappeared beneath a wave, one of the flippers rose from the foam.

"Wait a minute," Ernesto said, putting his hand on Manuel's shoulder. Another wave formed, peaked, and a man appeared at the top of the thin transparent crest, arms and legs akimbo.

"*Dios mio!*" Ernesto said.

"It's a swimmer."

"He's not swimming." Suddenly Ernesto felt protective of his little brother. "You better stay here."

"Why?"

"Because I'm telling you. Remember what Father said."

Manuel pouted. "I want to see."

"I'll be back in a minute."

The wave fell while they argued, and the man disappeared. Ernesto watched as another wave rose and the man appeared again. His arms flew up, as if he were signaling for help. This time he drifted all the way into shore, then out again until another wave pushed him up on the sand. His head was turned at an odd angle and his legs moved languidly on the foam. Ernesto thought they looked like the tentacles of a dead medusa. As he warily approached, he made a pact with himself. He could turn back whenever he wanted. To his surprise, he went on. The discovery of courage made him feel bold and grownup.

The man lay face down, one arm slung over his head. His legs moved when the water hissed over the sand. Ernesto tried not to look at them as he muttered a prayer and thought of what he would tell his friends. Filled with bravery, he nudged the body with his toe. It was heavy, inert, cold. He went around to the side the head was facing; when he saw the jelled eyes he ran back to his brother, sickened by the whiteness.

By noon the news had reached everyone who cared to listen. Since the *Elizabeth's Delight* was still moored in the harbor, and there were no reports of empty boats having come ashore, Harper's death was shrouded by a mystery that added interest to conversations throughout the town. Because the cause remained uncertain, it was only natural for people to speculate about other strange things that had happened in the channel. There was talk of shipwrecks; talk of two murderers who had taken refuge on Anacapa near the turn of the century. Some people revived the story of Juan Cabrillo, others that of Soledad, which had occurred within living memory and gave a certain legitimacy to the most farfetched speculations.

No one recalled Soledad's story more enthusiastically than O'Reilly, who greeted the news with a cackle and spent the better part of that evening at Esteban's recounting his experiences with the ghost woman who had killed the priest and returned a second time to claim the prideful bastard Henry Harper.

Esteban listened as he dried glasses behind the bar. He was not bothered by O'Reilly's remarks about Fray Santos. Personally, he had always considered the friar an old fool. But Harper had been a loyal patron, and he was not willing to tolerate O'Reilly's insults.

After he refilled the glasses of two men standing at the bar, he went over to the Irishman. "You forget something."

"And what might that be, your honor?"

"You were with them," Esteban said slowly, "told them she was there. When does she come for you?"

O'Reilly tried to ignore the insinuation in the interests of taking advantage of the free drinks that had been coming his way, but the Mexican's question lodged in his superstitious heart, destroying all his pleasure. Within the hour he abandoned his audience and returned to his boarding house where, toward midnight, he fell into a troubled sleep.

Early the next morning he appeared on the sidewalk in front of the St. Charles Hotel; a stagecoach was taking on passengers. He was last seen climbing into the stage by a drinking companion, and when the man asked where he was going, O'Reilly looked glumly out the window, saying only that he did not intend to stop until he was many miles from the sea.

# 24

♦ ♦ ♦

There are, inevitably, multiple interpretations of every story. Sometimes the public one, confidently inferred by a community, is oracular, differing only in a minor point or two from the actual events. In such instances, the difference is a matter of shading or emphasis, manifest and latent meanings lying close together, like two panes of glass. More often than not, radical misunderstandings divide the public and private versions, the community believing one thing while those involved live out a secret behind faces impenetrable as the carved masks of the Greeks.

Such was the case one March afternoon three months after Daniel wrote to Elizabeth about Harper's death. Returning to the town she believed she would never see again, Elizabeth descended from the coach in front of the St. Charles Hotel, aged far more than the six months she had been away. People who happened to be passing on the street that day saw in her face and the halting way she moved a widow so consumed by loss that it made their own loves seem pale. They began telling stories about her heroic love even as she was riding to her house with the drayman in his creaking wagon. But that was not what Daniel and Constancia saw when they went outside and found her staring at them with a bounteous grief. Her anguish was mostly for them, and as her eyes strayed across the house to the gazebo and back again, they knew it was also, still, for Soledad.

A similar misunderstanding occurred toward the end of that year when Daniel had begun working in the ship's chandlery he opened with the proceeds from the sale of the *Elizabeth's Delight*. Riders passing him on the road, fellow merchants and customers, saw a bereaved young man mourning his father's untimely death, never guessing that the true history of his pain had begun when he sailed away from San Nicolás, convinced that that moment was the watershed of his moral life. They never knew that over the next few days, despite his avowals to Constancia, he feared his conscience might get the better of him, forcing him to strike out for the island and in doing so cancel his revenge. Nothing in his face or eyes even remotely suggested how he had resisted out of principle, determined to wait until he was certain Harper had exhausted his provisions. Nor would they ever be privy to the fact that when he learned of Harper's death he understood that leaving the island had only been a cunningly wrought prologue to the guilt shadowing his days for which he desperately, futilely sought atonement.

It was no different with Constancia, who had moved into the house a few days after Harper's funeral; Susan Ludlow had agreed to let it be known that she had changed employment in order to help Harper's son. Whenever she went into town alone or with Angelita, people who once stared rudely at her shocking scars ignored them, seeing instead the face of charity they all approved of. They would never know that she had welcomed Harper's death as payment for his crimes against herself and Soledad, that she had forced herself to ignore her feelings about entering the house where she had been born and raped because she feared for Daniel's mind. They would never know that he suffered from raging headaches, which she tried to ease by massaging his temples until her fingers ached, or that she failed to relieve the pain because she could not reach its source.

So it was that they took up their lives in the house that Harper built, secure behind the masks invented for them. For weeks after Elizabeth's return, people reported seeing lights burning in the downstairs rooms into the small hours of the night, unaware that inside there were agonized discussions lasting for hours as she and Constancia vainly tried to convince Daniel that he was not responsible for his father's death. Night after night they beseeched him to listen to reason; night after night his answer was the same. He never doubted the justice of his plan, nor the need that led to its invention. All he knew was that in seeking redress for Constancia and Soledad, he had committed patricide. Time after time, in answer to their protests, he said, "I took him there. I left him." He had not shot Harper, nor poisoned him, nor driven a knife into his chest. But he believed that he had killed him nonetheless. It made no difference when Constancia insisted that in cutting short his exile Harper had acted of his own free will; whenever Daniel thought about the desperation that must have driven Harper to leave the island, he felt the thrumming of his conscience in his blood.

Finally the lights in the house no longer burned far into the night. While Elizabeth and Constancia offered comfort and consolation, there was nothing practical they could do. As time passed, Constancia began looking to her own life, and a year later found an unexpected occupation when the authorities in Mexico secularized the mission. Suddenly hundreds of neophytes were desperately looking for some way to live. She took them food and clothing, spoke as Daniel's emissary with ranchers in the valley, arranging work for as many as she could. Much later, when those she helped had taken up lives in huts on the verges of the fields, she often went to visit and engage in rites the friars had once condemned.

Elizabeth resumed her life in the house, passing her days doing needlework and gardening. There were times when she was almost happy seeing Daniel and Constancia together, but her pleasure was circumscribed by the price the children had had to pay. Soledad was always on her mind. She remembered the good times, the intimacies, as well as those which had scarred her soul. One of her memories took the form of a recurring dream of Harper's shadowy figure in the grove, his eyes red as the glow of his cheroot. When she tried to run away across the meadow, the air thickened with the scratches on his back; they held her helpless as an insect in a spider's web, bound her eyes open so that she had to watch him embracing Soledad.

Nobody knew about these things. They knew only that Harper's widow and son lived out their lives in the great white house looking down upon the mission, the abandoned huts, the sea. From time to time a guest or two was invited there, a carpenter would be summoned to make repairs, a crowd appeared for the wedding of Morales's daughter. But even on that festive day the house seemed like a hermitage.

Every four or five years Daniel painted it himself, spending long days crucified on a ladder, brush in one hand, bucket in the other. Because of his attention, the house was always bright as alabaster, pristine as a monument, although what it memorialized was inscribed only on the minds of those who lived inside. Sarcophagal, august, the white face glowed on sunny days when its windows, like great square eyes, mirrored the mission, the islands, and the sea, framing them in that looming presence which seemed to brood above the town.

THE PAINTED CAVE

The Bruja's House

EL CAMINO REAL

0        1/2        1

MILES

SANTA BÁRBARA

SAN
MIGUEL I.

SANTA BÁRBARA CHANNEL

LOS ANGELES

SANTA
ROSA I.

SANTA
CRUZ I.

SAN PEDRO CHANNEL

N

SANTA
BÁRBARA I.

SAN
NICOLÁS I.

SANTA
CATALINA I.

SAN
CLEMENTE I.

G. W. Ward